Beneath A Magi Sky

The Birth of Christ Consciousness

DJ Boyle

Dedicated
to my loving wife, Maureen,
to my sons, Sean and Kevin,
to my daughter-in-law, Galina,
and my granddaughter, Emma

ACKNOWLEDGEMENTS

I would like to acknowledge James Braha, my friend and astrology teacher, who brought Vedic astrology to the west. Laura LaBoone, my editor, whose guidance helped bring this book to fruition. Aroon Chaddha, my friend, who encouraged me to write and introduced me to the Scribes writing group. Maharishi Mahesh Yogi, who brought the wisdom of Vedic knowledge to millions. Deepak Chopra, for generously sharing his insight with everyone.

"Whenever dharma is in decay and adharma flourishes, O Bharata, then I create myself."
Bhagavad Gita Chapter 4 Verse 7

CONTENTS

Dedication
Acknowledgments
Epigraph
Silk Road Journey Map

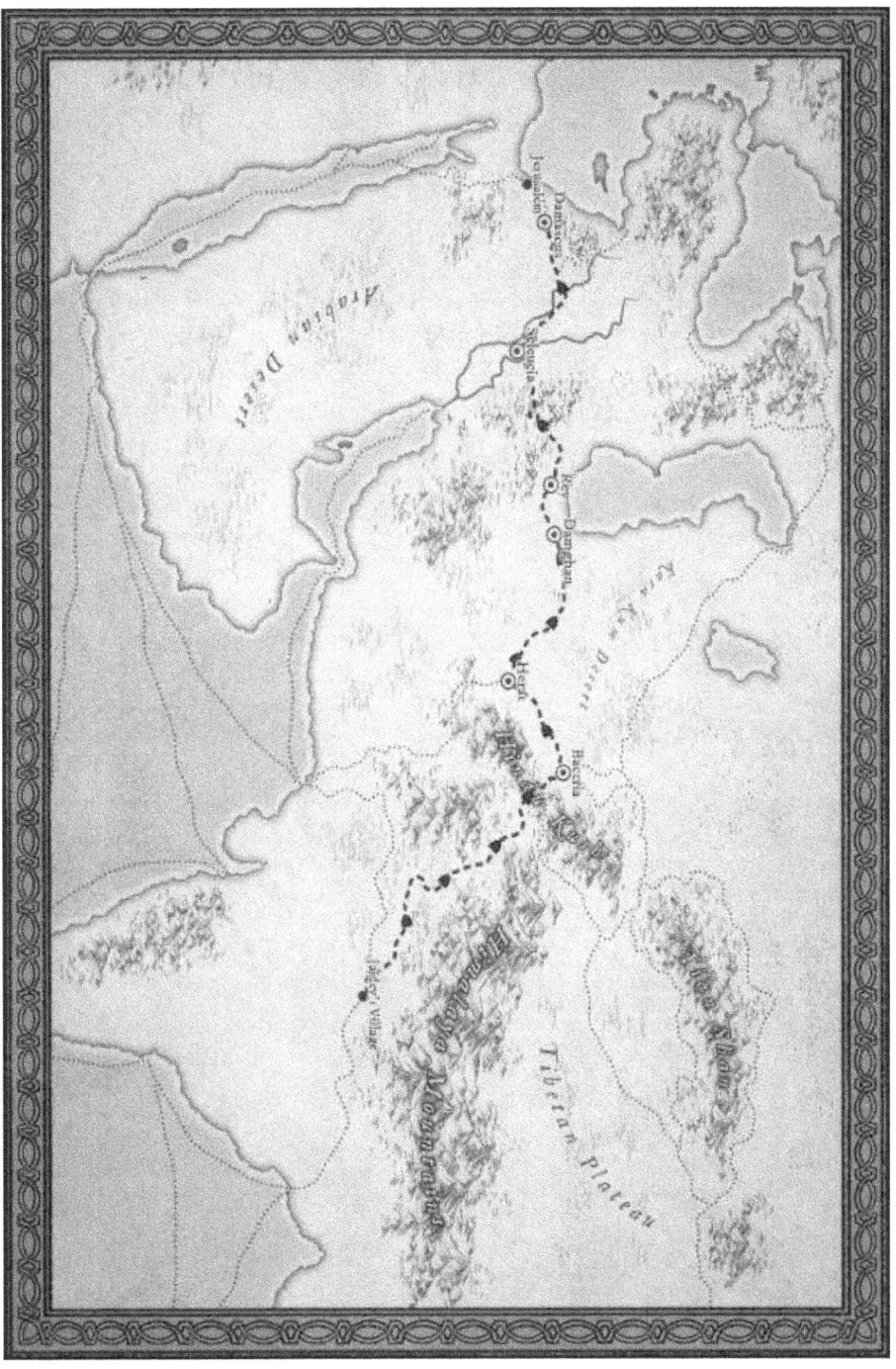

Figure 1: Magi Silk Road Journey

i

Chapter 1 - Four Friends

The stars spoke silently, filling Jaidev's mind with awe and wonder.

Jaidev was just a boy when he first felt the pull of the stars. They called out to him, drawing him into their mysterious world. They shared secret knowledge only the nine planets could tell—knowledge about the past, present, and future—each one with its own unique set of karmic tales. It dawned on Jaidev that he had an extraordinary gift. He could not only see these stories unfold in the sky but also feel their rhythms as if he were part of an ancient cosmic dance, each birth date, place, and time having a different meaning for one's life purpose, fortune, desires, and spiritual liberation.

The young Brahmin and Jyotishi, Jaidev, sat at the base of the Himalayas where three sacred rivers—Ganges, Yamuna, and Saraswati—flow. Gazing up at the sky whilst calculating a rare occurrence, his father, Mahesh, joined him to observe.

Bowing his head and clasping his hands in reverence, "Babaji," Jaidev said, "you have taught me to map the dance of divine forces through the heavens. This moment is scarcely seen—Jupiter and Saturn aligning three times in Pisces! I can feel the ripples of fate sweeping across the cosmos. Surely, something extraordinary awaits us."

Babaji was Jaidev's term of endearment for his father, Mahesh Trivedi. Mahesh taught his son well. The villagers revered

Mahesh's dedication to preserving the ancient teachings in their purest form. They considered Mahesh a Rishi, an enlightened knower of the Self, the Atma.

Mahesh raised his right hand, his usual gesture when he wanted to make an important point. His keen gaze locked onto Jaidev. He spoke of his grandfather's prophecy about a rare celestial event in Pisces, specifically in the lunar mansion of Revati[1], which would announce the advent of a remarkable soul, a Maha Atma. "We must examine this further to determine if this occurrence in Pisces is the foretold birth."

"Babaji, yes, that is what the Eye of the Veda is showing. Look here at this chart. See how the sign of Virgo, the Virgin, can bring forth a Maha Atma from the powerful aspects it receives from the planets in Pisces. The great soul will be born when the sign of the Virgin rises in the east in the lunar mansion of Hasta, the sign of blessing. In the west, Saturn, Jupiter, and the Moon are in Pisces and the lunar mansion of Revati. This sign of spiritual liberation will cast a powerful influence on the ascending sign. There is a great blessing coming to humankind," Jaidev said, his mind racing through the heavens, his heart exploding with excitement over his discovery.

---

[1] There are 27 lunar mansions known as nakshatras in Vedic astrology

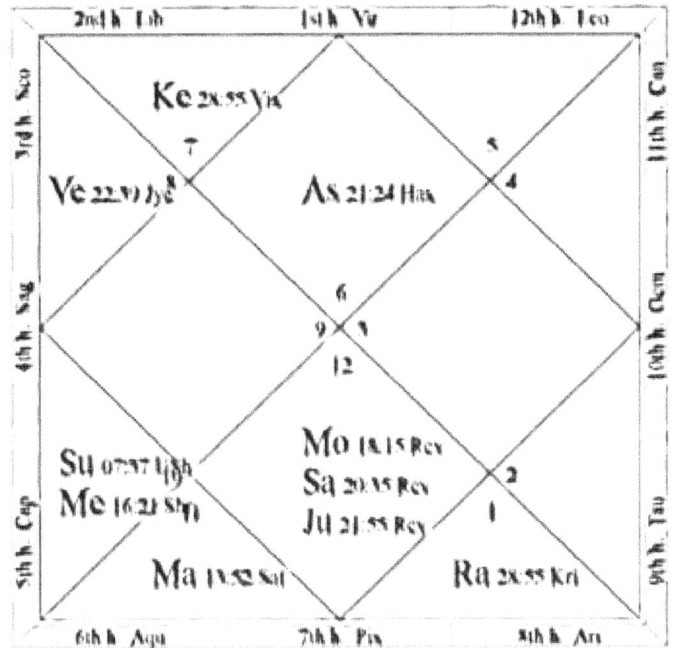

Mahesh intently studied the chart Jaidev had drawn. The great conjunction taking place in the western sky with Virgo as the ascendant sign was unlike anything Mahesh had ever analyzed before. The spiritual implications were astounding. Saturn and Jupiter aligned in Pisces and Revati three times, symbolizing the path to God through meditation and devotion. Following the third conjunction, Mercury, symbolizing Jnana yoga (God realization through knowledge), aligned with the Sun—indicative of the soul—in the powerful fifth house of children and creative intelligence.

Mahesh reached out and touched his son's arm. "Our Holy Gita teaches us that when dharma declines and adharma prevails, the Great Lord manifests repeatedly to restore dharma. This chart may signify the Lord's coming or, at the very least, the chart of an enlightened guru. You have found an auspicious message in the stars. We must analyze the many powerful yogas in this chart and calculate the dasha time periods to further understand how this life unfolds."

Closing his eyes, Mahesh reflected on the ancient texts and

teachings, pausing for a moment before continuing: "The person born will be bestowed with timeless knowledge; he will guide others to freedom through wisdom and devotion; he will inspire people to know God; he will enlighten man with his teachings of eternal life."

Mahesh held his only son, Jaidev, in awe and beamed with pride that such an accomplished Jyotishi was following in his footsteps. When casting Jaidev's chart at birth, his karmic greatness was evident—karma fitting for one from such a distinguished lineage. The Trivedi family went back to the very author of the Rig Veda, Vashista. Parashara, the grandson of Vashista, compiled the methods of understanding the star language in the Brihat Parasara Hora Sastra and called it Jyotish, the Science of Light. Even the famed sage Vyasa, author of the Bhagavad Gita, was a forbearer.

Jaidev's insights and intuition exceeded anything Mahesh acquired. Jaidev's understanding of the Vedas, The Upanishads, The Puranas, The Gita, and all the ancient texts was unparalleled. He had matured into a young man that any father would be proud of, whether the family dharma was Brahmin, the priests, Kshatriya, the warriors, Vaishya, the merchants, or Shudra, the laborers. The Trivedi family was also esteemed because it faithfully performed the sacred Yagyas, the prayer ceremonies, recited in the perfect tone and meter that was most pleasing to the gods.

The villagers noticed Jaidev's ascension amongst the young Brahmins and whispered that he was the next Jyotish Mati Pragya, one established in the awake field of intelligence that knows everything. Thus, they consulted Jaidev on all manner of questions.

The sunlight was still strong for several more hours, so Jaidev remained immersed in the charts. Making astrological calculations was a time-consuming and arduous task, but he loved interpreting the results. It could take days to follow the precise methods that were preserved for many generations on palm leaves—an ancient arithmetic handed down from generation to generation since Parashara discovered it in the earliest of times. The great conjunction in Pisces would occur over many months. Therefore, finding all the astrological intersections of planets, signs, houses, divisions of the chart called vargas, glances or aspects of the planets called drishtis, and timing of life events called dashas, was daunting.

However, the work did not deter Jaidev. He proceeded with his calculations fervently. Understanding the star's language led to insight into oneself, one's karma, and a stronger connection with God and Creation. This was his dharma, and it brought him great satisfaction.

He was interrupted by the snorts of a camel in a nearby field. A foreign voice called out from the hillside. "Bellows, what are you doing so far from our caravan? Do you think the grass is better on this hillside than down by the river?"

Jaidev watched as a bedraggled man walked towards the camel. As he neared, the man caught sight of Jaidev.

"I apologize for disturbing you, young man," the stranger said as he hustled to the camel, putting a rope around its neck to guide it back. "She can be stubborn and has a mind of her own."

Jaidev smiled warmly. "It is no disturbance, sir. Your camel is welcome to have as much of this grass as she likes. She must have been born with a malefic Saturn in her 5th house."

"I don't let this animal into any house—maybe a barn, but not a house," the stranger said, clearly not understanding Jaidev's jest. "I am Barbod. I am with the caravan camped down by the river."

"I am Jaidev, a Brahmin," Jaidev replied. "You and your camel are welcome anytime."

"You are most gracious, Jaidev. I will take Bellows back to my camp where she belongs. I hope we meet again."

"I too," Jaidev agreed, his intuition sensing something unexpectedly interesting about Barbod.

The breeze was soft, gently swaying the treetops. Jaidev continued working on his calculations as a familiar figure approached from the road. With his long stride, Aakash passed a cow slowly chewing grass along the edge of the road. Its large, soulful eyes watched him intently. A trail of dust kicked up from Aakash's sandals and followed as he walked along, intent on his destination.

"Pranam, Jaidev," Aakash greeted as he neared. "We are playing flutes and drums at the Holi festival. You will play with us, won't you? We are practicing tonight in the stable behind Ravi's home."

Jaidev always loved the festival and playing music with his friends Aakash and Ravi. Aakash was a slim, broad-shouldered, muscular young man with long, flowing black hair. The son of a Kshatriya, he had a protective, watchful manner and an energetic persona that enthusiastically embraced new challenges. His wide, engaging smile was hard to resist. It filled those who saw it with a glimpse of inner joy and appreciation for just being alive.

Aakash did not quite understand the deep mysteries of life that Jaidev comprehended. That was not his dharma. Jaidev knew from reading Aakash's Jyotish chart that his inner calling was to excel in sports and the art of self-defense—to be loyal, a good friend, and in the future, married to a loving woman and have several children. He was not someone to cross. His competitive nature could erupt quickly as anger and subside just as swiftly.

"I'm not so sure," Jaidev responded, smiling back at his invigorated friend. "Babaji has given me a task that may take a few days to work out."

"Jaidev, you must come. We have been doing this as a threesome for 13 years—since we were 7 years old. We can't replace you. Besides, Ravi's mom and sister Amrita make the best gujiya of the whole festival—maybe in the entire world. We can have some fresh from the oven tonight as they make them for Holi."

"I— I suppose I could come for a few hours," Jaidev concurred, checking Aakash's body posture and tone of voice for signs of tension. "It has nothing to do with the sweet treats, mind you. I just can't let my best friends down."

"Right, nothing to do with the gujiya," Aakash laughed. "I'll have yours then."

"I'll have some just to protect you from getting fat and sluggish," Jaidev shot back, toying with Aakash's fear of losing his athletic prowess. "You'll need your sharpest concentration for the archery contest."

Aakash's face lit up at the mention of archery. "Look, I have a new bow," he announced proudly, pulling forward a bow slung over his back. "It is of the finest black oak. A sadhu, a Holy Man, was using it as a walking stick when he came down from the forest seeking alms. Seeing me admire it, he claimed he had no attachment to it and offered it to me. I politely refused, but he insisted."

Pausing, Aakash added, "The sadhu told me that the bow revealed life's deepest lessons. Its efficient use was skill in action. 'To let the arrow fly, first pull back the bow,' he said. Then, he touched the bindi between his eyes saying, 'Whatever you set your attention and then intention on, must project forward from a mind fully established in the stillness. The arrow waits peacefully on the fully loaded bow to be released into action.' He then laid it at my feet and bowed. When I picked it up, it felt like I had been holding it my whole life, hitting my target constantly. It was like we made perfect music together. I have much to learn from this bow," Aakash declared.

Jaidev knew the sadhu had given his friend a very special gift. Such meetings and gifts were not haphazard events. Life's synchronicities happened for a reason—to propel one further along on one's dharmic path. For good or evil, one only had to choose to accept them or turn away.

"I will bless your bow and pray to Krishna that your aim is true at the Holi festival," Jaidev said. "You are in a Mars dasha, a good dasha for you to excel in sport."

"Yes, I feel like I can't miss," Aakash replied. "We will see at the festival in a couple of days. I'll meet you at Ravi's stable in a little while. By the way, Ravi said he invited someone from the caravan his father is trading with to practice with us."

"Jai Ram," Jaidev said, clasping his hands to his heart.

In the late afternoon, the air was cool, dry, and crisply clean as soft billowy clouds gently kissed the mountaintops in the distance. Jaidev Trivedi walked towards his friend Ravi's home, blowing a soft, slow melody on his flute. A bouquet of culinary delights wafted through the air from the village homes as Jaidev passed. One home smelled of fresh bread baking. Another of pungent curry. Another of chai. Holi brought the entire village alive with festive smells and colors. Powders of every shade of the rainbow were being prepared. Children waited anxiously for the festival fun to begin. *It was good to be alive and to live in such a beautiful place*, Jaidev thought, noticing his inner stillness was both within and without.

Ravi Bahira, a stout, muscular man, was the offspring of a renowned wealthy Vaishya. He had a zest for life, a remarkable dexterity in his words, and an insatiable appetite for worldly possessions.

Ravi's home was constantly alive with the chatter of women, both young and old. Women came from far and wide, wanting to get their hands on Sita's exquisite hand-embroidered fabrics. She was known as the finest seamstress in northern India. Ravi's sister, Amrita, inherited her mother's gift for sewing, and the demand for her exceptional embroidery was near her mother's.

Ravi's dad, Darmik Bahira, was a powerful merchant, a Vaishya. Trading herbs, spices, jewelry, perfumes, and fine cloths was lucrative along the trade routes between the Roman Empire to the far west, the Persian Valley and the South Indian villages, and China to the far east. The family boasted a stable of fine horses and hand-crafted leather saddles and bridles. Intricate carvings and artwork depicting the gods and demons, exquisite furniture, rugs, tapestries, and painted pottery adorned the Bahira house. A few of the prized horses were from far off Persia. Ravi's dad had accepted them as payment for the fine spices, cloth, and perfumes sent west to

Babylonia. Wonderful stories of far-off lands were told with each treasure.

Turning the corner, Jaidev heard a sound like nothing he had ever heard before. It was ethereal and hypnotic, filling the air with notes that were thin and fragile, yet deep and resonant. He quickened his pace as he neared Ravis's house. When he arrived, the sound grew stronger, mixing different rhythms and timbres to create an enchanting melody that touched his soul. Jaidev smiled in anticipation of the evening ahead—one that promised an exquisite experience for his ears.

Entering the stable, Jaidev saw Ravi sitting with a strange, turbaned, middle-aged man. The bearded man held an instrument resembling a curved bow with many strings attached. With the instrument on his lap, he nimbly plucked the strings with both hands to produce rhythmic sounds.

"Vaah," Jaidev uttered, his mouth gaping open and eyes wide with astonishment. "What is this?"

"This is a chang[2]," Ravi revealed. "Barbod here is traveling with a trading convoy heading back home to the west. It is a Persian instrument. I must have one, and I'm hoping he will bargain for it. I would love to learn to play it." Ravi moved his hands as he spoke, hoping to convey his words to Barbod, who understood much of the language.

Barbod's shaggy face smiled, bristling with stubble. An upper front tooth, prominently missing, stood out near the top of his smile like the peak of a mountain; still, his smile was warm and welcoming. His eyes met Jaidev's, glowing with recognition as if meeting an old friend.

"We met earlier today," Jaidev said. "He has a stubborn camel."

"Yes, how unexpected that we would meet again so soon,"

---

[2] Iranian harp

Barbod returned, bowing slightly. "I understand you play music with Dharmik's son."

"Yes," Jaidev said, showing his flute as Ravi played a few notes of an old Hindustani village song. Barbod listened attentively. Ravi played it a second time. This time Barbod moved his fingers and plucked the strings on the chang, mimicking the rhythm of the flute's notes. Smiling broadly, they both agreed that he mimicked it perfectly.

Jaidev realized that the stars destined Ravi's commanding presence and wealth. The benefic planets Jupiter and Venus blessed his second and eleventh houses—the houses that foretold wealth. His assertive presence was indicated by Mars positing the first house close to the ascendant. Stockier than Aakash, his fine clothes and strong self-assured persona made him a formidable young businessman. His social status was secondary to his friendship, however, and his admiration for his friends Aakash and Jaidev. It was Rahu in Ravi's second house, tightly aspecting his ascendant ruler positioned in his 10th house of career that concerned Jaidev. The allure of worldly possessions and prestige was strong in his chart and persona.

Each recitation of the song expanded the notes further. Soon Jaidev joined in and the three of them worked on a favorite Indian village song, communicating harmoniously.

Aakash walked into the stable, taking in the unfolding musical magic. He sat attentively with his drum until slowly and softly he matched the tempo of the music. The three of them seemed to have played music with Barbod for many years, the chang adding a new melodic dimension to the already harmonious sounds.

Jaidev watched Barbod as he gracefully plucked its strings. He recognized the auspiciousness of this common man and talented musician bringing a new instrument with unheard vibrations to Ravi's home, just as he found a rare and remarkable astrological occurrence in the sky—an occurrence that indicated a profound cosmic event and influence was coming their way. He studied Barbod's face and demeanor. His immersion in the music seemed to elevate him, only to return to his simplistic nature when the music stopped. "I have heard no one play so effortlessly; you seem to pick up our music like you have played it before," Jaidev said, curious about Barbod's response.

Barbod's face flushed, seeking to avoid self-recognition, simply uttering, "Thank you."

Saturn must hit his ascendant or ascendant ruler causing his shyness and lack of self-confidence, but his 3rd house of music must be blessed by benefics—Venus probably occupies it, Jaidev thought. A picture of Barbod's chakras opening and closing as he stepped in and out of his music role flashed through Jaidev's mind. *Still, he has an easy Jupiterian happiness about him.*

After a few hours of practice, Sita, Ravi's mom, poked her head into the stable. "My, you sound wonderful. I have some freshly baked gujiya here for you, along with some hot tea. Come and enjoy. It is best when still warm."

Aakash glanced at Jaidev and broke into his wide, infectious smile. They both were waiting to enjoy the scrumptious treats. The luscious aroma of sweet baked flour and hot aromatic chai was a perfect complement to the musical creations they were making.

"Thank you!" Aakash exclaimed. "Your divine cooking is deserving of the gods. We are fortunate to enjoy it."

As the platter floated around the small circle of musicians, Barbod's pupils dilated, eyeing the contents of the dish like a hawk circling its prey. Delicacies in his life were not frequent. Therefore, he could not hide his excitement at having his tastebuds treated to such delicious morsels.

"There is more inside if you like," Sita said softly, glancing at Ravi, who lightly nodded his approval. With a smile on his face, Barbod helped himself to an extra portion.

Finishing their tea, Jaidev spoke up. "Well, my friends," he said with a smile, "it is getting late. One more song and I should head home to help my father prepare for tomorrow's bonfire and festival."

After a lively raga, Jaidev expressed his awe. "That was amazing. I love the way the chang adds such dimension to the music." He grinned at everyone, adding, "I can't wait to play at the festival."

Jaidev bowed to his three bandmates before exiting the stable. He walked toward his dwelling just as the sun tucked beneath the western horizon and nightfall settled in from the east. Suddenly, a shooting star streaked across the sky, making him pause for a moment. He thought tonight he would burn the ghee lamp to finish working on his astrological calculations of the planets in Pisces.

Chapter 2 - The Decision

Jaidev felt his feet were not hitting solid ground as he walked. He rose ever so slowly from the road, floating three feet off the ground. Soon, he looked down and saw the treetops passing beneath him. Gazing at the distant Himalayan mountains, he effortlessly rose above the village and then to the highest peak. The gripping cold of the snow-capped mountains did not affect him. With his attention on the brightness of the full Moon, he ascended further into the sky. The Moon took his hand, gently rising with him. Peering deeper into the heavens, Jupiter and Saturn smiled, inviting him to come closer, to join them on their heavenly journey. Turning toward home, the Sun illuminated the edges of the Earth in a translucent golden glow. Rahu's grasping shadow tried to ensnarl the blue sphere, while Ketu's shadow slithered menacingly below.

"Jaidev, Jaidev, wake up," Mahesh's voice called from another world.

Jaidev's eyes fluttered open, the faint light of dawn diffusing through his window. He stretched out on the thin mat, then rose to a sitting position. A maze of symbols covered the parchment in front of him, each representing a celestial body and its meticulous placement. Jaidev spent the entire night studying and calculating their movements, falling asleep as his ghee lamp sputtered out.

"Look here Babaji, I have calculated back two thousand years," Jaidev said. "Never has this occurred. It almost came to pass about nine hundred years ago and again almost nine hundred years before that. But it was never so perfect."

Mahesh listened closely to every word Jaidev said.

"Babaji, 1,827 years ago, Saturn and Jupiter came together in Pisces. They united three times over a six-month period—two times in the lunar mansion of Uttara Bhadrapada and the last time in the mansion of Revati. Then Babaji, 973 years ago, they came together three times again in Pisces—all occurring in the lunar mansion of Uttara Bhadrapada. But this year is truly a wondrous and blessed event. In a little over two months from today, Saturn and Jupiter will reunite for the first time on May 27th in Pisces in the mansion of Revati. A few months later, on September 29th, they again will come together in Revati. And finally, on December 3rd, they will meet in Revati a third time."

Jaidev paused for a beat, letting the profundity of his words settle in before continuing.

"This is a time when a great soul, a Maha Atma, will be born. It will occur a few weeks after the last Saturn-Jupiter conjunction, when the benefic Moon joins them in the sky. All indications are that this birth will happen in the west. Pisces and Revati will be in the west, heralding and aspecting the rising ascendant in the east. Saturn and Jupiter in Pisces cast their most favorable glance to Virgo, the Virgin, and the lunar mansion of Hasta, bringing the highest blessings to this birth. Babaji, I ask for your blessing to travel to the west. I want to find and witness this birth the gods are foretelling in the heavens. When Saturn—representing Lord Shiva and meditation—and Jupiter—representing Brihaspati, the teacher of the gods—beckon, I must follow."

Mahesh gazed proudly and thoughtfully at Jaidev, taking it all in. "Son, we can pray about it and discuss it further after tomorrow. I am truly impressed by everything you have foreseen. Tonight is the Holi festival bonfire and tomorrow, Holi, celebrating love and the start of spring. We must prepare our sacrifice and prayers for this evening. Tonight is Purnima Tithi in Phalguna, the night when the

Moon is full and bright. Our prayers, the yagya for Holi, are sacred mantras and sacrifices that will enliven the gods that rule the forces of nature. We shall invoke the gods to bless us with good fortune—for the return of the light to bring spring warming, flowers, and bountiful crops."

At sunset, Jaidev, Mahesh, and several other priests performed the puja and yagya for the start of Holi. Aakash sat in the temple with other young Kshatriyas. Ravi, his father Dharmik, mother Sita, and sister Amrita sat with the wealthy merchant families on the other side of the temple. Occasionally, Aakash glanced in wonderment at Amrita, spellbound by her young beauty. When her full lips parted and eyes lowered in modest respect, his heart quickened. He had known her since she was 5 years old, and now, at 18, she had blossomed into her own. She shared her mother's sensuous brown eyes, flawless complexion, and flowing black hair. Her golden and turquoise sari wrapped delicately around her youthful figure and a simple bindi adorning her forehead mesmerized Aakash. When her eyes caught his, she smiled demurely. Aakash's face flushed. Her beauty enraptured him.

After the prayers concluded, Mahesh lit a torch and led Jaidev and the priests outside of the temple to the prepared woodpile for the Holika Dahan bonfire.

The elders sang a traditional mantra as Mahesh lit the sacred fire. The crackling flames illuminated enthusiastic faces, and the villagers broke out in joyous song, celebrating the victory of good over evil.

As the fire burned brightly, Jaidev made his way over to where Aakash was standing. "Aakash," he whispered, "there is a journey I must take. Saturn and Jupiter have written in the stars a wondrous event. It will occur in a far-off land to the west—lands I have only heard about from the caravans that have stopped here in our village."

"Jaidev, how will you do that? You have never traveled too far from the village. The lands to the west can be dangerous. The people do not honor our gods and customs. It can take many months to reach Damascus, where the caravans originate," Aakash explained, his eyes scanning Jaidev's face.

"I know," Jaidev said. "I don't know how I will do it yet, but I must go."

"Jaidev, Aakash, are you ready for tomorrow?" Ravi asked, joining them.

"Tomorrow? Yes. After tomorrow, who knows?" Aakash replied, grinning mischievously.

"What does that mean?" Ravi asked.

"I'll let Jaidev tell you," Aakash returned.

Jaidev placed a finger to his pursed lips. "Ravi, don't repeat this to anyone yet. I want to take a journey west, towards Damascus. There is a significant event coming—the stars say it is so—and I want to be there to witness it."

"But Jaidev, Brahmins don't take such journeys. We Vaishyas do and a Kshatriya like Aakash would, but a priest, a Brahmin, no way." Ravi shook his head incredulously.

"There is a first time for everything," Jaidev justified. "Besides, it is written in my chart at birth that I would travel to foreign lands."

"Jaidev, if you are going on this quest, as a Kshatriya, I feel it is my duty to go with you and protect you. But I must admit, I'm wary of what lies ahead. I don't know if I'm wise or brave enough to help," Aakash said firmly.

"It is essential that I join you on this journey as well," Ravi declared. "My talents for speaking multiple dialects and wheeling-and-dealing will come in handy. We can join a caravan that's heading westward and gain valuable insights into new products to bring back home. My father is searching for a silk thread of high quality to give as a gift to my mother, and I'm determined to help him locate a source."

"I am so fortunate to have you both as friends," Jaidev expressed. "We can make our plans for as soon as possible after the

Holi festival tomorrow."

"Okay, sleep well tonight. The festival starts at daybreak," Aakash said.

As Aakash walked away from the bonfire, he turned for one last look. Amrita's eyes were following him. His normal wide grin was strangely shy as he nodded goodnight. He turned away sighing and thought: *She will have many suitors, with money and many servants. I could never attract her.*

Aakash continued to walk towards his father's home, the bonfire gradually disappearing behind him. From the eastern sky, Capricorn rose slowly, taking over the heavens. Suddenly, a shooting star streaked across the horizon and vanished into the night.

Aakash turned onto his father's road to find a golden chariot waiting in front of him. Its ornate wooden wheels gleamed with polish and care, and five white horses pulled it. He stepped curiously into the chariot and the horses took off towards the once roaring bonfire. The crowd cheered as he passed by, and he could see Amrita standing among them, watching him with eyes like pools of water. The horses stopped right in front of her. She smiled at Aakash and stepped into the chariot. He whisked her away towards the moonlit river.

The plaintive, warbling trill of a blackbird floated through the open window, summoning Aakash from the dream realm. He slowly blinked his eyes open, and on a twiggy branch outside he spotted the cause: a glossy, black-feathered creature with a bright orange beak cocked mid-song, illuminated by the warm glow of morning light. He smiled wistfully at the bird, wishing his dream could have lasted just a few moments longer.

After washing himself in a basin of water in his room, he found some roti and dosas his mom had cooked the night before and stuffed his mouth with them. He then had some fresh water from the well, grabbed his drum and bow, placed them in a bag with some clean clothes, and headed towards the main village.

The village was alive with joyful sounds of laughter as the children scrambled around, throwing handfuls of vivid powders at each other. From every side, they dusted people and objects with bright colors—pinks, purples, blues, greens, reds, whites, and more—turning them into rainbow-hued works of art. Everyone from the Brahmins to the Shudras was showered with an array of vibrant hues that celebrated the arrival of spring.

Aakash, seeing a group of children readying a coat of powder for him, grabbed some from a jar left on a doorstep and ran towards the kids, letting loose a cloud of violet fog. The screeching kids pounced on him, immediately covering him with orange, red, blue, white, and green powder. Making a fierce demon face, he grabbed one of the young boys and flung him into the air, catching him as giggles of pleasure erupted. Suddenly, half a dozen kids waited for their turn to be unleashed into the sky—to fly momentarily like a bird, be caught, and safely returned to solid ground by Aakash's powerful arms. One after the other, he flung them into the heavens and caught them, gently placing their feet back on the earth. *I better save my arms for the archery contest later*, Aakash thought. He bowed to his young admirers and continued towards the main festival grounds.

Nearing the festival entrance, Aakash spotted Ravi and Amrita laughing as they covered each entrant to the festival grounds with colored powder. Aakash walked up and when they spied him, they readied another douse of powder just for him. Ravi threw first, a blue sapphire colored powder, and Amrita took some wetted red powder and painted Aakash's face gleefully. His skin memorized each brush of her fingers as if a first kiss. His heartbeat uncontrollably. Her smile was perfection, her lilting laugh a primordial harmony, her subtle floral perfume an invitation to discover sensuous delights. He thought he would burst but only showed his wide infectious grin, waving a finger in warning that he would repay them later. Amrita gave an alluring smile. "We'll see about that," she taunted.

As soon as Aakash stepped onto the festival grounds, energy

and anticipation swept over him. Everywhere he looked, people were bustling to get their stalls ready for the festivities. Nearby, children practiced their dance moves for the grand finale that would come later that day. He made his way to the riverbanks and saw other men already washing off the colors from their hair and clothes. Without hesitation, Aakash removed his clothing down to his loincloth and jumped into the crisp, ice-cold waters. He scrubbed himself with his hands, watching as the multicolored powders easily melted away in the current. After drying himself with his soiled clothes, Aakash pulled on a fresh pair of garments from his bag. His powerful frame stood out amongst all the others, a sharp contrast to their soft, aged muscles.

He took out his bow from its bag and secured it on his back in the typical manner. He wore it proudly. It showed he was a protector, a warrior, and that serving with his life was his duty.

The archery field teamed with young athletes and warriors honing their skills. Aakash chose his spot and measured out the distances of the targets from him—30 steps, then 60 steps, and finally, 100 steps. He glanced up at the treetops to gauge the strength and direction of the wind. Then, he tested his bow, pulling it to a half-draw, three-quarter draw, and full-draw. Calmly, he drew an arrow from his quiver and sighted in on the 30-step target. Steadying his footing, he notched the arrow onto the bowstring and raised the bow to rest by his cheek. His eyes never leaving the center of the target, he pulled back on the string, fully recoiling the bow, and squeezed his shoulder blades for that last inch before releasing. The thud of a perfect hit in dead center echoed through the field. After two more thuds hitting the 30- and 60-step targets, he carefully aimed at the 100-step target. A crow cawed as Aakash's arrow shot forward towards its mark but too far for Aakash to hear if it struck. He ran down the field to get a better view, and there it was—a perfectly placed shot in dead center! With this new bow, hitting any target seemed as effortless as thought itself; Aakash was ready to compete.

Waiting his turn, Aakash wandered the festival grounds. He saw the old sadhu meditating beneath a Sal tree with its large, fiery-colored leaves and decided to wait nearby until the sadhu opened his eyes. Birds chirped in the bushes, a gentle breeze blew through Aakash's hair, and the warm sun shined on his face. With eyes closed, his thoughts appeared like mist rising from a lake at dawn, forming clouds across the sky before wisping away, leaving a blank slate. A light gust of wind brushed his face, and Aakash opened his eyes to a smiling sadhu. "To let the arrow fly, first pull back the bow," the old man proclaimed before standing up. With an oddly graceful air about him, he bowed to Aakash and disappeared into the forest.

Aakash strode back to the archery field, feeling invigorated and ready to compete. As he prepared for his turn, he took in the sight of his rivals, anticipation building. His confidence was enough to unnerve the other Kshatriyas—word had already spread about the accuracy of his new bow. The competition was finally here, and he would hit his mark.

Summoned to the archery field in front of a crowd of villagers, enamored young girls waved at Aakash, yet he remained focused on the target ahead. He lifted and pulled back the bow, feeling an unspoken connection between himself and the weapon. He aimed at the 30-step target and let loose his arrow, hitting dead center. A collective gasp rang out over the field as he readied three arrows for the 60-step target. Unsurprisingly, he nailed three bullseyes in succession. Then, his eyes met the 100-step target. He scanned the treetops for any breezes before raising his arms with the arrow drawn, taking a deep breath, and releasing. An attendant alongside the target signaled another perfect strike, and the village erupted as Aakash was champion once again.

The crowd celebrated as Aakash lifted his prize, a wooden sculpture of Lord Shiva. He began to walk away with it when he spotted a crippled young boy, a Sudra, admiring him from afar. His heart opened wide, Aakash approached the boy and presented him with the statue. The child almost burst with joy that his hero had not only acknowledged his presence but blessed him with something so precious and expensive. Tears of gratitude streamed down his cheeks. Aakash embraced the boy and whispered a healing prayer in his ear: "Lord Shiva shows that your spirit is liberated in the dance." Watching the scene unfold, Amrita quickly brushed away a tear before anyone noticed.

A conch shell sounded from the tent area where the food was being prepared—it was time to eat. Villagers shared food and treats with everyone around them. Sita and Dharmik had a large tent set up and happily greeted each village neighbor. Their servants prepared generous dishes of food for each.

Jaidev, spotting Ravi, greeted him heartily, and they waited for Aakash to join them before eating. "Will Barbod be joining us later for the music?" Jaidev asked.

"Yes, he has his work to do but assured me he would be on time for our turn," Ravi said.

"Did you convince him to sell you the chang?" Jaidev asked. "That instrument is amazing."

"Not yet, I'm working on it," Ravi replied with a laugh. "Come, let's eat. Here comes Aakash."

"Aakash, congratulations. You never cease to amaze me," Jaidev exclaimed.

"Jai Ram. Did you see the sadhu earlier meditating under the Sal tree? I sat by him and fell into a deep, restful state just being near him. He is the one who gave me the bow. Who is he?" Aakash asked.

"Yes, I saw him sitting there. I hadn't seen him before. My father may know who he is. I'm starving," Jaidev said.

"Me too," Ravi chimed. "Come to my father's tent. The food is ready and there is plenty."

Sita and Dharmik's tent was filled with a variety of dishes. Jaidev, Aakash, and Ravi helped themselves to vegetable biryani, chana masala, lassi, gujiya, and rice kheer. The food was unmistakably festive and not something shared every day. Before they left, Ravi made a plate for Barbod, knowing he would appreciate the delicious offerings.

The four musicians met at the area where the late afternoon entertainment was held. A lone flutist played a soft raga as all the festive villagers assembled. Barbod, eyeing Ravi's plate of food for him, lit up like the Holi bonfire. Being treated with such thoughtfulness and kindness was rare. He devoured each bite like a kitten starved for milk, licking his fingers and plate so as not to miss one subtle taste of the amazing meal.

Aakash sat on the left side of the small, raised platform and began a gentle drumbeat, following the flutist. The gathering crowd clapped with appreciation when the flutist finished.

Barbod opened the case that held his chang and lifted it in the air. A murmur swept through the crowd, unfamiliar with the strange instrument. Their music was usually comprised of only drums, flutes, and a few horns from conch shells. While Barbod waited for the other musicians to be ready, he played a brief sequence of notes and chords. Everyone around him grew even more excited, shouting out to their friends and family to join them and witness this new musical device. Immediately, a throng of people flooded into the performance area.

Ravi started the performance with his flute, and Jaidev and Aakash followed with their own instruments. Barbod smiled as he noted the tempo and melody of the song from their earlier practice session. Gracefully moving his fingers, he plucked out notes that had never been heard in Northern India before. Everyone paused to listen to the ethereal music, except for one Brahmin who walked away disapprovingly, believing that the traditional music was being desecrated. When the second song began, many of the women rose, forming a line at the side of the stage and starting the classic Holi Kunitha dance. Sita and Amrita moved to the beat, swaying their arms in harmony with the other dancers and beckoning all to join in, every move connecting them as one.

The musicians played an old favorite, Barbod's instrument infusing it with new energy and carrying the audience away in a wave of joy and nostalgia. As the hour went by, the melodies grew more powerful and heartfelt. When the finale came, heads turned towards the stage with admiration and respect. Slowly, people rose from their seats and gathered around each other in an embrace of love and unity, swaying to the music of their shared culture.

Barbod gave a full strum, ending the song, and rose to bow with Ravi, Aakash, and Jaidev. The applause was raucous. It was a wonderful day of colors, contests, food, and song. Now it was time for a peaceful ending to the evening.

"Jaidev, tomorrow, I would like my father to meet with you and Aakash," Ravi said. "We have plans to make."

"Tomorrow then," Aakash agreed.

"Yes," Jaidev acknowledged.

Each bowed good night to all, hands clasped at the heart, and headed home. By the time Ravi walked towards his father's house, it was nightfall. A shooting star fell over the eastern horizon towards Pisces, still below the horizon.

Before retiring, Ravi took a lantern to the stable. His favorite horse, Tejomaya, snorted as he walked in, signaling that he wanted to be ridden. Ravi saddled him up and took Tejomaya out into the light of the full Moon, the smell of hay reminding him of his childhood at his father's stables. Tejomaya trotted down a path that led into the once familiar forest, which now seemed unrecognizable. Ravi felt vulnerable and alone in the darkness without his family nearby. Suddenly, an arrow whizzed by his ear and struck a tree limb in front of him. Ravi tensed and looked back, unable to tell how many were behind him. He gently kicked Tejomaya to run, and they galloped through the moonlit shadows and trees, his heart pumping with each stride. Strange voices yelled behind him in a threatening shriek.

Chapter 3 – The Meeting

"Ravi, wake up! Everyone is coming to meet with your father," Sita yelled into Ravi's room.

Ravi, Aakash, Jaidev, and his father, Mahesh, congregated in Dharmik's home. Ravi nervously fiddled with a cloth as his eyes shifted from side to side. The strange dream had unsettled him, and he was anxiously unsure if his dad would allow him to go on the journey.

Dharmik, taking control of the meeting, spoke first. "Jaidev, tell me about this trip you are contemplating."

"With deepest respect, I will try to convey to you the meaning of the stars and what is being foretold," Jaidev began. "Since the earliest Vedas, our Rishis have noted the lunar mansions, the movement of the grahas, and the seasons. Parashara told us that the planetary gods, the grahas, have a twofold purpose. One is to deliver to man his karmas. The other is the unborn Lord, as Janardan, as Vishnu, assumes the auspicious forms of these grahas to destroy the demons and sustain the divine beings. In our beloved Song of Life, The Bhagavad Gita, does not Krishna say that 'Whenever dharma is in decay and adharma flourishes, I create myself again and again to re-establish dharma?'" Jaidev continued. "The stars have foretold of many enlightened teachers. Our forefathers foretold Lord Krishna's birth. Now we have a unique and extremely rare occurrence in Pisces, the sign of the Fish. The grahas Saturn and Jupiter come together not just once, but three times over the next several months. This rare occurrence happens about every 900 years, though it has never happened that all three conjunctions will occur in Pisces in the final lunar mansion of Revati. This signifies the birth of a great Being to lead us to moksha, the liberation of the soul, with deep faith and devotion to God," Jaidev explained. "Shani as Saturn enlivens deep meditation while Guru as Jupiter enlivens devotion. This birth will be a teacher greater than the gods—a great light that will illuminate the gods themselves. Indeed, a Maha Atma is coming into the world to re-establish dharma and bring man closer to the One God, the unborn Father of Creation, Brahman. The birth will take place far west of our Ganges. I must meet this auspicious child," Jaidev concluded.

Aakash and Ravi sat fully awake to every word. Jaidev's explanation conveyed the special significance of the trip—the sense that something in the world was about to change and he may be part of it.

Jaidev glanced at Ravi who shivered slightly, still thinking of his dream. Jaidev thought to ask him after the meeting why he was uneasy.

Mahesh, sitting and listening thoughtfully, added, "Jaidev has calculated the grahas, rashis, and lunar mansions correctly. My grandfather also foresaw that this time would be a special event for humankind. I agree Jaidev should represent us at this event."

Dharmik moved to stand in front of the fireplace, and his eyes shifted between Ravi and Jaidev. "The Bahira clan owes a great debt to you and your father, Jaidev. You have been so wise in advising us on the best times to start projects, marry, and sow our crops; we've been blessed with abundance thanks to your knowledge of astrology. If I can assist you, then rest assured I will do my best."

Ravi's eyes grew wide. He wasn't sure how his father would react. His surprise spilled out, saying, "Father, we have your blessing, and I can join them?"

"Ravi, when I was a young man your age, I journeyed and made contacts that have served us well. It is time for you to make contacts of your own. Heed this, it is a tumultuous time in the west. The caravans that come through tell us that the west is ruled by Romans. They can be a brutal people, so do not cross them. They killed their emperor Julius Caesar several years ago and now Caesar Augustus, his step son, rules the Roman Empire. I hear stories of rebellion within the Roman territories that the Romans respond to harshly. Still, they have an appetite for our spices, perfumes, fabrics, and especially new silk thread from the far east, China. I would like to open more trade with them. I would also like to find a reliable silk supplier for our needs. So, yes, Ravi, you can not only join them, you will represent me and our family, our business, and our trading acumen on the journey. Our stables will supply three fine horses and two bullock carts of goods, and two of our servants will accompany you. We will send our finest cloths, spices, and perfumes with you to sell or trade for what you need. You will meet with the merchants of China and of the west and establish a relationship with them for our future suppliers and partners."

Mahesh raised his right hand, saying, "I have calculated the muhurta, the best starting time for this trip. It is tomorrow while the Moon is still almost full. Jaidev's natal chart confirms this. The transits to his house of fortune, knowledge, and long journeys, and his house of partners are very favorable, confirming that the trip should begin immediately under this full moon for the best possible success. The benefic Moon will be strong in the first lunar mansion of Ashwini in Aries, a time that favors journeys, trading, and if necessary, conquering enemies.

Dharmik unrolled an old map and paused, reading it carefully. "Ravi, Aakash, and Jaidev," he began, "here is a map that will take you through Persia to Damascus, where the trade routes originated. You will join a caravan of traders for protection and safety. The caravans move freely as trade is necessary and makes a country stronger. It is an older map, and alternative routes will have to be added as you travel. All accounts are that the west has been changing constantly over the last decade. The Persians, Greeks, and Romans have a very fragile alliance. There is much to be wary and careful of."

Mahesh, looking at the map, said, "When you reach Bactria, find my old friend Khartum. He came through our area many years ago with a trading caravan when Jaidev was just born. He had fallen very ill and had badly cut his right arm and broken his leg in a fall. We set his leg and nursed him in our home. His arm wound had become badly infected, so we treated it according to the teachings of Ayurveda, applying turmeric to stop the infection and then aloe vera to help with the healing. Without treating the infection, he would have lost his arm," Mahesh explained. "It's been 20 years since I have seen him. His heart is honorable and true. He will give you good counsel for your journey."

Sita and Amrita entered carrying hot tea and the gujiya made the day before. As they handed out the beverages and sweets, Aakash couldn't help but admire Sita's beauty. Even as she aged, her dark eyes framed by round cheeks and cherry lips kept their gentle glow. In comparison, Amrita was even more mesmerizing. Her soft brown eyes were like a captivating canvas of flowers, her lush red lips unveiling snow-white pearls when she smiled. Aakash wanted nothing more than to gaze at Amrita forever, yet he dared not look directly into her eyes, for she may sense his longing. As a warrior, he was fearless and free, but this woman could capture him with only a glance.

Dharmik, looking at Sita, said, "Dearest, our son Ravi and his young friends are preparing for a journey that will take them to foreign lands along the trade routes and beyond. They will leave tomorrow morning."

The usual serene look on Sita's face changed to surprise, then wonder and fear. Knowing that caravans traveled great distances over long periods of time, she was unprepared to see her son depart so quickly. "Why? What would cause this sudden journey?" Sita asked.

Dharmik replied, "Our young Brahmin here has discovered that a significant event will happen in the west. Through the Science of Light, he has found that a glorious light will come into the world—a Maha Atma for this age. It is a blessing that our son may witness it. Also, he will establish connections to trade our goods and bring goods from other lands back to us."

Amrita's shoulders drooped, her eyes not fixed on anyone, only inward. She stood alone feeling her upcoming loss. Sita gently put her arm around Amrita's shoulder, comforting her. "Your brother is a very strong, intelligent, and shrewd young man. He will be fine," she assured her. Amrita only shut her eyes and nodded, her thoughts and dreams holding her inner secret.

"That settles it," Dharmik said. "Ravi, take Jaidev and Aakash to the stable. Let them choose their travel companions. Ravi will take Tejomaya, his fine Arabian steed, and there are several amazing horses to pick from."

"I will help you, Jaidev," Ravi said. "I will match you with a horse you will feel a friendship with. There is a science and art to knowing a fine horse."

As the men hurried to the stable, Jaidev, thinking of Ravi's uneasiness, asked, "What was troubling you earlier?"

"I had a dream last night. I was being chased and hunted in strange woods," Ravi revealed.

Jaidev knew there was a meaning, a warning to his dream and this trip. He did not comment on it other than to reassure his friend. They both viewed the trip as an adventure—an exciting but possibly dangerous one. Nothing would deter them; they had already made up their minds.

Jaidev thought of Ravi's chart. He was a Leo ascendant and had just entered the dhasa-bhukti of Mercury-Ketu. Mercury was the ruler of his 11th and 2nd house. Forbidden secret desires were karmically attractive to him, and they would be particularly strong during this period. He recalled the time when Ravi was 13 and took some money from Dharmik's hidden drawer to buy a secret map to a treasure chest that a caravan fakir sold him. Dharmik was furious that Ravi was tricked by a common fakir into buying a worthless map and for taking his money without permission. Ravi swore he only borrowed the money without permission to put it back when he found the treasure. His desire to find a large fortune overcame him.

Amrita followed them into the stable. There were some twenty horses available to choose from. Aakash and Jaidev walked from stall to stall, considering each horse. Near the end of the stable, an anxious young stallion paced and snorted. "Maybe not that one, Aakash. He is a bit of a free spirit," Ravi said, laughing.

Aakash slowly approached the young stallion, his steps measured and cautious. As soon as he was within range, the horse snorted softly in greeting before gently whipping his tail. Aakash stopped in his tracks, feeling no fear or need to dominate the animal. He stared into the horse's eyes, searching for any trace of fear or intimidation that would make him back away. Their gaze remained locked until both man and horse came to an understanding—they were equals. Aakash reached out with a steady hand and stroked the steed's face. The horse bowed his head in response, accepting his touch. "What is your name?" he spoke softly, finally breaking the silence between them.

"He is Ojas," Amrita said. "Named for vigor, the essence of life. I named him from a dream I had when we received him."

"Perfect," Aakash replied. "I cannot take him if he is yours."

"This one only belongs to whom he chooses," Amrita affirmed. "He is a brother spirit to my horse, Sapna. Come with me. We will find a saddle that befits him and you."

In the saddle room, there were many to choose from. The artisans that served the Bahira family did the finest work. "Which one do you like?" Amrita asked.

Aakash looked them over pensively, grazing his fingers across the smooth tanned hides. "How about this one?" he asked Amrita.

"Yes," Amrita said, coming closer to Aakash and lowering her voice. Reaching into the folds of her sari, she pulled out a small red cloth and held it up for them both to see. Tiny stitches of gold thread created an intricate pattern depicting Lord Ganesha. "I don't mean to be so bold—I want you to have this," Amrita said shyly as she placed the cloth down onto the saddle.

"It is beautiful, Amrita, I—" Aakash fumbled for words.

"Shh," Amrita returned, drawing her finger to her pursed lips.

Aakash felt mesmerized by Amrita's beauty, her bold spirit, and her soft lips. He met her gaze, which was full of love, sending a thrill through his body. He leaned forward and their lips sealed together. With one muscular arm, he embraced her delicate frame while his other hand rhythmically ran through her long hair. As they pulled away from each other, Aakash saw tears streaming down Amrita's cheeks.

"I will always..." Aakash started, but Amrita put a finger to his lips to stop him from speaking.

"Just come back to me, Aakash," she whispered.

"I will, I promise," he assured, stunned. Amrita turned quickly, knowing their time alone could not be too long. She went back into the main stable.

Aakash folded the cloth and tucked it into his garment. He carried the saddle to Ojas. "Here boy, let's see if this saddle is the right one."

Jaidev and Ravi examined Gyatri, a graceful, poised, and attentive horse with a mane that flapped as she cantered. "She will be perfect," Ravi declared. "Let's take them out for a spin so we can get acquainted."

Amrita trudged back to her father's home and entered the room where her mother was located, her head hanging forlornly.

"Amrita, do not worry, all will be well."

"Mama, I'm worried."

"I know, my child," Sita consoled. "Aakash will keep them

safe, and your heart will be safe too."

"Mama?" Amrita responded quizzically.

"I understand, child. I have watched how you and Aakash played when you were very young. No one could keep you apart—no children were happier together. When your bodies changed, you avoided one another. Don't think I do not sense you are always aware of him, and he you. He has grown into a fine young Kshatriya, faithful and strong in his dharma. The gods did not mean his heart to be for any other but yours. A Jyotishi may read the stars to determine our dharma, artha, kama, and moksha—all of which are important—but it takes a mother to truly understand her child's heart."

"Oh, Mama," Amrita said, weeping softly as her mother welcomed her into her comforting arms.

Ravi, Aakash, and Jaidev rode the horses to the caravan camp. Barbod waved welcomingly when he saw them approach.

"Barbod, can you take me to the caravan leader?" Ravi asked.

"Yes," Barbod replied. "We know him as The Khabir, and his name is Nasir. Come, I will take you to his tent. It is a short distance."

Nasir was sitting outside his tent when they approached.

"Nasir, if I may, my friend Ravi would like to talk to you. He is Dharmik's son," Barbod requested.

Nasir, a portly, large, intimidating man with a turban and squinty eyes, looked Ravi over. "What is on your mind, young Ravi?" Nasir questioned.

"My two friends and I would like to join the caravan," Ravi declared. "We have goods to bring to Damascus and other business in the west. We are three riders on horseback and two bullock carts with two servants."

"What goods are you bringing?" Nasir asked.

"Spices, perfumes, and fine cloth," Ravi replied. "We will have two wagons worth of goods."

"The bullock carts will only be good for your journey to Bactria," Nasir said. "From there, you will need to exchange your bullock carts for camels to make the trek across the desert with us. I require payment before we leave. Our caravan's cook, Paloma, will supply a dinner each day as we make camp. We break camp and leave tomorrow at daybreak," he explained, spitting out a well-chewed betel nut between his rotting teeth.

"You are most gracious Nasir. We will be ready," Ravi said.

As they walked away, Barbod expressed, "I'm thrilled that you will be traveling with us. In Bactria, there is a merchant that makes beautiful changs. You won't need to buy mine. I will introduce you. He will sell you many."

"Excellent," Ravi exclaimed. "I will have my father send his most trusted servants with us. We can send them back home from Bactria with the bullock carts filled with changs and other goods for my father."

"Yes," Barbod affirmed. "I will see you early tomorrow as our journey begins."

Later that evening, Mahesh and Jaidev sat pensively, sharing their last dinner. The air was heavy. Jaidev gazed out the window and saw the stars twinkling in the night sky—a reminder of the many possibilities the future held.

As a boy, Jaidev thought of how he looked up to Mahesh. Jaidev would mimic his father's meditation position, sitting cross-legged with a straight back and steady head. He fondly recalled practicing Vedic chants with his father, who had a keen ear, correcting any mispronunciations. Mahesh taught him to understand the ancient texts, the chants carrying his ancestors' teachings inside them. No matter where life took him, he was never without their wisdom. Although many other young Brahmins memorized the texts for praise, Jaidev felt their vibrations alive in him. Every experience was an exaltation of the Vedic teachings—dynamic, ever-changing, yet never changing.

His father instructed him how to meditate properly on the Om, the reverberation that encompassed all other sounds. Gliding within, the Om guided Jaidev through the depths of his mind, settling at the source of thought, the silent observer now an ever-present part of him.

"Jaidev," Mahesh broke the silence at last, "your long adventure will begin tomorrow. New worlds will be before your eyes, fresh sounds before your ears, unfamiliar smells before your nose, new foods before your tongue, and new sensations before your skin." Mahesh forced a smile, sad that his son would be leaving him for such a long journey. "I will hold you in my heart until you return. Keep the Vedas always within you. Hold close the Smriti, that which is remembered, and the Shruti, that which is heard, of the Vedas."

"I will, father, and I will hold you close also in my heart until I return."

Meanwhile, Aakash was in turmoil, tossing and turning unable to sleep. He wanted more than anything to stay with Amrita, but he had committed to a journey that would take him away from her. He ached for her presence, his deepest desire to hold her in his arms. The thought of finally expressing his love for her had given him immense hope and joy, yet the prospect of leaving her now filled him with distress. He longed to be with her, to make plans with her, walk beside her, and feel her body against his own. All he could do was fight back his feelings—to suppress his anger at his fate, as the reality of his impending separation sank in.

Aakash stepped outside in the moonlight, his energy high and thoughts running wild. There in the shadows cast by the bright moon was the old sadhu, looking at him and smiling with clasped hands.

"What is your name, old sadhu?" Aakash asked, surprised to see him.

"There was a time when a name was important. Now the silence before and after the name is important. The silence from which the name emerges is all," said the sadhu.

"O nameless one, I need your wisdom. My thoughts are racing," Aakash declared.

"Yes, Aakash, questions and disturbances are within you. Rajas is guiding your thoughts," spoke the sadhu.

"My heart is torn between accompanying my friend on a journey I promised to go on and leaving my dream of the woman I have always desired," Aakash continued.

"All men must make choices. It is the nature of man. Even to choose no choice is a choice. Choice is the action of the wheel of karma, the wheel of the soul. Subtle impressions arise as samskara[3], memories, which leads to vasana, our desire, and then we choose to act, karma. The choice leaves a samskara from which another vasana and karma arise," the sadhu expounded.

"How do I choose? How do I know which action is right?" Aakash asked.

"The bow holds within it the seed of the tree, the potential of becoming, the warmth of the sun, the rain, the earth, wind, moon, stars, rainbows, and the memory of birds that nested in its arms. And now, after Shiva cast a thunderbolt separating the limb from its mother, its dharma arose. It has become one with your dharma and serves your spirit on its journey home—to the earth, water, sun, wind, stars, and rainbows. You will know all of this when you learn the secret of the bow: 'To let the arrow fly, first pull back the bow,'" the sadhu continued. "Men are bound by the three worlds of maya— of waking state, dream state, and deep sleep state. It is not until a man finds the fourth world called turiya, the pure awareness, that a man can be free from this bondage, and the three worlds united. The bow teaches us that it is by drawing it to the point of most dynamic stillness that the arrow's action can be most effective. You also must draw back your mind to the point of perfect stillness in the fourth world beyond the three worlds of maya. Filling the mind with the words of an old sadhu will teach nothing. Experience the stillness of the drawn bow and let the arrow fly," the sadhu instructed. "Sit and

---

[3] Subtle impressions that lead to memories

34

close your eyes; hear the sound of creation in your mind. Follow it to where it comes from and be."

Aakash sat beside the old sadhu and closed his eyes. When he opened them sometime later, the moon had moved across the sky, and the old sadhu was gone. He must hurry and pack for the journey.

Just before the sun rose, Ravi, Aakash, and Jaidev arrived at the stable. The servants prepared the horses for the journey, loading up the bullock carts with supplies. Dharmik's most faithful servant, Sanjeet, and his son Sanjaya were by their side.

Aakash spotted Amrita by a window in Dharmik's house. He motioned for her to meet him on the other side of the house. Walking to the rear of the home, he waited in the shadows until Amrita appeared in the doorway. Then he rushed to her, blurting, "In my mind, you will be with me every day, every night, in every dream." He held his hand on his heart as he spoke.

"Aakash, I have known since we were young that I would love you—that I do love you. I am sorry it is only now that you leave that I have made my heart known," she confessed.

"I too, Amrita. You are all I have ever dreamed about and all I will ever dream about. In the moonlight, on the walk over, this beautiful flower was waiting for me to bring it to you. Hold it with you as a sign of my love and the promise of our future together. I will return and be by your side for as long as the gods allow."

Aakash cupped the petals of a single red rose in his palm, intertwining their hands as they stood beneath the moonlight. He caressed her lips with his own, gently circling and exploring their softness, growing hungrier with each passing moment. His breath quickened as she clung to him, the warmth of her body pressing against his, their desire undeniable. Breaking away, he looked deep into her eyes, the longing still alive in the air between them. With one last kiss, Aakash released her hand and began his lonely walk back towards the stable, feeling a distinct chill as the distance grew between them.

"Aakash, let's get moving," Ravi said, mounting Tejomaya.

Aakash mounted Ojas, Jaidev mounted Gyatri, and Sanjeet lightly whipped the bullock carts forward. In the moonlight, they proceeded down the road towards the caravan. Sita and Dharmik waved them good fortune, while a lonely silhouette watched through the window. Saturn, Jupiter, and Mercury were rising in the sky as daybreak came.

Chapter 4 - The Journey Begins

"Ravi, have your group fall in behind the last camels," Nasir said, waving them to the position in the caravan. "The journey to Bactria will take a few weeks. I hope your asses toughen up." Nasir spit out a betel leaf and laughed.

Barbod, riding a camel, approached the three men. "Ravi, have you made a journey like this before?" he asked.

"No," Ravi said, his face wincing in disgust. "Barbod, how can you stand the smell of that beast? The stench would gag a goat."

"What smell?" Barbod laughed. "You'll get used to it."

Aakash shook his head and held his nose, agreeing with Ravi. "Ugh, that smell is putrid."

"Barbod, how did you come to work on a caravan?" Jaidev asked, curious about his life's journey.

Barbod recounted how his parents had joined a caravan when he was just a child. His father became the camel driver and his mother the cook. However, a scorpion sting killed his mother on her first trek across the desert. His dad then raised him until he was old enough to become a camel driver himself. "My father was a tough man; he didn't take to me playing music. He passed away from a fever while we camped in Bactria ten years ago."

"It must have been difficult to lose both your mother and father," Jaidev said, thinking Barbod must have an affliction to his 9th house of the father.

"When my mother was stung, I begged every god in creation

to save her. She swelled up from the sting and gasped for every breath to stay alive. Crying from the pain, her eyes were open when she took her last breath, still fighting to stay with us. I curse the god who made scorpions," Barbod declared.

"I'm sorry," Jaidev sympathized, convinced that indeed Barbod's 9th house had an affliction. Both his father and religion had bad samskaras.

"Have you any family other than your mother and father?" Ravi asked.

"I was their only child. My father's father was a warrior in the Seleucid army under the great general Surenas. All I know is that my grandfather was killed in a battle. Surenas defeated the Romans; then Julius Caesar and Marc Anthony, Caesar's general, defeated the Seleucids. Many of my people became Roman slaves, so the caravan is my only family. There are about 10 of us who always ride with Nasir. He appears gruff and ornery, but underneath, he is a good guy. The Romans also killed or sold his family into slavery," Barbod shared.

"These Romans, do they have armies here in the east?" Aakash asked.

"We may run into a contubernium when we are further west. That is a small unit of about 8 legionaries led by a decanate. They are scouts for larger units. They never bother the caravans, though. They protect them because caravans are vital suppliers to Rome," Barbod explained. "You need to get a head covering," he continued, pointing at his head wrap. "This one I wear is a keffiyeh. It protects the head from the sun, and, if the sand blows, can protect the mouth. It can even shield your delicate nose, Ravi, from the sweet perfume of my little Bellows here." Barbod stroked the caramel coat of the camel's long neck. "Ravi, she loves the flute, by the way. Perhaps you can serenade her later."

"I would like to learn to ride her, once I get used to that smell," Ravi said. "She moves gracefully, but not like my Tejomaya."

"Yes, she is very easy to ride. I will give you a sweet potato to feed her later. She will be friendly to anyone who gives her that treat. Women should be so easy," Barbod laughed.

"Were you ever married?" Aakash asked.

"No, thank goodness I have put no one through that hell," Barbod replied. "I've found a woman from time to time when my trading was fortunate enough to bring in the money. The caravanserais closer to Damascus have women, owned by Roman merchants, who sell their goods in the marketplace. Of course, no woman could possibly want me with this face here—" Barbod gestured at his weather-beaten skin, "carved by sand, wind, freezing rain, and blistering sun—greeting her every morning." He laughed.

Hours passed as the caravan moved north. Local villagers stood waving at them or watching them like they were a funeral procession. The trees, bushes, and hills Jaidev had seen his whole life filled the countryside. Thatched roofs and mud walls enclosed the village dwellings of families he was familiar with. Until now, Jaidev had never traveled farther than half a day's journey from his home. He was about to enter lands unknown to him. Despite feeling secure and recognized in these known places, he couldn't help but wonder about others' perceptions of him and his companions.

The caravan made its way through the valleys and forests at the base of the Himalayan mountains toward the Hindu Kush mountains. The late March weather was cool and crisp. With the monsoons still a few months away, they would be far from the drenching rains' reach by then. During the first few days, the caravan moved steadily toward Bactria. While Paloma's evening meals were simple dishes of rice and lentils, Jaidev was so hungry by mealtime that he thought the dishes were cooked for a king.

In the early afternoon of the fourth day, as the caravan came over a hill, a lake appeared. "We can stop for a rest here. The camels and horses could use a break," Barbod announced, knowing Nasir would stop by the lake.

"I need a break," Jaidev expressed. "I can't feel my legs and my butt has been killing me for several hours."

Ravi slid off Tejomaya, the white steed with dark, piercing eyes snorting gently. Stretching his back, he reached for the sky. "Ahh, smell that air—so fresh, so invigorating."

Aakash walked Ojas down to the lake. Mountains with russet rocky tops framed the shimmering water, and green trees crept down to the lake's edge. Ojas drank deeply from the cool water.

"When we make camp tonight, we will be by Wular Lake— where the snake dancers have settled," Barbod said.

"What are the snake dancers?" Ravi asked.

"They are nomads that move around India. Many migrated to Wular Lake, making their living with song, dance, and cobra charming," Barbod replied. "They are a very colorful and energetic people."

"Snake dancers!" Aakash exclaimed. "I can't wait to see them."

"Time to move on," Nasir announced, ending the break. "We want to make it to Wular Lake and set up camp for the night."

The caravan rounded the edge of the lake, revealing an expansive grassy field before them. In the distance, they could see a pack of dhole[4] with their reddish coats glimmering in the sun. They hovered around their kill, growling at any predators that drew too near. The travelers held their breath and watched the wild dogs warily, hoping they would remain unperturbed by their presence.

"They hunt by day and make a mournful cry at night," Barbod revealed, "but they usually don't bother with caravans like ours."

"Look, campfire smoke is up ahead," Jaidev pointed out, as the caravan continued its way toward it.

Standing on a hill watching the caravan approach were several men from the snake dancers' tribe. Their dress was colorful, and the patterns on their clothes formed intricate tapestries. Curious

---

[4] Asian wild dog

faces adorned with headbands or turbans watched the caravan through fierce, piercing eyes. They appeared to be of Indian heritage but seemed to have a wildness—a less civilized manner about them.

"They will welcome us tonight," Barbod assured. "They like to see what they can get from us in exchange for their food, song, and dance. Be careful, though; they are cunning. Keep an eye on your packs. Some have the hearts of a Chor. That's a thief, Jaidev," Barbod said with a telling laugh.

Finally, stopping for the night was a welcome respite for the weary travelers' aching bones. They set up camp and watered, fed, and tied up the horses and camels. After negotiating with a group of men, Nasir announced that the snake dancers would host them for the evening meal and entertain them with some song, dance, and snake charming. "Bring your chang!" he yelled back to Barbod.

"Ravi, Aakash, and Jaidev, bring your flutes and drum," Barbod requested. "Leave Sanjeet and Sanjaya to watch the horses and bullock carts."

Ravi and his companions approached the dera, the snake dancers' camp. The men and women stood to the side, their faces alight with curiosity as they eyed the newcomers. Ravi's gaze locked onto Sonal, the beautiful green-eyed daughter of Chetan, the snake dancers' chieftain. She wore an intricately decorated sari that clung to her slender frame, her shimmering black hair cascading down past her shoulders. As he passed by, she elbowed her friend and smiled seductively at him. Ravi felt his heart race as he tried to look away from her captivating eyes.

"Welcome Nasir and his traveling companions," a young man and snake dancer said. "Chetan, our chieftain, is away tonight. He and several of our tribal men are in the lowlands, snake hunting. We will prepare chapatti, dates, goat, and sheep's milk for your enjoyment. Come sit by the campfire and relax."

A turbaned old man sat by Jaidev and showed him his pungi, a flute-like instrument. Jaidev compared its shape and sound to his own flute. The bowl, just below the mouthpiece, was new to Jaidev. When he blew into it, the pungi made a terse hornlike sound, distinctly different from his mellow flute.

The pungi player signaled to a grinning man, who placed four knee-high covered baskets in front of Jaidev and himself. Swaying slightly as he played the pungi, the snake charmer looked up and smiled at Jaidev. He took another breath and reached over to open a basket held down by a woven strap. A large cobra, grayish green and copper red brown, swiftly emerged from the basket, mouth agape and fangs exposed. Jaidev's eyes grew wide as he froze, fear erupting in his heart. Aakash glared at the cobra dancing before them and pulled out an ornate katar from his belt, ready to strike the snake should it attack.

Laughter erupted from all the snake dancers at Jaidev's surprise. The cobra stood motionless in its strike position, transfixed by the music. The player removed a second basket top, and another cobra appeared, facing Jaidev and the young snake charmer. This time, Jaidev was ready for the snake. He sat scared and motionless as the pungi player waved his hand over yet another basket, revealing a third and then a fourth cobra. As the snakes swayed ever so slightly before them, Jaidev dared not move, afraid that one cobra would lose its trance and strike. Jaidev's fear amused the snake charmer even as his lips played the pungi. He casually replaced the tops on each basket until he covered the last one. Then, he stopped playing the pungi, laughing with delight at the group's surprise.

"Vaah, I have never been so scared in my life," Jaidev expressed, holding his chest in relief. "I have never seen such a thing."

"Come visit us in a few months during July/August," the young man said. "We have our festival then, and all the snake dancers and charmers in North India come together to celebrate Naga Panchami. We perform special yagyas for the occasion. Brahmin, you are welcome to join us."

"I would be honored," Jaidev replied. "Perhaps I can visit after our journey west. What is your name?"

"I am Chitranjan, brother of Sonal and son of Chetan," the young man said, pointing to Sonal, who was preparing food with the tribal women by another campfire.

"Rahu and Ketu must be prominent in your Rashi, the birth chart," Jaidev shared in a complimentary manner.

Chitranjan smiled and laughed with delight at the thought of the celestial grahas blessing him. The snake charmers felt a special affinity for Rahu and Ketu. Rahu was the serpent-like demon that became immortal by sneaking in line with the devas and drinking the ambrosia, the nectar of immortality. When the Sun and Moon saw Rahu drinking the Soma, they alerted Lord Vishnu, who threw his chakra, cutting Rahu in two. The head was Rahu, and the body became Ketu. Now they forever live in the shadow of the Sun and Moon, where eclipses occur, and exert their influence on humankind.

"Come eat. We will dance and sing after the meal. 'Atithi Devo Bhavah', meaning the guest is God," a smiling Sonal said, her eyes speaking directly to Ravi.

Ravi, like most Indian men, was unaccustomed to direct eye contact with a woman. The snake people seemed to have their own rules, though. He enjoyed the smiling eyes of such a beautiful creature.

"Mmm, this is delicious," Aakash proclaimed, ripping a piece of chapatti and dipping it into the milk and roasted meat.

Nasir's face lit up as the steaming bowl of stew was placed in front of him. He could smell the fragrant herbs and spices, the tender meat chunks, and the hint of sweetness from the milk. "Anything tastes delicious after a couple of days on the caravan," Nasir said appreciatively, savoring his first bite. "But this is worthy of praise. It smells incredible."

Jaidev received his bowl, clasping his hands together in the traditional Indian fashion.

The entire tribe of men, women, and children joined in and

shared in the community meal. "Sai Ram, our fortune has been good this year," Chitranjan declared.

"Come, come," Sonal said, clapping as everyone finished their meal. "It is time for music and dance."

Men grabbed their pungis, flutes, and drums called muflaks and dholas. The music's excited rhythm filled the air as they started a rigorous Matku raga. The women sprang to their feet, arms gracefully circling as they joined hands and formed a circle. They performed the traditional snake dance, undulating in unison to the beat of the drums. Sonal, wearing a bright green sari, stepped away from the formation, her hips swaying as she worked her way to the center of the group. Bending her lithe body over backward, her long hair cascaded down her back. Her hands on the ground supported her frame as she continued gyrating to the energetic, enchanting music.

Sonal's supple frame and graceful movements in the moonlight and campfire glow mesmerized Ravi. He and the other men clapped along with her dance and the rhythm of the snake dancer's song

Barbod picked up his chang and invited Ravi, Aakash, and Jaidev to join him. The unique sound of the traditional Indian music with the new instrument mesmerized the snake people. The men started singing the Shiva Shambho mantra, while the female dancers expressed homage to Shiva's pure consciousness through their movements. Sonal was one of these dancers, seemingly having an extra pair of arms—resembling Shiva in the cosmic dance.

Jaidev knew the mantra behind the Shiva Shambho dance well. Shiva was one of the triune Hindu Gods. There was Brahma, the God of Creation, Vishnu, the God of Preservation, and Shiva the God of Destruction. He closed his eyes and felt the primordial resonance within his Being.

While a slower raga was played, Sonal took a break and sat near Chitranjan, Jaidev, and Ravi. "Did you like the dance?" she asked

Ravi.

Somewhat unsettled by a young woman talking directly to him and not wanting to be rude, he said, "Yes, it was breathtaking," while thinking that Sonal was also breathtaking.

"There are many secrets to dance. The mystery, suspense, heartache, desire, and love," said Sonal, sounding wise beyond her years. "It is life itself."

"I never thought of it that way," Ravi replied.

Sonal smiled, raising her eyebrows and nodding knowingly, like a teacher to a student.

"Chitranjan, play!" Sonal called to her brother with a hint of mischief in her voice. She grabbed Ravi's hand, and they stepped into the center of the campfire light. As the melody swelled, Sonal swayed to its rhythm, inviting Ravi in by holding his gaze. He felt awkward at first, but as she spun around him gracefully and let out an infectious laugh, he instinctively stepped into her lead. Every movement—her swirling hair flying each time she spun—captivated him. He realized that this mysterious woman wasn't something he could control or possess. With each turn of her body, a web was woven around his heart. When the song concluded, Sonal playfully stroked Ravi's hair as if saying goodbye for now, sending him back to his seat by the campfire, his mind and heart ablaze.

Jaidev smiled as he watched, his hand keeping pace with the music. He was happy for his friend's expansion of heart and mind, but wary of the seeds of desire being planted. Ravi's path to moksha (liberation) had many obstacles in his chart. His artha and kama houses were strong. The pull of the grahas presented many karmic opportunities for riches and the desire to be prominent.

"Nasir, are you leaving tomorrow, or can you stay another night?" Chitranjan asked.

"We leave tomorrow at dawn," Nasir said.

"You should stay," Chitranjan insisted. "My father will be back in the late morning tomorrow and he may want to see your wares."

"Well, why didn't you say so?" Nasir replied, smiling. "How can I leave without visiting my old friend Chetan? We will leave at midday."

"We can show your travelers how to capture a snake in the dry brushland in the morning," Chitranjan suggested.

"I bet our Brahmin friend, Jaidev, can't wait," Nasir said, chuckling.

As they headed back to their camp, Ravi commented to Jaidev, "The women here are a lot more interesting than those at home. Did you see Sonal dance?"

"I did," Jaidev affirmed, smiling while patting his friend on the shoulder. "She is something."

At the camp, before retiring, Jaidev sat observantly and tracked the grahas' movement through the signs and lunar mansions. The moon was waning, becoming less visible each night. He reviewed his Prashna calculations—the chart cast when he first asked the stars whether to go west and search for the Maha-Atma. Based on his chart and the transits of the planetary gods during the journey, he anticipated danger in the coming days. Quietly, he recited a mantra to avert the karmic danger ahead.

When sunrise lit up the morning sky, Chitranjan came looking for Jaidev, Ravi, and Aakash. He wore a mischievous grin as he asked, "Are you ready to learn how to catch a cobra?" explaining they needed to venture about a mile away to an area with low vegetation and sandy soil. Cobras prefer those places.

The trees became scarce as they walked from camp. The grasslands turned to drier ground and then to sandy soil with small mounds, making it easy for small creatures to burrow and hide. Chitranjan dug into one burrow and reached deep inside a hole. Ravi, Jaidev, and Aakash watched nervously, expecting Chitranjan to be bitten by some exotic animal. With one fell swoop, he pulled out a large monitor lizard, holding it at arm's length to keep its sharp claws away from him.

"This one will make a nice drumhead for you, Aakash," he said, smiling and sticking the lizard in a bag.

A young snake dancer paused and pointed down the path to a shadow in the grass. It was a large cobra, freezing when it sensed their presence. Chitranjan crept up behind the snake and snatched it by the neck, gleeful at his catch. "Never approach from the front where they can strike," Chitranjan instructed, putting the snake in another bag. "Always from the rear."

The group spread out across the hills and brush, looking for snake trails in the sand or hiding places in the mounds. As Jaidev rounded a mound, he suddenly found himself face-to-face with a dhole, its fur matted with dirt and a seething mass of saliva frothing from its jaws. Haunched and ready to spring, it bared its teeth and snarled, eyes blazing with rage. Jaidev raised his arms in front of his face as he let out a scream, bracing himself for the agonizing bite that would bring death. Before the rabid animal could reach him, an arrow pierced its chest, and the dhole fell dead at Jaidev's feet. He lifted his gaze to see Aakash standing calmly, eyes focused on the target, another arrow already nocked just in case.

"Sai Ram, Aakash," Jaidev exclaimed as the others came running to see what the scream was about.

"I heard the creature's snarl, Jaidev. I'm thankful I arrived in time," said Aakash.

Chitranjan looked at Aakash admiringly, then examined the dead dhole with an arrow perfectly through its heart, foam still dripping from its mouth. "Come, we must get back to camp. There may be more of these diseased dholes nearby."

At camp, Nasir was finishing his deal with Chetan as the hunting group returned. The sound of laughter and shouting permeated the camp—a stark contrast to the quiet brushlands and the close call with the dhole. Jaidev sat silently on a log, a haunted expression on his face.

"What happened, Jaidev? You look like you've seen a ghost,"

Nasir voiced.

"I just missed being bitten by a rabid dhole. Aakash saved me just in time," Jaidev said as Aakash stood stoically by his side.

Chitranjan raised his chin with pride as he recounted the story. "It was like slow motion," he recalled. "The dhole leaped with its razor-sharp teeth bared and aimed for the Brahmin's throat when, out of nowhere, Aakash fired a perfect shot straight through its heart."

"The young Kshatriya will have many stories told about him," Chetan declared, observing Aakash.

"Come, it is time to leave our gracious hosts," Nasir said, bowing to Chetan.

As they mounted their horses and joined the bullock carts on the caravan, Ravi spotted Sonal watching from a distance. She grinned and nodded to him, letting her face settle back into its soft curves, her lips parting in a sweet invitation. Her green eyes sparkled with happiness. Ravi beamed a broad smile, trying to contain his joy as their eyes met one last time before parting ways.

He didn't know where; he didn't know when, but Ravi wanted to find his way back to the snake charmers and see Sonal again.

Chapter 5 – An Old Friend

"Our route will take us northwest, along the jagged edges of the Hindu Kush mountain range," Nasir announced while munching on his ever-present betel leaf. "We'll have to travel for a few days before reaching a pass that cuts through the mountains. We should be out of India by nightfall."

The hooves of the camels and horses clumped steadily along. Jaidev, having become accustomed to Gyatri's gait, could now pull out his flute and play melodies of home. Sometimes making up new ones, as the picturesque mountains and valleys inspired him.

Each day, the caravan slowly snaked along the dusty path, moving ever northward and westward. The majestic mountains rose around them like silent sentinels, their snow-capped peaks glistening in the sunlight. Occasionally, a cloud would drift through the mountaintops and obscure their view. Then the sun would break through behind them, bathing the rocky cliffs in a mystical glow. These peaks wore their white cloaks proudly, standing as a barrier between them and the adventures that lay beyond.

Barbod joined Jaidev, Aakash, and Ravi as the caravan trudged under the midday sun.

"My father told me the mountains were from the one source of all mountains, the Hara Berezaiti. These mountains are part of the High Hara and are the source of all rivers and waters of the world. It is one of the seven lands created by Ahura Mazda, the Zoroastrian God of creation, and is the center of creation," Barbod explained.

"We also have a story that Mount Meru is the center of creation," Jaidev said. "I wonder if our stories are from the same source, told by different storytellers?"

Barbod laughed at Jaidev's openness to his father's stories. "Yes, it appears we share many similar beliefs, though told in different ways," Barbod affirmed.

"And what of your God?" Jaidev asked. "How do you view God?"

"God, God—what is God to me? Show me God," Barbod responded, somewhat annoyed. "Roman gods, fight with Greek gods, fight with Chinese gods, fight with Egyptian gods... Picking the right God is harder than winning a game of dice. I know nothing of your gods, Jaidev. I don't mean to offend; I just have no use for the unseen gods. Music and song—that is a god to me. Food and wine—yes, another god."

"My old friend Cyrus and my father were Zoroastrian," Barbod continued. "Cyrus has grown old and can no longer travel with the caravan. He works at a caravanserai that we will reach in three days' time. I hope he is well and we can talk with him. He spoke of one God, Ahura Mazda, and how our deeds are measured at death, determining whether we go to heaven or hell. I don't know what happens after death. I only know I walk the one earth, am quenched by the one water, breathe the one air, am warmed by the one sun, and look into the one deep sky at night. One God makes sense to some; many gods make sense to others. I only know what my senses tell me. Beyond that, I do not know."

"You are a wise man, Barbod," Jaidev replied. "In my culture, there is one God: Brahman. Brahman is the changeless who becomes the many. We teach that we do not want to believe in God; we want to be friends with God—to know God."

Barbod looked at Jaidev, contemplating the meaning of his words. He had never heard such a description.

"The caravanserai is at the edge of the pass through the Hindu

Kush mountains. We will rest there for a few days before the arduous trek through the pass. Cyrus will enjoy talking with you, Jaidev—or talking at you," Barbod laughed. "I'm sure you will beseech your God Brahman to rescue your ears," he laughed once more.

Perhaps Shiva, Brahman's expression of the unmanifest made manifest, Jaidev thought, wondering what this Cyrus would be like.

Days rolled by as the caravan made its way to the caravanserai. Spring flowers and the smell of fresh blooms permeated the valleys. The night air was cool and crisp, filling the lungs with energizing prana. "Life in the mountains is harsh, but the wondrous beauty of moments like this makes it worthwhile," Aakash expressed, taking a deep breath of mountain air.

The shadows of the mountains grew closer as they neared the pass through the Hindu Kush. The snow-capped peaks glowing in the sunshine awed them with their impossible heights. On a hilltop, there was a low gate surrounded by fort-like walls. "There," Barbod said, pointing. "The caravanserai is just inside. Ahh, to sleep within walls again, near a hearth—I can't wait."

"Once we travel through these mountains, there will be more caravansaries," Barbod continued. "As the Romans' desire for silk and our spices, perfumes, and cloth grows, so does the road between east and west. They pay with silver, coins, and tools of iron."

Nasir halted the caravan. A man standing on the wall of the caravanserai waved a flag indicating that he recognized them. Nasir waved the blue flag of a friend in return, and the gate opened.

Inside, the caravanserai was like a small, bustling city. Local hunters and farmers had fresh meat, fruit, and vegetables to trade. Barbod scanned the faces of each person, looking anxiously for his old friend Cyrus. Recognizing a stable hand, he asked him where Cyrus was.

"He now works at the fruit traders' stall, trading apples and mangoes. He is growing older and stiffer and no longer does much lifting or man's work," the stable hand said.

Barbod spotted the fruit traders' cart and an old, wizened man. He sat quietly, watching the people feel his wares and bargaining prices. Age reduced Cyrus—from a proud old caravanner who made dozens of trips from Damascus through India to a fruit trader trying to earn enough to live on. It saddened Barbod to see his old friend aging so. He thought of how proud Cyrus was to be named after the great Persian conqueror and how he lived with a robustness worthy of such a name.

He approached his friend and called his name. "Cyrus, it's Barbod!"

"Barbod? Barbod? There is only one Barbod. My old friend, come take my hands," Cyrus said.

Grasping Cyrus's still iron grip made Barbod glad. He still had vigor and life in his arms, though his eyes were foggy—a little unfocused. Barbod had seen this before with the aged. It was difficult to see the path at night, and fine details were a strain to discern. Not blindness, but impaired seeing. Too many days squinting into the bright sunlight in the desert had dulled his eyes.

"Cyrus. Old friend, you look well," he said.

"Liar," Cyrus cried, laughing and hugging his friend tightly. "It is good to see what I can of you," he said. "We will have many stories to tell tonight. You will dine with me, yes?"

"I will, Cyrus, and I have friends from India here that are traveling to Damascus who will listen to our tales and fortunes," Barbod added.

"Wonderful, I have a few things to tell them about our days together," Cyrus replied, leaving his hand on Barbod's shoulder. Tears began to well up in his tired eyes. "Yes, many tales to tell," he laughed.

"Be kind, old friend," Barbod laughed, knowing that Cyrus had seen the best and worst of him.

As they gathered for the evening meal, Barbod helped Cyrus sit down with Ravi, Aakash, and Jaidev. "This is my old friend Cyrus.

We have had many adventures together."

Cyrus nodded at each of them and muttered greetings in a gravelly voice.

"Yes, many adventures. I would think three fine Indian men like yourselves would keep better company," Cyrus said, seeming to relish a new audience. "Let's enjoy some Greek wine tonight. I have been saving some for such an occasion as this. It's rare that an old fruit seller can tell the stories of years ago."

"Brahmin, you will love this wine," Cyrus continued. "If all could drink it, there would be peace between the gods. Some call it Soma; others call it ambrosia. I refer to it as the nectar of the gods," he said, acknowledging Jaidev.

"We have Soma in our rituals," Jaidev affirmed. "It is not from the grape, but from other plants. I will enjoy your wine and praise the gods that made it."

"The gods, yes, and the sweet feet of the maidens in Greece who crushed the grapes in vats," Cyrus laughed, pouring wooden cups for everyone. "You do not just drink this; you see its purity of dark color, inhale its nectar deeply, feel its wetness kiss your lips, taste its varied sweetness on different parts of your tongue, and hear the music and dance of life as it travels down your throat," he explained, showing everyone the proper way to enjoy the drink.

"Vaah," Ravi uttered. "This smells heavenly and has a subtleness of taste I have never enjoyed before."

Cyrus, closing his eyes, took another drink of the reddish-purple liquid, shaking his head slowly and reverently. "Has Barbod shown you the chang?" Cyrus asked, opening his eyes.

"Yes, it is a wonderful instrument," Jaidev replied, somewhat cautious of the warm glow he started to feel from the wine.

Cyrus laughed. "That old, chiseled face of Barbod's was never one to attract maidens, but when he took that chang out and played it before Greek, Roman, Persian, or any other woman, suddenly he looked like the Greek god Adonis," Cyrus shared, obviously enjoying having an audience.

"One time in Damascus, we were relaxing by the fire after a day of trading. Barbod serenaded a group of priestesses—Oracles we knew them as. They swooned to his music for several songs. Two priestesses, in particular, became so enchanted with Barbod that they took him for a private serenade. I didn't see him for the rest of the night. I even feared for his life! Barbod had a smile on his face for a week afterward," Cyrus laughed, raising the glass to toast his friend's music skills.

Barbod's eyes glistened with pride, his face breaking into that warm smile. "I wish I could remember all of it," he said. "Then, this mug was younger and more pleasant to gaze upon."

"Yes, and music and Greek wine changes the eyesight for the better," Cyrus added jestingly.

"You should talk, old man," Barbod taunted. "You found happiness with that old shepherdess from Babylonia until you learned she was married and her husband would return from the fields soon. We had to disguise you to get you out of the city before her husband cut your throat," Barbod shared, enjoying turning the tables on his old friend.

"That one could turn any lamb into a ram," Cyrus said with vigor, clenching his fist and holding his forearm to look like a rock-hard erection. "Those days were the best."

"What brings you three into this part of the world?" Cyrus asked.

"We are on our way west towards Damascus," Jaidev answered. "We are following the stars to find a great soul."

"And to find new trading partners for my father," Ravi added, not missing a chance to mention business.

"I knew priestesses in Greece that knew the star language and could predict the future with it. I've had a sense of awe and connection to the sky since," Cyrus suggested. "Hold out your cups. I have another jug of Greek wine here."

"The nights are getting darker. We are near the Amavasya, the new moon," Jaidev said.

"Our journey through the mountain pass will take many days. The nights will be frighteningly dark in the Hindu Kush valleys without the moonlight," Barbod replied.

"You have the young Kshatriya to protect you," Cyrus assured, looking at Aakash. "Just as I am named after a great king, in the western lands on the other side of the Hindu Kush, you are named after the greatest archer of all time, my young friend. Arash was the greatest archer in the history of the Persian land. He brought peace and tranquility to the land many ages ago. They will respect you for your name and bow and arrow throughout Persia. You better be good with it."

"I know the story," Barbod said. "Sepandarmaz, an angel, gave a special bow and arrow to Arash. He used it to settle the boundaries between the Turan and Zoroastrian kingdoms by shooting it from Mount Damavand."

"Aakash is the greatest archer in our land," Ravi said proudly.

Aakash's eyes widened with wonder. A holy man, a sadhu, also gave him a bow. *Was my bow made by a god?* he wondered.

"The days will pass quickly, my young friends," Cyrus advised. "You will be like me soon enough. The cycle of birth and death is ever-turning. I have found happiness in my old age. Ahura Mazda has favored me. Soon this old body will lie in the Tower of Silence and my spirit will go to the Bridge of Judgement for its fate."

"What happens then?" Jaidev asked with curiosity.

"At The Bridge of Judgement, I will encounter either a beautiful woman or a witch. She will judge whether my spirit goes to a place of reward or punishment. If my actions are deemed favorable, I will see the beautiful woman and continue to the House of Songs. If evil, I see the witch and will go to the House of Lies."

"I am sure The House of Lies wouldn't put up with you, old man. You'll make it to The House of Song; my friends and I will join you there and sing to you," Barbod declared.

"Your friends, yes. You? I'm not so sure," Cyrus laughed. "When you were a young boy, after your mother died, I would tell you about the beautiful House of Song she went to. I think that is why you have always been good with music; you want to be rejoined with her."

"I remember that. You also taught me to laugh at myself, old friend," Barbod said to Cyrus.

A serene silence fell over the group as they basked in the company of new and old friends.

"I will have more stories to tell tomorrow. Now these old eyes must shut for the night," Cyrus announced, as a meteor crossed the evening sky in the east.

As they headed towards their sleeping quarters, Barbod said, "I could never understand how Ahura Mazda creates us, then when we die, we either go to the House of Lies or the House of Song. The House of Song isn't a place I want to be if my mother or Cyrus aren't there."

"Barbod, Barbod, wake up," Cyrus interjected, beckoning Barbod to follow him.

Barbod slowly stood up. The night was dark and cloudy as if a black sheet had been drawn across the sky. The fog had rolled into the caravanserai in spooky wisps, creating billowy masses of whitish-gray smoke across the courtyard. Barbod was uneasy about what he saw out of the corner of his eye. He felt something else was there but couldn't make it out clearly. "Where do you want me to follow you to?"

"Here, down this alley. Hurry," Cyrus instructed. Barbod followed his shrouded friend until, suddenly, he found his feet weighed down by mud and slippery slime. He stumbled to the ground and pushed himself back up, covered in cold wet earth.

"Cyrus, where are we going?"

The figure's robes shifted and morphed, revealing a Roman

soldier with his sword raised, his face shadowed by a dark helmet. Barbod could feel the intensity of his piercing gaze as the shadow spoke menacingly. "Cyrus, who is Cyrus? Tell me where the boy hides—or your life." The soldier's arm tensed, preparing to strike, and Barbod could hear the metal of the sword hum.

Barbod cowered, waiting for the blow, when he heard Aakash's voice from outside his curtained bed. "Barbod, Barbod, wake up. I heard you screaming in your sleep."

"Aakash, I was dreaming. It was a terrible nightmare," Barbod whispered, trembling. "I haven't had a dream like that since I was a boy. I don't know what caused it."

"You are awake now. I'll sit with you awhile to make sure you are alright. We can let Jaidev know about it in the morning. Jaidev understands the meaning of these things."

Morning came quickly. The caravan took it easy for another day while the camels and horses rested for the mountain trek that would take them to Bactria. Fog and rain shrouded the day, enveloping the caravanserai in a dreary chill. As Barbod shivered, he wondered if it was the cold air or the dream that caused his body to tremble.

"Jaidev, Aakash, and Ravi, trade those Indian rags for some mountain and desert clothes. Believe me, when the wind and sand kick up in the weeks to come, you will know why," Nasir advised as they headed to the stables.

"We will. The mountains can be difficult, Barbod has told us," Ravi replied.

Nasir surveyed the group, his face etched with worry. "Yes, the camels and horses will make it okay," he affirmed. He gestured to the rocky landscape ahead. "I have seen the remains of bullock carts at the bottom of some cliffs. The roads here are not forgiving, so take what is valuable on your horses. I have heard that a late winter storm occurred, which will have swollen the rivers and left patches of ice and snow.

Jaidev and Ravi nodded with wide eyes. Aakash looked resolute—undeterred.

By midday, Cyrus was back at his fruit stand. Barbod sat with him, enjoying his last precious moments with a man he considered family. Cyrus knew his mother and father and remembered them both with fondness.

Unfastening a thick leather strap beneath his shirt, Cyrus revealed a golden medallion with intricate wings. "Barbod, I have something I would like you to carry on your journeys. This Faravahar, depicting the winged sun god of the Zoroastrians, has been my companion and protector for many years now. Take it with you. May it bring you good fortune."

"Cyrus, this is beautiful. I can't take it," Barbod stammered.

Cyrus held the medallion out in sun-spotted hands and leaned forward. "Please humor an old man. You are like a son to me; I have no other family. I want you to promise me you will carry on my legacy when I am gone," Cyrus urged, his voice raspy with emotion.

"You will be around a long time, old friend." Barbod placed a firm hand on Cyrus's shoulder.

"I don't think so, Barbod," Cyrus said, raising a craggy hand to his forehead and sighing wearily. Age lined his face, and his eyes seemed to have grown dimmer since he last saw his friend. "It's not just my eyes that are sometimes weak. An old man knows when his days are declining; it is something that all men must accept. I know how your father was very hard on you—how he didn't think your music was manly and wanted you to learn wrestling and become a horseback rider. He wanted you to be an athlete like his father and like he wanted to be. He made you attend religious rituals when you were small. You would sneak into my tent and cry that you hated him and his silly religion. Religion should not be about rituals, my friend; it should be about making a man aware of his mortal flesh and immortal soul. Our flesh wears out, but our souls continue on. Wear the Faravahar and think of me and these words. It would honor me."

"I will wear it with pride," Barbod affirmed, bowing to his old friend. "When we come back this way on our return trip, you will be here and we will tell stories, laugh, and share wine again."

"Yes, the stories will still be told," his friend said, not acknowledging that he would be around to tell them.

As Aakash, Jaidev, and Ravi entered the stables, Sanjeet and Sanjay were caring for Gyatri and Tejomaya. "What about Ojas?" Aakash asked. "Don't you give him your fine attention, too?" Anger rose through his spine, thinking his horse was being neglected.

Sanjeet and Sanjay looked at each other, both hesitating to answer. Finally, Sanjeet spoke up. "My Lord, we are willing to take care of Ojas, but none of us can touch him as he won't let anyone but you near him. His defiance is like nothing I've ever seen before." Sanjay nodded in agreement.

Aakash smiled at Sanjeet's words, his anger subsiding quickly. "We have a special bond. We are alike in spirit."

Ojas stamped his hoof and snorted eagerly as Aakash approached him with a brush. "I'll work with him," Aakash declared, running the bristles through Ojas's mane lovingly. "We'll climb the mountains and head into deep valleys tomorrow," he murmured to the horse's ear. "Look, I have an apple from Cyrus's stand for you." He held out the fruit to Ojas, who gently nibbled it from his hand without hurting him. Aakash rubbed his neck gratefully to show appreciation for his loyalty.

"I will stay and tend to Ojas," Aakash announced. "I'll meet you at dinner."

As Jaidev and Ravi walked towards the main caravanserai, a large eagle circled overhead. Jaidev pointed to the eagle, smiling with excitement. "Look, it is Garuda, a sign from Lord Vishnu that our journey through the mountains will go well."

As they met up with Barbod and Cyrus, a warm, earthy smell of meat and spices floated through the air.

Cyrus's voice was deep and worldly as he said, "Tonight's

dinner will be special. I am having a lamb stew prepared with herbs and beans and fruit afterward, of course." He pointed to the kitchen area and urged them to take a whiff.

"This kitchen smells wonderful," Ravi remarked.

"Yes, I am hungry already," Jaidev agreed while thinking, I'll pick out the meat and give it to Aakash later.

When dinner time arrived, Barbod, Cyrus, Aakash, Ravi, and Jaidev gathered again. After setting out dishes of the delicious stew, Cyrus smiled in satisfaction. "Tear off a piece of Sangak bread and dip it in the stew like this," he explained, demonstrating how to properly enjoy the meal.

Barbod pulled a large jug from his bag and placed it on the table. He filled small clay cups with the dark red liquid and passed them around. "Tonight, the wine is on me," he said, smiling. "Raise your cups to Cyrus, our host! May the gods favor him always. He is a great friend."

When everyone had their cups in hand, Barbod raised his cup. "To Cyrus!" he proclaimed, before taking a sip of the sweet-smelling liquid.

"To Cyrus," everyone echoed, as Cyrus grinned proudly at his old and new friends.

Cyrus leaned back in his chair, sipping his wine thoughtfully. "You know," he started, "I've got another Barbod story for you before we call it a night." He paused for effect. "Barbod was born a few weeks before the autumnal equinox almost 40 years ago. His mother called for a midwife under a Mehregan[5] moon and delivered shortly after noon. The old midwife at the caravanserai near Seleucia saw he had a birthmark on his left shoulder and claimed it was an omen of greatness. What exactly that 'greatness' entailed, she never specified."

Jaidev's ears perked up. He would cast a chart later to see

---

[5] Last quarter waning moon

where the planets were some forty years ago and a few weeks before the autumnal equinox during a last quarter Moon. He knew synchronistic stories like this were part of a larger design.

Chapter 6 - The Mountain Pass

On the morning of departure, Nasir was on edge as his caravan lined up to leave the caravanserai. The mountain pass was unpredictable and always presented unique challenges. To guarantee a safe journey through the mountains, he hired two Kalasha guides who rode ahead of the caravan in case a rockslide or flood blocked their path. Once everyone was ready, he gestured for the caravan to move, shouting out a warning to be careful.

Jaidev, Ravi, Aakash, and Barbod rode behind the two bullock carts. "Who are the Kalasha guides?" Jaidev asked Barbod.

"The Kalasha are a very industrious people who claim to be descendants of Alexander the Great. They keep to themselves mostly, and live off herding, farming, and guiding travelers through the dangerous mountain passes," Barbod answered.

The caravan started its long climb up the steep mountain pass. A river rushed through the valley below them, tossing rapids and rocks in its way. After a few hours, the cedars were replaced with soft oak and walnut trees, and the road they followed shrank until it was nothing more than a cart-wide footpath with a dangerous drop off to one side. With the bullock carts barely fitting through, the camels and horses had to walk single file. As they ascended higher, the cedar trees that lined the path eventually gave way to towering firs.

Suddenly, the Kalasha raced back to the caravan, jumping over rocks and pointing frantically toward the pass ahead. Their words were a flurry of excitement and warning as they tried to explain how the melting snow had caused a massive rockslide, blocking their path completely.

Nasir gestured wildly towards a sharp incline that seemed to be the only way around the rockslide. The Kalasha took off up the slope to investigate whether they could use it as a path. Soon after, they returned with a negative gesture, indicating that this option wouldn't work.

Barbod joined the Kalasha and Nasir's huddle on how to get through the blocked route. Backing down the mountain would take them a day, and they would have to cross the raging river to reach the other side. It seemed like a difficult route.

Nasir announced to Barbod and the Kalasha that he was going to climb the mountain and assess the closed-off trail himself. He ordered the caravan to remain while he inspected how serious the blockade was.

Nasir crested the ridge and surveyed the scene before him, holding onto a tree and breathing heavily from the climb. A wall of sediment, rock, and mud had tumbled down from the mountain, completely blocking the road. He glanced over his shoulder at the caravan stretched out behind him in a line. He estimated that with 20 strong backs and several horses, they could remove enough boulders and flatten enough mud to move over the impasse. It would be a backbreaking two days of labor, but without it, they could not cross the mountains. Until the new path was finished, they'd have to make do with camping on the rocky slopes and sheltering as best as they could.

"Get to work, everyone! We need all able-bodied men to dig out the landslide so we can get the caravan through."

The group tackled the landslide with picks and shovels. As the tedious work continued into the late afternoon, the sun cast long shadows over the mountains. An icy wind accompanied by a thunderous howl came sweeping from the north, shaking Jaidev and the others digging on the path. The sound seemed to be that of an asura—a mythological demon—taunting and daring them to pass through the mountain. Jaidev said a mantra to Ganesha, the remover of obstacles, as he worked. His blistered hands and aching back were not used to the harsh physical labor.

Hours passed. The group grunted and sweat as they pried, shoveled, and rolled small boulders over the mountainside to the valley below. The night grew even colder, forcing the caravanners to retreat to the campfires a hundred yards back. Shadows danced on the mountainside as Jaidev and the others huddled closer around the fire, sharing Paloma's meager meal of lentils and hot tea. It was too frigid to play music.

Barbod summoned the Kalasha to join them, seeking advice on how to make it through the frigid night on a windswept mountainside in the open. The Kalasha instructed them to find natural shelters from the wind, using the bullock carts to cover themselves and huddling together for additional warmth. The night was pitch dark, with no moonlight peeking out from the clouds. Small critters screeched in the chilly air, and the rushing water below seemed to grow louder whenever the wind paused from its own cacophony.

Jaidev, Ravi, Aakash, Sanjeet, and Sanjay huddled in a bullock cart, blocking the wind as best they could. When the clouds cleared away, thousands of stars illuminated the night, the high altitude making them brighter. Jaidev could see that Jupiter and Saturn had moved even closer in the sky.

"I've never been so sore, cold, and miserable," Ravi complained, his teeth chattering. "There must be an easier way to the west than over these mountains!"

"Man has the ability—the intelligence—to find new and better ways to accomplish his desires. Who knows, someday not only may we travel to the west easier; we may travel to the stars above us," Jaidev mused. "For man, nothing is impossible because he can contact the source of all possibilities."

"I'd be happy with just walls and a fire right now. I miss home and a warm bed," Ravi grumbled, pulling his blanket closer.

"I'm happy I took Nasir's advice and bought warmer clothes at the caravanserai," Aakash declared, shutting his eyes.

When daybreak came, rigid hands, legs, and backs stretched and came alive. Paloma stirred the campfire back to life with some hot tea and lentils. Another day of hard labor lay before them.

After finishing the small breakfast, the stiffened bodies made their way to the landslide and began the arduous task of clearing the rocks and dirt from the precipitous path. The Kalasha seemed to be in a good mood, enjoying the hard work. When the morning winds quieted down, the sounds of birds filled the air. The camels' bellowing, bleating, and low rumbling roars accompanied the shovels and picks hitting dirt and rock.

"Good work. This is going faster than I thought," Nasir said. "With a little luck, we should be through this landslide by midday. I would hate to have to stay another night in this godforsaken place."

Nasir's words were music to Aakash, Jaidev, and Ravi's ears. They had not slept well during the night and could feel it in their bones.

The Kalasha directed the work, securing the path to ensure that it wouldn't shift as the caravan moved over it. Just wide enough to fit the bullock carts, it was easier to smooth over the top of the landslide and make a fresh path than to dig out the original one. It presented a small hump in the path that would require some effort to get the bullock carts over, but not untraversable.

Nasir placed his hands on his hips and nodded with satisfaction at the newly formed path. At last, he gestured for the caravan to move forward. The camels were led across first, followed by one bullock cart at a time. Each turn of a wheel was carefully watched as the Kalasha and others strained their backs to keep the carts from slipping down into the cavern below.

"Stop!" the Kalasha yelled, as the ground began to slide away bringing one of the bullock cart's wheels perilously close to the edge. "We can't move; it will go over the edge."

The oxen moaned, their eyes widening as they sensed the cart could pull them over the cliff.

"We have to let that one go. Untether the animals!" Nasir yelled to Ravi, surveying the hopeless position the cart had slid into.

"We have to try to save it! I can't just let it go over the cliff," Ravi responded.

"No, we can still get it through," Aakash assured as he stepped forward, determined to save the cart. "Get some ropes and tie them to the cart. We can wrap them around those trees up ahead and keep the cart from slipping off as the animals pull it forward," he directed. "It won't be able to slide back."

As the cart inched forward, Aakash and the other men pulled the ropes, keeping them taut and secured to the trees. After a few feet, the cart was past the danger point and back on solid ground. Their faces shone with triumph as the cart rolled further from the cliff's edge.

"Well done," Nasir congratulated everyone. "Aakash, your idea saved Ravi's cart from certain doom."

The group erupted in jubilant applause and cheer. Nasir hugged the Kalasha, their faces crinkling in surprise. "This is how Alexander took an entire army across the mountains!" he exclaimed.

The caravan inched forward, though their pace continued to be slow. The path abruptly changed direction as they traversed through each peak and valley, winding up and down continuously.

Nasir gestured towards a clearing in the distance below. "Let's make camp for the night."

The setting sun cast a golden hue over the grassy knoll. Long blades of grass waved invitingly in the breeze as the river sparkled in the last rays of sunshine, enticing the animals. It would provide much-needed water for the camels and horses.

Jaidev gazed up at the grand mountains surrounding them, their snow-capped peaks now snuggled close. As the sun set before them, marking the westward direction, a pair of stoic Ibex stood sentinel on a peak across the divide. Jaidev noticed Libra would be the rising constellation once the night had fully descended, with Jupiter, Saturn, and Mercury following suit in the east before sunrise. He uttered a special mantra to honor Budha and Guru, the deities that enlivened Mercury and Jupiter, who were in perfect alignment this spring night. The waning Moon smiled from Aquarius. "This is a very special night for the Maha Atma. Guru and Budha have joined energies in an auspicious alignment, heralding his birth."

Aakash listened to Jaidev's words with reverence. When Jaidev spoke in that tone of voice, he knew he was interpreting cosmic forces that only someone with Jaidev's deep knowledge and intuition could read.

As the first rays of sunlight peaked over the mountain range, Jaidev sat cross-legged a few meters away from the caravan. He lit a small fire in his puja bowl, and its flames danced to the rhythm of his chanting. As ancient mantras flowed from his lips, the air around him felt charged with spirit. Aakash and Ravi watched from a distance, waiting for Jaidev to finish his prayer before breaking camp and joining the winding caravan.

"Barbod, how many more days until we make it through the pass?" Ravi asked.

"We should come out on the other side tomorrow afternoon," Barbod replied. "There is another caravanserai at that end. From there, we will make our way to Bactria over several days' time. Bactria is a large trading city. Travelers and merchants from all over the world meet there and trade their wares. You can make or lose a fortune, so do not rush into any deals, Ravi. There will always be another deal tomorrow. Get your bearings on prices and value before actually trading," Barbod counselled.

After making camp that night, Barbod sat by Jaidev. "How do

the planets and planetary gods have their effects?" he asked.

Jaidev's eyes gleamed with wisdom as he drew a slow breath, searching for the right words.

"The planets deliver our karmas—the rewards and punishments for our past deeds," he began. "Ultimately, karma is unfathomable. It says so in our Holy Book, the Gita. Understanding the planets and charts helps us understand the karmic influences playing out in our lives. In the Vedic view of Creation, Brahman—the totality, the one source—is unmanifest. In its unmanifest state, it recognizes itself as pure consciousness. This is the quality of Rishi, Devata, and Chandas—or the Knower, the Process of Knowing, and the Known—and all are Brahman. As Creation begins its vibrations, the Gunas of Sattva, Rajas, and Tamas—the aspects of creativity, maintenance, and dissolution—come into being. They embody the triune gods of Brahma and Saraswati, Vishnu and Lakshmi, and Shiva and Shakti. No male energy realizes its full power without its complimentary female energy in dualistic Creation."

Jaidev paused for a moment to let the words settle, his voice rich with the resonance of timeless wisdom.

"From the Gunas, the Pancha Maha Bhutas emerge: earth, air, fire, water, and ether. This is manifest Creation or the Creation we see around us. All aspects of Creation then take on distinct qualities. They can be sattvic, rajasic, or tamasic—meaning they can be life-enhancing and evolutionary, life-maintaining through activity, or life-devolving forces," he explained. "We seek to be sattvic in our living, so we don't create negative karma and suffer. Through the planets, the planetary gods deliver those karmas to us from lifetime to lifetime. For the individual, the Pancha Maha Bhutas combine to form the doshas of Vata, Pitta, and Kapha. These combinations make up the physical and subtle body. These qualities are also reflected in the planets," Jaidev concluded.

"That is a lot to digest," Barbod remarked, "but what about Hanuman, Krishna, Ganesha, and all these other gods I hear about?"

he asked with a touch of skepticism.

"Brahman, through the triune gods, can manifest as any shape or form. That is why so many gods are in our teachings," Jaidev replied simply.

Barbod nodded slightly, his brow furrowing with contemplation. "I'm beginning to understand, but it will take a lot of thought. So, tell me, how does this Maha Atma that is coming into the world fit into all of this?" he asked.

"The Maha Atma's—incarnations of God, not men—come into the world to re-establish dharma, so says our Holy Book, the Gita. Dharma is that which upholds evolution, bringing us into realization with Brahman," Jaidev explained. "'Whenever dharma is in decay and adharma flourishes, I recreate myself again and again in order to reestablish dharma,' Krishna tells Arjuna."

"Uh, I think I will need to sleep on all of this," Barbod said with a wide smile.

Jaidev laughed when he saw Barbod's quizzical smile. "Yes," he agreed.

The following day, they followed a steep and winding trail through the mountainside, finally emerging at the top of a grassy hill. Below them was a wide expanse of lush grasslands, colorful wildflowers, and towering oak trees. In the distance, nestled between two hills, stood the caravanserai, its stone walls shining in the midmorning light.

"Look! I see it!" Ravi exclaimed excitedly.

Nasir waved the blue flag from the mountainside. A flag waved back, and the door creaked open.

Upon entering the caravanserai, the Kalasha tribesmen were warmly welcomed home. Nasir bowed and expressed his gratitude to the two guides. It was clear they were proud of themselves, for it takes a special knowledge and courage to maneuver through those mountains safely.

Barbod had been to this caravanserai several times, so he

showed Jaidev, Aakash, and Ravi around. Sanjay and Sanjeet walked the horses to the stables and led the oxen and camels to a small spring-fed lake with fresh water and grazing land.

"They have an old woman here who makes a delicious dish called abgoosht. It is prepared by mixing chickpeas, lamb parts, potatoes, and other ingredients in a clay pot. The pot is then sealed and buried in the ashes of the stove until it is ready. After so many frosty nights in the mountains, this will taste like heaven. I'll go and make sure the old cook prepares some for us. Sleeping quarters are on the second floor up that stairway. See the guy in the turban over there to get a room," Barbod instructed.

"Have her prepare the dish for Sanjay and Sanjeet as well," Ravi added. "Point me to the baths. My legs ache from all of that walking through the mountains. I will be happy just to soak for an hour, then explore the bazaar."

An hour later Ravi, Jaidev, and Aakash wandered through the busy bazaar. Traders barked out their wares, selling a wide range of fruits, nuts, grains, rice, woolen goods, cotton goods, baskets, wines, and other goods. Some were selling horses, camels, mules, goats, sheep, chickens, and camels. Shimmering knives were also openly bargained for. Aakash picked up a Persian khyber knife with his right hand and spun it in the air above his head. It resembled a sword and had a pleasant feel and balance to it. Ravi examined a Persian kard knife, sliding it out of its raised wooden sheath with his fingers in one swift motion. It had a shorter blade than the khyber and was worn on the belt.

"These differ from our Kanda swords," Aakash observed, waving the long knife in front of him. "They sharpen only on one side while we sharpen ours on both sides. The workmanship isn't bad."

Seeing interest in the knives, the merchant shouted out a price in Sogdian, a Persian dialect. Aakash, unsure of what he said, laid the knife back down. Ravi understood some but not all of what the merchant was shouting. He put his knife back and nodded respectfully to the merchant, stating in broken Sogdian that they would be back while gesturing with his hands. They had to learn how to deal and trade in the common dialect of the Silk Road.

Jaidev noticed Barbod deep in conversation with a younger man. They rushed over to him. "Barbod," Jaidev called out. "We need your help. We're not able to understand the merchants. We need you to be there when we talk to them."

Barbod cleared his throat, and in a low rumble, said, "I can teach you some Sogdian—the dialect we use for bartering. It's easy to pick up some basics, like 'How much?' and 'No, no, too much.' Say 'Okay,' but throw a bit of skepticism into the mix. Never say yes too quickly," he continued. "Make them think you're walking away before deciding."

As night fell, the aroma of delicious fresh-baked bread and abgoosht filled the air. Barbod brought Ravi, Aakash, Jaidev, Sanjeet, and Sanjay to the caravanserai kitchen where an elderly woman waited for them. She spread out a rug near a firepit and placed six clay pots in front of the travelers. The pots were filled with stewed lamb, chickpeas, carrots, potatoes, and other ingredients, which they ate with fresh bread and water.

Barbod reveled in the wonderful taste of the food. "This woman's abgoosht is the best in all of Persia. It could even get praise from my father when he was with us. Believe me, praise from my father was rarer than a dancing camel in a sandstorm," he declared as he savored a mouthful.

The others nodded, their mouths too full of the savory stew to laugh. Jaidev ate everything but the lamb and gave that part of the dish to Aakash, who gratefully accepted, respecting Jaidev's desire to avoid eating flesh.

"Tonight, we sleep in warm beds. Tomorrow, we head to Bactria," Barbod announced.

Chapter 7 - Bactria

As the caravan approached Bactria, Jaidev was awestruck. The buildings spread out as far as he could see, crowding the landscape on all sides. A large building loomed in the distance, surrounded by a sea of smaller white stone buildings.

"There is much to see—much to learn here, Jaidev. This is the main crossroad on the Silk Road. A variety of people from the far east to the far west frequent here. You will see Romans, Greeks, Persians, Chinese, and others. They speak many tongues," Barbod shared.

"My father has an old friend here that I would like to find. His name is Khartum," Jaidev said.

"We can stop at the marketplace. With some luck, someone there will probably know him," Barbod replied.

The sheer size of the city astonished Ravi and Aakash. "I am hoping to find some quality suppliers for my father's business here," Ravi said eagerly, "and to meet the chang builder you mentioned, Barbod."

Nasir scanned the horizon and pointed to a grassy field with a small group of trees by the river just outside the city walls. "We will set up camp there," he declared. Several members of their group would leave the caravan and stay in Bactria, while others would join the caravan on the next leg of the journey. Nasir announced that they'd be there for several weeks before heading westwards to Damascus.

The pulsing energy of the large city was new to Jaidev. Activity was everywhere. The calls of merchants echoed between the tents and stalls. Carts moved goods from one place to another. People bustled about, moving from this something to that something and then on to the next something. There was a palpable smell in the spring air—meats cooking, breads baking, and spices simmering. Animals lazily squatted or lay down in their pens, ever watchful for predators. Dogs scampered in and out of tents looking for scraps while being careful not to be seen by owners. Some sniffed warily until they got close enough to find familiar faces or recognizable smells, growling threateningly at unfamiliar passersby.

"Vah," Jaidev remarked in wide-eyed wonder. "Aakash and Ravi, did you ever imagine it would be like this?"

"I have heard stories of these cities, but they don't compare to the real thing," Ravi replied. "Let's head over to the marketplace."

After tethering their horses to a hitching post, they stepped into the bustling city streets. Everywhere they looked, people shilled their bright apples, fragrant spices, and spools of colorful fabrics. They wandered the marketplace in awe, making sure not to miss out on any of its wonders.

"I would like to find a silk dealer," Ravi announced. "The cloth is incredibly light, soft, and holds dye well. Silkworms make it in the Orient. It is the most valuable cloth there is. I have been told the Romans use it and it quickly becomes popular with women. Amrita and Sita will want some."

Jaidev approached an aged grain seller and inquired if he was familiar with the location of Khartum.

"Yes, yes. Khartum is one of our elders. He can be found in the primary plaza," the old trader answered, happy to be helpful. "It is a thousand steps down that path."

The trio headed down the road towards the plaza. Trading tents gave way to modest, sun-drenched buildings of mud and clay. The plaza soon became visible before them—a large open courtyard with a building made of granite blocks and columns and steps leading to a covered landing where several elderly distinguished-looking gentlemen gathered.

"Does anyone know where we can find Khartum?" Jaidev asked.

Eyes flickered over the three young Indian men.

"Who is asking for Khartum?" a tall, bearded, turbaned man with a pronounced hooked nose asked. He was an imposing figure— his voice low and deep and his frame large.

"My father, Mahesh Trivedi, is his friend," Jaidev replied.

"Mahesh, Mahesh! I praise the God of Creation who brought you to us. I'm Khartum. Your father saved my life when I was young and made me realize what a gift life is. Welcome to Bactria, son of Mahesh! And what might your name be? Are your companions also Mahesh's children?" he asked, staring at Ravi and Aakash.

"My name is Jaidev, and this is Aakash and Ravi, my lifelong friends."

"Ah, Jaidev, you were just a baby when I recovered under the care of your mother and father. Everyone, please come to my place. I'll prepare some drinks and snacks, and I'd love to hear all about you and why you've come here," Khartum exclaimed, excitedly waving his hands to follow him.

Khartum's home was a modest one-story dwelling made of sturdy stone, with an immaculate garden and wooden shutters adorning the windows. He had been respected as a town elder for many years. Although his status came not from wealth or power, but from a life of wisdom, experience, and compassion shared by his loving wife Parisa and their son Akim.

Khartum graciously stepped into the house and called to his wife. "Parisa, please get some refreshments for our visitors, Jaidev, Ravi, and Aakash. Jaidev is the son of Mahesh, who saved my life years ago." Khartum turned to his guests. "Please, have a seat. I'm eager to learn all about your travels."

"My father spoke fondly of you. He told me he taught you about Jyotish and how we can determine a person's birth karma and significant life events through the position of the stars at their birth," Jaidev said.

"Yes, Jaidev, your father taught me that, and much more. He showed me how to enjoy this," Khartum replied, pointing to his temple. "How to enjoy subtler and finer levels of thought and finally go beyond even the subtlest of the subtle to just Being, the field of all. He demonstrated that to grow a thriving flower, the gardener must understand the root, because that's where it gets its nourishment. Mahesh also showed me how to contact the root of my thinking—the source from which all thought springs, for we are the gardeners of our thoughts. I practice what he taught me every day and have a much deeper understanding of our Persian God, Ahura Mazda, as a result."

"You have done well to still remember those lessons," Jaidev remarked.

"It was in understanding this that a great peace came to me. Your father revealed how action is born of the three Gunas or forces of life. He showed me how to act in accordance with Sattva, pure evolutionary life-enhancing action, to avoid Tamas, impure life-destroying inertia, and to moderate Rajas, life-perpetuating self-centered action," Khartum shared.

"My father said you were a very wise man. I can see why he spoke so highly of you," Jaidev said.

"Since your father introduced me to the language of the stars, I have become a student of a great Persian astrologer, but I can tell you more about that later. Tell me, why you are here?"

"We are traveling to the west, to Damascus. The stars are foretelling the birth of a great spiritual being that will bring blessings to humanity," Jaidev declared.

"I think we are seeing a similar message in the stars. There is a great conjunction in Pisces occurring," Khartum affirmed, stroking his chin.

"Yes, yes, and it casts a very significant aspect on the Virgo ascendant. That is why we are traveling west. When the Virgin rises in the East, it is the conjunction in the western sky, in Pisces, that emanates such spiritual power," Jaidev explained.

"We Persians consider Pisces the sign of the Judea nation, which is now under Roman rule. The child will be born into a Judean family. Can you show me the chart you cast? I would like to study it tonight," Khartum added.

"Yes, I'll draw it here. I welcome talking about this more with you," Jaidev responded.

"Parisa, please get Akim from the field. I want him to meet these young men," Khartum said, calling to another room.

Khartum's gaze shifted to Ravi and Aakash, who had accepted refreshments from Parisa. "Are you two also interpreters of the stars?"

"I am not trained in the science of the stars," Ravi replied. "I am here to assist Jaidev on his journey and to meet with suppliers for my family's trading business. Bactria is said to be a hub where all the newest products are found."

"Well, Bactria certainly offers that," Khartum confirmed as his gaze swept across the bustling city, gesturing eastward with an outstretched arm. "Over there, you will find a Chinese area full of its signature silks and porcelains. A short walk south and you come across the Greek district which overflows with wines, cheeses, and olives. As for us Persians, we offer a multitude of riches—music, sculptures, fine steeds, artfully crafted woolen rugs, and bows befitting of a master archer. Look to our western side and you'll find leather goods from the Romans and some of the finest iron tools, blades, and swords." His face lit up as he spoke about his beloved homeland. "It will take you some time to make your way through all our traders and areas."

"Tomorrow, I would like to visit the Chinese on the east side.

I would like to procure silk to send home," Ravi declared.

A tall, lightly bearded young man entered the room, the pronounced hook of his nose unmistakably matching Khartum's.

"This is my son Akim. He is becoming one of the finest horsemen in Bactria," Khartum announced. Akim bowed gently, his eyes studying each of the newcomers.

"You and your friends shall dine with us tonight, Jaidev. Go and rest up and come back at sunset, for we will prepare a special welcoming meal."

"Namaste, Khartum," Jaidev replied, clasping his hands together and bowing in respect and reverence.

As they walked back towards their camp, Aakash grew tense, seeming to sense that they were being followed. After they rounded a turn in the road, he beckoned the others to continue, while he hid in the bushes, waiting to see who was following them. Jaidev and Ravi exchanged worried glances but proceeded as Aakash instructed them to do. A few moments later, a figure crept around the bend. It was Akim.

"Why are you shadowing us? What is your purpose?" Aakash asked, confronting Akim.

"I mean no harm. My father often speaks of Jaidev's father. He told us about the special powers, Siddhis, that the ancient yogis gained—how they could levitate, walk through walls and on water, be in two places at the same time, and other special powers and gifts. I wanted to see if Jaidev would walk in the air."

"I have heard of the powers of the great Siddhas, Akim, but it is a rare adept who has accomplished them. And not before my eyes. If Jaidev possesses such ability, he does not show it. I believe one such adept gave me my beloved bow. It too has a special power. Its arrow always finds its target. I am still learning its teaching and message," Aakash explained.

"Learning to shoot a bow like our Persian legend, Arash, is my deepest wish," Akim shared, admiring Aakash.

"If your father gives permission, it would be my great honor to teach you, Akim," Aakash replied.

"My father will surely approve. When you come to dinner later, I'll ask him," Akim said as he excitedly pivoted on his heel and made his way back to his father's house.

On the walk to Khartum's home for dinner, Ravi stopped to pick up some wine from a dealer in the marketplace. "My father always said you should bring an appetite, wine, and grand stories when invited as a dinner guest."

Aakash smiled as he recalled, "Dinner at your place always brought amazing stories. My favorite was about Rama, one of Vishnu's avatars, and how he broke the bow of Lord Shiva that King Janaka possessed and then married Sita."

"I can see why that would be your favorite," Jaidev said quietly to Aakash.

As Khartum's guests entered his house, the pungent aroma of simmering curry and freshly baked bread filled their nostrils. Khartum's deep, bellowing voice welcomed them heartily. In the corner sat an elderly man, wrapped in a brown shawl. "Welcome! Welcome! I have invited my astrology mentor Zirgan to join us tonight," Khartum said, gesturing towards the frail man.

"Zirgan, this is Jaidev, Ravi, and Aakash. Jaidev is the son of my old friend, Mahesh. Mahesh saved my life years ago and introduced me to the language of the stars."

Zirgan slowly raised his head, his left eye peering out from beneath the string of a patch covering the other. With a gesture, he asked Jaidev to come and sit near him. In front of Zirgan was a pinax, an astrological board with an inner and outer ring. Inside the board were intricately carved figures representing the planets. The inner and outer rings held the position of the planets for the birthdate and transits, and the planets could be moved as the dates changed.

"Khartum told me you have seen the triple conjunction in Pisces that is upon us," Zirgan stated. "The heavens are singing to us, and all of creation is awaiting this event. A child born of this alignment will bring great blessings to the world. Come, look at the positions of the planets on the pinax."

Jaidev leaned in to get a better look as Zirgan gestured towards the board.

"Here, see, the birth will occur when the shadows, the nodes, are least effective. Rahu has just entered Aries, and Ketu has just entered Libra. When the shadows are yet awakened in their new signs, the child will be born." Zirgan traced his finger emphatically across the pinax. "Also, note how all the planets are in between the nodes, thus signifying a high birth. To many, this high birth means the status of a king, but that is a misconception. It means that a soul capable of enlightening men will be born amongst us."

Jaidev was thrilled at the advanced astrological knowledge Zirgan expressed.

"When the planets are all between the nodes, we call it a Kala Sarpa Yoga, meaning between the serpents of time. It is a very auspicious formation, for it is written that to be born with the stars in this position, one killed a serpent in a past life. And see here the position of Mars in the 6th house of service and enemies. Mars is the 3rd Lord positing the 6th, indicating that the child's service will include healing, and he will be a hands-on healer," Jaidev observed.

"Yes, yes, but it also forebodes that this birth will have great enemies. Mars is a malefic that activates the malefic influence of enemies," Zirgan added. "Beware in your travels who you share the news of this child with. His enemies will be powerful."

Zirgan's words made Jaidev and Khartum shudder. They shared a look of mutual acknowledgment that they needed to pay attention. Ravi's dream of being chased and Barbod's dream of the Roman soldier flashed through Jaidev's mind.

"The seven wandering planets, or grahas as you call them, here in this portion of the pinax are placed where they would be on the birthdate of the Maha Atma," Zirgan pointed out. "But see here the transit positions of the wandering stars. A wise old Chaldean teacher once showed me a method whereby the sign the ascendant is in at birth will be the sign the Moon is in at conception. Here we have the Moon transiting Virgo on March 13th, nine months before the birth. Note that this is the day of a full Moon. The sun is with Saturn in Pisces and is very auspicious for the ascendant of a Virgo birth in late December."

"Sai Ram, Sai Ram," Jaidev expressed, his eyes widening, face glowing with excitement, and hands raising to the heavens. "The Maha Atma was conceived, the seed was planted, on our feast day of Holi. Holi is our celebration of the day the Light returns to Earth. Zirgan, you have shown me something miraculous in this ever-unfolding chart of miracles. The Maha Atma was conceived on Holi, while the full Moon was in the sign of the Virgin. And the birth will take place when the sign of the Virgin ascends and Jupiter, Saturn, and the Moon are in the nakshatra of Revati. Thus, the planets in Pisces will be aspecting the ascendant tightly. Revati is a moksha or spiritual liberation nakshatra, as is Hasta, where the Moon was at conception. The full Moon at conception indicates that the Maha Atma will be known by the masses."

"Jaidev and Zirgan, I have goosebumps hearing you discuss this," Khartum remarked. "God and the heavens are speaking to us through the Virgin. When your father introduced me to astrology when I was a young man, he showed me how your teachers calculated a chart—how the zodiac and the 27 nakshatras defined the sections of the chart. I have shown that to Zirgan. The Chaldean teachers also produced our charts based on the ascendant sign and zodiac. They further defined the chart into decans, where each sign is divided into three sections of 10 degrees. Your lunar mansions or nakshatras are 13 degrees 20 minutes each based on the movement of the Moon through the skies, and the influences your ancient sages recorded correspond to each. So, our charts are very similar overall, with some distinctions."

"Zoroaster and the Buddha were both born with a Jupiter-Saturn conjunction, and this chart heralds the birth of another great soul," Zirgan said. "I am in awe of the power of this chart. The most positive planet in our Chaldean chart is Venus, signifying great love—indeed a great brotherly love for Venus is in the house of brothers. Venus is unafflicted in the 3rd house. By sectile, it aspects the very auspicious 5th house, positing the Sun which signifies leadership and Mercury which signifies a great mind. It also aspects Pisces in the 7th by trine, bringing a very benefic loving energy to the Moon, Jupiter, and Saturn. The ascendant is also in a sextile to Venus and a trine to the Sun and Mercury in the Capricorn 5th. The chart just rejoices in heralding the ascendant."

"Yes, our charts and techniques agree," Jaidev confirmed. "The grandson of Sage Parashara was Sage Jaimini. He made further distinctions and refined how we read the stars. Jaimini would see Venus, the planet in the highest degree in the chart, as the Atmakaraka, or significator of the soul. We entirely agree on that point."

Khartum's wife, Parisa, glided into the room with a soft rustle of her skirt. Her dark hair was pulled back, framing her face in an elegant bun, emphasizing her warm smile. "Dinner is served!" she exclaimed, gesturing to a low wooden table set against one wall. Plump pillows lined the edge of the tabletop, and a delicious aroma emanated from the dishes arranged upon it. "Come and sit at our table. We have prepared a special evening repast for you."

"And I have bought some wine bottles to share with everyone," Ravi added. "It is a Persian wine called Mey."

Khartum poured glasses of the deep red wine. "You know the story of Persian wine?" he asked, his eyes sparkling with mischief. "It's said that a young girl, jilted by her lover, tried to end her life by eating rotting table grapes. She became intoxicated, fell into a drunken slumber and when she woke up, she realized life was worth living after all. She started making wine from fermented grapes in celebration of life."

He handed a glass to each guest, and they clinked them together, savoring the rich taste of the ancient libation.

"That is a story I will repeat often. I would like to meet such an incredible female," Ravi said, expressing his strong desire.

Khartum looked into his wife's eyes and smiled, raising his cup in a toast. "Ahhh, I hope you find her. My Parisa is all that I need to intoxicate my senses." As the words lingered in the air, Khartum noticed a rosy flush creeping up from her neck to her cheeks.

"To Parisa," Ravi chimed, as all acknowledged her with gratitude for the meal.

As the meal wound down, Akim caught the eye of Aakash. Aakash remembered that he had promised to teach Akim how to shoot a bow. "With your permission, Khartum, I have promised Akim a lesson in archery, if you are agreeable," Aakash said.

Khartum looked at Aakash with an encouraging smile, gesturing towards a grassy hill in the distance. "Yes, of course, Aakash. There's a field on the north side that would be perfect for you to practice. The sun will set in an hour or so—go give it your all."

"Come, young Akim, we will practice there," Aakash announced, grabbing his bow. "Do you have a bow?"

Akim gingerly retrieved a dark, intricately carved wooden bow from nearby. "This was a gift from one of our mighty Sparabarra— the mounted warriors and bowmen of Persia," he said proudly as he delicately caressed the wood. "They follow a strict code that requires them to be skilled riders, archers, and speakers of truth."

"There is wisdom in that. Speaking the truth helps develop a quality of mind that trains the eye to focus one-pointedly on the goal," Aakash affirmed.

Arriving at the field, Aakash took an arrow and pointed it at a tree about 50 steps away. He effortlessly pulled his bow back and released the arrow dead center into the tree.

"Let me see how you do with your bow," he told Akim.

Akim's hands shook as he reached for an arrow, clumsily inserted it onto the bowstring, and tried to draw it back with a steady hand. He released the arrow, but it flew off course and landed in the dirt just inches short of its target.

"We will start with the basics and then the secret," Aakash declared. "Begin by finding a draw length that feels comfortable and repeatable. The arm extended in front of you should be relaxed and in line with your frame, not bent or leaning into the bow. As you pull back on the string, bring it to a consistent spot, ideally using your jawline as an anchor point. Let's practice this method a few times."

Akim stood steadfast, mimicking his stance. Holding his left arm out straight, he pulled the bowstring back to his jaw and loosed the arrow. It caught the target on the outer edge. Aakash watched as Akim shot arrow after arrow, offering encouraging advice after each shot.

"Very good, Akim. Practice that again and again. If you accomplish that with consistency, you will have an excellent start," Aakash said. "We better go back to your father's house. It will be dark soon. We can meet again in a few days for more tips and pointers."

Akim lifted his chin and lengthened his strides as he walked beside Aakash. He felt an unfamiliar surge of energy fill his veins and a newfound sense of purpose radiating from his heart. His steps were filled with the excitement of finding a lifelong passion, as well as pride, as if finally passing from boyhood to adulthood.

As Aakash and Akim returned to the dining room, Khartum was passing a large bowl of fresh cherries around the table. Akim rushed to grab a handful of his favorite fruit. "Father, Aakash showed me how to shoot a bow. I hit more targets than I missed."

Aakash smiled at Akim's exuberance. "Akim has a keen eye and a powerful arm for archery; I believe he will excel at it," he shared. "I can also teach him some basic kalaripayattu, our Indian art of self-defense. Did I miss anything while we were practicing?"

"Khartum is thinking of joining us on our journey," Ravi

replied. "Tomorrow he will ask his brother to take over his business and watch over Parisa and Akim."

Khartum, seeing the miracle in the stars, felt a duty to witness it in person. "All of us must honor it," he concurred. "This baby will be born in Judea yet will be a beacon to all humanity. This astrological event is without precedent; I feel compelled to represent our Persian culture. The Zoroastrian scriptures have foretold the birth of a Saoshyant, a Savior from a Virgin, who will do battle with Angra Mainyu, the demon. I'm certain this is that long-awaited child, and the Virgin is undoubtedly the sign of Virgo."

"You will be a most welcome addition to our small group. My father will be so happy to know that his old friend will honor us with his presence on our journey," Jaidev remarked.

"Can I go, father?" Akim asked.

Khartum stood in front of his son, gripping his square shoulders with a calloused hand. "No son, I need you here to help your mother and my brother Farhad and to practice your archery skills. When a great archer like Aakash says you have promise, then it must be allowed to come to fruition. Zirgan showed me when you were born that you will excel at sporting challenges," Khartum explained.

Zirgan looked into the young man's eyes, his voice gentle and earnest. "Stars have a way of speaking to us about our destiny," he said softly. "Hear their whispers and you will find success with the support of Ahura Mazda, the Creator himself. But if you ignore them, be warned: Angra Mainyu's chaos and destruction may ensnare your heart."

Akim's eyes widened in awe and fear. He did not want Angra Mainyu to enter his heart. He felt connected to his destiny and enthusiastic about learning archery.

Jaidev declared that it was time to thank their hosts for dinner and the amazing hospitality. He bowed his head, offering a "Namaste" of appreciation to Zirgan, Khartum, Parisa, and Akim.

"Jaidev, you are welcome to join me in three days for lunch. A group of men from all the various quarters here in Bactria get together every other week and discuss ideas and other topics of knowledge," Khartum offered.

"I would be honored," Jaidev replied. "I am very curious about all the different people I see here."

"Khoda hafez, meaning God keep you safe." Khartum bowed as the others clasped their hands.

Jaidev, Ravi, and Aakash walked to their camp. The late May moon was waning half-full and hung heavy in the sky. As white stars flickered against a deep blue backdrop, a shooting star streaked down the eastern sky.

When the shooting star hit the horizon, a fireball erupted into the sky. As the light subsided, Jaidev could make out hundreds of rabbits running towards them, carrying their babies on their backs. Thousands of rats chased them with large cutting teeth, gnashing and snarling. "Don't let them escape!" a large commanding rat yelled. As the rabbits ran by, they were followed by dozens of columns of vermin, like a small version of an invading force. The rats started attacking, and Ravi and Aakash swatted them away. "God help us!" Jaidev tried to yell, but only a shriek came out.

"Jaidev, Jaidev, wake up!" Aakash called from his bed. "You are thrashing and squirming in your sleep."

Jaidev's eyes flickered open, his skin still clammy from the dream. The colors and images were vivid, and Jaidev was certain it was connected to Ravi and Barbod's dreams and Zirgan's strange warning. He lay still in bed for a few moments, trying to make sense of the confusing images before finally allowing himself to drift off again.

A cock crowed as the sun came up over the horizon the next morning. Jaidev was sitting in meditation as Aakash arose. Sensing his friend stirring, Jaidev opened his eyes.

"Where is Ravi?" Aakash asked.

"I'm not sure. Perhaps he went to find some fresh fruit and bread for breakfast," Jaidev said. "I am hungry this morning."

"Knowing Ravi and his robust appetite, he will come back with a basket of food and a story to go with it," Aakash remarked.

Ravi flung open the door, with Barbod trailing behind him. "Come, there's plenty of food here," he exclaimed. "Bread, butter, apricot jam, feta cheese, and walnuts! We have quite a bit to do today—we're off to the chang builder so I can buy a dozen to send home. India will soon develop an appetite for stringed instruments."

Barbod, smiling as always when food was around, said, "After we meet with the chang dealer, I know an old woman who can read fortunes by looking into a goblet and observing how certain items move inside it. Her prophetic gifts are legendary."

"Maybe she can tell me where to find the best silk dealer," Ravi replied, tongue in cheek.

"It is going to be an interesting day," Aakash noted.

Barbod's face broke into a wide smile as he glanced at the spread of food on the table. "I would love some bread, cheese, and walnuts. We will need our strength," he said, grabbing a hunk of crusty, warm bread from the basket. "The chang builder is about an hour's walk from here."

After their morning meal, they ventured into the ancient area of Bactria. There, they found potters, rug merchants, and other craftsmen, each with their own shop. On this day, the sky was a crystal-clear blue with a gentle wind and a pleasant temperature. Jaidev filled his lungs with the crisp, sweet morning air. He closed his eyes and smiled, feeling the warm sunshine on his face. "Brahma has truly created a beautiful day for us to enjoy," he said.

The city was coming to life, as merchants opened their yurts for people to shop. "The ancient Persians used yurts such as these for shelter," Barbod explained. "They are critical for keeping out the blistering sun, chilling wind, dust, flies, and wild animals."

As the four men walked down the road, a young boy about 13

ran up to them. "Come, come to my father's yurt. He makes the best waterskins. They hold more and fit on your belt or across your shoulder."

"What is your name, boy?" Ravi asked.

"I am Darab, son of Sam, the flask maker. See my waterskin? It is the finest leather and stitching. It can carry enough water for an entire day," Darab said.

"What is that inscription engraved on your waterskin, boy?" Aakash asked. "I have not seen it before."

"It is a hamsa, to ward off the evil eye. My father says it will protect me from evil."

"Take us to your father. I would like to meet him," Ravi declared.

After following the boy into a disheveled yurt, Darab yelled out excitedly. "Father, father, these travelers are interested in your skins."

A middle-aged man, bald with a beard and brawny forearms, approached. His brown eyes shone with wisdom, and the wrinkles around them deepened as he spoke. "Darab, your mother needs you to go to the well for water," he said in a gentle yet authoritative voice. "Hurry, boy, your mother can be impatient about these things."

"Yes, Papa," Darab replied, hurrying out the rear of the yurt.

"Your boy showed us his waterskin. I would like to see what you have," Ravi stated.

"I have several here in this basket, each with a slightly unique twist on the neck. I use the finest sheep skin, and it remains soft and pliable for years."

"I may like one, if the price is right," Ravi expressed.

"I can let you have one for three drachmas or three for eight drachmas," Sam offered.

"I will pay two drachmas for one," Ravi said sternly.

"Three for seven drachmas," Sam countered.

"Three for six drachmas is my last offer," Ravi replied.

Sam leaned over the bazaar stall, pointing to a stack of waterskins. "Six drachmas for three of these," he confirmed in a low voice. "I'll take 6 drachmas today—but keep it between us, okay?" He passed the waterskins across the counter.

"Agreed," Ravi said, taking six drachmas from his coin pouch. "If I like the quality, I will return in a week and discuss a large purchase."

"Thank you. I look forward to your return," Sam responded.

As they left the yurt and strolled up the dusty road, Barbod clapped a hand on Ravi's shoulder. "That was masterful. It doesn't take you long to catch onto how things work out here."

Ravi puffed out his chest proudly. "It is in my blood; I am the son of a great Vaishya," he declared, his eyes sparkling with newfound confidence and a hint of arrogance.

The sun was at its highest point as they made their way to the chang dealer's modest shop. Several mules stood tethered outside the hut. Barbod approached the doorway and yelled, "Yaser! Yaser, are you here?"

"Who is calling Yaser?" a grave voice questioned from behind the door.

"It is I, Barbod, you crusty old goat," Barbod yelled back.

"Did you lose another chang gambling?" Yaser chided as he opened the door.

Barbod's arms opened slowly as he stepped forward, his weathered face creasing into a wide smile. Yaser dropped his tools and leapt from the porch to meet him halfway, engulfing Barbod in an embrace.

"Come here you old snake," Yaser uttered, his voice grizzled with emotion. "You're like a bad dust storm. Every year you come around to torture me."

"Yaser, you never change. The only man I know who is even uglier than me. You have gotten fatter—business must be good. I have someone to introduce you to," Barbod announced, holding

Yaser's shoulders at arm's length so he could get a good look at him. "Ravi, Jaidev, and Aakash, this is Yaser, one of my oldest and dearest friends."

Barbod directed his attention back to Yaser. "Can you believe that these fine Indian gentlemen had never heard a chang until our caravan visited their village in North India?"

"Their ears must have thought they were hearing an instrument of heaven until they looked at that grizzly old face," Yaser said with a mirthful look.

"Barbod says you are the best chang maker in Bactria," Ravi stated.

"Bactria? No, no, no," Yaser remarked, shaking his finger. "I'm the best in the world!"

Yaser stepped aside and gestured behind him. "Come, come inside. I'll make some tea and show you the beauty of the chang."

Yaser prepared a pot of tea as Ravi and Barbod observed the various changs in the room.

"That one is very special. I made it out of mahogany wood, and it has a sound sweeter than honey," Yaser declared.

Barbod carefully strummed its strings, savoring the delicate notes that filled the room. His calloused fingers moved with a graceful ease, eliciting a level of emotion in his melody that felt almost spiritual. The music seemed to wrap around Barbod like a comforting blanket as he smiled and proclaimed, "Yes, this one has a resonance that has no equal."

"It is my prized chang. Note the smoothness and exquisite grain pattern. It gives the notes a beautiful depth of vibration. I can supply many of these for you," Yaser said to Ravi.

"I think they will add a new exciting sound to our traditional Indian music," Ravi affirmed.

"They will beautifully complement our Ghandarva Veda melodies," Jaidev added.

Yaser smiled as he said, "It pleases me to think that the

melodic tunes of this instrument will become part of your culture."

"Can you prepare 12 for my servants to return to India with? And at what price would such a large and continuous order bring?" Ravi asked.

"The first order will cost 10 drachma each, or 120 drachma. I usually sell them for 14 drachma each, but I'm giving a special price to Barbod's friends. How many times a year will you require them?" Yaser asked.

"I expect to have them shipped to us three times a year, with different caravans that come to India," Ravi informed.

"In each shipment after this, I will include one free with the order. I am never this generous, but it does my heart good to spread the music," Yaser said.

Barbod nodded his head, pursing his lips in approval of the price.

"Done," Ravi announced, extending his hand to shake on the agreement.

Yaser grabbed it firmly.

"I will send my men to you in two weeks to pick up the changs for their trip back home," Ravi added, smiling broadly and bowing to Yaser.

"It is my pleasure." Yaser returned the bow, quite satisfied with his new deal.

"Come, it is time to visit the fortune teller Barbod told us about," Ravi said. "I'm curious about this Seer."

"Ahhhh, beware of the sounds from the Seer Stella's mouth," Yaser said disparagingly, shaking his head.

As the sun beat down on them, the group of intrepid adventurers trekked up a winding hill, snacking on walnuts and apricots as they walked. They could see in the distance a gate and fence surrounding an emerald-green garden where cows and sheep grazed peacefully. As they rounded a bend, an old woman slowly made her way along with the assistance of a stick. Barbod quickly warned everyone in a low voice not to stare into her eyes, for she was an enchantress said to have powerful magic.

"Who comes to Stella's house? What is your purpose? Stella does not see everyone. Have you brought tribute for Stella?" the old woman asked suspiciously, eyeing the group.

"It is I, Barbod, and my friends," Barbod replied.

"I remember you. Twenty years ago, you sought the advice from the Seer of the house."

"Yes, I was a much younger man then," Barbod remarked.

"I have had more days in the sunshine than most. The sun has withered my skin but not my eyes—no, not my eyes," the old woman declared.

"You must be Stella," Ravi said.

"No longer. The Seer Stella is my daughter now. Tribute first," the old woman asserted, holding out her hand.

Ravi looked at Barbod, who motioned to give one drachma. Ravi took a coin from his change pouch and handed it to the old woman.

"Hmmmpphhh," the old woman snorted and waved the foursome into the house.

As they passed the threshold, their eyes grew wide as they adjusted to the faint light. A figure stood in the corner by the hearth where a fire burned behind a curtain, which kept the light subdued. A whiff of lotus perfume was noticeable. Ravi inhaled deeply.

The figure stepped into the light, and the four men regarded their host in awe. She stood with a powerful elegance before them. Her eyes glittered in the dimness while she spoke in a melodic voice: "The fragrance you inhale is called Nenufar. My mother made this fragrance for the queen of Egypt."

Barbod, Aakash, and Jaidev stared, transfixed on the alluring creature. Ravi stood straight with his jaw ajar, mesmerized by the vision of beauty only a young woman can conjure. Long flowing hair cascaded over delicate shoulders leading to firm supple breasts. Her dress hugged each curve of her body, highlighting her thin waist and long legs. As she moved, everything flowed, giving the appearance of floating. *Only a goddess could possess such beauty,* he thought.

"I am the Seer Stella," the woman announced. "Why do you seek me?"

"We have come to hear your foretelling of the future," Ravi answered.

"The light and darkness that is to come is on its journey to us. For some, the shadows of darkness outweigh the dawning of light. For others, the dawning of light dispels the darkness. The Seer Stella is only the reader of these shadows. I do not change the light or darkness."

They felt the energy in the room rise around them, as if an otherworldly spirit was making their hair stand on end.

The Seer Stella unveiled the curtain to show a hearth with a pot boiling on the fire. Strange talismans adorned the mantle.

"And what is your question? The answers lie within," Stella said, pointing to the boiling pot.

"We are traveling to the west to witness the birth of a special child," Barbod shared. "What does the journey hold in store for us?"

Stella placed an item in each of their hands—Barbod, a seed representing earth; Ravi, a feather for air; Jaidev, sunflower petals for fire; and Aakash, a grape for water.

While saying an incantation, she motioned for each to place their item into the pot.

"The wind can whisper, whine, and whip; the ground can growl, grow, and grip; the sun can fire, flash, and flick; and the water can drown, drench, and drip. We drop all of this into the pot. What will be and what will naught. We stir and see just what we wrought." As the Seer Stella chanted, she laughed, twirled, stirred, and whirled. Then, she pulled the pot and placed it on the floor before them. Catching the items with a ladle, she poured them into a goblet and watched, bending to see how the items settled. For a moment, her eyes seemed incredulous. She squinted at the goblet and placed her hand over her mouth, blinking and looking again even closer. She stood back, locking eyes with Jaidev.

The Seer Stella's eyes widened, her gaze fixed passionately on Jaidev. "You," she said, slowly pointing at him. "You can read the Light." She paused for a moment and bowed her head in understanding of Jaidev's gift. When she looked up again, her expression had turned grave. "There is more darkness and light here than I've ever seen. The forces of darkness are trying to get to the babe when it is born, and those of Light are desperately trying to protect it. The baby will be wrapped in simple cloth so that none may recognize its grandeur. Be wary, young travelers—the darkness seeks to use you."

A chill ran across the group and Barbod's face drained of color. Aakash inconspicuously felt along his belt for the reassuring hilt of a hidden knife. Jaidev gritted his teeth and steeled himself with unwavering resolve, while Ravi remained captive to Stella's beauty, unable to look away. His eyes grew heavy with desire, a burning passion consuming him as he recalled memories of Sonal and imagined her graceful dance. The other travelers remained oblivious to the hunger filling Ravi's gaze.

"Know that the angels themselves will be your guides. You are part of a new era for humanity. Keep your senses sharp and follow the path set by your heart," Stella concluded.

Barbod was the first to break the silence. "I still remember your mother's readings from many years ago. It was an experience that stuck with me for a long time. She told me I would witness the rise of a new king someday. I think this is what she was referring to."

"The warp and weft of our Persian rug makers are not seen from the beautiful top of the rug. One must know to look behind the rug," Stella said. "Like the rug makers, we bowl readers see the designs behind our lives in the bowl. It is both a gift and a curse."

"How should we prepare for these dark forces? What

weapons will defeat them?" Aakash asked.

"There is no weapon made on Earth that can defeat darkness. Darkness is only defeated by the light. If there is darkness in your heart, the dark forces will find you, cling to you, and possess you, obscuring the light in your heart. You have with you someone who knows the light," she said, looking deeply at Jaidev. "Shadows rise and fall, dancing on my walls as the candlelight and hearth fire embrace. The sun rises and falls, taking its sunlight with it. The light you seek never flickers, never rises or falls, and is beyond what your eyes can see, your ears can hear, your tongue can taste, your nose can smell, and your skin can feel," the Seer explained, sitting wearily into a chair.

"Understand this!" she continued, waving a foreboding finger. "It is desire that drives men to the Seer Stella—to the darkness or to the Light. Understand the desire that creeps into the mind— becoming thoughts, becoming actions, becoming deeds. As is your desire, so you are!"

Appearing fatigued, Stella stated, "I must ask for your leave now. This reading has drained me." She placed the back of her hand over her eyes.

Ravi spoke out, looking for justification to see the Seer Stella again. "Can you make more of the Nenufar aroma? Can I buy some from you? My dad and I are merchants from India. We could sell this scent to women throughout our country."

The Seer Stella looked at Ravi. She pursed her lips as her eyes focused on him with a mirthful, seductive glance. "Come tomorrow in the mid-afternoon and we can discuss it," Stella said, nodding towards the doorway, indicating that the four should take their leave.

As they walked back through the gardens to the road, Aakash asked Jaidev, "What do you make of the bowl reader?"

"These abilities are beyond the mind and intellect. They emerge from the field of possibilities, the Akash, where the vibrations of the past and future possibilities are held. It is the field from which creation, space, and time emerge. A Seer such as this, and still possessed of the ego, can either clearly read the message or manipulate the message for the ego's desired outcome. I think the Seer Stella was speaking with accuracy and good intent on this matter," Jaidev responded.

"And Ravi, what do you think?" Barbod asked playfully.

Ravi, caught up in his fantasy of the Seer Stella, admitted, "I thought she was stunning—fairer and lighter-haired than Indian women. Her perfume was enticing. If I can get her to make it for me or let me know the ingredients so we can make it, I will be thrilled."

Jaidev could see the samskaras of desire emerging in Ravi's mind—desires that could take him further from the light. He hoped to gently influence Ravi towards life-supporting sattvic desires and away from rajasic and tamasic desires. Rahu was very strong in his chart. With so little benefic energy to his moksha houses, Ravi would have to develop a desire for moksha in order to use his strong Rahu to achieve it.

"What should we make of these warnings, dreams, Zirgan's prediction, and now the Seer Stella's vision? Are we going to make it safely back to India?" Aakash wondered.

"I have marked the time of your question, Aakash, and I will cast a prashna chart that will answer it," Jaidev assured.

When the group was back at their quarters, Jaidev cast the prashna chart. All eyes sat transfixed on him, waiting to hear what the stars had to say.

"The prashna chart shows that the artha houses are well aspected. It will be a trip that earns the money and trade that Ravi is procuring for his father. The house of enemies has a lot of malefic energy to it, but it also is ruled by Jupiter, which is well placed in the 9th house—the best placement on the chart. So, although we will have challenges, we will defeat them. Jupiter aspects the ascendant lightly from the 9th house, so the ascendant is well protected on this journey. I believe we will be guided through this and return home safely. There are indications from the house of long journeys that there will be travel by water ahead of us," Jaidev explained with firm conviction.

Chapter 8 - Silk Connections

On the morning of his afternoon meeting with the Seer Stella, Ravi told everyone that he knew the way and that he would take his white stallion, Tejomaya, to the meeting. "He could use a good run," Ravi said, creating a ruse to break free from the group.

"When do you want to go visit the Chinese silk traders?" Barbod asked.

"Let's postpone it until tomorrow morning. I want to be sure my time is not cut short. If you could ask around today and find out which traders offer the best silk and the best prices, I would be grateful," Ravi replied.

"Of course," Barbod agreed.

"I will ride Ojas over to Khartum's and give his son another archery lesson," Aakash announced.

Ravi rode up the hill on Tejomaya, his white horse. The sun darted in and out behind lazily drifting clouds. When he arrived at the garden, Ravi could see the silhouette of an old woman framed in the doorway. As he approached, she stepped out into the light and said with a cool authority, "State your purpose here, sir."

"I am here to discuss perfume with the Seer," Ravi confirmed.

The old woman squinted her piercing eyes and nodded slowly. "Ahhh, yes. You were here yesterday, and I recall some mention of your visit today." She shuffled through the door, creaking it open to reveal a dimly lit room. A haze hung in the air. "I will see if the Seer is free," she stated before disappearing back behind the door.

"She will be just a moment," the old woman said when she reemerged from the doorway. "You can tie your fine-looking horse there and wait in that chair."

"Thank you, ummm... what did you say your name was?"

The old woman shook her head, a musical laugh bubbling in her chest like an ancient river. "My name is Anahita, though you will know that soon enough. I used to be a courtesan myself. Now I teach them the tricks of the trade," she winked.

"How do you come to be with the Seer?" Ravi asked.

Anahita's lips narrowed to a thin line as she spoke, and her eyes seemed to penetrate whatever lay beyond the horizon. "The Seer teaches men how to view the world through fresh eyes," she replied with assurance. "I can see the hearts of men and teach those skills to the Seer, but I can no longer see the future. That ability has now passed to my daughter." She paused for a moment, her gaze remaining focused on something distant.

A small chime rang from inside the house. "The Seer Stella will see you now," Anahita declared. "It is customary to give a tribute for a meeting with the Seer."

"I am not here for a reading," Ravi explained, not understanding the request.

Anahita blocked the door, extending her open hand. Ravi rummaged through his coin pouch and pulled out a drachma.

"It's two drachmas today," Anahita asserted.

Ravi placed a second coin in her palm, and, with that, she smiled contentedly, gesturing to enter.

Ravi opened the door to find a flickering candle, casting light on his face for a moment. Glancing around, he saw other candles illuminating the small home. The faint smell of the Nenufar perfume permeated the air.

A figure appeared, dancing slowly in a corner. As Ravi focused his eyes, he could see the Seer Stella gesturing to him to come closer. Her hands were graceful and free, almost as if she had no bones. She wore a very thin white veil, almost transparent, like gauze sticking to her skin. It enhanced her body, giving it a ghostlike appearance.

As he approached, the scent of the Nenufar became heavy, making his head feel light. A warm sensation coursed through his body, awakening his senses. As his eyes adjusted, he could make out every inch of her body. She looked both erotic and natural in her sheer-clothed nakedness.

"Sit here," the Seer Stella instructed with a sexual playfulness in her voice. "Breathe deeply of the Nenufar. Its blue lotus scents will bring you to another world." She held some steeping Nenufar to his nostrils.

Ravi lowered himself into a chair, the plush cushions enveloping him like a comforting hug. He breathed in the mysterious scent wafting through the air and felt a strange lightness enter his body. The lights in the room flickered, and he could hear the rapid beat of his own heart. His fingers explored curious textures on the armrests and fabric of his clothing that he'd never noticed before.

"You see, Ravi, Nenufar is the perfume of passion. It is the perfume that all seek in perfumes." The Seer Stella came closer, bending to whisper. Her locks fell away from her shoulders, her breasts teasingly visible to him. "Let yourself enjoy, for the body is made for pleasure," she whispered, lightly brushing his hair. Her lips moved close to his. "The lips are the portal of passion," she said, gently kissing him. Her finger traced his lips. Ravi could not move away, nor did he want to. "The lips are to be delighted, every finger's width of lip to be caressed, both the upper and lower to be surrendered to your partner." Seer Stella nibbled lightly on his lips, her nose brushing his as their lips entwined. The heat of her soft breath teasingly enticed him.

Anahita joined them, her eyes locked with the Seer Stella's as they stood just within Ravi's reach. For a moment, they seemed Inseparable. Ravi felt his heart race as he watched them merge into one being. The Seer Stella's voice softened as she spoke. Her hand swept over Ravi's chest, gentle yet electrifying. He could feel a delirious power radiating from them both as she continued, her deep brown eyes never leaving him. "Our moments of pleasure are fleeting, our entire bodies becoming as sensual as our lips when we open the gates," she whispered. "The goddess Ishtar guides us beyond the gates."

Anahita changed from the Seer Stella to the old woman, to a young girl, appearing to float off the floor. Ravi couldn't tell who was the Seer Stella and who was Anahita.

"Nenufar is the secret of the goddesses, of the sirens, of the secret courtesans of many generations. Its secret was lost because of man's arrogance, thinking he controlled life. Nenufar unleashes a man from his boundaries and takes him to the gate of the goddess. To enter beyond those gates, one must let go of the entrapment of the mind. His senses must be open to experience without inhibitions," the Seer whispered.

Ravi's legs felt like they were made of stone and his chest felt compressed by a heavy weight. He wanted to flee but couldn't will himself to move. Anahita and Stella stepped away from him.

"You are not ready for the goddess's temple yet," Stella said softly. The words hung in the air as Stella touched her fingertips to Ravi's eyelids. His entire body slackened under her magic, and he faded into a deep slumber.

Sometime later, he opened his eyes, his mind engulfed in confusion. He did not know how long he had been asleep, and a feeling of embarrassment swept over him as he slowly realized this. Vaguely aware of the presence of others around him, he hesitantly spoke up. "How long have I been out?" he asked apprehensively.

"Half an hour or so," replied Seer Stella, approaching him with a steaming cup of tea. She was wearing a stunning dress that accentuated her figure. Ravi thought this mysterious woman could make anything look sensual. His head pulsed slightly.

"You had the privilege of glimpsing the goddess Ishtar's secret temple today. Nenufar guides you to the temple, but entrance is not for everyone. The goddess chooses her followers carefully, and today she allowed you to glimpse her through the Nenufar. As you can see, it is incredibly potent."

"I was so under its spell. I couldn't move. Is it meant to do that?" Ravi asked.

Stella leaned forward, her piercing gaze locked onto his. She spoke in a hushed tone. "It is a precious secret, known only to the most devoted of Ishtar's followers. The poppy used in its creation has special powers beyond compare." Stella hesitated before adding, "I cannot sell it to you or tell you its secret ingredients. It is not meant for anyone but those who worship the goddess herself."

"All I know is, I want to come back and experience the Nenufar again," Ravi declared.

"We will see. You did well today for one so inexperienced with the goddess," the Seer Stella remarked. "It is up to the goddess to call you."

She motioned for Ravi to stand up. As he did, he noticed how unsteady he was and braced against the wall as he gained his footing.

"Go slowly, Ravi. The effects have almost worn off—they will be soon. Drink plenty of water today."

Ravi felt a sudden rush of affection and reached out his arms. The Seer Stella let him hug her. "You are amazing, thank you!"

"Go now." She gently guided him to the door Anahita held open. "Take this as a gift. Use it sparingly." She handed him a vial of the Nenufar.

Back at the stable, Aakash stood looking over Ojas. He had just come back from teaching Akim archery at Khartum's home. As he affectionately stroked and brushed the horse's mane, a soft melody hummed from his lips. He carefully laid the cloth with the Lord Ganesha embroidery across Ojas's back, reminding him of the moment Amrita had gifted it to him. Thoughts of Amrita filled his head; he wished for nothing more than to be close to her, to talk with her, share his feelings and desires, and kiss her again. With eyes closed, Aakash said a silent prayer to Lord Ganesha, asking that any hindrance between him and Amrita be removed. When Aakash opened his eyes, Jaidev was standing nearby.

"I came in to check on my horse, Gyatri," Jaidev announced, knowing he had caught Aakash in a private moment.

Aakash smiled at his friend and slowly folded and tucked the cloth into his garment.

"That is a beautiful embroidery of Lord Ganesha. May I see it?" Jaidev asked politely.

Aakash carefully unfolded the delicate cloth, revealing the intricate pattern woven with golden threads. Jaidev admired the craftsmanship, tracing his fingers along its edges. "A fine artisan did the work," he remarked. "Embroidery like this I've only seen done by Sita and Amrita's hands."

"Yes, Jaidev, Amrita gave it to me as we were leaving. Please keep it between you and me."

"Of course, my friend. Your request will be honored."

"Someday, I would like to marry and have children. What do the stars say for me?" Aakash asked.

"You are a Kshatriya, and you have a strong Mars in your 7th house of marriage, tightly aspecting your ascendant. We know this as a Kujadosha and it is not auspicious for marriage. From the 7th house, it also aspects your 10th house of life's work. This gives you the dharma of a great warrior," Jaidev explained.

Hanging his head, Aakash felt the weight of disappointment press down on him and sighed heavily. Jaidev reached out a hand and placed it on his shoulder, giving it an affectionate squeeze. His voice was warm and comforting. "Do not despair, my friend! There is still good news yet to be heard. It is said that someone with Kujadosha makes an excellent match for you, and I have located such a person. She has exceptional talent in her hands too, making artwork of extraordinary quality. What you hold is just such artwork." He gestured to the intricately crafted cloth in Aakash's hands as his cheeks widened to a grin.

Aakash returned Jaidev's smile with his own broad smile, both relieved and ecstatic to hear that Amrita would be a suitable match for him. "How long have you known?" Aakash asked.

"A few years ago, Sita asked my father to look at Amrita's chart to see if there was a match for her. I was sitting in the next room and heard their discussion. My father explained the Kujadosha to her and said that your chart had similar indications. It thrilled Sita to hear this news. She considered you to be a fine match even if you were not of the Vaishya's."

"Why didn't you tell me?" Aakash asked.

"The stars reveal their karmic secrets to us through the grahas and the timing through the dashas and transits. You are in a Jupiter antardasha, a good period for you to gain knowledge," Jaidev shared.

"Jaidev, sometimes when you explain the stars' language, I am lost. But I am grateful for you sharing this information with me."

"When the time is right, we will pick a good muhurta, an auspicious timing for you to begin that part of your life," Jaidev declared.

"Jaidev, I appreciate it. We Kshatriyas are schooled in kallaripayattu, the art of self-defense. Unfortunately, I'm unaware of Lord Kama's teachings related to love," Aakash replied.

Jaidev laughed. "I will tell you what the scriptures say. Our tantric teaching is the most intimate art of lovemaking. Sharing love with a partner fulfills the promise of the union of our trinity Gods and Goddesses, Shiva-Shakti, Vishnu-Lakshmi, and Brahma-Saraswati. We must enrich the three bodies—this is the divine union," Jaidev explained.

"Three bodies?" Aakash looked inquisitively. "I have heard you talk about them before. Please explain them again."

A wide smile spread across Jaidev's face. Having someone to explain his understanding to made his brown eyes dance with pleasure.

"Aakash, a woman or a man may satisfy their partner's physical needs by understanding how to enliven the five senses—the touch, the alluring smell of jasmine, wearing beautiful adornments for the sight, a sweet speech for the ears, and the taste of a kiss so divine. We can excite the physical body using these five senses. A man can be brought to ecstasy and back with the gifts of the first body. Enjoying only this level brings pleasure, but not union. We can get stuck in this pleasure and never move beyond. This leads to entrapment and sin, and we become darker in our hearts. The union of Vishnu-Lakshmi and its gifts are realized by being fully awake in all three bodies. So, we must nourish and enrich the second and third body also, Aakash."

"I am remiss in not having learned these things before," Aakash confessed.

Jaidev laughed with delight at his ability to capture Aakash in the discourse. "Aakash, the subtle second body also contains three parts. Our heart/mind that holds the promise of eternity—of learning the very secrets of creation—is the foremost part of the second body. Our intellect, which gives us the ability to discern what brings us light and what brings us darkness, is the second of the three parts. It is the third part of the subtle body that is most difficult to bring into union."

"And what is that?" Aakash asked, mesmerized by Jaidev's discourse.

"The third is the great grasper, the inner gravity called the ego," Jaidev revealed. "It is the part of the subtle body that wants to attract and view all things in terms of itself. It is our greatest challenge and what keeps us out of union with our third body. When in harmony, it completes the union of Brahma-Saraswati. To fully know your partner, you must engage your heart/mind with hers, your intellect must discern what is most pleasurable for her, and your ego must withdraw from its never-ending inner dialogue. In this way, you are both the giver of pleasure, the enjoyer, and the witness to the enjoyment."

A look of profound insight dawned on Aakash's face. He knew he didn't completely understand what he was hearing, but he grasped the basics of it and pressed on. "Please explain the third body," Aakash requested. "I'll ask more questions about the first two after I hear the complete description."

Jaidev's eyes flashed through the heavens. He took in the surrounding stable. A soft breeze blew through the door, and they heard a robin singing on the fig tree outside. His eyes glossed over, seeming almost trance-like. Through a soft smile, Jaidev said, "The third body, our causal body, contains our soul—that which holds our karmas, our samskaras or memories, and the seed of our vasanas or desires. Our soul connects us to everything around us, to the gods and goddesses of natural law, and to Brahman, the Totality. While we think it is beyond our knowing, in truth, it is merely hidden in the fog created by the ego."

"What do you know of it? How did you find it?" Aakash asked.

"When I am most at peace, it brings deeper peace. When I am most alive, it brings more life. The skilled teachers of the past show us the way. Our Bhagavad Gita says that weapons cannot cleave it, fire cannot burn it, water cannot wet it, wind cannot dry it. It is eternal; it is unborn and never dies. I know it as the inner watcher, witnessing everything I do. I desire that it always be the light of my mind guiding me. Meditation allows the mind to access it. Shakti and her union with Shiva are the journey and destination. The tantric teachings tell us that when Shiva and Shakti unite, it is done in the very womb of creation, and from their ecstatic dance, all of creation emerges. This union brings the kundalini to life, harmonizing and energizing the subtle and physical body. This is the fulfillment of the triune gods of the three bodies in the one eternal Brahman. The atma joins the Para-atma. Thus, our ancient sages declared, 'Aham Brahmasmi; All is Brahman'."

"Jaidev, your speech is an inspiration, but I am a Kshatriya.

How am I to understand this?" Aakash questioned.

"Each day, Aakash, you travel through three worlds—the world of waking, the world of dreaming, and the world of deep sleep. In the waking world, you experience the two bodies—the physical body of the senses and prana, and the subtle body of the mind, intellect, and ego. The causal body, although ever-present, is not yet awake. When you enter the dream state at night, you experience the one body, the subtle body. The mind is awake, creating and observing our dreams, while the five senses sleep. The causal body is still not yet awake. In deep sleep, neither the physical nor subtle body is awake. The sages say that the causal body is awake, but you do not remember it."

"Please explain, Jaidev. How do I awaken the causal body?" Aakash asked.

"The causal body is awakened through Turiya, the fourth world, Aakash. To enter Turiya, we start from the waking world. As it was taught by the ancient sages, we slowly withdraw the senses from their activity by allowing the primordial vibrations to bring the endless stream of thinking to its cessation and origination. The mind becomes less and less engaged in thought as the senses become quiet. When all thought and sensory activity stops, we enter the fourth world of Turiya—a state of just being aware, without an object of awareness. An arrow poised without a target. This is the initial experience of the third body awakening."

"Jaidev, is this what the old sadhu meant when he told me, 'To let the arrow fly, first pull back the bow'? That I must enter the fourth world of Turiya—the state of no-thingness as you are describing it?"

"The old sadhu told you a deep secret. It's the same secret that was taught to Arjuna by Lord Krishna on the battlefield of Kurukshetra," Jaidev replied. "The experience of Turiya takes us from activity to infinity, and from infinity to activity."

"How do I learn the primordial vibration?" Aakash asked.

"We teach it one on one, Brahmin to student. I will teach it to you tomorrow at the full moon if you wish," Jaidev offered, bowing reverently.

Jaidev and Aakash watched as Ravi cantered into the stable on Tejomaya and dismounted awkwardly. He waved to them, and they nodded back, grinning.

"Ravi, how was your meeting with the Seer Stella? Will you be bringing the perfume of Cleopatra back to India?" Jaidev asked.

"I don't think we can make the fragrance in India. The ingredients are foreign to us," Ravi fumbled for the words.

"Are you okay, Ravi? You look a bit disheveled and dazed," Aakash remarked.

Ravi shifted his weight from foot to foot, avoiding eye contact. His dark skin was beaded with sweat, and he seemed to hold his breath. "Just something I ate... it won't last. I'll be okay in a bit," he managed to get out, holding onto Tejomaya to steady himself.

Jaidev stared at his two friends. They were so different, yet both incredibly dear to him and needed for his journey.

Barbod yelled out to his friends, barely able to contain his excitement. He had stumbled upon a silk trader in Bactria who was said to be the best in the region. Bringing everyone closer, Barbod unveiled a piece of fine fabric with threads that were soft and light, yet resilient to the touch. The sun illuminated the intricate colors and patterns, so different from the dull hues of wool clothing.

Ravi inspected the silk approvingly. "This is amazing. The fact that worms make it is astonishing."

Barbod's eyes glowed with zeal as he described the threads. "Not just any worms. These are mulberry silkworms. They feed them a special diet of mulberry leaves to produce this beautiful and durable thread. Worms given other diets simply cannot make this exquisite quality." Barbod rubbed his hands together in anticipation. "The trader is a follower of The Awakened One, so we can trust that our dealings will be fair and respectful."

"This thread is gorgeous," Ravi commented, examining it. "My father, mother, and sister will be very pleased with it."

"The trader, Zhang Qian, is interested in acquiring perfumes, spices, and especially horses for the silk," Barbod informed.

"I can't wait to meet him tomorrow," Ravi exclaimed. "We have the spices and perfumes, but the finest horses are here in Bactria. Perhaps we can partner with Khartum and corner the market to supply Zhang Qian with all the products he needs," Ravi suggested.

"Who is 'The Awakened One'?" Aakash asked.

"The Awakened One was an Indian prince. His teachings were brought to China by his devotees. The Awakened One sought the elimination of suffering for mankind and gave up his birthright to bring peace to all," Jaidev explained.

"How do you reconcile that The Awakened One was once of your Hindu faith and now has started his own faith?" Barbod asked.

"Our rituals and traditions are meant to bring us to a greater realization of life. They are not meant to bind one to ideas and beliefs that are not naturally uplifting for the soul. The Awakened One is not to be dismissed, rather his teachings and techniques are to be explored and embraced if one feels they can learn and benefit from them. Abundance in all things is a quality of enlightenment. The Awakened One shows us the value of watering the root to enjoy the fruit," Jaidev said respectfully.

"Let's head to Khartum's house and discuss a strategy for acquiring the silk with him," Ravi suggested.

Khartum was sitting on intricate carpets and sipping tea with his brother Farhad when the four travelers arrived.

Khartum gestured to the young man standing next to him. "This is Farhad, my brother and dearest companion," he announced. "I've shared with him the prophecy of Saoshyant, how the stars suggest a Savior will soon be born. He has graciously consented to care for my business and family while I'm away."

"That's the purpose of our gathering," Ravi began, "to discuss the possibility of a business collaboration. Tomorrow we're meeting Zhang Qian, the Chinese silk trader with the best silk on this side of the world. We intend to trade him our Indian spices and perfumes plus your Arabian horses for exclusive rights to his silk. My father and I will appoint you as our representative here in Bactria. If you cooperate with us, it could be lucrative for both you and your family."

"My brother Farhad has the finest horses in Bactria. He, not me, is the one you should deal with regarding this," Khartum informed, pointing to Farhad.

Farhad gazed intently at the young man before him, taking in his features as he spoke. "I have heard much about you from my brother. He speaks of India with great fondness and admiration, and of those who helped save his life and nurse him back to health. I have sent several fine horses there over the years. I believe I may even have traded some with your father in the past—if Dharmik is indeed your father."

"Yes, Dharmik is my father, and he has acquired some fine Arabian horses over the years. The horses we ride here are from the Arabian line," Ravi shared.

"I saw you ride in on them. The one you rode has the spirit of a true Obajan," Farhad remarked, pointing to Aakash.

"Obajan? If that means independent then, yes, he is all of that. His name is Ojas," Aakash said.

"His mother was one of the greatest horses I have known," Farhad declared.

"So, will you be interested in working with us?" Ravi asked.

"Your proposition is worth discussing further over a bottle of fine Greek wine," Farhad proposed. "The wine, cheese, olives, bread, and dates are on me tonight, my friends. Come, let us all go down to the taverna and talk."

"It is strange to talk business when you are drinking wine. Wine changes our thinking," Aakash whispered to Barbod.

Laughing, Barbod answered, "It is a Persian ritual to drink

wine while talking business. Persians will use it to their advantage to strike a better deal when the other's guard is lowered."

Ravi slid into the seat beside Farhad, while the rest of their companions shuffled in around them. The taverna owner approached with a wide smile, cradling an ornate bottle. "This, my friends," he began, uncorking the wine, "is a rare vintage. From grapes grown only on the sun-drenched hills of Greece." He filled Farhad's cup first. "If I didn't have this taverna to run," he continued, "I'd be out there among those vines myself." Farhad took a sip and leaned back in his chair with a blissful sigh.

Ravi gingerly swirled the dark purple liquid around in his cup, savoring the aroma before taking a sip. His eyes widened momentarily as the subtle notes of oak and plums graced his tongue. With an appreciative nod to his host, he spoke with enthusiasm. "This is truly something special! You have outstanding taste."

"It is a reserved wine. We keep it in simple casks that are unremarkable to the eye, so it does not attract the attention of thieves. The Romans, Greeks, Jews, and Persians seek it, and now we have added India to the list," Farhad said, laughing.

Ravi declared, "We need to get some of this shipped off to India. But tonight, our focus should be on the silk." He continued, "We can supply plenty of spices and fragrances for you as a bartering tool when acquiring the silk from Zhang Qian. In exchange, we offer you five percent of each transaction."

Farhad's face drooped, and his brows furrowed at the offer. His eyes squinted in disappointment. "Listen to me carefully. It is not easy for me to commit the resources necessary to warehouse your goods and get them ready for trading with Zhang Qian at such a paltry amount. Ten percent of your profits seems a fair compensation for my services."

Ravi was delighted with the counteroffer his host presented him. It was evident in his expression that he would not compromise on his own proposition; rather, he recognized it was a starting point.

In his head, he calculated how much he could raise the price of the silk back home in order to cover any additional costs.

"We never offer over five percent; it is unheard of. We want the silk and I think you will be a good fit for our business. I will go to seven percent, nothing higher. My father will disown me if I don't get a good deal with you."

Farhad replied with a furrowed brow, "Seven and a half percent." He fixed his gaze, waiting for a response.

Ravi picked up his cup and held it up to the light, noting the ruby hue of the wine inside. He set it back down and looked his business partner in the eye. "You will need to throw in some of this Greek wine with each shipment if I am to convince my father to give his final approval."

Farhad relaxed as he leaned forward. His eyes glinted with triumph, and a broad grin split his face as he declared, "It is not just the grapes that have been squeezed here tonight. We have a deal!"

"Yes, my friend, may we drink to our success and profits," Ravi exclaimed, raising his cup.

"To a long and prosperous friendship," Farhad chimed, taking a sip and grabbing a handful of olives.

"Tomorrow, we meet with Zhang Qian," Ravi affirmed.

As Aakash and Ravi strolled back to their sleeping quarters, Aakash glanced at Ravi and asked curiously, "You had little to say about your morning with the Seer Stella. What was it like?" The wind rustled through the leaves of the nearby trees, sending a slight chill down Ravi's spine.

"The Nenufar does strange things to the senses. It makes the heart pound, figures and shapes change, and sounds become more melodic and have an energy to them. The Nenufar is unlike anything I've ever smelled. Pulses of scent waft around the room, while shadows of light dance before you. Voices sound like angelic harmonies. The Seer Stella and the old woman seemed to merge in and out of each other. They playfully exchanged bodies as the

Nenufar took effect. I don't know how to describe it. It is both pleasant and fearful at the same time. It is an experience that is not of this world," Ravi described. Lowering his gaze in embarrassment, he added, "I passed out."

"Wow, I'll stick to the world I know," Aakash replied, laughing.

"It is not for our Indian women. The Seer gifted me a bottle of it," Ravi shared hesitantly.

When the sun broke the next morning, Jaidev did his calculations of the planets. *There will be a full moon this night. Venus, Mercury, and the Moon are in Cancer aspected by Jupiter. At 4:30 this evening, it will be an auspicious time to teach Aakash meditation. Cancer will be in the 9th house of learning*, Jaidev thought.

Ravi awoke with enthusiasm about what the day would bring. He was eager to get to the Chinese settlement in Bactria and meet Zhang Qian. Jaidev had informed him that the muhurta showed 8:30 a.m. would be an ideal time to start his journey to the Chinese side of Bactria.

Aakash came into the room, and Jaidev greeted him. "This afternoon at 4:30 p.m., the Moon will be full and in the house of learning, aspected by Jupiter from the 5th house of the mind. I will teach you meditation then, Aakash."

"I will be ready," Aakash affirmed.

"If someone learns this meditation, will they become a better musician?" Barbod asked.

"You can experience the source of all music in meditation. It will also bring you deeper rest, more awareness, and clearer sensory perception," Jaidev explained.

"Then will you teach me too?" Barbod asked.

"Yes, of course. Come with Aakash later," Jaidev suggested.

"Come, let us eat something, Barbod. Then we'll gather our horses and meet with Farhad and Khartum and make our way over to Zhang Qian's encampment," Ravi declared.

Two hours later, they arrived in East Bactria, the Chinese

region. It had a distinctive look and feel of China. People wore long robes and bamboo hats, and the native language was completely new to them. There were makeshift shops and carts selling jade, porcelain, and silk. Ravi paused and inspected one of the silks—it was coarse with a yellow hue and dark patterns.

"I'll offer you a great deal for this fabric," the merchant said excitedly. "It's from Huozhou, where the best silk is produced!" His Sogdian dialect was heavily laced with tones of China.

Ravi stared at Farhad and Barbod, a look of disappointment on his face. He slowly shook his head and set the spool of thread down. With a heavy sigh, he uttered, "It's not what we're looking for." Then turned and walked away resolutely.

"That will give us something to compare Zhang Qian's goods to," Ravi shared with them.

"Good. Zhang Qian's house is just a few minutes ahead," Barbod said.

Zhang Qian stood at the threshold of his home, a creased smile making dimples in his weathered face. His triangular beard grew white like snow and framed a set of kind, gentle eyes. Bowing ever so slightly with his hands clasped prayerfully, Zhang Qian said, "May you be well and happy."

As they returned his bow, he ushered them inside, indicating to a young servant to bring tea.

"Zhang Qian, we are honored to meet with you," Ravi began, mirroring the respectful nature of Zhang Qian. "We have heard so much about the fine silk that you trade."

"Yes, our silk is like no other," Zhang Qian replied as he gestured with his hands and smiled. "It is strong, light, and holds dyes well. Why, just one thread from one of our silkworms can be over one mile long."

The coolie nearby shuffled over, carrying a burlap sack, and set it down in front of Zhang Qian. He untied the sack and carefully pulled out a roll of fine white silk. It had a shimmer that seemed like sunlight dancing on a lake, and it appeared weightless as he unrolled it before them.

"This is exquisite—so pure, so unique," Farhad remarked.

"To dye it, use the best indigo for the finest blue dyes, madder root for a deep red, iron vitriol for black, and turmeric for gold." He spoke Chinese Mandarin to one coolie who hustled in small wrapped parcels of each color.

"My sister and mother will be thrilled to receive this fine cloth, Zhang Qian. My father supplies goods to all of India and we would like to buy as much as you can sell us."

"And what do you offer to my Lord and Master for it?" Zhang Qian asked. "Our silk is in much demand. The Romans have a robust appetite for it."

Ravi was alert to the subtle shifts in Zhang Qian's attitude when he spoke of the Romans. Knowing that he did not favor them, Ravi hoped to use this to his advantage. He bowed and said, "We share a bond with The Awakened One and would be pleased to trade with one of his followers."

While Jaidev rarely interrupted Ravi's business, he spoke about the shared teachings of karma, dharma, moksha, and rebirth with followers of The Awakened One. "There are many devotees of the Buddha that will treasure your silk in India."

Zhang Qian's face lit up with delight. His mind filled with the image of devoted followers of Buddha wearing his exquisite silk clothing in India. A pleasant tingle spread through him.

"We can offer you the finest perfumes, spices, and Arabian horses in trade," Ravi declared.

"Our horses are the envy of the eastern world. We have a few outside that we can show you," Farhad added.

"I would like to see the perfumes, spices, and especially the horses," Zhang Qian requested in his quiet demeanor.

"Come walk with us and we can show you," Ravi replied in his best welcoming, friendly sales voice.

Zhang Qian spoke in Mandarin to one laborer, who then sprinted off and returned with a second worker. "This is Sun Yang," Zhang Qian introduced. "He looks after our team of horses and oversees our stable."

Sun Yang went over to one horse Ravi had brought. He carefully examined it from head to foot, taking time to look in the ears, inspect the teeth, and feel the legs and feet. He spoke Mandarin while nodding his approval to Zhang Qian.

Zhang Qian stood tall with a stoic expression and his hands clasped together authoritatively. "We will pay thirty bolts of silk for each horse, and six bolts of silk for each cart of spices and perfumes," he declared.

"Thirty bolts? The Romans will pay much more. It is too little," Farhad protested.

"Thirty-five bolts each," Zhang Qian countered.

"You know our Arabian horses are hardy. They can find food in the frozen steppes. They are strong, long-lived, and stately in the way they stand. We will take forty-five bolts for them," Farhad said.

"We must cultivate the mulberry silkworm with a special diet and in special conditions. It does not breed like a horse. We must nurture them. Producing such pure silk is not a simple process," Zhang Qian responded.

Ravi and Farhad avoided eye contact, while Zhang Qian stared straight ahead. An awkward tension filled the air as they all seemed to be locked in a silent duel of negotiations. Ravi slowly stood and turned, breaking the stalemate. He cleared his throat and sighed heavily. "It seems we can't come to an agreement today," he stated. Farhad followed suit, standing as if to leave.

After a brief hesitation, Zhang Qian spoke. "Thirty-eight bolts per horse is my final and best offer."

Farhad leaned in, his eyes focused intensely as he extended a rough hand with calloused fingers. "I will shake on it at forty bolts and we can celebrate," his voice took on a conspiratorial tone, "and make plans to exchange our goods."

Zhang Qian's eyes fluttered shut and his lips moved in a silent conversation as if pondering an unseen answer. He opened his eyes again, and they twinkled with satisfaction. He brought his hands together like he was about to pray before extending them outwards to seal the deal. A wide smile spread across his face that seemed to carry centuries of wisdom as he bowed slightly to his visitors. "We have a deal," he said.

Ravi extended his arms around Farhad and Zhang Qian. "We will make our countries proud."

"A long and prosperous relationship," Zhang Qian affirmed.

As they mounted their steeds, Ravi's chest puffed out, his gaze filled with triumph.

"Your father will be very pleased with this silk," Jaidev said.

"Yes, it will bring great prestige and riches to our family," Ravi agreed, his pride and accomplishment bursting forth.

Jaidev thought of the time Ravi's father gave Ravi a gold chain with his name engraved on it when he was just becoming a teenager. Ravi showed it to everybody with such pride. It meant so much to him to have Dharmik's approval. Jaidev also appreciated the approval and praise of his own father for his spiritual and Jyotish learning. They both had parents that furthered their karmic paths, albeit vastly different paths.

As they rode their steeds back to the stable, Aakash asked Jaidev, "Do I need anything for our meeting in a few hours?"

"It is respectful to bring some fruit and flowers to the ceremony, in honor of our tradition of teachers," Jaidev replied.

Chapter 9 - Lessons

At 4:30, Jaidev prepared the puja ceremony to guide Aakash and Barbod in meditation. When they arrived at the small room, Jaidev gestured for them to sit and collected the pieces of fruit Aakash had brought. The sweet smell of sandalwood incense burning on an altar filled the room. Jaidev explained that he would perform a traditional chant to cultivate sattvic purity. Then, he asked Barbod to remain outside for a few minutes as he taught Aakash individually. He started by reciting a short mantra. "Now repeat after me, Aakash," Jaidev said, softly speaking a mantra.

"Now repeat it more softly and close your eyes," Jaidev advised.

Aakash repeated the mantra as instructed.

"Now whisper it," Jaidev stated.

After a few more repetitions, Jaidev said, "Now repeat it to yourself without mouthing the words."

Aakash sat cross-legged on the floor, his hands resting on his knees and his eyes closed. He silently intoned the mantra as Jaidev observed. As Aakash repeated the mantra inwardly, his breathing grew slower and steadier until it was barely detectable. His posture became more and more relaxed as he focused on the rhythm of the mantra. Jaidev waited in silence for what seemed like an eternity until finally, he stated, "You can stop now and slowly open your eyes. Is it comfortable? Easy?"

Aakash nodded.

"Fine meditation is just that simple. There is no need to force or concentrate. When you find yourself thinking about a thought or emotion, just bring the mantra back gently. Don't try to change it, and if it does, just observe and continue. Now please step outside and continue to meditate while I bring Barbod in and teach him his mantra.

Barbod sat before the altar as Jaidev guided him through the short ritual, softly reciting Barbod's mantra to him and instructing him as he did Aakash. After watching Barbod meditate for a short time, Jaidev instructed him to sit next to Aakash and continue meditating, with Jaidev joining them.

They sat together, eyes closed, enjoying the quietness and subtle awareness of the meditative state.

After about 20 minutes, Jaidev softly announced, "Now let's stop repeating the mantra. Take a minute or two before slowly opening the eyes."

"It was easy? Natural?" Jaidev inquired, as Aakash and Barbod's eyelids peeled open.

Aakash slowly nodded in agreement, his eyes taking in the space illuminated by a warm yellow hue. He felt a deep sense of well-being and understanding that hummed through every cell in his body. The corners of his lips lifted into a gentle smile as he realized he was gaining invaluable knowledge.

Barbod nodded as well.

"Wonderful," Jaidev expressed. "We will meditate together tomorrow morning. I will answer any questions you have and provide further knowledge about this."

The sun-drenched landscape enveloped Aakash with warmth and clarity as he stepped outside. Everywhere he looked, he could sense life. The grass, lush and vibrant, seemed to ripple with each gentle breath of wind. The trees stood tall and proud, their leaves swaying to the rhythm of the breeze. Aakash felt as if his eyes were seeing more than usual; colors were richer, smells were sharper, and sounds seemed to resonate deeply. He settled himself down on the ground, leaning back against an ancient tree trunk, and let his thoughts run free. As they did, he considered the words of the old sadhu—words that now seemed to take on new meaning.

Later that night, Akash sat beneath the starlit sky, lost in thought over the lessons he had learned and the new experience of meditation. A comet streaked across the sky. He drifted into a deep sleep and awakened in the dream world. Amrita was smiling and waving at him. He returned the wave from a hilltop. Suddenly, his gaze fell upon a group of Roman soldiers riding up the well-worn path towards her. Sensing danger, Aakash spurred Ojas on, beckoning Amrita to look behind her. She stood waving gently at him as the soldiers rode right past, chasing a lamb up the hill. Without wasting a moment, he jumped off Ojas and snatched up the innocent lamb, slinging it onto his back as he leapt atop his horse again. As he galloped away, a swirling white fog surrounded him, obscuring him from the soldiers' view.

"Wake up, Aakash." Ravi nudged him. "You fell asleep. Get to your bed; you will feel much more refreshed in the morning."

The following day, Jaidev was tending to Gyatri when Aakash stepped into the stable. "How did you sleep?" Jaidev inquired.

"I fell into a deep dream state while sitting under the stars last night. I had a dream about rescuing a lamb from soldiers I had never seen before. It was so real," Aakash remarked.

"Reality is real for whichever of the four worlds we are in," Jaidev explained. "But I think your dream has a message we need to be alert to. There are indications both in the charts and our dream worlds of danger for us and the child who will be born. We must heed this when we get to Damascus and Jerusalem."

Barbod joined them in the stable. He seemed happy and alert.

"Can we meditate again?" Aakash asked.

"Yes, let's all sit comfortably over there, and I will lead us in meditation," Jaidev declared.

"Sit comfortably and close your eyes," he instructed. "Take a moment to observe the rhythm of your breathing before we start. Then begin by asking yourself these soul questions, pausing after each one for any responses that arise. Who am I?" Jaidev paused for a moment before repeating, "Who am I?"

After a minute, Jaidev continued. "What do I want? What do I really want?"

After another minute, "What is my Dharma or purpose in life?"

And finally, "What am I grateful for?"

The questions lingered in the empty space for another minute or two.

"Now take a breath in, let it out, and begin to slowly recite your mantra. Don't mind the time. I'll whisper when it is time to end meditation."

After about twenty minutes, Jaidev broke the silence. "Now let's stop repeating the mantra."

Aakash took a deep breath and opened his eyes, taking in the room around him. He felt an unexpected sense of clarity and focus as he looked around, and a wide smile spread across his face. "Wow," he whispered. "I'm amazed at how clear my thoughts are when I come out of meditation—how calm my mind is."

Barbod also sat smiling serenely.

"Yesterday, I explained to you the concept of the four worlds. But today, I want to briefly delve deeper into the fifth world," Jaidev began. "Remember that in whichever world we exist, reality is real. As we become more familiar with the fourth realm, Turiya, something changes within us. For some it happens quickly; for others it takes time. Nonetheless, it happens. The experience of Turiya—an awareness without a specific object of attention—begins to grow in our daily lives, coexisting with our thoughts and experiences. When this state of awareness becomes fully established in the three worlds—waking, dreaming, and sleeping—we call it the fifth world:

Turyatita, or Atma Consciousness. The senses no longer dominate our inner awakening. Instead, the Atma, our soul, envelops us like cloth fully immersed many times in dye until it becomes colorfast."

"Are you or your father in this consciousness?" Aakash asked innocently.

"I can't speak for my father, but I can say that I simply enjoy the world as I experience it," Jaidev replied, not directly answering the question.

"This is something I have never thought about," Aakash said.

"Meditate tonight, and we can meet here tomorrow to meditate together again. Today, I would like to visit Zhang Qian again and ask him about the Compassionate One," Jaidev expressed.

"I will accompany you," Aakash declared. "I want to be sure that you travel safely. There is much about Bactria that we still don't know."

Acknowledging Aakash with a nod, Jaidev said, "Ojas and Gyatri will appreciate the ride."

Aakash and Jaidev arrived at Zhang Qian's house on their horses. A petite woman with hair in two tight braids opened the door. She clasped her hands as she bowed to them.

"Greetings," Jaidev said. "Would the master be available for us to visit?"

The young girl nodded meekly before stepping aside to let them into the home. After a moment, a fierce-looking, heavy-set guard appeared. He sized Aakash up and motioned for them to enter.

Zhang Qian emerged from a back room and looked pleased to meet them. "Where is Ravi?" he asked.

"He is meeting with different suppliers for Greek and Roman goods," Aakash replied.

"Are you here to discuss our arrangement?" Zhang Qian asked quizzically.

"No, we leave that to Ravi. I am curious about your experience with The Awakened One's teachings," Jaidev explained.

Zhang Qian smiled, his eyes reflecting the peace that had settled in his heart since The Awakened One entered his life. "When I was young," he said, motioning to Aakash with a slight nod, "I was once a warrior like our friend here. I spent years learning from masters of ancient martial arts in China. Now come, let us sit for some tea and I can share my story for a bit before I must prepare for another meeting."

"I have heard that The Awakened One was once a great Prince in India," Aakash shared.

"Yes, renouncing his royal birthright, Siddhartha Gautama left the palace in search of enlightenment. After many teachers without success, he chose a seat beneath the sheltering branches of a bodhi tree. He vowed not to rise until he found inner peace and wisdom. Aroused by this challenge, Mara—Lord of Death and Desire—unleashed wave after wave of temptation. First, a shower of flowers rained down upon him; then beautiful women swayed temptingly before him, yet still, he remained resolute. When this didn't work, Mara hurled flaming arrows and storm clouds at the Buddha in defiance. But nothing could penetrate his meditation and, finally, Mara's fury subsided. With profound insight and understanding, Gautama reached enlightenment."

"And you?" Jaidev asked.

"I had lived the life of a warrior, having inflicted pain and misery on countless individuals in battle. Always full of anger and distress, I once marched into a village ready to slay a monk—someone devoted to The Enlightened One. As I pointed my sword at his chest, it surprised me to see no fear in his gaze. It was then that I asked: 'Aren't you afraid?' The monk's face was serene as he replied, 'No, for fear is not a state of mind that can coexist with stillness, inner bliss, and satisfaction. I have no desire to stand in the way of your wishes. If it pleases you, you may take my life.' Killing this monk would have had no effect on him. He had achieved something I never thought possible, much less attempted. He was beyond the reach of pain—of desire. I decided I would not kill him until I had learned his secrets. I put my sword away and never used it again."

"How did you end up here, in Bactria?" Aakash asked.

"I followed the teachings and became a monk. Although I tried my hardest, I could not achieve the level of austerity required to realize true enlightenment. When my teacher passed away, a wealthy silk trader befriended me. He was a devotee of The Enlightened One. We became friends, and I have come here as his representative."

"That is an incredible story. It is amazing the effect The Compassionate One has on men and women," Jaidev remarked.

"Yes, I am in his debt. Buddha has brought me great peace," Zhang Qian affirmed.

"And do you have other thoughts on it?" Jaidev asked.

"A thought is but a fleeting thing. It arises and crests and another takes its place like waves rippling on a lake. We string them together for a continuum of shared creation, but this is not what the Buddha teaches. It is the canvas on which our thoughts are painted that is the art and masterpiece of Buddha," Zhang Qian explained with a bow. "Perhaps we can sit and talk more about this at another time," he added. "Right now, I have to attend another meeting."

Jaidev put his hands together in the blessing position followed by Aakash and Zhang Qian. With a bow, they walked out the door.

As Aakash and Jaidev headed back to their stable, Aakash inquired, "How does Buddha's teaching compare with ours?"

Jaidev's voice rang with conviction. "The Sanatana Dharma, the everlasting truth, proclaims 'Paths are many. Truth is one.' Ultimately, we follow similar teachings. The Awakened One is but one aspect of the ways Shiva has told us about. Buddha has found the ocean of eternal truth. His methods are to be honored. If one finds that his teaching is attractive to one's heart, then following him is a natural dharma."

"His meditation—is it the same as ours?" Aakash queried.

Jaidev spoke cheerfully as he explained that there are various types of meditation, all of which are beneficial. He cited the Buddha's technique as a mindfulness practice unique to the individual. He also explained how there are guided focus meditations in which thoughts are directed towards an objective. He then described how his Atma meditation takes an inward journey back to a place called Turiya, a source of enlightenment. Jaidev concluded by saying that you can do each of these meditations, although not at the same time.

"Did the Buddha experience Turiya and Turiyatit?" Aakash asked.

"The Buddha was clearly established in the Self. Notice that Mara could not hit Buddha with water, fire, weapons, etc. This is like our Gita saying: 'Weapons cannot cleave it; Fire cannot burn it; Water cannot wet it; Wind cannot dry it. It is eternal. It is unborn, and it never dies.' Being established in Turiyatit would certainly produce that result. There are other refinements to Turiyatit that we can discuss tomorrow after our meditation. We can look at them and see if Buddha may have achieved them," Jaidev said.

The June breeze picked up each second, with gusts of wind blowing the white clouds across the sky. Aakash's eyes squinted in the sunlight to survey the horizon while he held on tightly to the reins for support. He noticed one particular cloud, a large one, resembling a deva with wings against an otherwise clear sky.

"Look at that cloud," Aakash said excitedly, pointing toward it. "It looks like it is pointing towards the western horizon."

"A sign telling us to continue towards the Maha Atma's birth," Jaidev remarked.

The next morning, Aakash, Barbod, and Jaidev again met in the stable. Sitting near each other, Jaidev said, "Let's close our eyes and put our attention on our breath." After a minute, he added, "Now let's begin by asking ourselves the four soul questions. Who Am I? Who Am I?"

After a pause, Jaidev continued. "What do I want? What do I

really want?"

After another minute, "What is my dharma or purpose in life? How can I serve?"

And finally, "What am I grateful for?"

After letting the questions linger a moment longer, Jaidev continued. "Now take a deep breath in, let it out, and let it go. Let's begin our meditation. Remember the mantra may change as we observe it. We do not force a clear pronunciation; we follow it where it goes. When you notice it is gone, reintroduce it. Don't mind the time. I'll whisper when it is time to stop meditating."

After about twenty minutes, Jaidev said, "Now let's stop repeating the mantra. After a minute or two, slowly open the eyes."

When Aakash opened his eyes, again his big infectious grin overtook his face. "It is so simple, yet so profound, this inner silence," he expressed.

"It is as easy and effortless as thinking a thought. Yesterday, we explored Turiyatit. There are two refinements to Turiyatit that an enlightened man comes to realize. The Upanishads say, 'Tat Tuam Asi,' or 'I am That,' 'Thou are That,' and 'All This is That.' Here we find the clues to the sixth and seventh states of consciousness. The sixth state is the recognition that the inner silence at my core is also at the core of others. That silence awakens in our perception of others. We call this state God Consciousness. Even so, it becomes even further refined. Eventually, we perceive the inner silence in everything. There isn't anything that isn't 'That'. This is called Unity Consciousness. Here, the sages declared 'Aham Brahmasmi,' or 'All is Brahman.'"

"And do you think the Buddha was in Unity Consciousness?" Aakash asked.

"We can only guess from what he accomplished with his heart and teachings," Jaidev replied, his face glowing with a soft smile.

"Jaidev, I don't understand what you mean by God Consciousness. Are you saying that a Zoroastrian sees Ahura Mazda or a Jew sees Jehovah or a Greek, Zeus?" Barbod asked. "Personally,

I don't believe in this believing stuff."

"This is not a technique that asks anyone to believe in anything. It is a technique that awakens in a man his inner sight. This inner sight has been covered by thoughts, ideas, the mind, intellect, and ego. It is an experience, not a belief. Once that subtle inner sight opens, the sages say that you no longer have to believe in God. God, as the source of all, is impossible to avoid. We take it one step at a time. For now, it is like when we first learned to play the chang or flute. We learned the notes, but it was through repetition and practice that our musical abilities blossomed. Meditation is the same. It is through repetition and practice that our inner sight, the self that is changeless, blossoms."

"I understand the musical analogy, but I'm still not so sure about this God stuff," Barbod expressed.

"If I described a ripe cherry to you—the tart yet sweet taste, the cool juice, the different textures of skin, fruit, and pit on your tongue—you still would not know the taste of a cherry until you actually bit into one," Jaidev explained.

"Now that I understand," Barbod said.

"Tomorrow I am invited to lunch at Khartum's. He meets with a group of men to discuss ideas and other topics. Aakash, why don't you ride over with me and give another lesson to Akim?" Jaidev suggested.

"Sure, Ojas could use the exercise, and I enjoy teaching Akim. He is eager to learn and excel," Aakash replied.

The following day, Jaidev and Aakash rode to Khartum's. Aakash went back to the field where Akim was practicing his bow. Parisa escorted Jaidev to her sunbathed garden, where a group of men were standing and talking. A low table was set before them.

"Welcome, Jaidev. We are happy you could join us. Come, let me introduce you to our friends and guests. This fair-skinned scoundrel is Konstantinos from Greece. Next to him is Ptahotep, an Egyptian trader. Holding a goblet there is Phillipus, our Roman guest, and next to him is Benjamin from the Israeli territory. Then we have Li Wei—he is a Taoist from China—and finally, that broad-shouldered fellow with the iron grip is Jahan, from the mountains of Pamir to our north. My friends, this is Jaidev, the son of my very dear friend in India, and a remarkably intelligent young man," Khartum announced.

The diverse group of men smiled and bowed respectfully to their young visitor.

"Our group, Jaidev, gathers to discuss topics of interest, from mathematics to philosophy, art, music, architecture, science, astronomy, and current world affairs. At each meeting, one of us opens with a topic for the day, giving a brief explanation. We then go around the table and share our own ideas about the topic. Our discussions can get quite lively, even heated. One can express themselves with all the vigor they want, and there is a lot of cajoling of each other. The one unbreakable rule is we never attack another personally. All comments are directed to the topic," Khartum instructed.

"That way, we don't need a bodyguard to get us safely back home," Ptahotep remarked, as everyone laughed.

"If nothing else, you'll learn the fine art of laughing at yourself," Phillipus added, slapping Benjamin on the back.

"Come, let us take our seats around the table. Lunch is a flatbread with melted cheese and olives. We have wine, tea, and water for drinks," Khartum stated.

Each settled around the low table made of short stone legs and a slab of teak across it, their robes tucked neatly around them. Goblets of wine or cups of tea were poured for each.

Benjamin spoke first. "Today, our topic is presented by our Greek friend Konstantinos. Hopefully, it will be a better subject than the last meeting's discussion on bridge architecture techniques from our Roman friend."

"Was that what it was about? I fell asleep during the explanation," Jahan teased, appearing to shut his eyes and yawn.

"Today, my friends, I have a subject that only the deep mind of our famous Greek philosopher Plato could conceive," Konstantinos announced light-heartedly as the mood in the room shifted to respect and thoughtfulness.

After pausing a moment to let everyone's attention settle in, Konstantinos began. "In his distinguished work, the Republic, Plato explains his understanding of The Good. He believed that there exists a perfect, eternal, and unchanging form of The Good. This form goes beyond our material world and even beyond the constraints of time. He suggests that The Good is the basis for understanding all other forms. It allows us to comprehend justice, virtue, and the essence of reality. He likens it to the Sun. Just as the Sun illuminates the visible realm, the form of The Good illuminates the intelligible realm. It is not only the cause of knowledge and truth but also an object."

With eyes peering deeply at Konstantinos, the men stroked their beards, rested their fingers on their temples, studied their wine goblets, and nodded their heads slowly.

Konstantinos let a smile seep to the edges of his beard and mustache. "The form of The Good serves as the origin of knowledge, although it is not knowledge itself. From The Good, things that are just and true derive their usefulness and value. Plato tells us that humans are inherently oriented toward seeking The Good. However, true understanding of The Good requires philosophical reasoning. True knowledge investigates the purer, more perfect patterns—the models from which all created beings are derived. He goes as far as to say that Philosopher Kings should rule because they understand The Good. So, with that in mind, we Greeks should rule the world," Konstantinos concluded with a mirthful glance around the table.

"As today's host, I will go around the table and hear each one's thoughts on the subject. Let's start with Ptahotep, our Egyptian friend," Khartum said.

Ptahotep fingered his necklace amulet, hidden beneath his robe. "Such a primitive idea, this Good. Keep in mind that our

Pharaohs were building great pyramids and sphinxes while the Greeks were still trying to put two stones together."

Jahan almost choked on his flatbread as the others cackled at the good-natured ribbing.

"I do not want to do injustice to my namesake, the venerable Ptahhotep, author of The Wisdom. He teaches us to be good listeners. I cannot say for sure that my forbearers considered such a concept as The Good. Our god Thoth embodies our sacred texts, mathematics, and the sciences. We see Thoth as having the means to convey wisdom about all things. So, I think it would be Thoth that holds the notion of the philosopher Plato's The Good. On further thought, Thoth probably visited Plato and helped him with the idea." Ptohotep's teeth glistened as a large smile stretched across his cheeks.

Konstantinos shook his head into his wine goblet.

"Our Roman friend, Phillipus, is next," Khartum declared.

"It's a good thing Rome conquered Greece so we could set her straight," Phillipus began, trying to rile Konstantinos. "You say that Plato had this crazy notion of The Good, some untouchable gobbledy gook about pure forms and ideas from which forms and ideas come. Our Roman view is much like the Greek stoics, not like our Platonist friend here. Virtue is the only good and is all a man needs to lead a good life. We believe it is how a man acts, not how he thinks or where his thoughts and ideas come from, that is important. Where most Romans seek virtue, my one complaint is that our Roman Emperor has adopted the Greek epicurean method of seeking pleasure, not virtue. Both have their practical value while this Platonic, head-in-the-clouds approach of The Good has no utility for our farmers, soldiers, builders, and certainly not for our slaves. What proof did Plato offer for this Good? I can prove that this wine is red, that I am a man, not a woman, that the sun rises and falls, and that the rivers run to the sea. We believe in the laws of nature—of natural law. That is why we have many gods and goddesses ruling different parts of

Creation," Phillipus explained.

"I would like to remind my Roman friend that Greece was never conquered. You cannot conquer ideas, philosophy, art, architecture, and culture. We figured that the easiest way to spread the superiority of Greek art, philosophy, and science was to let ourselves be absorbed into Roman society, and our plan is working. It's like we marched in backward, telling them we're leaving," Konstantinos quipped as Phillipus pursed his lips and shook his head. "Who cares who the tax collector is? And, by the way, Rome adopted our gods and goddesses and merely gave them a Roman name," Konstantinos grinned, throwing in a last dig.

"Well, I see that there is much to be pondered here today," Khartum remarked. "Let's give our eastern friend Li Wei a chance to speak."

"Thank you," Li Wei nodded respectfully while slowly refilling his teacup. "I tend to agree with Konstantinos. While The Good is described as the formless form of all things, the Tao flows through all things without form. Harmony lies in the balance—the yin and yang, the heaven and earth, harmonizing silk cloth and iron swords. the Tao is ineffable, formless like The Good, and beyond comprehension. It is the Tao that harmonizes, bringing inner tranquility to man. Virtue could not exist without the Tao, for virtue is an expression of the Tao. How can the Romans know virtue without the form of virtue in heaven? We know it as 'wu wei' the effortless dance between action and nonaction," he said, looking at Phillipus. "Sometimes we confuse the thunder with the rain. Ice does not try to melt, rain does not try to fall, and the river does not try to run to the sea. These are done by the natural order of things. The highest virtue is to be as the water, knowing the ice, rain clouds, and river, following the natural order and without a sense of self."

"Yes, yes. It is the Tao that allows the Greeks to conquer the Romans from within, for that is the natural order," Konstantinos said, seeing another chance to rib his friend and Roman antagonist.

Phillipus nodded, raising his cup to acknowledge the statement while chuckling.

"Benjamin, what say the Israelis about all of this?" Khartum asked.

"Are you sure Plato didn't have some Jewish blood?" Benjamin asked. "There are distinct similarities between The Good and our teaching, our Law, and some major differences that are perhaps reconcilable. Perhaps!" Benjamin waved his finger for emphasis. "Plato sees The Good as the source of all ideas and universal forms, such as justice, beauty, courage, and morality. We view the Creator 'Yahweh' as the source of all Creation, including truth, justice, and all moral laws. Thus, if there are universal forms, Yahweh created them. Plato says that The Good can be realized through reasoning. We see that God can be realized through examination of His Word and the word of his prophets through the Scripture, His covenant, and our faithfulness. So, we have a difference there. To put it more plainly, it is Divine Revelation, not reason, that reveals to us the source of The Good. Some may even argue that reason was the fall of Man. Man fell from knowledge and communion with Yahweh when the snake persuaded him that he could obtain wisdom on his own without God's guidance. My view is that Man needs both reason and knowledge that is beyond reason, for the God of Creation is beyond reason," Benjamin explained. "So, the more I think about it, I don't see a reconcilable path for the two. Reason may give a glimpse of the Divine Good but can never totally reveal it."

"Well said, Benjamin. Jahan, what do you think of this?" Khartum asked.

"I was once tracking a brown bear," Jahan began. "By its paw prints, it was the biggest bear in the Pamir Mountains. Legend had it that the bear was the Bear of Virtue, a guardian of all that was good and noble in the wild. I tracked it through dense forests, across icy streams, and up steep slopes. As days turned into weeks, my hunger increased, my limbs grew tired, and my eyes were dazzled and blinded by the whiteness of the snow. My desire to know the secrets of the bear, how it came to be known as the Bear of Virtue, never wavered. I wanted to learn its fabled secrets of conquering the mountains. I never knew the Bear of Virtue could teach me the secrets that you call The Good. One moonlit night, I tracked the Bear to a secluded glade. There, beneath a silver birch tree, was the bear— just steps from me."

Jahan paused as if reliving the moment, his eyes fixed on something distant.

"I froze as she looked at me," he continued. "She walked around me, stood on her hind legs, towered over me, and sniffed for fear. I could feel her warm breath on my face. She gazed into my eyes, searching for my reason to track her. 'I want to know the secrets of the Bear of Virtue,' I blurted out. 'Walk with me,' the Bear said. For several weeks, I walked and watched the Bear of Virtue share its catch with little cubs, defending them against harm and sheltering them from the storms. As the seasons changed, I walked with the Bear, but the Bear never changed. It never took what it did not need; it never destroyed so it could be called a great Bear. It lived as one with the mountain and in service to it. After many months, she spoke again, 'Tell me, what have you learned?' She looked at me with eyes that showed countless stars and worlds within them. 'You have shown me that Good and Virtue is not a lofty peak to climb but a thousand small steps we take to care for and nurture our world and environment. I thought I was going to find the secret of dominating the mountains, but instead, I found the secret of living a life of service.' The Bear said, 'Walk on your own now,' and so I am here with you, enjoying lunch and stimulating conversation."

Jaidev looked at Jahan, gleaming with admiration for this rugged man who had learned the secrets of the Bear of Virtue.

"Jahan, your stories always have an unexpected point of view," Khartum said. "I will go next. Jaidev, you are welcome to speak after me, if you wish."

Khartum directed his attention to the full table. "Thank you for your topic, Konstantinos. Plato may not have had Jewish blood, but I think he shared a few wine bottles with an ancient Zoroastrian. We have a very similar concept that we have deified, and we call it Vohu Manah. It represents divine wisdom, illumination, and love. It produces the Good state of mind that a man must acquire in order to fulfill his duties. We often call Vohu Manah 'Good Thought' or 'Good Purpose.' So you see, we have developed before Plato the concept of The Good. When one evokes Vohu Manah, he thinks Good thoughts, which lead to Good actions and thus Good deeds. Good deeds lead us to the House of Song when we die. In this way, Zoroastrianism takes Plato's understanding of The Good to completion. We don't just leave it hanging as Plato has done, but apply it to the entire cycle of life," Khartum concluded. "I will leave it there for now. I want to leave some time for individual discussion, and of course, our guest Jaidev is welcome to speak."

Jaidev nodded, taking a deep breath. His eyes were steadfast, reading thoughts from the deep illumination of his mind. "My father, Mahesh, Khartum's dear friend, once said, 'It is the joy of man to know the complete range of Creation.' This means from the unmanifest to the manifest—from the causal body to the subtle body to the physical body. The Good that Plato refers to, he found through reason by the intellect illuminated in the mind. It manifests from the causal body that holds all forms in their pure unmanifest state and is shared by and accessible to all men. This is because Man's mind can extend from the finite to infinity. If we listen to the music of the chang, we hear the joy of the note. Man also can hear within him the joy of the entire Song of Creation because man has access to the infinite field of unmanifest Being within him." Pausing for a moment to let his words sink in, he continued. "This is beyond the senses. The source of The Good is beyond the senses, even beyond the inner sense of feeling. We know it and feel it as it manifests in the mind, but its source is found in the unmanifest. Each of you has spoken wisely from traditions that bring forward the transcendent radiance of the Creator. Meetings and discussions such as this provide valuable insights to the manifest minds of men. It is a great honor to sit among you." Jaidev bowed, clasping his hands in front of his eyes.

"Thank you, Jaidev—a beautiful perspective worthy of Mahesh himself," Khartum observed. "We now finish our lunch and talk more amongst ourselves."

As the afternoon continued, each of the guests stopped by and gave a warm welcome to Jaidev. Most expressed a desire to visit and learn more about India and his culture.

Aakash and Akim waved from the garden entryway. Khartum and Jaidev went to greet them.

"Akim is showing remarkable progress. He has a natural ability with the bow," Aakash shared.

Khartum looked with pride at Akim. "It seems we both have learned much from our Indian friends."

Chapter 10 - Leaving Bactria

Throughout the month, Ravi bartered with locals, acquiring goods to send home to India via Sanjeet and Sanjaya. The ox carts were fully loaded for their journey back over the Hindu Kush mountain range, and they found a caravan for them to join. As their time in Bactria was winding down, Nasir declared that the group heading towards Damascus would depart in three days' time.

Ravi looked at Sanjeet, his dark eyes intense. "I want you to take the bolts of silk directly to my father and mother. My mother will be so pleased. Let my father pick who he sells the changs to— someone with a good ear for music. Keep the chang with the inscription safe for me. Finally, the last bundle of silk must go to Sonal, daughter of Chetan, of the snake dancers."

Sanjeet bowed, understanding Ravi's desire without saying it aloud.

As the caravan back to India lined up to begin its journey, Aakash quietly approached Sanjeet. He held out a small hand-carved box with a silk golden ribbon tied around it. "Please bring this small gift back with you and deliver it privately to Amrita," Aakash requested.

Looking into his eyes with understanding, Sanjeet replied, "It will be done."

Jaidev took a deep breath before approaching Sanjeet. He spoke with determination in his voice. "Tell my father that all is well and I can't wait to be home again. Tell him Kharlum will travel with us." His hands held Sanjeet's firmly in a clasp of goodbye.

Again, Sanjeet understood, bowed, and repeated, "It shall be done."

With a blare from a horn, the caravan back to India was ordered by its Khabir to move forward.

Ravi, Aakash, Jaidev, and Barbod watched silently as it departed, heading back to their homeland and loved ones. Among them, there was a feeling of separateness and homesickness, accompanied by a desire to go back home.

"Well, let's prepare for our caravan's departure. Nasir will call us to leave in just a couple of days," Barbod said, breaking the melancholy mood.

"Khartum has invited us to dinner at his house tomorrow night before we leave," Jaidev announced. "I am looking forward to getting back on the road."

"Let's bring our instruments and Barbod can play the chang with us, like at the Holi festival," Aakash suggested.

"Excellent," Ravi added.

Barbod's voice was deep and soothing, and he gestured with his hands as he spoke. "The desert will be long and arduous, hot and filled with sand and pesky flies. But don't fret! Along the route, there are some great caravansaries that provide a welcome respite. An evening of music before we begin the journey will be a pleasant memory."

In the afternoon, Aakash gave an archery lesson to Akim. He watched Akim pull back the bowstring, fit an arrow into the groove, and take aim. His brow scrunched as he concentrated, and his lips moved silently as he counted to three before releasing the arrow. "I'm going to ask my father if I can come with you," Akim said. He leaned against the bow, a look of longing in his eyes. "I want to continue to have archery lessons and learn more about the ways of kalaripayattu."

"Akim, the desert, they tell me, is long and arduous. It will not be an easy trip. There will be many hardships," Aakash warned.

Akim flexed his young arm muscles and patted his broadening chest. "I have seen young children traveling with some caravans over the years," he said confidently. "I am older and stronger than many of them—I know I can do it."

"You certainly have done well with your archery lessons and kalaripayattu. I think you can handle the journey if your father agrees to let you come," Aakash replied.

"I am going to ask him when we are done. Will you come with me?" Akim asked.

"Let's do it now," Aakash responded.

Khartum was sitting and having tea when Akim and Aakash walked in. "Father, I have a request," Akim announced.

"Yes?" Khartum acknowledged, raising his right eyebrow.

Akim stood before his father with pleading eyes. He wanted to go on the journey to search for the Maha Atma but knew his father would be hesitant. He clasped his hands together and spoke with passion. "I want to continue learning archery and kalaripayattu from Aakash, father. Please allow me to come. I swear I will be a great help, not a burden." His voice was firm, hope shining in his eyes.

"Akim, I need you to stay with your mother while I am gone."

"But father, I can prove myself. I'm not a little boy anymore. I tend the horses. I can do a man's day's work as well as anyone. I'm strong. I have been studying archery and self-defense with Aakash, and he says I'm better than most men. Besides, you traveled to India when you were just a little older than I am. I want to see the world— to learn about people and places in distant lands. I have heard the stories you have told and want to have stories to tell like you. Please, father, I need to go with you."

"I want my son to see the birth of the great soul into this world. Your desire for adventure is much like mine. But I need to think of your mother."

"Father, I have to come with you. Mother will be alright. She has your brother and his wife and is highly respected in the city. Everyone will look out for her," Akim urged.

Khartum looked at his son's pleading eyes. He knew he could not disappoint him when his heart was so resolute. "If you are sure that you want to come on this journey, then I will not only not deny you, I will be happy to have you with me," Khartum declared.

"Father, father, thank you!" Akim exclaimed, gushing with excitement.

Aakash grinned proudly as his gaze followed the young boy, who had a quiver of arrows strapped to his back and a bow in hand. "Your son has taken to his archery and defense lessons with zeal. His hero is the ancient Persian archer, Arash. His skills are already far beyond the common shooter. He has both the outer fortitude and inner temperament to lead men someday," Aakash expressed. "I can continue to help him develop his skills by having him with us."

Khartum sighed heavily as he clasped Aakash's shoulder. "You have been a significant influence on him, Aakash. He talks about your lessons all the time, and I am in debt to you for teaching him archery." Akim fidgeted with a quiver at his side. "I will let your mother know," Khartum continued slowly. "She will be sad, but that is a mother's burden, for there always comes a time when a child leaves."

Akim nodded respectfully.

Preparing for the next part of their journey, Barbod and Ravi visited a camel dealer. There, Ravi bought three camels to ride and take some of the load off the horses.

"These camels look strong and suitable for the journey." Barbod ran his experienced hands over the camels, examining each one thoroughly. "They have healthy, full humps and are not overweight. A healthy hump is important for desert travel. And their eyes are alert and not skittish." Barbod felt the camels' legs and examined their hooves and temperament. "They have firm large hoofs providing them with ample stability even on shifting sand," Barbod remarked.

"Whew, do they all have such an offensive smell?" Ravi asked, holding his nose.

Barbod grinned as he watched Ravi's scrunched face. He gestured towards the camel that stood just a few feet away, its thick fur matted with sweat and dust from days of travel through the desert. "Camels pee down their legs to help keep cool, which is one cause of that distinctive smell. They also regurgitate and re-chew their food, causing an unpleasant belching gas. They don't get to bathe, but thankfully their thick heavy wool helps keep their skin from getting too hot. But best of all, they can sniff out water that can be more than a day's journey away—sometimes up to thirty or forty miles away! And they can go many days without water and carry heavy loads on their backs. You will come to love them like I love my Bellows," Barbod assured with an instructive tone.

Ravi's lips pursed and his face twisted in revulsion as he shook his head. "No, I don't think I'll ever get used to this," he replied with a disgusted grunt. "Let's get back and clean up before tonight's dinner."

Back at their rooms, Ravi washed up. Barbod decided to meditate to refresh himself. When he opened his eyes, he froze. As he sat on the floor with his legs crossed, a scorpion was now perched on his sandal, poised to strike. His inner calm quickly turned to terror. He trembled and began to sweat, afraid to move.

Ravi and Aakash knocked on his door. "Barbod, Barbod!" Ravi yelled. "Are you in there? He said he was going to rest for a while. Maybe he is sleeping."

Aakash carefully pushed the door open and peeked in. Barbod sat terrified, wide-eyed, and ashen white.

"Don't move, Barbod. I have trapped many scorpions back home," Aakash assured. Moving slowly but deliberately, he picked up a jar and took out his katar knife. Very delicately, he brought the mouth of the jar near the scorpion. With his katar knife in his other hand, he delicately slid it under the scorpion, lifting and depositing it in the jar.

Seeing the scorpion safely removed, Barbod sprang to his feet and stepped back. "I thought I was going to be stung and die. One of those bastards killed my mother."

Jaidev entered the room and observed Barbod's trembling and terror.

"You're okay now," Ravi reassured him.

"My father was never afraid of scorpions. He used to hold them near me, tease me with them, and tell me not to be afraid. But it just made me more afraid. I would have nightmares about them crawling on me," he stuttered and shuttered thinking about it.

Jaidev listened closely to Barbod's explanation. "It is understandable that the scorpion causing the loss of your mother when you were very young has left a deep samskara that will continue to emerge until it is healed. The surface approach of trying to conquer the effects of a samskara by directly confronting it as your father hoped, does not erase the deep impression it has made. When we cut ourselves, the skin heals from underneath until eventually, the scab falls off. We must follow nature's guidance and heal the samskara from underneath, from deep within, with meditation and positive healing waves of energy and thought, releasing the toxic fear that comes with the samskara. This will allow the chakra that is being blocked due to this deep stress to begin to clear and the part of the body that it most affects to be healed."

"I don't want to carry this fear of scorpions any longer. What do you mean about blocked chakras and the body holding fear?" Barbod asked.

"The samskara can manifest as many things. Because it is tied to your mother and then your father, it could inhibit you from expressing love through your heart chakra. Your mother's death removed love, leaving you afraid to love again. Your father's tough attitude may have inhibited your throat chakra because you wanted to speak out against him scaring you with other scorpions but couldn't because you were too young," Jaidev speculated.

"Cyrus told me I used to come to his tent when I was upset with my father," Barbod shared, failing to admit that he would go there to cry.

"I will prepare a program for you that will help heal it," Jaidev said.

"Right now, I'd like to heal this hunger I'm feeling," Ravi declared. "Let's head over to Khartum's."

Parisa and her maidens had planned for a banquet. The feast consisted of apricots, grapes, pears, dates, olives, cheese, artichokes, breads, roast lamb and chicken, traditional sesame seed cookies, wine, and beer—a drink brewed from fermented barley.

"Come, try this beer. It isn't commonly found in Persia. I think you will enjoy it," Farhad suggested.

"Ugh, it is not for me," Ravi replied, taking a cup and swallowing the pungent concoction. "It is too bitter and earthy."

Farhad's lips curved into a mischievous grin as he looked around the group. "That's what we all thought the first time. After your second cup, you'll be begging for more." His laughter filled the room.

"I'll stick to the red wine I know and love," Ravi replied, putting the cup aside.

Barbod lifted the cup to his lips. As the liquid slid down his throat, delight flooded his face. "Ahh, this is what I remember!" he exclaimed. His eyes brightened and an energetic spark lit within him. Grinning, he looked across at Farhad with a grateful nod. "A few of these and my chang playing takes on a whole new rhythm."

"First, our meal prayer, the Baj. Then we eat," Khartum announced, bowing his head. "Zirgan, will you honor our meal?"

"In the name of Ahura Mazda, giver of all good things, the generous-spirited and loving. Here we revere Ahura Mazda, who created the animals, grains, waters, and plants—who created the sky and the earth and all good things," Zirgan intoned, then raised his head.

"Enjoy!" Khartum added.

As Parisa watched her guests, she felt a strange mix of emotions. On one hand, she was pleased that her culinary efforts were so well-received. On the other, she had an uneasy feeling in the pit of her stomach. Her husband had just informed her that he and their son would be leaving for a mysterious journey together. As the plentiful food was devoured, her anxiety grew.

Khartum savored the meal—a feast of spices and flavors from across the region. "This truly is a gift from heaven," he declared. He looked at their guests with an expression of warmth and generosity. "Now, it is our honor to have you share some music from your home with us: a kirtan."

Jaidev, Ravi, Aakash, and Barbod all took up their instruments. Ravi counted out the beat, and they began a harmonic tune. Jaidev set his flute aside and sang a hymn to Lord Krishna, uttering each verse as a chant. Aakash, carrying the beat on his drum, repeated each of Jaidev's verses in unison. Barbod, playing the chang, added another layer to the music that made it more vibrant with each stanza.

Jaidev started the second song with a call and response, repeating the chant slowly and having each guest sing it after him. The tempo increased as the song went on, with Khartum, Parisa, and Akim all joining in. When the song finished, Akim felt his heart open and quietly approached Barbod to inquire if he knew the Persian Mater song.

"Yes, I remember it," Barbod said, nodding. "It goes like this."

Barbod strummed the chang softly.

Akim sang a song in honor of his dear mother. Khartum sensed the special message in Akim's voice and joined in on the singing. Her son's serenade mesmerized Parisa, her heart overflowing with emotion. Farhad and the servants all joined for the last verse, tears streaming down Parisa's cheeks as she listened. Holding her hand over her heart, she thanked everyone who sang and bowed in appreciation. As soon as the song ended, she threw her arms around Akim and wept joyfully. She knew this was Akim's way of saying goodbye before he and his father left on their long journey.

"Wine and fruit," Khartum ordered the servants with a clap when the song was over, breaking the heartwarming spell.

Barbod played the Persian Song of Joy next. Ravi, Jaidev, and Aakash caught on quickly and joined in as the chang's melody filled the room.

The night and music slowly faded away, and the attendees said their goodbyes to Parisa, Khartum, and Akim. Khartum held Parisa tenderly as they settled in for the night. As he drifted off to sleep, a dream enveloped him. He saw his mother smiling at him, but when he tried to embrace her, she transformed into a young woman wearing a blue tichel scarf around her head. Her round eyes seemed bottomless, resembling the depths of the night sky, radiating love. She was cradling an infant beneath her breast. As she reached down to uncover his face, the sun shone brightly from her bosom, jolting Khartum awake with intense emotion. Khartum lay in bed, mesmerized by the dream, while watching Parisa sleep peacefully.

Chapter 11 - The Long Desert

Nasir gazed up at the rising sun on a mid-June morning, wiping his brow and then grimacing as he held his chest. "Damn heartburn," he uttered to anyone that would hear. His eyes met with a brilliant sky in the steadily increasing temperatures. By mid-afternoon, it would be sweltering outside. Summer had officially arrived.

"Make sure you water your animals and pack your belongings securely. We leave in an hour," Nasir announced. "We have many new travelers in our caravan. Barbod, you and your friends will move up and ride behind me. Let the Greeks and Moroccans bring up the rear."

Barbod returned to collect Ravi, Jaidev, and Aakash. After saddling the camels so they could sit atop, they tied their belongings to the sides of each saddle.

"Khartum and Akim, help Ravi, Jaidev, and Aakash get on their camels and start moving," Barbod ordered. "They'll become used to riding them in no time. We can have the horses follow behind the camels."

The camels snorted when they were mounted and walked to their position in the caravan line.

"Once I get used to riding this beast, there are several traders in the caravan that I want to talk with on the journey and learn what I can about their goods," Ravi said.

"The journey to Damascus will take three full moons," Barbod informed. "We will soon travel during the cool of night so we can avoid the punishing heat. We shall take our time and rest during the hottest hours of the day."

The caravan lumbered away from Bactria. Jaidev looked back one last time. It was a different world than his home in India—the multitude of cultures and ideas he encountered was a real eye-opener. The meeting with Zirgan, Zhang Qian, and the Seer Stella; the lunch and discussion at Khartum's; the marketplace with Greeks, Romans, Egyptians, Chinese, Persians, and other traders all with different ideas about life and Creation... *Truly, the Creator speaks to all in their own manner*, he thought.

"There is a caravanserai within each day's travel," Barbod said. "The road is challenging, but we will sleep in a protected area. It will take us about 17 days to reach Herat. There is a great bazaar in Herat, and the Citadel of Alexander is a sight to behold."

As they traveled southwest, Jaidev saw a flock of vultures circling overhead.

Barbod followed Jaidev's gaze to the clusters of vultures circling in the sky, his face grim. "There must be carrion for them to feed on or they wouldn't be circling like that," he observed, tugging at his beard and nodding toward the horizon. "We will see soon enough; we are heading in that direction. The vulture is a carnivorous creature."

The dirt road snaked through the rolling steppes, turning this way and that as the mountain range rose to the right. Reaching a hill's crest, they were greeted with a gruesome sight: vultures tearing apart an ibex, its long horns and distinct beard still recognizable amidst the horrific scene.

"Jackals probably took it down," Barbod said quietly, watching as the birds tore at the meat.

"Keep up the pace!" Nasir shouted back. "We have to reach the caravanserai before dusk."

Jaidev mused that nature has a purpose for every living thing. Even the lowly vulture, with its scavenging, removed the decaying flesh of the ibex from its bones, thereby cleansing it.

"Barbod, I have been thinking about your samskaras—your deep-seated pain of your mother's death from the scorpion and your father's coldness. The foundation of Vedic knowledge is the establishment of wholeness. When we are blocked by samskaras, we forget our wholeness and it must be reawakened. So, our approach is to prescribe both inner and outer methods to help facilitate the experience of wholeness. With that in mind, I want to make suggestions that can help achieve the desired result. First, let me explain the inner approach. When you sit to meditate and ask yourself the soul questions, bring this to mind when asking 'What do I want?': you want to heal this samskara—to be free of the emotional blockage it is causing you. Bring your awareness to your heart area then throat area and feel healing emerging from within. Then, when you go beyond the samskara in meditation, you will bring the light of awareness and healing to it."

"How long will I need to do that?" Barbod asked.

"It is a process that cannot be measured by time. For some, it heals quickly and for others, it takes longer. Try it for a while and see how you feel," Jaidev advised. "In our view, when these samskaras cause imbalance, our doshas become imbalanced. Our doshas are Vata, Pitta, and Kapha. When a samskara causes anxiety and fear, our Vata dosha can become imbalanced. When we hold resentment and anger, our Pitta dosha can come out of balance. We want to bring these back into balance, which we can do by practicing pranayama, or breathing techniques. There are many breathing techniques. Let's start with a basic pranayam called Nadi Shodhana. In this technique, we breathe through alternate nostrils. I'll show you how. Follow my lead and close off your nostrils, inhaling and exhaling as I do."

After a few minutes of practicing Nadi Shodhana, Barbod seemed more settled.

"Very good," Jaidev affirmed. "Practice this for a few minutes before each meditation. The Vedic approach is complete, so we will look at what you are eating and drinking and make adjustments where necessary. I will also perform a yagya for you that will mitigate any negative karmic energy coming your way. Finally, we will enhance your primary planet Jupiter, a very positive benefic, by wearing a gem that enhances Jupiterian energy. I can tell that you are mostly Jupiterian. The gem for Jupiter is the yellow sapphire. We will find a nice one and fashion it to wear properly. Usually, one would wear it in a ring, but we don't want to draw attention to a gem while on the caravan, so we will fashion one to wear against your skin under your robe," Jaidev suggested.

"I am already wearing a gold faravahar that Cyrus gifted to me," Barbod said.

"Perhaps we can add a suitable yellow sapphire to it—if you are comfortable with that. It will take a while to find a gem, so you can think about it," Jaidev added. "So, as you can see, our approach to re-establishing wholeness is one of fullness, seeking to bring the support of nature from the causal, to the subtle, and to the physical."

"I have never tried such a full approach. Usually, when I'm not feeling well, Paloma will prepare a tea and tell me to rest," Barbod replied.

"Rest is the basis for both activity and healing, so Paloma is wise in knowing that. Sleep is a restful dullness whereas meditation is a restful awareness. That is why we lay down to sleep and sit up to meditate. Meditation brings deep rest, and sometimes the wisdom of the body will seek sleep when we meditate. There isn't anything wrong when that happens. It is natural. When we realize we have been sleeping instead of meditating, we simply end with a few minutes of meditation," Jaidev explained.

"Thank you, Jaidev. I'm looking forward to seeing some results. I hate these nightmares about scorpions and the panic I feel when near one."

"You may find it interesting that Scorpio, the scorpion, is the natural 8th house in Jyotish. It is a dusthana house, meaning grief-producing. It can cause great disease, fear, misfortune, and even death. This practice will help ease any 8th house ailments," Jaidev added. "But that is for another day. Be encouraged, for the 8th house is also one of the three moksha houses, meaning it is connected to liberation."

Jaidev looked at Barbod, who was lost in thought, practicing the pranayam as Bellows clumped forward.

The days inched by, one after the other. Each night, they found respite from the heat at a caravanserai to eat and rest.

Finally, after many long days of travel, the caravan made its way into Herat. People stopped to gawk, and children pointed gleefully at the tired travelers. The buildings basked in the sun, spread out on dusty roads, while the Citadel of Alexander proudly overlooked the modest adobe houses.

"Vah, that is a magnificent building. How did Alexander build such a citadel?" Aakash asked.

Ravi stared up in awe at the building rising over the desert; it seemed to reach into the sky. "The Citadel is way beyond anything we have built back in India," he mumbled, more to himself than anyone else. "It is huge."

"Behold one of the impressive architectural feats of the Greeks and Romans. You will be amazed as we head further westward; there are incredible structures in the west," Barbod remarked enthusiastically.

"The animals can water and graze down by the Hari River," Nasir announced. His sun-weathered face cracked into a broad smile as he thought of the two days they would have to rest. "I plan to enjoy the succulent kebabs, crispy flatbreads, and sweet pastries in the bazaar while savoring some of the finest wine Persia offers."

"Superb wine and food await," Barbod proclaimed. "My favorite dish is Herat style kitchiri rice mixed with beef and moong beans. It is good with or without the beef, Jaidev."

"I'm famished," Ravi said. "Let's head to the bazaar."

As they entered the bustling bazaar, a scrawny, blind beggar in a soiled robe sat at the entrance. He held his bowl out with one hand and tapped a stick on the ground with the other. "Love and mercy," he called out in a raspy voice.

"Love and mercy to you," Jaidev replied, stopping and reaching for a coin as the others walked on.

"The light be with you," the beggar said.

Jaidev squinted at the aged blind beggar before him, watching his lined face for any hint of recognition. "How does a blind beggar know the light?" Jaidev asked.

The old beggar bowed his head, and silver whiskers framed the creases of joy on his tan face. With arms outstretched, he spoke in a low sing-song voice. "I am blessed to know light where many know darkness. I know the light in the voice of compassion and in the sparrow's song, in the sweet juice of an apple and the warmth and satisfaction of bread in my belly, in the touch of a hand on my shoulder guiding me down the street, and in the fragrance of the flower and the rain as it comes on the winds. Beyond these lights, I know the light behind the eyes showing me the way," the old beggar said.

Jaidev stared in disbelief at the blind beggar, his heart swelling, astonished that such wisdom could come from this frail man. "Your understanding far surpasses most men with eyesight," he replied with reverence. "Our Rig Veda says, 'The Light of God which we experience within our own transcendental consciousness is found shining throughout the whole creation to the farthest point.' God is truly with you, old man. We are now journeying to find the birth of a great soul who will be the light of men."

The old beggar's voice was full of affirmation. "You will find him in a manger. The beasts of the earth will gather around him at his birth. I have seen it in my dreams, and you have affirmed this truth." His unfocused eyes twinkled with delight.

"Love and mercy. I am so honored to have crossed your path,"

Jaidev expressed.

"And I, yours," the old beggar agreed, his eyes seeming to see within.

Jaidev hurried to catch up with the others, still deeply engrossed in his conversation.

"You seem to have enjoyed your conversation with the old blind man," Aakash remarked, knowing his friend.

"Some men see more without eyes than those with," Jaidev said.

"Indeed," Aakash acknowledged. I'm going to give Akim another archery lesson and some training on hand-to-hand combat. We'll meet you for dinner in a while."

Aakash and Akim found a quiet spot in a garden not far from the inn where they would sleep that night. Akim was excelling at his archery and eager to learn the lessons of hand-to-hand combat. Aakash had him exercise his breath control as they worked. "Control the breath to conserve your energy as your opponent expels his," Aakash instructed. "Inhale as you prepare to strike and exhale as you execute."

After several tries, Akim said, "I can feel the difference. I feel more focused."

"Come, let's get washed up and rest before dinner," Aakash proposed.

As they turned into an alley, they saw several teenage boys watching another teen pin a young girl against a wall. She looked terrified, afraid of being raped. Aakash felt a rush of anger surge through him. The thought of a young woman being dishonored and forced against her will infuriated him. "Stop," he commanded.

One young man grimaced at Aakash. "There are seven of us and two of you. Move on," he responded.

Aakash looked at Akim whose eyes were wide with uncertainty. Seeing Aakash's eyes burn with inner fire and his body move into a fighting position, he mimicked his teacher.

The cocky teenagers looked back, one picking up a large stick to swing. "This is none of your business. Move on!" he yelled.

"The girl comes with me," Aakash demanded, moving towards the biggest teen holding the stick.

The teen rushed at Aakash, preparing to strike. Aakash swiftly and gracefully avoided the blow, kicking the teen hard in the stomach and taking his breath from him. He continued to twist into his attacker, striking his throat and disarming him from the stick. The boy fell. A second boy came up from behind and Akim instinctively swept his feet with a kick, sending the young man face down into the dirt. Aakash threw a third young man head-first into the building. The four others decided it was safer to run than tangle with Aakash and Akim. They didn't have any knowledge of fighting beyond their bravado.

The first three limped off, afraid to anger Aakash further. The young girl looked up and, being closer to Akim, ran into his arms. "Thanks," she cried.

Akim whispered to her, "You're safe now. Be easy."

"What is your name, child?" Aakash asked.

"I am Leila, the daughter of a baker. We live down the street there." She pointed down the alley.

"Come, we will walk you home," Aakash said.

Her eyes met Akim's who had never had a young woman in his arms. He gently released her, as pride rose through his chest at being a defender. He placed a comforting hand on her back. "Come," he whispered.

When they arrived at her father's bakery, Leila burst into tears. "These men saved me!" she cried. "Several young rukhkhana[6] attacked me and these two gentlemen defended and saved me."

"I am Aakash, and this is Akim," Aakash said. "We came across your daughter in peril and defended her. We defeated and disposed of the attackers."

---

[6] Caravan raiders

"Papa, they took on seven young men and defeated them," Leila gushed.

"We are in your debt. Thank you, thank you. I must give you something. Here, loaves of the freshest and best bread in the city," the father offered.

"Nothing is necessary; it was an honor. I am most proud of my young student, Akim. He showed courage and a clear mind," Aakash said.

"Leila, get those loaves for these young men. We are so fortunate to have you show up."

"We are honored. Your bread smells fantastic," Aakash replied. Leila handed some loaves to Akim, looking admiringly into his eyes.

Akim blushed, unable to look away.

"We will be going back to our inn," Aakash announced. Akim bowed as he moved away, still transfixed on Leila's eyes.

As they walked into the inn, they met Jaidev and Khartum.

"What happened?" Jaidev asked, noting the loaves and Akim's excited look.

"We saved a young girl who was being attacked. Aakash and I gave them a lesson," Akim gushed. "Her father is a baker and gave us some loaves in thanks."

"Akim handled himself admirably. I couldn't have helped her without him," Aakash acknowledged, being sure to direct praise to his younger student.

"Are you okay, Akim?" his father asked, concerned.

"Yes, father. No need to worry. Aakash's lessons made it easy," Akim assured proudly, his newfound confidence glowing. His body assumed the strike position to demonstrate what he had learned.

Jaidev looked at Aakash, proud of his friend for defending a young girl. However, he could see by the way Aakash avoided his eyes that something was privately bothering him.

"Let's get some rest before dinner," Aakash said.

Back in the room, Jaidev suggested to Aakash that they meditate after sleeping a few hours and before dinner. "You seem uneasy my friend," Jaidev remarked.

"It is this inner anger that comes from nowhere at times," Aakash explained in frustration. "It was hard not to seriously hurt one of those attackers because of my anger. Our Gita says, 'It is anger born of Rajo Guna, all-consuming and most evil; know this to be the enemy here on earth.' And, at times, it controls me."

"You are truly a man who acts in accordance with his dharma," Jaidev encouraged. "Our Gita also says that there is nothing better for a kshatriya than a battle in accord with dharma. You are right—our Gita says that from anger arises delusion, from delusion arises unsteadiness of memory, and from unsteadiness of memory, destruction of the intellect. That is why, in this meditation, we go beyond the three Gunas, beyond Rajo Guna, and establish ourselves in Yoga before taking action. Before you meditate, when we ask the soul question of 'What do I want?' bring this to mind, let it go, and let nature dissolve the samskara of anger that troubles you."

"I'll try Jaidev," Aakash replied. "Thanks, I'll ponder it."

Jaidev thought of Aakash's chart. Mars was prominent in his chart being in the 7th house and tightly aspecting his ascendant. He was ending a Mars-Rahu Dasha-Bhukti and entering a Mars-Jupiter Dasha-Bhukti. Jupiter was in his 11th house of desires and aspecting his 5th house of Purva Punya, or past life credit, and 7th house of marriage. He was a Gemini ascendant, so Jupiter ruled his 10th and 7th. This Dasha-Bhukti was going to be a good time for fulfilling his desire of controlling his anger.

Once gathered for dinner, Nasir clapped and shouted for everyone's attention. "Let it be known that we will set off on our journey tomorrow at dusk," he announced. "We will need to travel in the cooler night hours to protect our camels and horses from the intense midday heat. May the stars light our way."

As dusk fell, the caravan lined up to move forward. Jaidev, Ravi, Aakash, and Barbod each mounted their camels with their horses tied behind them. Khartum and Akim followed.

"Tonight, the sun will set in Gemini, as Sagittarius rises in the east," Jaidev declared. "Venus and Mercury will be in Cancer, just above the western horizon. The Moon and Mars will be in Scorpio and Virgo respectively in the south-eastern sky. I will point them out to you as they appear when the sky darkens. Tomorrow night is Guru Purnima, the full Moon after the summer solstice when we honor our teachers. In observance of this, I will travel in silence tomorrow night."

"Move out!" Nasir barked at the caravan. "We have many nights before we arrive in the great city, Damghan."

The darkness of the night was a blanket that muffled sound and hid the world in shadow. The path ahead seemed to stretch endlessly, lit by the stars shimmering against the ink-black sky and the almost full Moon.

The caravan slowly wound its way through the night, the muted clomp of hooves on brittle desert soil and the occasional barked command puncturing the still air. Jaidev felt enlivened by the night sky, the expansiveness of eternity all around him. He leaned back in his saddle as they drifted along, eyes closed to the star-speckled sky above. He could hear the Vedas silently emerging in his mind's eye, the primordial vibrations of creation's organization and expansion, recited for generations by his family.

Feeling inspired, Jaidev spoke to Barbod and Aakash. "When we look at the star-filled sky, we sense the unboundedness of the Creator. This same unboundedness exists within us as well, for if it was not within us, we could not experience it through the light perceived with our eyes. Unboundedness is everywhere. It is the glory of man that he can know it."

"Jaidev, how is unboundedness both within us and around us in the heavens?" Barbod asked.

"Our forefathers knew that man's Being is also the Being of all. This was revealed to them through the 'shruti', meaning 'that which is heard'. The subtle vibrations that precede creation are also the subtle vibrations at the source of thought. Our Vedic rishis could perceive these vibrations. They knew the unboundedness within and found that it expresses itself unboundedly—it cannot be lessened. Unboundedness from unboundedness remains unboundedness This is how we get unboundedness from the largest of the large and the smallest of the small to the subtlest of the subtle."

"But why don't I know this unboundedness?" Barbod questioned.

"It is the subtle body that conceals this, causing our unknowing. Unboundedness expresses itself as our intellect, mind, and ego. The ego grasps everything in terms of itself, hiding unboundedness from perception. For example, we see things as my horse, my wife, my knife, my camel, my bow, etc. However, this is maya, the illusion," Jaidev explained.

Barbod scanned the sky, shaking his head. "It sounds like we are self-imprisoned—we are each our own jailers. How do I free myself from the prison of the subtle mind and ego?" Barbod asked, mustering a sense of resolve rather than defeat.

Jaidev looked at Barbod with admiration. "You have a sharp intellect, my friend. The light of knowledge must burn away ignorance. We gain this knowledge not from without, but from within. So, we turn our attention to that state where the senses are quiet, so they do not fill the mind with activity, making it alert. By remaining alert when thoughts cease, the state of unboundedness is achieved in its purest form."

"So, if I can gain the unboundedness, the illusions of the mind—the ego—all go away?" Barbod asked.

Jaidev's voice resonated softly like a melody of the flute. "When we gain unboundedness, the ignorance fades away. The intellect, mind, and ego no longer function at the level of boundaries.

We see the boundaries for what they are. The illusion of being bound within boundaries dissolves."

"How long does it take to gain this unboundedness?" Aakash asked, listening intently to the discussion.

"The paths we each take are different," Jaidev replied softly. "But in the end, we all have the same destination. For now, just enjoy the unboundedness of the starry sky and the inner quiet of meditation. Absorb the light and the stillness of the stars within you."

The next night, the travelers moved in near silence, with only whispers exchanged between them. They all made gestures and motions with their hands—a sign of respect for Jaidev's observance of Guru Purnima.

The following night, the summer stars shone brightly overhead.

"I have been thinking about our discussion two nights ago. I'm still trying to grasp how this unboundedness unfolds or shows itself to me," Barbod remarked, sounding perplexed.

"As we encounter unboundedness, there are two experiences. We know one as nirvikalpa, the eternal unboundedness or unboundedness that doesn't break. We know the other as sarvikalpa, the unboundedness that breaks," Jaidev stated.

"Why would it break?" Barbod asked.

"It is a perception of breaking because our minds are not yet ready to accept it as ever-present. The cycle of action, memory, and desire dominates the mind. As we meditate, the mantra slows and changes. This is the first stage. When the mantra only becomes a sense, a faint knowing, this is the second stage. When the mantra is no longer even a faint hum in the mind, this is 'am-ness', the experience of pure Being. And this is the third stage. This experience begins to come and go in the waking state, as it becomes more present in our awareness. When this 'am-ness', or Turiya, becomes always present, it is no longer lost in the three worlds of waking, dreaming, and sleeping—we have achieved the ever-present unboundedness. We are then a Jivan Mukti, meaning inner freedom amongst outward activity. We are no longer attached to karma," Jaidev explained.

"I keep thinking of the lesson from the old saddhu that gave me my bow: 'To let the arrow fly, first pull back the bow.' Is one who has mastered this a Jivan Mukti?" Aakash asked.

"All stages of the experience of unboundedness are present in the saddhu's words," Jaidev said reassuringly.

"I still have much to learn about the bow," Aakash mused.

"There are two types of knowledge: knowledge that is experiential and knowledge that is theoretical. Both must be present for knowledge to be verifiable. When the teachings of the Vedas are alive in experience, one is a Jivan Mukti," Jaidev said.

"The old saddhu that I met must have been a Jivan Mukti," Aakash determined.

As the night's shadows disappeared with the morning sun, a caravanserai emerged.

Barbod stretched his arms out wide and let out a giant yawn, his voice heavy with exhaustion. "I'm looking forward to a meal and laying my bones down on a nice soft bed."

Aakash nodded in agreement as a meteor streaked down the western horizon.

As they rode slowly into the caravanserai, a lone figure sat cross-legged at the gate. Sunken eyes peered out from a hooded shroud. Aakash recognized the face as the old saddhu. He motioned for Aakash to come and sit beside him. As Aakash sat down, the old saddhu looked deeply into his eyes. His face changed to Lord Krishna's, and he unfolded a cloth with a picture resembling his beloved Amrita embroidered into it. Upon closer look, Aakash saw that it was a young woman like Amrita but holding a child who emitted a warm, rich golden light. The child's hand was positioned in the sign of blessing. Aakash could feel his heart warmed by the love flowing from the child's hand. Suddenly, a bell tolled in the distance, and he could hear Akim calling to him from his deep sleep.

"Aakash, look! Roman soldiers are entering the caravanserai! They're pulling slaves in chains!"

Shaking off his reverie, Aakash arose from his bed. He went to the window and stood alongside Akim to witness the scene.

Horses dragged the captured men by their arms, each barefoot and wearing a tattered tunic. Patches of dirt, grime, and dried blood covered their skin. Their faces were swollen from punches, and their bodies were littered with bruises of purple and blue.

"These swine are enemies of Rome and King Herod," the lead soldier announced. "No one is to feed or give water to them or they will join them in chains." The lead soldier led the slaves to a corner of the stable and chained them in a horse stall with a guard stationed nearby.

Aakash studied the soldiers closely, noting their swords, spears, and bows with arrows tightly strapped to their backs. Protective helmets and chest plates shimmered in the light. *They will be formidable adversaries*, he thought.

Nasir's booming voice echoed through the stone-laid courtyard. "Grab a bite to eat. We leave for our night's journey in three hours."

"Jaidev, what did you think of the prisoners and slaves the Romans captured?" Barbod asked as the caravan departed the caravanserai. "They showed them no mercy."

Jaidev glinted, speaking with a compassionate tone. "It is a travesty that men seek to enslave other men. A man is born to be free. Beware, my friend. Men can be bound into slavery not just by other men but by an unbalanced mind. A man's mind can become attached and enslaved to rajasic and tamasic activities, where all he thinks of is anger and passion. On the other hand, a man physically enslaved can be free if his mind is not bound," Jaidev explained.

"Do the stars tell us if a man is to be imprisoned or enslaved?"

Aakash wondered.

"The twelfth house can tell us if a man is karmically inclined towards enslavement or moksha, though the whole chart must be considered," Jaidev replied as his finger traced a circular motion, stopping just before its starting point.

"What does the chart show for the Maha Atma?" Aakash asked.

Jaidev's voice betrayed a hint of awe as he spoke. "The Maha Atma will have great enemies, but nothing that man or Asura does can enslave him. He will walk the earth unbound and unfettered. He will show men the way to their own liberation. By shining his inner light before men, he will illuminate the darkness within them. He will free men from the enslavement of their sins."

As the sun set the following night, the caravan advanced slowly. Jaidev took out his flute and started playing a gentle tune. The music had a seductive and entrancing rhythm.

"What are you playing?" Barbod asked, riding Bellows next to Jaidev and Aakash.

"This is a Ghandarva Veda tune. It is a pitta beat—the vibratory quality meant to soothe and harmonize with the setting sun," Jaidev replied.

"How does it work?" Barbod asked.

As Jaidev spoke, Barbod could feel the mysticism in his words. "The seers of our Vedic tradition could access the hidden rhythms in all of nature. When we learn to listen, we can hear and feel these same vibrations within us. Ghandarva Veda music helps us tune into this inner harmony."

"When you taught me how to meditate, you gave me a sound and vibration to repeat. Is this similar?" Barbod asked.

"When we play music together, all our instruments must come into harmony for a song to be played and enjoyed. If an instrument is out of harmony, all within earshot know it immediately. Recall how a misplayed note feels in your gut and sends a shiver down your spine. Now think about how a perfect harmony of instruments feels. I think you recognize this distinction well," Jaidev said.

"That's what makes music so enjoyable and pleasing—the harmony and rhythmic beauty it creates," Barbod affirmed with a nod.

Jaidev smiled in agreement. "All of creation is a harmony of the Creator. We are notes in the Creator's melody. Our vibrations must be in rhythm with the Song of the Creator. That is the purpose of the Vedic wisdom. Ayurveda, Ghandarva Veda, Vaastu, and Jyotish—these are different instruments to bring us in tune with the Song of Creation. Meditation is the most powerful instrument. It brings the mind to the source, the point of stillness where we are observers of the Creator's Song and the Song itself," Jaidev explained.

"How do the stars, planets, and what they tell you contribute to this harmony?" Barbod asked.

"The stars and planets we see above us are reflected within us. At birth, the outer planets reflect our inner planets, and they show us our karmic harmony and disharmony. Parashara taught us that the Sun is our soul, our casual body. It can become hidden by the clouds of the mind, intellect, and ego, and it must be awakened. Our inner small Sun must be harmonized with the inner big Sun, the Creator."

"How do the other planets contribute to this harmony?" Barbod asked.

"The Moon is reflected through the waves of our emotions. One day, we feel our emotions arise as fear; another, as jealousy; another, as empathy and compassion; another, as wholeness. We must recognize these emotions and anchor ourselves not to the surface waves of change but to the depths of the silent ocean. When the water is still, we see the clear depth of the water, and the reflection of the Sun is full," Jaidev said.

"You have told me I have a strong Mars. How does this bring harmony to the Creator's song?" Aakash asked.

"Mars brings us energy and motivation. We must harmonize

Mars with the Creator's Song through yoga, meditation, and seva or service to others. It is a warrior's dharma to serve and protect. When it is out of tune, we often express our vibrations as anger, rajas, violence, and ego defensiveness," Jaidev replied.

"What is my dominant planet and how does it connect?" Barbod asked.

Jaidev grinned appreciatively at Barbod. "You are mostly Jupiterian. You enjoy fun and the fullness of things like good food, excellent wine, and wonderful music. Jupiter harmonizes through the expansion of the heart and mind, which brings more and more fullness to life. When the heart feels fullness, a man becomes more devoted to the Creator."

"I have never felt a devotion to God, but since you have taught me meditation, I appreciate what is around me more," Barbod remarked.

"That is a sign that meditation is working," Jaidev smiled.

"And the other planets?" Aakash asked.

"Mercury is intelligence. It orients outer information by making sense of things through the intellect. It harmonizes by growing from outer intelligence to inner intelligence. In this way, we see the measurable in the light of the immeasurable. Venus is the planet of love," Jaidev continued. "The ego can contain love and become possessive and obsessive. It harmonizes with the wonder and joy of life's beauty and is often expressed through art and music. In perfect harmony, life expresses the spiritual heart. Barbod, I don't know your birth date, place, and time, but I would guess you have a well-placed Venus in your third house giving you musical ability," Jaidev added.

"And when we feel love for someone that we want to be with?" Aakash asked, clutching the cloth Amrita gave him in his cloak.

"It is by loving ourselves that we can truly love another person. And this inner harmonization of Venus brings forth the love of self. We can then express this purely in the flow of love to another.

Water the roots of inner love by harmonizing Venus and the fruits of our outer love will be fulfilling," Jaidev stated, recognizing the intention behind Aakash's question.

Aakash listened intently and nodded in understanding.

"Saturn harmonizes by bringing order and structure to the Song of Creation," Jaidev continued. "Each note contributes to the whole. If Saturn is out of harmony, we get stuck and repeat a note over and over, and the song loses its melody. Saturn brings each note to its conclusion so a fresh note can arise in the Song of Creation."

"My mother always feared Rahu and Ketu," Aakash noted with hesitation.

"The two shadows, Rahu and Ketu, are best understood through myth. Rahu, an Asura, snuck into the line of Devas waiting to drink the Amrita of immortality. When the Sun and Moon discovered Rahu, they alerted Lord Vishnu, who threw his chakra and cut Rahu in two. But because he had already drunk the Amrita, both parts became immortal. They became the points in the outer and inner sky where eclipses of the Sun and Moon occur. Rahu harmonizes by eliminating the shadows and illusions of our memories and desires, the cessation of the insatiable. Ketu is the mystical attraction of secrets harmonized with the secrets of the Divine."

"What happens once we harmonize the inner planets?" Aakash asked.

"The inner harmony of the self is the foundation for an expanding chorus of music. It is the Chetana, or consciousness, of Turiya, our Atma, and becomes ever present in our awareness. In this state, one can no longer be impacted by pain" Jaidev said. "As we continue to grow, our inner harmony is felt and heard within others. We perceive that the Song of the Creator, the silence from which all songs emerge, is also present in others. The silent waves of harmony flow from us to others and waves of harmony flow from others to us. We see and hear all creatures in the silent harmony of the Creator. This is Bhagavat Chetana, or God consciousness," Jaidev added.

"Does the song end there?" Barbod asked.

Jaidev laughed in appreciation of the question. "The song never ends. The ever-present 'am-ness' is always expanding. Waves of bliss flow not only from within us but also from other creatures as we perceive the 'am-ness' in them. We hear the Creator's Song sung by all of Creation. This is Brahmi Chetana or Unity consciousness."

"As a man who loves music, I hope to hear this song," Barbod declared.

"You spoke of this a little when you taught us meditation. It is becoming clearer now," Aakash said.

The morning sun rose, its rays revealing the travelers' tired faces as they arrived at yet another caravanserai. Exhausted after nights spent riding camels through barren deserts, the travelers silently made their way to their sleeping quarters while Nasir shouted words of encouragement: "We'll make it to Damghan by tomorrow!"

Chapter 12 - Three Cities

As the caravan approached the entrance to Damghan, Barbod's enthusiasm soared. "We're almost there! Damghan is known for its delicious pistachios—they have a rich flavor that can't be found anywhere else. I'll take you around the bazaar, Ravi," he promised.

Ravi groaned and stretched his back, wincing from the pain. He had been riding a camel all night and was exhausted. He could still smell the animal's musky scent emanating from his clothes. "I think I just want to take a long bath and sleep," he said.

"Ahhh, but you will be missing some true delicacies," Barbod exclaimed to Ravi. "Khartum, you will be interested to know that there is an ancient Zoroastrian temple in Damghan, a fire temple!" Barbod yelled back to Khartum.

"How long will the caravan be in the city?" Khartum called.

"Nasir will probably stay for about a week. That's long enough to devour a few kilos of pistachios. He enjoys pistachios almost as much as a betel leaf," Barbod grinned.

Barbod wove his way through the caravan camp, passing camels, wagons, and tents. He found Nasir in his tent, gasping for breath. Sweat poured down Nasir's face, and his eyes were wide with fear.

"What is it Nasir? You don't look well," Barbod asked, concern ringing in his voice.

Nasir could only manage a raspy whisper. "Something... in the air..." he said between gasps. "I think I just need sleep and rest, Barbod. I haven't felt well for several days now."

Barbod reached out and gently squeezed his shoulder. His caramel eyes filled with worry as he nodded and said, "Don't worry about the caravan. I'll make sure it's taken care of. Paloma will come to look after you while you rest. Everything will be alright."

Nasir smiled slyly, revealing yellowed teeth beneath cracked lips. His sunken eyes and hollow cheeks made it clear he was unwell, yet his words were met with humor. "Thanks, Barbod. I'm not paying you any extra."

Barbod's face was heavy with concern. "If you did, I would think you are really not feeling well. Take some time to rest and get better."

While Aakash and Akim took care of the horses, Khartum and Jaidev made sure they had adequate lodging. "Let's get some sleep and check out what this town offers," Jaidev suggested.

About midday, Jaidev walked to his window and breathed in the heated air. The sun was high in the sky, but the streets were empty, with hardly a breeze to stir up dust.

"Everyone takes refuge from the heat during the day," Barbod informed, looking up at him from his bed. "It's too hot to do much, but soon it will begin to cool and people will get back to their daily lives."

The sound of a fist pounding on the door startled them. It was Paloma, frantic and crying. "Barbod, come quick! Nasir is breathing strangely, and I can't wake him up!"

Barbod, Jaidev, and Aakash raced to Nasir's quarters, their robes billowing behind them. As they entered the room, they found Nasir breathing laboriously and doubled over in pain, gripping his chest with one hand as sweat poured down his face. "We must get him help!" Barbod shouted. "Find a physician—quickly!"

Jaidev stepped forward and gently took Nasir's wrist in his hand. He closed his eyes for a moment, feeling the pulse of life beat like a racing swan beneath his fingertips. When he opened them again, they had gained an intensity that frightened the others. "His heart is beating fast, and he's burning up. Quickly now—wet some rags with cold water and place them on his neck, wrists, and forehead. It will help to bring his fever down."

Paloma rushed in with the bowl of water and rags, her face pale with worry. Nasir lay on the bed, his eyes wide and bulging as he gasped for air. She carefully pressed a wet cloth against his forehead, as Jaidev applied the other wet rags to his vital points. Paloma placed one hand on his chest and murmured soft, calming words.

After a few minutes, his breathing evened out. He tried to sit up and motioned towards the water. "Just a small sip," Jaidev said firmly. "You're too overheated to drink much right now. You can have more when you return to normal but eat nothing until I check on you later."

Khartum had observed with fascination as Jaidev gently touched Nasir's wrist, sensing the pulse beneath his fingertips. "What was that you did?" he asked.

"That was Nadi Vijnanam. Our forefathers taught it as part of Ayurveda. The pulse tells us much about a person's health. Nasir showed a kapha heart rate. His heart is hardening. He will need to change his diet, lose weight, and exercise or his heart may stop beating. The heat has intensified his distress. He is very unhealthy," Jaidev explained.

"I remember your father holding my wrist when he healed me years ago," Khartum remarked.

Jaidev paused for a moment, stroking his chin thoughtfully. "Yes," he said finally. "I believe a diet change would be wise for Nasir. But, for now, he needs rest."

Khartum, hearing Nasir was settled for now, suggested, "Let's eat and take it easy while Nasir recovers. Then maybe we can go see the Zoroastrian temple."

Jaidev and Barbod strode side-by-side through the camp.

Jaidev's voice was quiet and taut with concern. "Nasir is very ill," he confided to Barbod. "His heart... it's so weak. I fear he won't make it to Damascus."

Barbod met Jaidev's gaze with a tender expression. He thought of all the years Nasir and he had been companions, living and working together, and how their caravan was now the only family Nasir had left.

"Tell everyone to make sure he doesn't exert himself too much," Jaidev said.

After several days, the color returned to Nasir's cheeks as he regained his strength. He looked and sounded much better. "We leave on the eighth day," he declared. "Enough of this lying around. It will take us many nights to travel to Ray, the next city."

Jaidev, always monitoring the position of the planets, announced that the sky would be dark, as it was the night of a new moon.

When the departure day approached, the caravan of camels and horses snaked out of Damghan. The night air grew warmer with each footstep, a warm breeze ruffling their robes.

Barbod leaned forward on Bellows, his face scrunched in concentration. "Jaidev, how do we lose the harmony, the melody of unboundedness, the Song of Creation you taught us about the other night?"

"You are the Song of Creation expressed as a note in the Song. Understand that when the Song of Creation flows, it does so as three: the Observer of the Song, the Song itself, and the Process of Knowing the Song. There is the Knower, the Known, and the Knowing, and there are no boundaries between them. They are One—One Universal Mind, One 'Intellect', One 'I', and One Song. Boundaries only occur within the boundless. The individual note has a boundary because it is manifest, while the Song is unbounded because it is unmanifest. Yet, this boundless silence from which a bounded note arises and exists is also One with the note," Jaidev explained, pausing for a breath to let his words settle.

Barbod listened intently, his gaze unwavering.

"Through Pragyapradh, the 'mistake of the intellect', this unbounded eternal silence underlying the Song of Creation is forgotten," he continued. "It is overshadowed by the boundaries of the manifest. The intellect, mind, and ego forget their unboundedness and perceive only the boundaries of the manifest. When this happens, the individual notes of the Song become out of tune, and this disharmony is expressed in all manner of pain and suffering. The individual must be brought back into tune by remembering he is the Silence—the unmanifest Being from which the original Song of Creation emerges. He is Unboundedness and Bliss. It is lost only at the level of the individual. The Universal Song continues to play even though he has forgotten it. And, because the Song of Creation is ever present, the individual can be brought back into harmony with it anytime by opening the mind, intellect, and ego to it. Pragyapradh can be corrected, the Unboundedness remembered, and the individual can live in harmony and unity with the Song of Creation once again," Jaidev concluded.

Barbod closed his eyes and sighed as he spoke. "Oh, to feel the Unboundedness within me—to be taken away by the Song of Creation, to be filled with bliss, love, and inner calm," he whispered, his words seeming to evaporate into the space between them.

"Simply continue the path of meditation and right action and listen with your heart. It is a Song that is beyond the ears," Jaidev counseled.

That night, the next caravanserai came into view, and with the light of burning torches, Jaidev could make out dunes of sand piled around the walls. The air hung heavy, carrying a sense of foreboding, as if something dark lurked beneath the surface.

Barbod looked stunned. "I remember this caravanserai as vibrant and robust. Now it is covered by a blanket of sand and dust."

"What causes this?" Jaidev asked.

"In this part of the desert, violent dust storms come this time of year. It is as if the very gates of hell are descending on you. Dark clouds of swirling sand and choking dust roll through, blackening the sky. It is a fearful sight," Barbod revealed.

Nasir coughed and wheezed as he shouted, "Let's get the animals taken care of! Feed them first, then make sure they're all settled in." He wiped the beading sweat from his brow.

The dust-coated caravanserai was a dour sight. The walls lost the fight against the relentless desert sand, and the sweltering temperature gave no relief, even in the shade. Sand and filth were everywhere.

"I'll be happy to move out of this place," Ravi remarked.

"Let's get some sleep," Khartum suggested.

The animals stirred in the late morning as the air grew thicker. The camels let out deep bellows, while the horses nervously pranced and snorted in their stalls. Aakash glanced out the window to check on them. The sight of a dark, rolling cloud of sand and dust descending towards the caravanserai made his stomach churn.

"Barbod!" he yelled. "There is a sandstorm coming!"

Barbod squinted against the blowing sand and saw the angry clouds rolling in from the east. He shouted orders to everyone. "Hurry! Get the horses under cover! Put their halters on and get them into the stable so none of this grit gets in their eyes and nostrils. And put your keffiyehs over your faces!" The roiling wind nearly swallowed his words.

Jaidev, Aakash, Barbod, Akim, Khartum, and Ravi sprinted towards the stable as the fierce wind stirred up thick clouds of dust and sand. It was like an avalanche descending upon them, howling viciously and carrying bits of debris. The horses were skittish with fear, their whinnies echoing through the caravanserai. Nasir commanded everyone to move items away from the windward side of the buildings.

The dust clouds came in a wave, engulfing the buildings and

blurring out any sight of movement around them. Jaidev, Aakash, Ravi, Khartum, and Akim braced for cover against the walls of the stable, hunching over to shield their faces. Urgent shouts for help could be heard, but the deafening roar of the storm quickly drowned them out. After what seemed like an eternity, the wind gradually died down, leaving only a heavy layer of dust hanging in the air.

The caravanserai slowly reemerged from the storm. People wandered around and called for one another. As the group recollected, Aakash spotted a large hump covered in sand and dust on the road. It moved ever so slightly. Aakash sprinted over to the huddled form.

"It is Nasir! Come help me get him inside!" Aakash yelled.

Barbod, Ravi, Khartum, Akim, and Jaidev quickly rushed to lift Nasir's heavy frame out of the sand pile and under shelter. Jaidev felt Nasir's wrist for a pulse. "He has exhausted himself," Jaivev whispered urgently. "His heart can't pump enough blood through his body—he's dying."

Barbod's face drained of all color when he saw Nasir lying still. He shook his head and kneeled beside him, grasping one of Nasir's limp hands in both of his own. His voice cracked as he pleaded for a miracle. "Please, stay with us, Nasir... we need you."

Nasir slowly peeled open his eyes, struggling to bring Barbod's blurry shape into focus. His voice was a raspy whisper. "Barbod, I need you to take over the caravan. I cannot go on." He paused, searching for the strength to continue. "You've been with me since the beginning; you know the route." Nasir closed his eyes, exhaustion settling heavily over his body.

"I can do it, but you are coming with us," Barbod declared. "We can make you comfortable in a wagon."

Nasir's chest heaved with each labored breath as he looked out into the distance, his eyes narrowing. "I can see my father now. He is beckoning me," he whispered, a distant smile on his lips. A moment later, Nasir's breathing stopped, and he was still.

"He is gone. May Krishna guide his journey," Jaidev said, gently laying down his wrist.

Barbod slumped tears streaming down his face as he gently laid his forehead against Nasir's chest. He wept silently for what felt like an eternity before finally lifting his head. Clutching the fabric of Nasir's shirt, Barbod said a last goodbye and thanked him for all the years of companionship they shared. With one last glance, he whispered, "Until we meet again in heaven."

Turning to everyone, Barbod said, "He once told me he liked the customs of the Pharaohs in Egypt and the Jews in the west. He wanted to be buried in the earth."

"We will prepare a place," Aakash replied.

Barbod bowed his head and spoke in a low voice. "At the setting of the sun, we will honor our dear friend's life and lay him to rest, according to Zoroastrian custom. We shall then carry on with our journey just before nightfall tomorrow."

Aakash, Akim, and Khartum prepared the grave, carefully placing Nasir's body into a deep hole in the earth. His skin was decorated with sacred oils and herbs, and he was draped in a shimmering white shroud. Khartum stepped forward and bowed his head towards Nasir's ear, reciting the Zoroastrian prayer, the ashem vohu. He stood back from the grave and offered Barbod a white cloth to hold in grief. With their heads bowed, Khartum led them in reciting the ahunavaiti gatha, the burial prayer. When the prayer was finished, they all paused for a moment in respect before slowly stepping away from the gravesite. Barbod, still overwhelmed by emotion, silently wiped tears from his eyes.

Jaidev placed his hand on Barbod's shoulder and, with a serious tone, said, "You are now 'The Khabir', Barbod. We will help you in any way we can."

Barbod nodded slowly in understanding and appreciation.

At dusk the next evening, Barbod took his position in the caravan's lead. Jaidev, Ravi, and Aakash joined him, with Khartum and Akim right behind.

Barbod inhaled deeply and slowly raised his arm, signaling Bellows to walk. The clump of hooves against the hard ground and the clanking of supplies shifting on the camels' backs were all that could be heard as their journey commenced.

Barbod waved his hand, motioning for Jaidev to join him. The heaviness of loss still overwhelming him, he asked Jaidev, "What causes this grief?"

"It is caused by attachment to the transient things of life, forgetting the unchanging nature of the soul. Once our unchanging nature is forgotten, we see ourselves through the eyes of the ego. The ego likes to see everything in terms of itself, not the unchanging Self. It seeks to avoid what it doesn't want, and it doesn't want death. As a result of this desire to avoid death and falsely seeing the loss of the body as death, the ego and the subtle and physical body become immersed in pain. Our Vedic forefathers showed us that the cycle is not life and death, it is birth and death. Life is ongoing. I know these words are distant to your experience, my friend. It will take some time for this pain to wash away. What are your best memories of Nasir?"

"Nasir was tough and appeared gruff and angry. He carried himself with an assuredness that revealed this man had seen more than his share of danger and lived to tell the tale. But after years of travel through the unforgiving deserts and mountains, something changed in him. Though he kept his hard exterior, when he laughed, it was like a beacon of warmth and joy amidst the barren landscape. I will always remember the sound of Nasir's laughter most of all," Barbod expressed.

Jaidev's face creased into an appreciative smile as he listened to his friend. He chuckled a little, thinking of Nasir's hearty laughter. "Fear constricts and has its beginning and end. But joy and laughter are a quality of the ever-expanding self whose nature is bliss. Remember Nasir by laughing often, my friend." Jaidev's voice had taken on a gentle, understanding tone.

A smile spread across Barbod's face as he recalled Nasir's hearty laughter. "We were crossing a river on a sweltering day, and one of the travelers had a particularly stubborn camel," he began. "As the man tugged fruitlessly on the reins, the animal simply settled itself at the edge of the riverbank enjoying the cool mud. Nasir came over to see what was causing the hold-up and soon found himself cajoling the stubborn camel to move. Finally, the owner tried pushing the camel, and as he pushed the camel got up and moved so abruptly that the owner fell full-faced into the mud. Nasir laughed so hard he was breathless. His laughter was contagious and soon everyone was laughing at the poor miserable camel driver. Even he, knowing how ridiculous he looked covered in mud, laughed along. Later, Nasir brought a carrot back to the camel for giving him the greatest laugh he had in years. He told that story around the nightly campfire a thousand times. Each time the poor camel driver was covered in thicker and deeper mud." Barbod found himself laughing as he recalled the story.

Jaidev shook his head, laughing and enjoying the story.

"We will arrive in Rey in a few days. Rey is a major city with many cultures inhabiting it," Barbod informed.

The air was hot even in the midnight stillness. The caravan trekked steadily across the sand dunes, Barbod following ancient pathways and using the stars as guidance. "You know, it is funny, we caravan travelers have always used the stars for guidance across the desert at night. I never thought that they also foretold the destiny of man as you see them, Jaidev," Barbod remarked.

"The stars can guide both our inner and outer journeys," Jaidev replied.

Several nights later, the fires of Rey could be seen from the hillside as they approached.

"Khartum, you will be interested to know that a Zoroastrian Fire Temple stands in the old section of Rey. It was built in the east and west direction so it could greet the morning sun as it rises and face the evening sun as it sets," Barbod announced loudly.

As the caravan entered Rey in the morning, the city was just awakening. The roosters crowed and the smell of fresh bread baking filled the air.

"Let's get a few hours' sleep and then look around," Ravi declared.

Clouds filled the sky as the afternoon sun bore down, providing some respite from the usual daunting heat. Ravi called the others to join him, and they headed towards the bazaar.

A merchant selling figs and olives drew Jaidev's attention. "I have the best olives at the best prices. Here, try these olives," the merchant offered.

"Vah, these are superb," Jaidev exclaimed.

"They are from a special grove maintained by our people," the merchant replied.

"Are your people from here?" Jaidev asked.

The merchant looked around cautiously, as though he expected unwanted visitors, then spoke in a low voice. "My people were brought here centuries ago as slaves. King Darius of Persia freed us. We have lived peacefully amongst the Persian people ever since. We are proud to be descendants of Adam, the first man, and Abraham, our lineage's father. The one God and Creator, Yahweh, is who we worship." His words resonated in the air before fading into silence.

"Our people also see creation as coming from one source. We are heading to Damascus. We have seen the coming birth of a Great Soul in the stars and want to be there to honor him," Jaidev shared with some excitement.

"Our elders, the wise ones who study the teachings of the prophets, would be keen to learn your views. Would you like to break bread with me this evening so I can introduce you to our esteemed Rabbi?"

"I would be honored," said Jaidev.

"My name is Ezra. I live in the Jewish settlement on the western side of town. If you wait at the well by the synagogue, one of my sons will come to show you to my house. Bring your companions as well," the merchant added, nodding towards Barbod.

Jaidev spoke with a proud and dignified voice. "I am Jaidev Trivedi, son of Mahesh from northern India where the three holy rivers of Ganges, Yamuna, and Saraswati join together."

"We will have a good discussion," Ezra declared.

"We are also seeking a gem seller. Do you know of one?" Jaidev asked.

"Yes, Jeremiah sells gems and jewelry. He has the shop with the yellow pendants down that street there. Tell him Ezra sent you."

"Many thanks," Barbod replied.

When they arrived at Jeremiah's shop, they were greeted by an elderly man.

"We are looking for Jeremiah, the gem dealer," Barbod announced.

"My son is Jeremiah. I will let him know you are here."

The old man disappeared behind the door, and a short, portly man with a welcoming smile appeared. "How can I help you gentleman today? I'm Jeremiah."

"We are looking for a yellow sapphire. Do you have any?" Barbod asked.

"Yes, I only have a few. Their demand isn't as high as other gems and colors. Wait here."

Jeremiah retrieved a small satchel from another room and opened it cautiously, laying the contents on a small tray. "These sapphires are of Persian origin. They have a beautiful clarity and a shimmering, rich, canary yellow. Here, let me bring them over to the sunlight where they can be better observed."

"These are of beautiful quality," Jaidev said, examining them. He moved three from the small lot towards one side of the tray.

Ravi picked up each gem and examined them in different lights. Holding them to the sunlight, the door light, and the candlelight. "These three are appropriate for what you are seeking, Barbod."

"I have never wanted to buy a gem before. I don't know how to go about it," Barbod admitted.

"Once you verify that the gem is of high quality, simply let the gem speak to you. See which gem you are most attracted to. You will have it for a long time, and you want it to give you a positive feeling every time you look at it. So, having an affection for it is important," Jaidev explained.

Barbod picked up each gem and held it up to the sunlight, peering into its depth and beauty.

"Just let the gem sit quietly within you. You don't have to decide right away. We can come back in a day or two if one calls to you," Jaidev said.

"How much are these gems?" Barbod hesitated.

"They are all in the 5-drachma range, I made a large purchase at a great price and can give you a good deal," Jeremiah suggested, smiling.

"Let me think about it," Barbod replied.

"You also make jewelry. Can you set a stone in his necklace?" Jaidev asked, motioning for Barbod to show Jeremiah his faravahar.

"Yes, I can set it in the necklace easily. It won't come loose," Jeremiah affirmed.

"We will let you know," Barbod said.

As they walked away, Barbod looked at Jaidev and Ravi for guidance. "Tell me, did you have a feeling or attraction to one gem more than another?" Jaidev asked.

"Yes, there was one gem I felt very attracted to. I have never thought about buying a gem and never had a desire or felt attracted to one. I want to wait. Drachmas don't come easily to a caravanner, and I want to see if the feeling stays with me," Barbod said.

"Yes, you will know if it is right after some thought," Jaidev affirmed.

Later that afternoon, Barbod sat under an olive tree and shut his eyes as he held the faravahar. He thought of Nasir and the extra money he had for taking over as Kabir—more than enough to pay for the sapphire. Thoughts of his mother flashed through his mind. He remembered his father smiling and calling his mother 'My Sapphira, my little gem.'

That's it, Barbod thought. The gem he was most attracted to brought back memories of his mother. He would purchase that one.

When he found Jaidev and Ravi sipping tea at the inn, Barbod blurted, "Jaidev, I have decided to purchase the gem. I know it is right."

"Very good," Jaidev replied.

"Leave the negotiating to me. I will get the best price," Ravi declared, as they headed back to Jeremiah's shop.

"You are back," his father greeted them again at the door.

"Yes, we have decided on the gem," Ravi announced, taking over.

Jeremiah's father bowed slightly and went inside. Jeremiah soon emerged, his arms and smile wide open in a welcoming gesture. "So good to see you. You have decided, yes?" he asked. "Come into the shop and I will get the stones again."

Jeremiah laid the three stones back out and Barbod pointed to the one that most attracted him.

Ravi nodded. "You said these were 5 drachmas each and that you could place the gem in the necklace securely."

"Yes, it will take only an hour to have it ready," Jeremiah replied.

"We are on our way to Damascus where there are many gem dealers, so I think we may do better in a large city, but let's talk," Ravi said.

"I know many of the dealers in Damascus, and I can tell you, I am priced very well."

Ravi held up each gem, examined them, and grimaced like he detected a flaw. Jeremiah picked one up and held it to the light to see if he missed something.

"I don't know," Ravi uttered. "I'm sure I can do better in a large city. He motioned to Barbod and Jaidev that they should leave.

"Well, I could do a little better," Jeremiah said.

"Jeremiah, we can look at them again on our return trip from Damascus. As you said, this color isn't as popular as a red ruby, blue sapphire, or green emerald. It won't hurt to wait." Ravi turned from Jeremiah and winked at Barbod.

Jeremiah swallowed. He wanted to move his inventory and make some money.

"I can go to 4 drachmas, and I'll throw in the necklace setting if you buy before you leave for Damascus," Jeremiah proposed.

"I paid just 3 drachmas in India for such a stone. I would say 3 and a half drachmas; you throw in the setting," Ravi countered.

"If you buy right now, I'll do that deal," Jeremiah replied eagerly.

"Done," Ravi said, grinning and extending his hand. "We can wait while you set the stone in the necklace," he added, motioning to Barbod to give Jeremiah his faravahar.

Jeremiah's eyes glistened, happy to have made a large sale. "Father, get these gentlemen some cool water while they wait." He got to work on setting the stone in the necklace.

About an hour later, he held up the completed necklace, inspecting every final detail and putting on a finishing polish.

"Wow, I love it," Barbod expressed, pulling the money out of a hidden purse.

Taking the necklace in his hands, he showed it to Jaidev and Ravi.

"It is perfect," Jaidev remarked. "The gold in the faravahar helps the gem transmit the planetary energy of Jupiter in the yellow sapphire. It is a perfect balance and will serve you well. It promotes wisdom and harmony and will increase life energy. Jupiter is in its own sign in Pisces, and today is Thursday, Jupiter's day. It is an auspicious time to begin wearing the gem."

After final acknowledgment to Jeremiah and his father, they walked into the street. "We have a dinner tonight with Ezra. He will be happy to know that his gem dealer recommendation worked out," Ravi said.

Barbod put the necklace on, holding his hand to his heart and feeling a new connection to his faravahar.

A little later, Jaidev, Khartum, Barbod, Aakash, Ravi, and Akim gathered at the well. An unfamiliar young man around Akim's age came up to them. Unable to communicate in Sogdian, he motioned for them to follow him. Instead of leading them to Ezra's home, he took them to the local synagogue. The building radiated a feeling of holiness as the group was guided into a room with a table full of delicious breads, olives, figs, cheeses, and fruits. At the end of the table sat an elderly Rabbi with a white beard and staff. He was accompanied by two assistant Rabbis and Ezra, the merchant from the bazaar.

The Rabbi sitting at the head of the large, wooden table gestured for everyone to take their seats. He smiled warmly at Jaidev and motioned him closer, pointing for him to sit next to Ezra.

"Shalom," the Rabbi greeted. "I am Mezriani, a descendant of Malki Tzedek, a priest of Abraham, our forbearer. We are honored to have you. This is Rabbi Mordecai and next to him is Rabbi Menahem. You have met Ezra, who is hosting our meal together."

"Peace, I am Jaidev Trivedi, a Brahmin or priest of our people. With me are Aakash, Ravi, Barbod, Khartum, and Akim. We have been on a journey from the east for many moons now," Jaidev proclaimed.

"Ezra told me you have traveled from the east to observe a momentous spiritual event—a birth, indicated by the stars," Mezriani replied.

"Yes, we have seen it in the stars. There is a triple conjunction of Jupiter and Saturn heralding a great birth. Does your religion know the language of the stars?" Jaidev asked.

"Our learned Kabbalah elders understand the language of the stars. The Menorah, a seven-candled light illuminating our Temple, is commonly viewed as a symbol of the seven days of Creation. Some respected teachers of the Kabbalah view the Menorah's seven lights to represent the seven wandering stars that travel through the night sky," Mezriani explained.

"We also follow the seven wandering stars and what they tell us. Our Chaldean and Zoroastrian teachers know the language well," Khartum informed his hosts.

"The stars shine their light and wisdom on us all equally. In that way, we are all connected. Our Kabbalist teachers show us through the Sefir Yetzira, the Book of Formation, that everything in creation depends on, is intertwined with, and affects everything else," Mezriani said.

Jaidev nodded affirmatively. "We agree on the interconnectedness of all things."

Mezriani pointed to an illustration from a book he possessed and explained, "According to our mystical interpretation, the seven days of Creation in the Bible correspond to the planets or 'Ruling' stars moving through the twelve tribes, or sons of Jacob. We view this as the planets moving through the constellations."

Menachem and Mordecai nodded in agreement.

"Our lessons teach us that people are mirror images of the cosmos. Knowledge is not a physical power; it is the foundation from which Creation began. The teaching proclaims, 'What lies above is also found below, and what lies below is mirrored above,'" Mordecai added.

Barbod spoke up with enthusiasm. "It is as if we are branches of the same tree," he said, his voice filled with awe.

"Exactly, for when we look closely at the tree, we find that the same source of nourishment that fuels the growth of the roots, trunk, limbs, crown, and leaves also creates the fruit on the tree," Jaidev pointed out. His knowledge made Mezriani's eyes shine with admiration. "It is the unseen energy in the tree's sap that transforms into every part."

Mordecai stated, "It is Yahweh, or God, who gives life and movement to this energy."

"Our Vedic masters and your tradition have much in common," Jaidev declared.

"This Infinite Divine source connects everything. The Sefirot is the channel of divine manifestation and is depicted as the Tree of Life that you mentioned," Mezriani continued. "The divine energies are expressed through the celestial bodies. The conjunction of Jupiter and Saturn in Pisces shows that this birth will bring spiritual awakening. Pisces is a sign of compassionate service, kindness, and empathy towards all. This birth will be a great healer of men's souls."

"This chart we are exploring shows the father's house, the 9th house, to be in the constellation of Taurus. The house of Judah is Taurus in our Kabbalah astrology," Mordecai added. "Our prophecy is that a messiah would be born to the house of Judah. If this birth is of our people, it could be the prophesied birth."

"Mezriani, you must consider joining these travelers in their search for this birth," Menahem suggested.

"You are most welcome to travel with us," Jaidev expressed.

"I am old for such a journey, but it would fill my heart with joy to witness this birth," Mezriani remarked. "So be it."

"Our departure for Seleucia is tomorrow night," Barbod informed. "We're getting closer to our destination, Damascus."

The following evening, as dusk approached, Mezriani joined the caravan with his nephew, Shimon. "Shimon will make sure that my old bones do not slow you down," Mezriani declared.

"Shalom, Shimon," Barbod said.

"Shalom." Shimon bowed slightly as the caravan lumbered

forward.

It took three full weeks to traverse the dusty road from Rey to Seleucia. On the morning of the fifteenth day, the night travelers arrived at an inn operated by a young Nabatean. After several hours' rest and sleep, a shofar horn echoed through the walls of the caravanserai.

"Jaidev, Barbod, Aakash," Ravi said. "Come hear this instrument. It has a wondrous sound."

"That is the shofar. It's an ancient instrument of the Israelites," Barbod informed.

"Let's go listen," Ravi proposed.

The four friends headed toward the music emanating from the corner of the caravanserai until they reached the musician.

"What a deep, beautiful sound," Ravi exclaimed.

"Thank you," the musician replied. "It has been part of our people's tradition for many centuries."

"We are also musicians. We play the flute, drums, and chang," Ravi shared. "This is Jaidev, Aakash, Barbod, and I am Ravi."

"Shalom, I am Ghaffar. I am traveling to Seleucia to meet with the Essenes. My brother is a leader of their community, and I am studying their teachings." Ghaffar bowed his head and folded his hands in greeting.

"Love and mercy," Jaidev said. "Our caravan is heading to Seleucia too. Would you like to ride with us? It can be a long journey alone."

"You are most gracious, but I have no money to pay for your caravan," Ghaffar replied.

Barbod, stepping into his role as Kabir, announced, "You can pay for your transport by tending to our horses and camels and doing other errands for the caravan."

"That is a deal," Ghaffar smiled, shaking Barbod's hand.

"We leave at dusk. Meet me an hour before and I will show you what to do," Barbod declared.

"Thank you, Shalom," Ghaffar replied.

"Shalom," Barbod repeated.

As the caravan traversed the night sky, Jaidev noticed that Jupiter and Saturn had moved closer together once more.

On the fourth night of travel, Ghaffar approached Jaidev as they took a break.

"May I ask you something?" Ghaffar asked Jaidev.

"Of course," Jaidev responded.

"Some in the caravan say you are a Magi. Is that so?"

Jaidev grinned. "In Bactria, they named those who interpreted the celestial language Magi. So, in that sense, yes. Do the Essenes also look to the stars for guidance?" he inquired.

"My brother has talked about it, but it isn't something an initiate like me would know about," Ghaffar replied.

"Tell me about the Essenes," Jaidev said.

"When I get to Qumran, I will put on the white robe of an initiate. We believe that men have a soul and that the soul survives death. After we die, the soul can ascend to higher levels of Being, depending on our actions in this life. So, we practice purity and dedicate ourselves to God," Ghaffar explained.

Jaidev nodded sagely. "This is a fundamental belief in my culture as well," he said. "The results of our actions, or karma, determine the fate of our soul, or Atma, after death."

"I have heard that you are seeking the birth of a Great Soul," Ghaffar stated.

"Yes, my friends, Khartum and his son, the Rabbi, Mezriani, and his nephew are all seeking the birth of a great soul," Jaidev affirmed.

"Khartum is Persian and Mezriani is Jewish, and you are all on the same quest?" Ghaffar asked, a little puzzled.

"We all follow the star language according to each of our teachings, and the star language is pointing the way to a Maha Atma or Great Soul being born in the west," Jaidev declared.

"I have heard a rumor that this birth is going to be a great king," Ghaffar remarked.

"You spoke of the ascension of the Soul in terms of higher states of Being," Jaidev replied. "This birth will be a realization of the highest state. To those unaware of these states, it may appear to be the coronation of a king."

"I am unfamiliar with the star language," Ghaffar expressed. "However, my brother in Qumran would be keen to learn it. I'd like to be present at this birth so I can tell him about it."

"You are welcome to join us," Jaidev affirmed.

As they approached Seleucia, the caravan could see a party of Roman soldiers coming their way. The lead soldier was on horseback, and the troops behind him were whipping a group of seven men carrying large wooden beams. Further down the road, several crucifixes stood in the distance. The lead soldier sent a few troops forward to meet the caravan.

"Stop. Herod the Great commands you to witness the sentence of these criminals under the rule of Rome," the lead soldier demanded.

Barbod, visibly anxious, signaled for the caravan to halt. He shouted, urging everyone to obey the Roman soldiers' instructions.

The condemned men lined up on both sides of the road as the sun began to rise.

A slender, scared young man pleaded his case desperately. "Please, I'm innocent—I have a family to provide for! I haven't ever disobeyed the Emperor or King Herod!"

"Are you saying the Emperor made a mistake by condemning you?" the soldier probed.

"Yes, yes," the young man pleaded. "I am innocent."

The soldier sneered. "He dares to say the Emperor made a mistake. We shall nail him up first as punishment for his crime against Rome."

The soldier swung his spear with a grunt, smashing the blunt end into the young man's stomach, knocking the wind out of him. With one swift movement, he brought the other end of his spear down on the young man's knees, knocking them out from under him and sending him to the ground. They tied his arms to the beam, holding them as they hammered thick iron nails through his wrist, missing the vein. The man vomited, filling the air with a putrid smell. An ox cart pulled up with a large stack of lumber. Two soldiers grabbed the longest piece of wood—longer than both of their heights—and dragged it to the man nailed on the beam. They secured the beam tightly to it, forming a crucifix with a thick rope and two heavy iron nails. Then they carried and hoisted it into a newly dug earthen hole. Stakes were driven around the edges of the cross, ensuring it wouldn't topple over. The hung man screamed in agony.

The caravan travelers looked on in shock as the soldiers nailed one man after the other until all seven were hanging. Jaidev's eyes filled with sadness, his face solemn. Aakash remained silent and composed. Barbod held out a warning hand, gesturing that they should stay still and not interfere.

One of the hanging men shouted a string of curses at the Roman soldiers, his voice growing hoarse as he made one last plea for them to end his torture with the thrust of a spear. One soldier stepped forward, gripping a heavy hammer tightly in his fist. With a sneering grimace, he raised the hammer and brought it down on the man's legs with calculated force, breaking the bones with a sickening crunch.

"Please kill me now," the man cried out, losing consciousness.

The soldiers remained impassive as they followed orders. They marched with robotic strides, unmoved by the sight of suffering men and the blood and destruction around them. Their faces were hardened like stone masks, their eyes emotionless and fixed straight ahead. The commander barked out his orders, to which they obediently responded.

"God have mercy on them," Ghaffar said.

As the morning light brightened, the Roman officer motioned for the caravan to move on. The crucified men were still gasping for breath and staring up at nothing. As the caravan passed by, the Romans shot intimidating looks that begged to pillage the caravan. Thankfully, the commander shook his head 'no,' understanding that trade between east and west was important for Rome. As soon as they passed, the soldiers plunged swords and spears into the nearly lifeless bodies hanging from the crosses. They wanted to quickly end the ordeal before the midday heat arrived.

"What will happen to the bodies?" Aakash asked Mezriani.

Mezriani's voice trembled slightly as he spoke. "They will leave those bodies there to serve as a warning—a reminder to all of us never to cross the Roman law." He paused for a moment before pointing to the other crucifixes and continuing in a somber tone. "They crucified those men over there a few days ago, and their corpses are rotting. They are now nothing more than food for carrion and crows."

"According to the Essenes, this is a battle of light against darkness, with the Romans symbolizing darkness and needing to be overcome by the light," Ghaffar proclaimed.

Jaidev responded agreeably. "My tradition also believes that light destroys darkness. The Brihadaranyaka Upanishad says, 'Lead me from the unreal to the real. Lead me from darkness to light. Lead me from death to immortality.' This shows us that seeking truth, knowledge, and enlightenment can transcend ignorance, darkness, and mortality."

"You will enjoy meeting my brother, Basil, and discussing these things with him," Ghaffar said in a solemn tone.

"What could those men have possibly done to suffer so much?" Barbod asked, the fear, horror, and revulsion etched on his face.

"The horror we have just witnessed has many victims. As horrific as their suffering is, the poor souls hanging are only part of the suffering. Every man by his every thought, word, and action vibrates the entire Song of Creation, and the entire Song lies in every individual. The individual note and the entire Song are interdependent. When a man acts in harmony with the Song, the Song responds by supporting the individual. In the same way, when a man acts in disharmony and causes suffering to others, the Law of Karma returns the suffering to us," Jaidev explained.

"Our Bible states, 'They sow the wind and reap the whirlwind,' the bastards," Mezriani said with disgust.

"We Kshatriyas are taught to fight in accordance with our dharma, but that is certainly sin, not dharma. Those soldiers are weak, not strong," Aakash remarked, suppressing his inner anger.

"Yes, our Sanatana Dharma teaches the Law of Karma," Jaidev said. "Those soldiers by their sin have created waves in the lake of their karma, acting contrary to their dharma. They are also the victims of their actions. Wrongs, once done, cannot be undone. The Law of Karma will come back to them, causing them to suffer."

"I can only hope to be around to see it," Shimon mumbled, his body tense and eyes full of righteous rage. "It is written, 'An eye for an eye, a tooth for a tooth. Whatever injury he has given a person shall be given to him.'"

"They will get their deserved suffering at the Bridge of Judgement. The House of Lies and the suffering of hell awaits them," Khartum declared.

"It is also written, 'Vengeance is mine, sayeth the Lord.' We must have faith in God's ways," Mezriani added, counseling his nephew.

"Forgive me, uncle," Shimon replied.

"We are all sickened by what we have witnessed, nephew. Your anger and disgust are only human," Mezriani assured.

"A man must take responsibility for his actions. Certainly, we want to act in accordance with the Song of Creation. Acting with all the Song's harmony—its peace, happiness, unbounded Love, and actions of serenity and grace—is within the capacity of man because he can know the Song of Creation within him," Jaidev added.

A solemn silence descended on the caravan as it slowly progressed into the city, each processing the horror in their own way.

"We will be in Seleucia for two days. Then, we will make our way to Damascus to end our trek to the west. Rest up and try to enjoy this beautiful old city," Barbod announced, breaking the silence.

"I can't sleep or eat after what I saw this morning," Ravi proclaimed, his voice drenched in sadness. "I think I'll wander around the city and walk off this morning's horror."

"There are some interesting shops in the bazaar," Barbod said.

"I'll take a look," Ravi replied. "But my heart's not in it."

Aakash called out to Akim. "Come and help me with these horses. I have something for you to see."

Aakash walked with determination towards the stables. "Akim, this is our opportunity to review the weak spots in a Roman soldier's armor. Aim your arrow for either their throat or thighs for your strike. You can also attack the hands, elbows, knees, and feet as secondary targets. Anything else on their body is likely to be well-protected; you never know when we may have to use our training to protect ourselves or get away."

"I have never seen a man suffer and die before. I am sick inside from what we saw," Akim expressed.

"That is why we must prepare. We never know when we will have to defend ourselves from unrighteousness," Aakash explained.

"I wanted to save those poor men—such terrible suffering. I felt helpless," Akim remarked.

"I wanted to save them as well. If we had taken action, however, the Romans would have held an enormous advantage. They would have defeated us, resulting in an attack on our friends and fellow caravanners. A warrior does not act out of anger and rage. Lord Rama defeated the demon Ravana, who had abducted Lord Rama's wife, Sita, because he used Ravana's rage against him. Lord Rama remained calm and composed amidst the battle," Aakash stated.

"Controlling my anger is something I have to work on," Akim shared.

"A warrior knows there are many ways to win a battle. Fighting is not the only way," Aakash added.

"How would you pick the right target if we had to fight the Romans?" Akim asked.

Aakash raised his arm, aiming an imaginary bow and arrow at an invisible soldier. "If I wanted to incapacitate the soldier and escape," he said, "I would go for the thigh. It's bigger and easier to hit while you're moving." He paused as if visualizing the scene. "But if I needed to silence him so he didn't alert other soldiers, then—" His eyes dropped to the target shaped like a human torso in the distance. "The neck is almost surely a death strike, but it's harder to hit if you are moving." Aakash lowered his arm and turned to face Akim with a determined expression. "We will practice shooting from a riding position tomorrow before we leave."

"Do you think we will need it against the Romans?" Akim asked.

"We will be prepared for all possibilities. They are not a people that respect human life," Aakash replied.

Barbod walked aimlessly through the bazaar and streets, processing the crucifixion he had witnessed. He could hear Ravi calling out, "C'mon, one time. Lakshmi, smile on me."

Barbod turned the corner and saw Ravi throwing dice with several men gathered around him.

A burly man nodded sympathetically. "Ah, that's too bad, Ravi," he said. "You were doing great. Don't worry, you'll win it back in the next round."

Barbod watched as Ravi pulled out a drachma and held it in his hand. He had clearly gotten in over his head with some street ruffians. They cheered in a mocking tone that Ravi didn't recognize.

Alarmed by the situation, Barbod yelled out at Ravi from across the street. "Hey, Ravi! Come quickly, your horse is sick!"

Alarmed, Ravi rose swiftly. "I'll be back. Keep the dice warm," he said.

Once they turned a corner, Barbod stopped and said, "Those men were taking advantage of you. It's an old trick used against inexperienced players. They let you win a few rounds before they pounce on you and win all your money. They had three people rolling loaded dice, so you had little chance. How much did you lose?"

"Just a few coins. I didn't know," Ravi admitted, feeling embarrassed.

"They have a hawk's eye for a mark," Barbod commented. "I speak from experience—I learned the hard way. Good thing you didn't lose too much."

"A few drachmas and my pride," Ravi said.

"Let's get out of here. This part of Seleucia feels dangerous," Barbod declared.

Chapter 13 - The Road to Damascus

The caravan congregated to embark on the last stretch of the Silk Road to Damascus. Barbod signaled the start of the journey, announcing, "Let's roll. It is a three-week journey to Damascus."

Jaidev rode beside Barbod, Ravi, and Aakash. Barbod gazed at his companion inquisitively, rubbing his chin in thought. "Why is it," he spoke slowly, "that in your culture, Aakash is a protector, Ravi a producer, you a teacher, and me? What am I?"

"We would know you as a Sudra, a provider," Jaidev replied.

"Is that good, bad, high, or lowly?" Barbod asked.

Jaidev spoke in a deep, soothing timbre. He extended his hands outward as if to emphasize the enormity of the concept. "Our varna is a way or station of life that most supports our evolution, unlocking our innermost potential. We are not bound by it. We use it to carry us closer to knowing the Song of Creation within us. If we fulfill our varna with sattvic action and avoid rajasic and tamasic action, our consciousness and heart expand," Jaidev explained.

"How do I know this sattvic action?" Barbod questioned.

"We know it intuitively if we bring the attention within. That which makes us feel lighter brings us closer to the enlightenment of the Song of Creation. That which makes us feel heavier or duller—out of tune, so to speak—takes us further from knowing the unboundedness of the Song of Creation," Jaidev stated.

"So, I am a Sudra, a provider. But when I became the Kabir, a leader, did I remain a Sudra?" Barbod asked, curious to understand his role.

"For many years you fulfilled your Sudra duties with sattvic devotion to doing a good job as you worked under Nasir. This hard work and devotion have led you to a fresh path—that of a Vaishya, a producer. You now produce goods and services for the entire caravan. More importantly, your dharma is devotion. I mentioned to you some nights ago that you were mostly Jupiterian. Jupiter is the planetary energy of devotion in its sattvic expression. Continue to serve in your new varna through devotion, and it will continue to carry you towards knowing the Song of Creation," Jaidev declared with a certain wisdom.

"So, I was not destined to always be a Sudra?" Barbod asked.

"If you follow your dharma—that which upholds your evolution, that which you know in the innermost regions of your heart—you can be anything," Jaidev proclaimed. "You are the unbounded Song of Creation. All things are possible if we are in tune with the Song. Whether you feel your dharma is remaining a Sudra, becoming a Vaishya, a Kshatriya, or a Brahmin is all within your potential as a man."

Barbod looked at the star-filled sky and took a deep breath. A peaceful calm engulfed him. He felt a sense of oneness with the stars and connected to the space between them. The clouds were no longer separate from him; the cool breeze was his lungs. *I am starting to understand Jaidev's teachings*, he thought.

Jaidev smiled, seeing the expanding Song developing within Barbod.

"My friend, what is this thing called karma that you talk about when you read the stars?" Barbod asked.

Jaidev leaned forward on his camel. "Action causing karma arises through the vasanas or the desire for something. These desires come forth through memory or subtle past resonances called samskaras. These samskaras then become a vasana which creates a new action or karma. For example, when you desire dinner, the memory of dinner causes that desire. So, from the memory and desire, you eat dinner and create a new karma, an action," Jaidev explained.

"That seems simple enough. How does my karma end up in the stars you read?" Barbod asked, grasping to comprehend the entire picture.

"When we know ourselves as the note and not the Song of Creation, we think our actions are held within the boundaries of the note. Anything we do by thought, word, or action ripples on and on as the vibrations reach all of Creation. Thus, the individual serves all of Creation. Creation responds by serving the individual—by continually supporting him towards evolution. The stars reflect the individual's past karma that he brings into this life. A Jyotishi reads and brings light to these karmas for man's evolution."

"How does this happen? How can I understand this?" Barbod asked.

"As we appear to go from body to body, we drop the physical and subtle body, but the causal body remains. Our Jiva, or individual soul, holds the subtle vibrations of our past karma. We choose our new body when the planets mirror these karmas by their position in the signs and bhavas, or houses. When we read the stars, we interpret the vibrations or karmas that we are going to replay, re-hear, and resolve," Jaidev said.

"Why do you say appear to go?" Barbod asked.

"Because you were never in the body. The body is in you. We were never a sole note in the Song of Creation. We are the Song of Creation, expressing itself as a note. It is simply a matter of our vibration changing to understand that the boundaries of the note were never real," Jaidev declared.

Barbod shook his head, smiling. "I'm glad you're the teacher, my friend."

"I'm glad you're my friend," Jaidev remarked, smiling back.

"I was listening," Aakash interrupted. "We have many kinds of karmas, I have been told."

"Yes, in general, there are four kinds of karma. Sanchita is the storehouse of all our karma; prarabdha is the karma we bring into this life; kriyamana is the karma we are creating; agama is future karma. Karma is unfathomable, our Gita tells us. Like a stone thrown into a pond, it sets off ripples that travel the whole pond. We can reduce our negative karma and enhance our positive karma through acts such as yagyas, mantras, and good works. Additionally, we can transcend it when the bow is pulled back to its fullest extent—when the mind reaches its still point," he explained, referring to the bow gifted to his companion by the old saddhu.

"If we can transcend our karma and our bad karma is mitigated by good works, yagyas, and mantras, what is the purpose of the Maha Atma?" Barbod questioned.

"When discordance and disharmony are flourishing, the Song of Creation sings a perfect tone to restore equilibrium and attune us once more. The resonant pitch creates vibrations that elevate all notes," Jaidev proclaimed.

"And that is the Maha Atma?" Barbod asked.

"Yes." Jaidev nodded.

"Wow, no wonder you want to be at the birth. When the caravan disbands in Damascus, I would like to accompany you to the birth of the Maha Atma," Barbod proclaimed.

"That would please me immensely," Jaidev said.

"Jaidev is a great Brahmin. He is someone that you should listen to. He and his father's guidance have been immeasurable to my family's success," Ravi remarked.

"How do you mean? Do you know the Song of Creation that Jaidev talks about?" Barbod asked.

"I don't think in those terms. We Vaishyas are meant to uphold the economic well-being of society. We do this through productive work, supporting our spiritual teachers, and almsgiving," Ravi replied.

"So, your dharma is to uphold society by making money?" Barbod asked.

"We produce goods for which we are rewarded. It is natural for us to do this. We Bahiras have been making money for generations. We are good at it, and it is my desire to continue our family tradition," Ravi explained.

"Jaidev was just talking about desire. He called it a vasana," Barbod said.

"Since I was a little boy, my father taught me the ways of the world. He showed me how to trade and how to value art, land, gold, jewelry, precious stones, and fine craftsmen's work. I know I am fortunate to be born into such a family. I accept and do this full-heartedly. I enjoy it," Ravi declared. "Jaidev and his father Mahesh have guided us with their wisdom, telling us when we have the most support of nature for our goals and warning us when negative karma is coming our way."

As Ravi spoke, Jaidev thought of his chart—how it favored wealth and fulfillment of desire. He was a Leo ascendant, giving him leadership ability. The Sun, his ascendant lord, was in his 10th house, giving him a successful career, respect, and fame. He was career-minded and easily rose to a position of authority. Venus was in his 4th house, aspecting his 10th house beneficially. He was also blessed with a Lakshmi yoga—a yoga that gives wealth—in his 1st house, with the Moon and Mars conjunct and the Moon in the higher degree.

"But don't you want to know the Song of Creation?" Barbod asked.

"This mystical stuff doesn't attract me. I love to hear Mahesh and Jaidev talk about it, but my desire is to expand our family business and increase our influence," Ravi said.

Jaidev knew this was true. Ravi would not seek spiritual knowledge until his Wisdom stage of life—his old age when he was in his Moon Venus dasha.

"My thoughts have also been toward my dharma. I have

wanted to be a great archer and warrior for as long as I can remember. I view myself as a protector of society. My childhood heroes were all stories of heroism and valor. Self-discipline is necessary to achieve my goals," Aakash shared'

"But you have been practicing the meditation... to hear the Song of Creation?" Barbod asked inquisitively.

"We have many great Kshatriyas in our tradition. The greatest Kshatriya was Arjuna, the hero of our beloved Bhagavad Gita. He learned the greatest lesson from Lord Krishna—how to perform action in Yoga. That is my greatest desire. 'Established in Yoga, perform action,' Krishna told him," Aakash said.

"Krishna instructed Arjuna to go beyond the three Gunas. This is the technique of our meditation—to go beyond the most primordial impulses of manifest creation. When this happens, only pure awareness—the awareness without an object of awareness—remains. The 'I Am' shines brightly, unclouded by the mayas, the sheaths that cover pure awareness," Jaidev added. "So, Aakash is following the method that Arjuna himself followed."

"I don't know if this is the same, but when Akim and I were rescuing the young girl, I watched as an inner anger arose and subsided. When we went into action, fighting to rescue the young woman, I didn't feel that Aakash was doing anything. I was witnessing the action as I was doing it," Aakash remarked.

"How can you act without doing anything?" Barbod asked.

"Recognizing the silent witness in your awareness is a wonderful step in your growth to Turiyatit consciousness. Watching your anger arise and subside without engaging in action born of anger is the state that Arjuna achieved," Jaidev explained.

"It wasn't some earth-shattering event. It was very subtle. I was even reluctant to mention it," Aakash acknowledged.

"Yes, it happens very slowly, without fanfare. When you go to sleep each night, spend some time reflecting on the activities of the day and whether the witness experience comes and goes," Jaidev suggested. "When you ask yourself before meditation the soul question 'Who Am I?' also bring that experience of 'I Am' to your awareness."

"And what about you, Jaidev? You are a Brahmin and a Jyotishi. I am someone who has done physical labor all my life. What is the role of a Brahmin and Jyotishi?" Barbod asked.

"Brahmins are meant to be knowers of Brahman and perform the sacred yagyas and pujas to bring the Song of Creation into awareness. By the perfect recitation of the sacred mantras, we enliven in Creation the different qualities—the different vibrations of the Song of Creation. The beautiful diversity of the Song is unified by the silent field from which the Song emerges—the Unity of the entire Song and the Unity of the Silence. When one knows the Song of Creation and the Unity in Diversity, life flows effortlessly. Desires are fulfilled with the support of nature," Jaidev revealed.

"Did this show up in your star chart?" Barbod asked.

"I was born with a Raj Yoga in my 5th house of Purva Punya, or past life credit. It supports awakening the Song of Creation within. Even so, I have the free will to do as I please. But this path is my choice; it is my dharma, and it pleases me. Venus, the ruler of my 12th Moksha house, is conjunct Jupiter in the 5th house which is Libra. Venus also rules my 5th house, and I am a Gemini ascendant. This also supports my dharma and spiritual desire," Jaidev elaborated.

"It sounds like you were born under lucky stars for what you want to do," Barbod said.

"Yes, most men think they are born under lucky stars. For me, the stars are born of and within me," Jaidev replied with a wide grin, pointing to the heavens and his forehead as an effervescent joy bubbled from within.

"I can only join in your laughing, Jaidev. I don't quite get what you mean all the time," Barbod remarked, shaking his head with a smile.

As the sun sank below the horizon, a chill settled over the

desert, accompanied by a light breeze. With each step on their trek toward Damascus, the stars grew brighter, and the night air grew cooler.

"Tomorrow, we arrive at Damascus," Barbod announced, wearing warm garments to shield his body from the chill night temperatures.

"Ahhh, I love this air," Aakash exclaimed, reaching outward and inhaling deeply.

Mezriani and Khartum moved up in the caravan to ride next to Jaidev and Barbod.

"Damascus is a prosperous city under Roman rule," Mezriani shared, "with a perimeter wall featuring seven entrances representing the planets."

"Many cultures have followed the planets over vast periods of time, each understanding the star language in their own fashion. Jaidev's father originally introduced me to the language when I was a young man traveling through his village. When I returned home, I met Zirgan, a teacher from my culture, who further instructed me," Khartum said.

Mezriani proposed, "Let's meet with the renowned Roman mathematici Lucius while we are in Damascus, for the Romans also look to the stars for knowledge of men."

"I would like that," Jaidev replied.

Chapter 14 - Damascus and Meeting Herod

Barbod pointed eagerly toward a wall emerging on the western horizon. "Behold, there stands the Gate of the Sun, the eastern gate of Damascus! They positioned it eastward to meet the morning sun."

"An east-facing entrance is very auspicious in Vaastu, the Indian art of building," Jaidev declared, observing the look of relief on everyone's face.

Ravi sighed heavily as he scanned the wall. They had been traveling for months, and he could see that everyone was exhausted from the long journey. "Finally, we have reached the west," he exclaimed with a hint of triumph in his voice. "It seems like we left our homes ages ago."

"I will disband the caravan this morning at the gate. We have completed the journey," Barbod announced with relief. "You go on through the gates. Bellows, Paloma, Ghaffar, and I will bid farewell to each of our caravan travelers here."

Jaidev and the others moved through the entrance. Barbod sat glowingly on Bellows, greeting each camel and its riders and wishing them well. Each of them expressed their profound thanks, and many gave a gift to Barbod and Paloma in gratitude for their safe journey.

"Let's seek our accommodations and give our animals some rest," Ravi suggested. "Tonight, we honor our Kabir, Barbod, with a feast of food and drinks."

Mezriani gestured down the bustling road to an old inn, its walls showing signs of aging plaster. "Come on, I bet I can get us a good deal," Mezriani said with a wink.

The early morning air in Damascus was alive with the aroma of freshly baked bread. A welcome cool breeze refreshed them after the arid desert heat. The travelers made their way down the awakening street towards the inn.

As they entered through the front door, Mezriani yelled, "Anybody here?"

"Who wants to know?" a voice answered behind a door.

Mezriani cried out, "Ah, cousin Rubin! It has been far too long since I have seen your face!"

Rubin joyfully exclaimed, "Praise Jehovah! It's always a pleasure to see you, Mezriani."

"I've been wandering through the desert and found these companions from the east. We need rooms for everyone," Mezriani said.

"Of course," Rubin replied.

Mezriani added with emphasis, "And I'd prefer beds that feel like the softness of wool, not the stone slabs of Moses!"

"That's extra," Rubin said with a twinkle.

"And you'll join us for dinner later, cousin," Mezriani declared.

"If you're buying, I'm coming," Rubin remarked.

"You never change, cousin," Mezriani said, shaking his head and grinning. "Do you know where I can find the mathematici Lucius?" Mezriani asked.

"We frequently spot him at the taverna with a Greek friend. They both regale patrons with tales of the stars," Rubin shared.

"Then we visit the taverna before dinner. Meet me here later," Mezriani stated, turning towards Jaidev.

"Let's rest up," Ravi suggested.

As Jaidev stirred from his sleep, a gentle breeze caressed his face, and the warmth of the sun soothed his skin. He peered out the window to see it was well past midday. The rhythmic clopping of hooves soon caught his ear. He watched as a group of Roman soldiers marched down the street, their polished armor glinting in the sunlight.

Mezriani was in the middle of a conversation with his cousin

Rubin as Jaidev walked into the main room of the inn. They fell silent, looking rather anxious.

"Jaidev, come. We are just reminiscing," Mezriani said.

"The others will be down soon. I saw Ghaffar, Aakash, and Khartum moving about," Jaidev informed.

"Rubin will go to the taverna and check out the situation. If it's full of drunken Roman soldiers, we're all better off staying away. The Romans are always looking to challenge strangers as a show of strength," Mezriani warned.

"If the mathematici is inside, I'll go in and ask him to come out. The Romans recognize me and leave me be," Rubin said.

Jaidev's jaw tightened. "Thanks. We have seen the evil deaths of men crucified on the road into Damghan. The Romans are a brutal people."

"Their culture has achieved many great things—roads, buildings, water aqueducts, and more. They use men they enslave to do the work," Mezriani declared.

Ravi descended the staircase, his tired body refreshed from sleep. He asked where they should go later to eat and honor their friend Barbod. They had braved scorching sun, blustery bone-chilling cold, perilous mountains, and a baking desert. It was time to celebrate their journey.

"Rubin has arranged a private room where we can dine. I hope the mathematici can join us," Mezriani said with a nod of gratitude towards Rubin.

"That would be wonderful," Jaidev remarked.

"Your animals are in excellent hands with plenty of food and water," Rubin assured. "Mezriani has told me of your journey, and I'm honored that he is joining you. We all consider him family here; now we consider you family too."

"Thank you," Jaidev replied.

Rubin gestured to the spread on the table. "Help yourself to the cool water, wine, olives, cheese, and grapes. I'm off to the taverna to see if the mathematici is there. I'll be back soon."

As Rubin opened the front door to leave, he turned back, saying, "We are going to get some rain soon. I can smell it coming. The wind is picking up and the cooler air is moving in."

Mezriani added, "Here, we are closer to the sea. It rains more than out east in the desert. Tomorrow night marks the start of our sacred Sabbath day—a day of rest, according to our scriptures. God made Creation in six days and on the seventh day He ceased His labor and blessed it. The Lord instructs us to keep this day holy by resting from all labors."

"It is a beautiful practice. It is when we are still and at rest that we come to know the Creator," Jaidev remarked.

Mezriani's eyes followed Jaidev. Recognizing his wisdom, he said, "Indeed, for our scripture says to 'Be still and know that I Am God'."

Shortly after, the room fell silent as Rubin strode in, followed by two men—one with an olive complexion and an amiable smile, and the other tall and lean. Both men wore simple tunics with leather belts. Rubin introduced them to the assembly. "This is Lucius, the Roman mathematici, and his Greek friend Ambrose."

Lucius's face held an expression of superiority.

"Your presence honors us. Allow me to introduce our guests: Jaidev, a Magi from India, and his friends, Ravi and Aakash; Khartum, a Magi from Bactria, and his son, Akim; Ghaffar, an Essene; and Barbod, a musician and the caravan Kabir who brought them all to Damascus; Shimon, my nephew; and I am Mezriani, a Rabbi and Kabbala reader of the stars."

"Have some wine, cheese, and olives," Rubin offered. "We have a dinner being prepared. It will be ready shortly."

"Why have you come to a mathematici, my friends? Is it the celestial alignment of the stars and planets?" Lucius inquired.

"Yes, we foresee the appearance of a Maha Atma or great soul by the conjunction of Saturn and Jupiter," Jaidev declared.

"We have been following this great conjunction. It is a rare celestial event," Lucius agreed.

Jaidev explained that this rare alignment of Jupiter and Saturn happened three times from May to December. On December 24th at 10:50 pm here in the west, after the third conjunction when the Moon was in its most influential position, the birth would take place.

"Pisces is a water sign, the last sign of the Zodiac," Ambrose added.

"Yes, the birth will happen as Virgo rises in the east—when Pisces is in the western sky," Jaidev said.

Ambrose squinted, scanning the chart Jaidev opened before him. Pausing, he pointed to the symbols. "See here, the Sun and Mercury in Capricorn are in a powerful trine with Virgo. Venus there in the 3rd house is forming a quintile—not as powerful but still a significant influence." He tapped his finger against Saturn, Jupiter, and the Moon in conjunction. "No planets opposing Pisces," he observed with a nod. "But this birth you are predicting? It doesn't align with our view. From our view, it's these two planets—the Sun and Mercury in Capricorn—here in the 5th house that give the primary understanding of this chart."

Lucius's eyes glinted as he spoke, and a note of pride rang through his words. "Our celestial gods do not recognize this 'Maha Atma' you are seeing," he stated. "Just as the fallacy of One God that the Israelites profess is not the Roman and Greek view. Our gods and goddesses, if angered or insulted, can manifest their wrath with ferocity and retribution." He peered into his wine cup, seeming to ponder life deeply, then scoffed, "Do you now understand why the Israelites are under our Roman rule?"

Lucius's gaze met Ambrose's, and he smiled at his Greek friend, who nodded in agreement.

"Still, this is a powerful chart of significant change for men," Lucius continued. "Jupiter or Zeus, as my Greek friend insists on calling him, is associated with kingship, prosperity, and expansion.

And Saturn—Kronos in Greek—stands for structure and rulership. We see it as a birth heralding a change in the rulers of the world. The birth will occur when Pisces is the rising sign, Mars is in the 12th house, and the Sun and Mercury are in the 11th."

"Your chart is not, as we say in Greek, the 'Christos' or anointed one," Ambrose declared.

"I respect your learned knowledge," Jaidev replied, understanding that astrologers often see things differently. "Your grasp of the astrological movements is remarkable."

"Tomorrow, I'm going to meet Quintus Aemilius Lepidus, a Roman senator who's visiting Damascus," Lucius began. "I'll tell him about your journey through our Roman territory and he may want to hear more from you in person."

Mezriani surveyed the table where servants placed steaming dishes of succulent meats, fragrant vegetables, and freshly baked bread. "Come," he said with a wide smile, nodding towards Rubin. "Let's enjoy this scrumptious meal that our generous host has prepared."

Khartum exhaled deeply. "We can all agree on that," he said with a contented smile. "I'm ready for something that will satiate my taste buds and soothe my soul."

Barbod's eyes twinkled in the candlelight. "It's the simple things in life—fine food, a good bottle of wine, a decent night's sleep, and being able to greet the day feeling refreshed—that I enjoy most."

Rubin raised his glass, filled with the deep red wine. "Here's to our guests, Lucius and Ambrose," he announced. "L'chaim, to Life!" He smiled around the table as he brought the cup to his lips.

"L'chaim!" Mezriani repeated.

As the meal was complete and the wine well into many cups, it was time to turn in. Barbod glanced over his shoulder and sighed. Time seemed to freeze for a moment as he looked at the night's darkness spread across the sky. "It will be good," he murmured, "to return to our beds at night and wake during the day. The night travel always leaves me a little uneasy."

Jaidev tilted his head back. "Our body knows what it needs," he agreed. "It does best following the natural rhythms of nature."

As Barbod's head hit his pillow, a meteor flashed down the eastern sky.

Barbod stirred from the sound of a baby's cry and leapt out of bed. He tip-toed down the hallway, following the noise to an open nursery. There he found a little boy standing up in his crib, reaching out both arms towards him.

Barbod knelt to scoop the baby up. The infant looked into his eyes and reached out, wrapping a chubby hand around Barbod's neck. He instinctively pulled the child closer to him. He could feel the warmth radiating from this little being and felt an overwhelming surge of love wash over him. "There, there, little guy, no one is going to hurt you," Barbod said. "I am here."

The child stared up at Barbod with wide, curious eyes. He felt as if an invisible thread connected them, weightless and timeless that seemed to stretch on forever. "What is your name, child?" Barbod asked.

"Whose name? Whose name?" Barbod heard Aakash saying from a distance.

With a cracked voice, Barbod uttered, "I was dreaming. It was nothing," and slowly closed his eyes as a wave of relief soothed him into a deep, restful sleep.

Hours later, he opened his eyes, and the first streaks of daylight warmed his face. A buzz of energy flowed through him as he stretched out in bed. Taking a deep breath, Barbod sat up, cleared his mind, and settled into Jaidev's meditation practice. His thoughts slowly faded away, and he grew aware of the mantra playing in the background. The mantra felt familiar now; it just bubbled from inside him, then gradually became softer and slower until it was just a faint notion, and then he just was.

When thoughts arose again, he was unsure how long he was

without them. He wasn't asleep, just aware. As he slowly came out of meditation and got up effortlessly, his body felt grounded yet light. He paused, scanning himself internally for any signs of unease or discomfort, finding instead a newfound sense of calm and peace. A warmth spread through his chest and an ever-growing love filled him from within. Barbod felt connected to everything and almost weightless as he walked towards the door.

"C'mon, Barbod. You are just in time. Jaidev and I are going to find some breakfast," Aakash said.

Barbod rubbed his hands together. "Yes, yes," he replied with enthusiasm. "I'd love some falafel, goat cheese, and sesame seeds with tea. I know a shop nearby that serves generous portions."

"Big portions sound good to me," Aakash affirmed, as they headed in the direction of the shop.

"Since I woke up this morning, there has been a strange sensation of being totally alive, yet there is a quiet stillness. Every sight, sound, and smell seems new to me, yet these feelings come and go, almost like I'm an observer from outside myself," Barbod expressed, taking a deep breath.

Jaidev joyfully declared, "You are beginning to recognize your true Self, which remains unchanged amidst the ever-changing, mind, ego, and physical body. It's an extraordinary sensation, a feeling of lightness. Your awareness is increasing."

Aakash chimed in. "I have felt that way when competing in archery. I feel I am acting kind of in the flow of things—that I'm not the one doing the action."

Jaidev calmly responded, "When we can act without the ego or the pragya pradh of the intellect, our actions are most powerful."

Aakash gasped, a wide grin spreading across his face. His eyes widened, his gaze piercing as he muttered a sudden epiphany. "That's it!" he exclaimed in jubilation. "This is what that old saddhu meant when he said, 'to let the arrow fly, first pull back the bow.' The point of stillness is the unchanging Self in awareness."

"Yes, the inner point of stillness is where the Song of Creation emerges. Waves of love emerge from the bliss of stillness," Jaidev said.

"What do you mean? I don't feel those waves of love. Why do you know them and not me?" Barbod asked.

"When we have closed off our hearts, allowing anger and resentment to fill them instead of love, these fruits of tamas and rajas dull the mind and heart, and we don't recognize the Song. This closing off is due to past samskaras—memories that have caused blocks within us. Some describe it as the muddy water of a pond, preventing us from knowing its depth," Jaidev explained. "Opening up to the Song of Creation, to the ever-present stillness you described, causes the mud to settle and be flushed out, so the depth can be known. Then, we can feel the infinite love radiating from it, and our hearts flood with love, compassion, understanding, and clarity as it resonates with the Song."

"I had a dream last night that a baby reached up to me and I could feel this incredible love radiating from him," Barbod shared. "I thought it might be a dream of the Maha Atma."

Jaidev looked at Barbod. He spoke with a peaceful yet powerful voice, filled with a gentle joy that connected deeply to the hearts of Barbod and Aakash. "Yes, the Maha Atma is always within us. The infinite love you felt could not exist in a dream if it were not already within you. When you woke up, you knew it as a dream. You are waking up from what we know as waking state to another state, turiyatit chetana, or soul consciousness."

"Whatever it is, I could get used to it. I never felt so good," Barbod smiled. "We have arrived, this is the shop."

"Let's pick a table where we can talk. I have something to show Barbod," Jaidev suggested.

Once they were settled and had ordered their food, Jaidev pulled some charts from his cloak.

"I have been looking at some charts that I thought could be

your birth chart, and I have found one that rectifies with what we know about you. You were born on September 5th, 40 years ago, shortly after noon when the Moon was Mehregan. You are a Sagittarius ascendant, and your ascendant ruler Jupiter is in a powerful Kendra Trikona Raj Yoga with Mercury in your 11th house of friends, desires, dreams, aspirations, and long-term gains," Jaidev explained.

He pointed to the ascendant and then Jupiter, showing Barbod the placement of the planets and houses.

"You have a second powerful Yoga of the 5th and 9th lords of the two best houses in the chart, conjunct in the 10th. Ketu is in your ascendant, which can cause shyness, but also indicates an interest in enlightenment or Moksha. Saturn is with Venus in the 12th house, a Moksha house, in your natal chart." Pointing to a second chart, Jaidev added, "Right now, you are in a dasha-bhukti of Saturn and Ketu. This is a time when your 12th house gets a lot of energy. Additionally, a very important transit is occurring. Venus is transiting your 12th house and is tight with your natal Saturn right now. Venus is the planet of love, and it is said that Venus can forgive anything. Jupiter is transiting Pisces with Saturn in your 4th house—also a Moksha house—bringing sattvic energy to your 4th and 12th houses through its 9th house aspect. Saturn, the planet of meditation, is also bringing sattvic energy from its transit of Pisces to your ascendant and natal Ketu, enhancing your ability to achieve enlightenment. The energies are very favorable for the forgiveness of those who have hurt you, thus opening the heart and mind to Moksha," Jaidev concluded.

Barbod gazed at the charts for a moment, taking it all in before looking up at Jaidev. "Can you explain Moksha?" he asked.

"Moksha is a state where the Song of Creation is awake in everything. It is freedom from the cycle of birth and death and the suffering of karma. In this state, one has transcended the cycle, and inner bliss and peace are ever-present," Jaidev replied.

Barbod looked intently at the charts, trying to absorb this new knowledge. "I don't understand the star language, but I would love to experience Moksha," he said. "I'm wondering, do the stars tell us about our mother and father?"

"Yes, the 4th house tells us about your mother and the 9th house tells us about your father," Jaidev affirmed, pointing to the first chart. The ruler of the 4th, Jupiter, is in a Kendra Trikona Yoga with Mercury in the 11th. Jupiter is hemmed in by benefics Mercury and Venus. The 4th house shows us not only the mother but also happiness. You have a very happy nature, indicated by the ruler Jupiter being so well disposed. The 4th is also aspected by the Sun and Mars from the 10th. They are both malefics and Mars is combust. Even though they bring energy to the career house, the malefic aspects hurt your mother's house, bringing the pain you have felt in your heart by your mother's death. Other indications in the chart confirm this. The Moon, a feminine planet, represents the mother. In your chart, the Moon is conjunct Rahu, a malefic, in your 7th house, indicating that your mother was overprotective of you, almost smothering—probably to protect you from your father. Your father is represented by the 9th house and the Sun. Mars is with the Sun in the 10th, indicating a very assertive and dominant father. Although Mars is combust, it still harms the Sun some, indicating that your father had some damage to his own assertiveness, which he appears to have taken out on you. There is one more planet to look at and that is Venus, a feminine planet and the planet of love. Venus is conjunct Saturn in the dusthana 12th house, which is not a good natal placement. The overall indication is that you were restricted the benefits of feeling loved by your mother and probably your father as well. Fortunately, it is not a very tight conjunction, and the transits and dasha you are in now favor great healing and gains towards Moksha." Jaidev traced his finger through the 1st chart as he spoke and ended at the 2nd.

Tears welled up in Barbod's eyes as he nodded in agreement. He recognized that his anger towards his father was waning, and he was opening inside. He placed his hand on his heart, lightly pressing the faravahar, feeling the inner warmth and love nurturing him. "I have one more question. Does music and my musical ability show up in the chart?"

"Yes, it is quite clear that you have a strong desire and ability for music. It is not easy to see from your natal chart. However, it is seen through a chart my father teaches called the Bhava Chalit or Bhava chart. In the Bhava chart, Venus joins Jupiter, influencing the 11th house. This gives you great desire and talent in the musical arts." Jaidev pointed to Venus moving to the 11th house and joining Jupiter.

Barbod shook his head in amazement at Jaidev's knowledge, pondering quietly.

Jaidev glanced back and forth between Aakash and Barbod, his brown eyes glimmering with understanding. Sensing his quiet presence was enough and words weren't necessary, he slowly nodded in agreement. The three of them sat together, eating the breakfast placed before them, each lost in their own thoughts and inner silence.

Upon returning to the inn, they found Mezriani with Rubin. He welcomed Jaidev, Aakash, and Barbod to sit with them. "Lucius dropped by earlier," Mezriani began. "Quintus Aemilius Lepidus has requested our presence at his villa later today."

Rubin's face was grave as he spoke. "He is a close ally of Herod," he said. "Be very careful what you say, for everything we discuss will eventually make its way to Herod's ears."

"Do we have anything to worry about?" Aakash inquired.

Rubin adjusted his robe and regarded the group with a serious gaze. "No, the meeting will be cordial," he said. "The Romans can be both brutal and diplomatic. A senator will show his welcoming diplomatic hand, but make no mistake—he will send a report to Herod of your presence and mission."

"Choose your words carefully," Mezriani warned.

The sun was high in the sky as the group set off on the short walk up the hill to Quintus Aemilius Lepidus's villa. The hilltop offered a spectacular view of Damascus. When they arrived at the entrance, two Roman soldiers wearing polished armor stepped forward with their spears drawn. They instructed them to leave all weapons at the gate.

Aakash cautiously extended his hand, offering his katar to the waiting Roman soldiers. The soldier gently touched the sharp blade and admired its craftsmanship, while another looked at the detailed carvings on the handle. With a slight nod of approval, the leader stated that it would wait for him at the gate when they finished their task. Aakash bowed his head in respect and thanked them as he handed over his beloved weapon.

The villa was immaculate, every blade of grass perfectly manicured. Well-tended gardens lined the path to the front door. Colorful blossoms cascaded down trellises and vibrant green shrubs bursting with life adorned them. Overhead, majestic trees shaded the path from the afternoon sun, forming an arch that provided a canopy of respite for the visitors. As they approached the entrance, a beautiful young maiden stepped out, carrying a tray of cool water flavored with hibiscus petals. Each of them gratefully accepted their cup with a nod and smile.

A small-framed man wearing a white robe and a large golden ring of Caesar's head on his right hand greeted them. Lucious and Ambrose followed behind. "So, this must be the Magi I have heard about," Quintus Aemilius said.

Mezriani, bowing slightly, spoke first. "We are honored, Senator."

Quintus Amelius, a distinguished scholar with salt and pepper hair and deep-set eyes, bowed his head to the Rabbi. "Thank you," he replied in his low, resonant voice. "It is the far easterners that I am most interested in hearing today."

Jaidev stepped forward. "Namaste, meaning the divine in me, honors the divine in you. Your home and this fine land are splendid."

Quintus Amelius squinted his eyes, furrowed his brows, and leaned back slightly as he studied the strangers. "I have not heard your accent before," he said cautiously.

"My home is far to the south of Bactria, beyond the majestic Hindu Kush mountains," Jaidev replied.

"You are a long way from home. What brings you to these lands?" Quintus Amelius asked.

"Our forefathers learned the lessons of the stars, and they speak to us today. The stars are announcing the birth of a great soul, a Maha Atma," Jaidev declared.

"What is the purpose of this Maha Atma?" Quintus Amelius queried.

Mezriani began to speak, hoping to frame the message, but Quintus Amelius raised his hand in silence. "I would like to hear it from the far easterners, Rabbi."

"The Maha Atma's dharma is to lead men to spiritual knowledge, to knowledge of God," Jaidev explained, meeting the senator's eyes so he could see he was being truthful.

Quintus Amelius fixed his gaze on Khartum and asked, "My friend, where is your home? And what insight do you have about this newborn?"

"I am from Bactria. I too have foreseen the birth of this child in the stars," Khartum affirmed.

"Show me these star charts that you are referring to," Quintus Amelius demanded.

Jaidev unrolled the chart he carried and pointed to its symbols. "Here we see that a triple conjunction of Jupiter and Saturn has been happening in the sign of Pisces, the fish. It is the conjunction known as a Raj Yoga, or royal union, and signifies that the birth will be here in the west when Virgo, the Virgin, rises in the east."

Quintus Amelius leaned forward, scrutinizing the chart before him. He wanted more answers to the reason for the child's birth. "Lucius," he began, his voice keen with expectation, "states that his understanding of the stars is that Jupiter represents kingship. Does this birth signal the coming of a king?"

Jaidev spoke in a clear, sonorous tone. "The birth of a Maha Atma is to liberate man—to reveal his soul and the beauty of the Song of Creation." He took a long slow breath, silently measuring the weight of his words before continuing. Speaking slowly and carefully so as not to raise suspicions, he hoped the Romans would not see his message as a threat.

Quintus Amelius's rich voice spoke mirthfully. "I always thought those dazzling lights in the sky were for us to make love to beautiful maidens and sleep under," eliciting laughter from his entourage and the maidens serving him.

Mezriani, picking up on the lighthearted jest, said, "You are right, Senator, and may you have many nights of pleasure under the stars."

Quintus Amelius's words were firm and clear. "I am sending word to Herod in Jerusalem of your visit to our lands," he said with a wave of his arm. "When you arrive, you must stop and see King Herod. He will want to hear of your journey and let me tell you—he is very fond of fine silk from the Orientals through Bactria." A hint of a smile appeared on Quintus's lips as he concluded.

"We understand," Mezriani replied.

Quintus Amelius paused for a moment and narrowed his eyes. Then with one firm sweep of his arm, he dismissed the visitors.

As they walked away, Mezriani nervously wrung his hands and glanced at the men around him. "We should go to Jerusalem tomorrow," he said, a hint of desperation in his voice. "The sooner we get the meeting with Herod out of the way, the better off we will be. If we keep him waiting too long, he'll become suspicious of us."

Rubin spoke with certainty. "Herod is growing old. He has been ruling the area on behalf of Caesar for 35 years. To rule so long under Rome says a lot. He is a cunning, shrewd, and ruthless ruler. Very suspicious of anything that can challenge his hold on the throne, he will do anything to maintain control."

Mezriani added, "Time is working against him. He has now grown old and feeble. His days are numbered, but still, he maintains an iron grip."

"It is rumored he executed his own son recently. No one has seen his son in months," Rubin said.

"He appreciates fine art, architecture, music, and books. He was born a son of Judea, but in truth, he worships only power and Rome," Mezriani declared.

"I have some beautiful fine silk I can present him," Ravi offered.

"And I can play the chang for him. Its sweet music can soothe any man's soul," Barbod added.

"Fine, we leave tomorrow for Jerusalem," Mezriani announced.

As the sun rose over the ancient city of Damascus, the air was still chilly from the night before. Ravi, Jaidev, and Aakash were ready to begin their journey to Jerusalem. They mounted their horses, Ojas, Tejomaya, and Gyatri respectively. Barbod rode Bellows and Mezriani, Shimon, Ghaffar, Khartum, and Akim each rode their camels. Other camels, loaded with supplies, followed. It would take several days to reach Jerusalem on the long, dusty road before them.

"It feels good to have Ojas beneath me again. I can sense he likes it," Aakash said.

"Tejomaya is also eager to have me ride him," Ravi added.

Mezriani paused, scanning their surroundings. "Keep your eyes and ears open," he warned, his voice barely audible above the crunch of gravel underfoot. "The Romans spy on those they're suspicious of." He glanced at his companions with a grim expression. "I wouldn't put it past Quintus Amelius to have us followed until we meet with Herod." After a moment, Mezriani continued. "They routinely followed my cousin around Damascus. The Romans seek insurgents and those who may support them. Being Jewish makes us a target of their untrusting eyes."

The group walked on in silence for a few moments, each lost in their own thoughts about the dangers ahead.

Mezriani sighed as he spoke, his voice carrying a reverence that hushed the group. "Ancient Jerusalem has been the home of my people since King Solomon, the son of King David, built the first temple. After being destroyed in the great war with the Babylonians hundreds of years ago, Cyrus the Great allowed us to reclaim it. When the Romans took control of the region, Herod was made king, and the Romans were now our overlords. Herod later reconstructed the temple, and Jerusalem has been a holy place for us ever since." He paused for a moment, soaking in the sacredness of its history.

Barbod leaned in towards Ravi, his eyes twinkling. He gestured grandly with one hand. "And in Jerusalem," he said loudly enough for all to hear, "they make a delicious baklava that rivals your mom's sweet gujiya."

"Nothing beats my mom's gujiya," Ravi retorted.

Barbod put his hand on Bellows's neck and stroked it. "It will take us a few days to get there," he said, gazing into the horizon, "but we will be there soon enough."

The sun was sinking lower in the sky as Aakash glanced over his shoulder and thought he saw a figure atop a horse, cloaked in shadow against the hill behind them.

With the autumnal equinox behind them and the winter solstice not far off, the days were growing shorter and cooler. *The birth of the Maha Atma is drawing near*, Jaidev thought.

Upon reaching the summit of Mount Scopus, Barbod cheered as he saw Jerusalem sprawled out before them. Mezriani took a deep breath and spread his arms wide as he exclaimed with some emotion, "Praise God; it is the place God has chosen! Our forefathers called it 'The City of David.'"

"You are blessed, for the Maha Atma will be born in these lands," Jaidev said.

Mezriani looked lovingly at the vast city before them. "Come, let us descend from this Mount and enter our beloved city."

As they neared the city gate, Aakash clearly saw a lone figure on horseback descending the ridge of Mount Scopus. Glancing over his shoulder, he said to Jaidev, "Don't look back, but I think we've had a shadower on our heels since Damascus."

Jaidev nodded, scanning the sky above them. "The shadows are moving into position in the sky as well. Rahu and Ketu are forming the Kala Sarpa Yoga. All the planets will soon be between them."

Mezriani led the group through the Gate of Damascus, the towering northern entrance to Jerusalem. The avenue before them bustled with activity as vendors hawked their wares and citizens wandered between the markets.

"This is the Gate of Damascus, the northern gate of Jerusalem. Welcome to the most beautiful city in the world," Mezriani announced. "I will show you the way to the inn we recommend, and then I must go to the temple. I will ask for an audience with King Herod while I am there. His palace is nearby."

Jaidev smiled and addressed Ravi and Aakash, who stood beside him. He gestured to Barbod, who was a few feet away, saying, "Diwali is here. We will light the traditional candles this evening to symbolize the victory of Light over darkness. You are welcome to join us."

Ravi lit up as he spoke. "Afterwards, how about some of that baklava Barbod was talking about? It'll be just like home. We always had treats afterward."

"Wonderful," Barbod said. "I'm honored to join you."

Jaidev placed five candles in the center of the room. He cupped his hands around them as he lit each one, shielding the tiny flame from any slight movements of air. The five candles represented the light of Diwali. With eyes closed, he chanted in Sanskrit, calling the gods to protect them from darkness. As he finished chanting, Jaidev opened his eyes and explained the story of Diwali. "When Ram rescued Sita and returned home with her after 14 years in exile, there was a glorious celebration, for darkness is only temporary. The Light that is within us and without us always shines. Carry the Light of Diwali within you and remember it on your darkest days. At home, we celebrate for five days. Here in this land, we will celebrate tonight and remember our homes."

Aakash held the embroidered cloth Amrita had given him during the puja. "I really miss our lives back home," he said softly, his voice lonely for home and Amrita.

Ravi nodded solemnly and rubbed his hands together. "Yes, we all do. I'm sure that once the Maha Atma is born, we'll be heading back home." He grinned widely. "Now let's see if Barbod's baklava treat is as good as our gujiya. He says it is."

"Coming right up," Barbod exclaimed. "I have the baklava as well as a meal being prepared for us at the inn. Let's go there and continue our celebration."

"Our next Diwali will be back home," Aakash said nostalgically. "Let's eat."

Once they finished their meal, Barbod dished each a helping of the specially prepared baklava. He watched as Ravi took a bite and his eyes glowed with delight, waving his fingers at the treat in appreciation. "See, it is as good as any treat in the world." Barbod bragged.

Mezriani popped his head into the room. "We meet with Herod mid-morning tomorrow. Let's meet here early and talk before seeing him."

"We'll see you in the morning," Jaidev said.

Jaidev left one of the Diwali candles burning on his windowsill as he settled into bed. A gentle breeze flickered light and shadows through the room as he drifted off to sleep.

Suddenly, a haunting melody stirred him from his slumber. He rubbed his eyes and saw an ethereal light floating where the candle had been. The light pulsed in time with the surrounding tune. Hands of cloud and mist stroked the strings of a chang-like instrument.

"Who are you?" Jaidev asked, awestruck.

The light being continued to strum the strings, otherworldly notes filling the room.

"Are you a god?" Jaidev whispered, barely believing what he was seeing.

A gentle light shone around the being, illuminating it in soft hues of gold and silver. It looked at Jaidev with its large, luminous eyes. Its voice was low and resonant as it spoke. "I am a servant of the Light, the one God. Some call me an angel, others a deva."

"You play the instrument beautifully," Jaidev said, feeling a warmth wash over him.

"It is easy to play when the Song of Creation is known within," the angel replied.

"Why have you visited me this night?" Jaidev asked.

The angel's voice became like a whisper in the wind, his wings shimmering in the candlelight. He smiled and spoke of the coming Maha Atma. "You are blessed, for you are chosen to help guide him to safety. There is great darkness that seeks to consume the Light, but you and your friends must guide him away from it. Follow the Song of Creation, and you will lead many to the same path. Go south, for there lies a haven where the darkness cannot touch."

Suddenly, the Diwali candle sparked, and the flame regained its shape as it burned. Jaidev felt a peace settle over him as he looked out of the window and saw Jupiter and Saturn drawing closer in the night sky. He lay back down in his bed feeling the embrace of grace and soon drifted off into a dream-filled sleep.

The morning sky was heavy with gloomy rain clouds, a chill breeze wafting through the air. As Mezriani addressed the group, he spoke slowly and deliberately. "Herod remains in power for these many years because of his shrewdness and cunning. Never forget that his warm welcome is all part of an elaborate ploy to gain information from us. He's already had Quintus Amelius compile a report on us, so be wary of what you say. He's a dangerous man who seeks to exploit the birth child. We should return his pleasantries and give him the impression that we're working together to fulfill his goals."

"What do you think his greatest fear is?" Aakash asked.

"His greatest fear is losing his crown. He doesn't have many years left, but he doesn't want to admit it and thinks he will live and rule forever," Mezriani replied.

"Countless slaves endured great suffering to construct Herod's palace, a magnificent building on a hill."

Mezriani swept his arm towards the horizon where three towering spires of Herod's buildings soared skyward. "Herod has built many remarkable structures in Jerusalem. He senses the city's desire for beauty," he said.

"Truly, this palace is an amazing sight," Ravi agreed.

They slowly approached the entrance to Herod's palace, where two statuesque guards flanked each side of the doorway. As they drew closer, one guard stepped forward and held his spear menacingly in front of them. His expression was harsh and unforgiving as he gripped the weapon and bellowed, "Who approaches?"

Mezriani stepped forward. "It is I, Mezriani," he said with a confident air. "I arrived yesterday, and King Herod requested that my entourage have an audience with him."

The guard gestured to the towering stone walls, where archers were positioned on each parapet. "King Herod has granted you entrance," the guard said, his voice stern yet reassuring. He looked them up and down, assessing their weapons before speaking again. "First, you must leave any sharp blades or bows here at the gate."

Aakash and Mezriani both left their weapons near the entrance—Aakash leaving his katar and Mezriani a small dagger. Two guards appeared in the hallway to guide them back to Herod's great hall.

When they arrived, the throne was empty, and the guards motioned for everyone to wait. After a few moments, a curtain behind the throne opened, and an aide stepped out to support King Herod, who was wearing a silk robe. His steps were unsteady as he walked closer to his guests. The guard loudly proclaimed, "All hail King Herod!"

Slowly, Herod sat on the intricately carved throne and surveyed the travelers with an imperious gaze. Lucius and Ambrose stood at the king's side, their faces expressionless.

"I understand that our guests have traveled from distant lands. Please come forward and introduce yourselves," Herod commanded in a faltering baritone.

Jaidev stepped forward confidently, gesturing to the others behind him. "Greetings," he began. "I am Jaidev Trivedi, from India, and these are my friends Aakash, Ravi, Rabbi Mezriani, Shimon, Khartum and his son Akim, Ghaffar, and Barbod," pointing at each of them.

Herod leaned forward, squinting to see better in the light. "I understand you are a Magi, following the stars," he said.

Jaidev continued, placing his left hand on his chest while seeming to embrace the others with his outstretched right arm. "I am a Brahmin and Jyotishi. I know the star language, as do Khartum and Mezriani. These others are companions and friends," Jaidev replied.

Herod raised an eyebrow and pressed his lips together in a thin line. He continued to lean forward slightly with an expectant posture. His voice carried the weight of command as he asked, "Explain this star language to me. Why have you traveled so far?"

Jaidev raised his right hand with a finger pointing upward. "Our forefathers have shown us how the stars foretell human events. Khartum and Mezriani have each learned to read the stars from their traditions," he said, his voice confident and unwavering. "We have all seen a powerful conjunction occurring in Pisces, a rare and powerful alignment of the stars that foretells a great birth."

Herod's brow furrowed as he spoke, his voice thick with doubt. "What makes this birth so 'great,' exactly?" He couldn't keep the skepticism from his tone as he shifted his gaze to Mezriani.

Mezriani, holding his arms shoulder-high and his palms toward King Herod, said, "We see this birth as a message from our Creator, who set the lights in the sky and the stars in motion."

"You are Judean? Are you not?" Herod questioned Mezriani.

Mezriani bowed low and lowered his gaze. "Yes, Highness. I am a Rabbi of long-standing, trained in the teachings of our tradition—the Torah and Kabbala," he said reverently.

Herod squinted his eyes, unsatisfied with the Rabbi's answer. "I understand, but please, explain to me why this child is so special," he demanded sternly.

The Rabbi expected such a question and remained composed while gathering his thoughts before answering. "Highness, this blessed birth marks the arrival of one who will serve in the Light of God." Mezriani picked his words carefully.

"As Jews, do you and I not serve God?" Herod pressed.

Mezriani bowed low and murmured, "Yes, Highness." He raised his head and met Herod's gaze with an expression of reverence and awe. "This birth will lead our people to the light, as Moses led us out of Egypt." He touched his forehead in a sign of respect.

Herod continued to lean forward, his brow furrowed in suspicion. "So, you say this child will be a leader of Israel," he said. "Tell me more about this 'Royal Yoga' you were describing to Lucius," his eyes glaring as he awaited the answer.

"A Yoga or union of two planets enhances their ability for better or worse. A Raj or Royal Yoga increases the benefic effects of the planetary energy. In the Raj Yoga of Jupiter and Saturn in Pisces, the benefits of devotion from Jupiter and the spiritual benefits of meditation from Saturn are enhanced. A king has nothing to fear from this yoga," Jaidev declared with conviction.

Herod glanced at Lucius and Ambrose. "Hmmmm, there is much to ponder here. And tell me, how will you find and know this birth?" Herod asked.

"The birth will occur after the winter solstice and the third conjunction of Jupiter and Saturn when the benefic Moon joins the conjunction. That date is the night of December 24th. We will scour the area and find every birth that is about to occur around that date and time. We will know the birth child when we know the baby born at that instant in time," Jaidev explained.

Herod's voice was stern as he leaned back into the throne. "So, you will be in our lands looking for the proclaimed baby," he said. "And then what? What will you do once you find it?"

Jaidev bowed his head, a deeply reverent look on his face. He raised his voice in solemnity so that it echoed through the chamber. "We will pay due respect and homage to him. To bear witness to such a high birth is a great honor for all beings."

Herod clenched his jaw, and his voice was tight with restrained emotion. "I too would like to pay homage to this great Being. I will organize a grand celebration for the winter solstice. All of you are invited to attend and inform me of where this special child is found."

"It will be an honor," Mezriani said.

Barbod cleared his throat, lifted his chin, and spoke with a slight quaver in his voice. "Highness, if it pleases you, my friends and I can entertain with our music during the festivities."

Herod smiled slyly. "I have a love for fine music. I will welcome your performance."

Mezriani bowed and stepped back. "With your permission, we will take your leave now, Highness."

"Go, and report back to me. I look forward to honoring this child and his parents," Herod said, trying to conceal his seething anger.

Herod watched the group as they quietly shuffled away. He

turned to his advisor, narrowing his eyes. "Make sure you keep your eyes on them. Immediately report back to me if they reach their destination or do anything out of character. Especially follow the Rabbi. I suspect he has ties to the insurrectionists."

Chapter 15 - The Maha Atma

The morning after the meeting with Herod, Jaidev awoke before dawn, tucked his blanket aside, and dressed. He walked through Jerusalem, taking in the sights and sounds of the awakening city. There were tens of thousands of busy inhabitants. The surrounding area held thousands more. *There must be 500 births a month in this area*, he thought. Probably 150 births in the week he calculated for the Maha Atma's arrival, and finding one among them would be no easy task. He sighed heavily and continued walking.

Mezriani was sitting in the main room having a steeping cup of tea when Jaidev returned to the inn.

"Mezriani, I was just trying to calculate how many babies would be born in this period. There will be many. How do you know when a baby is born?" Jaidev asked.

"Our custom is that each newborn be presented at the temple each week for a blessing. There are many, many presentations of newborns. I would expect that hundreds of births will need to be considered before finding the right one," Mezriani said. "Our midwives know when a maiden is with child. We will have to consult them to know who will be ready to give birth at the designated time. Also, there is a mikvah near the Temple, where a mother's 40-day purification after giving birth is observed."

"We should talk with these midwives and be receptive to their wisdom," Jaidev declared. "And we must keep not only our minds open but our hearts as well, for our hearts know and hear the Song of Creation's loving notes. To hear its song, we must be established in love."

"What do you mean?" Barbod asked, joining them.

"When we close off our hearts, allowing anger and resentment—the fruits of tamas and rajas—to fill them, the flow of love is restricted. As we open up to the Song of Creation, we can experience its infinite love. Our hearts then flood with love, compassion, understanding, and clarity as they resonate with the Song."

"How will this help us find the Maha Atma?" Barbod asked.

Light streamed through the windows and illuminated Jaidev's face as he spoke. "Miracles are always around us. They are the expression of the Song of Creation's loving harmony. When we fully open our hearts, we can receive the miracles surrounding us with clarity. So, by opening our hearts, we will be open to the miracle of the Maha Atma's birth. There is nothing more to do than allow, not resist. Resisting is the ego."

"How do I just allow?" Barbod questioned.

"Just Be, for just Being is allowing. That is how you allow miracles to happen." Jaidev let his words hang in the air, then added, "Allow your inner peace to be your guide."

Mezriani ran his fingers through his hair and let out a long sigh as he pondered the task at hand. "I will have to organize gathering the information from the midwives," he said.

Aakash, Ravi, Akim, Ghaffar, and Khartum joined them, and Jaidev filled them in on the task at hand. "Mezriani will gather a list of women who are due to give birth during this time period. We'll need to talk to each of them and trust our intuition to guide us," he explained. "We should split up to cover more ground."

"There may be many who are not of Judea who may give birth. Aakash, Ravi, Akim, Barbod, and I will keep our eyes open for any non-Judeans as well," Khartum added thoughtfully.

"In the Maha Atma's birth chart, the father's house is Taurus, showing that he will be born into the House of David," Mezriani said. "Still, we should be open to all births. I will visit with the temple elders today and start looking for the maiden. Herod will have his spies following us, so be discreet."

Aakash, Akim, and Khartum headed down the dusty road west of Jerusalem to start searching. They asked each villager they encountered if any maiden was about to bring new life into the world. The locals pointed them towards distant hamlets in small villages, where the trio continued their search.

Ravi, Jaidev, Ghaffar, and Barbod journeyed south, asking anyone they encountered about who may be with child, stopping at homes, small farms, and roadside inns.

Mezriani spent weeks collecting the names of young expectant mothers. He visited each one to determine when they were due and if they suspected anything special about their soon-to-be-born child. After consulting with a rabbi, he heard a story about an older woman who had recently given birth despite being past her childbearing years. Rumors spread that the birth was miraculous.

When Jaidev returned to Jerusalem, Mezriani informed him of this birth.

"There may be a connection to the Maha Atma's birth," Jaidev remarked.

"The woman whispered to a midwife that her younger cousin was carrying a miraculous conception. They are from Ein Karem, just west of Jerusalem. We should go there immediately," Mezriani suggested.

As they traveled west of Jerusalem, the sun moved across the midday sky. The clouds took the shape of angels blowing trumpets, floating across the heavens.

"Look, look at that!" Barbod exclaimed, pointing excitedly to the sky.

"Sai Ram, that is majestically beautiful," Jaidev agreed.

As the breeze blew gently, a dove landed in front of them and walked into a doorway. Curious, Mezriani looked in the doorway and saw an old woman cradling a newborn. "Praise God, you are devout in your faithfulness to God. You must be the woman who has been told to us," he said.

The old woman's wrinkled face lit up when she saw the Rabbi. She clasped her hands together and spoke with excitement. "I have seen angels from heaven! They came to me in the sky and told me wonderful news—a son of Judah blessed by God is coming!"

"God has favored you, and you are a new mother, are you not?" Mezriani asked.

The old woman nodded slowly as she spoke, her brown eyes twinkling with wisdom. "Yes," she affirmed, her thin lips forming a knowing smile. "I prayed to bring a baby into the world. God has blessed me in my late age with my son, John. Fear not, for a son of Judah is coming to bring light, the Shekhinah,[7] to all men."

"You are steadfast in your faith," Mezriani declared. "These men of the east with me have also seen the signs in the heavens of this birth."

"We wish to find this child and honor him," Jaidev said.

"His birth will be a simple one. He comes without fanfare of the things of men but can be seen by the hearts of the faithful. That is why his angels are all around us," the old woman stated.

Jaidev replied with a gentle voice, "Your sight is opened through your heart and crown, filling you with light."

"I have felt as light as a dove's feather for months. My joy is full," the old, wizened woman expressed.

Still speaking softly, Jaidev said, "I hear the Song of Creation in your words—feel its vibrations in your heart. You are a sign to us that we will find the child."

"He is the Light. He will shine before you and lead you to him. I can't tell you more than that," she added, winking with an unspoken

---

[7] Radiance, Light, the halo around angels and saints

knowing.

"All Glory to the Divine Teacher," Jaidev proclaimed.

"All Glory to God," the old woman rejoiced.

As they rode back to the inn, a profound sense of peace settled among them. The miracles that surrounded them this day brought a sense of awe and wonder to their beings.

Several days later, after interviewing dozens more maidens, Jaidev, Khartum, and Mezriani did not yet feel they had found the right woman and child.

"The old woman said that the Child would find us," Mezriani said. "I have faith in that, but I thought we would have found the mother more easily."

"We have to prepare to report back to Herod," Khartum declared.

Mezriani sighed heavily. "Yes, Herod will be suspicious that we haven't found the maiden yet. We need to spin the story so it seems like we're making progress, even if it's slow. We'll let him know when we've identified the birth mother," he said with a frown.

"Beware, I have identified two of Herod's spies following you," Aakash revealed. "They know everywhere you have been."

"Tomorrow night is the winter solstice," Jaidev began. "Herod is expecting us to report back, and I fear he will not be happy with us. I know a special song to melt his heart—a Sama Veda melody that will awaken the vibrations of the Song of Creation in even Herod's cold heart. It flows effortlessly and our flutes, drum, and Barbod's chang will be perfect for it." He paused for a moment, his voice hushed with excitement. "It will be the last song of our performance after several ragas we have played for our village."

"Can you teach it to us?" Barbod asked eagerly.

"It is Smriti, that which is remembered. It came to me in meditation earlier," Jaidev said. "Come sit quietly with me and close your eyes. I will lead you to it."

A soft breeze washed over them as they sat with their eyes

closed. A fountain bubbling nearby and children playing in the distance were heard as they settled their awareness. Jaidev began reciting a sacred chant of soft vibrations with meticulously spaced tonality. After several minutes of repeating the chant, he mimicked it with his flute. Smiles spread over the faces of Barbod, Ravi, and Aakash. The music was transcendent, ethereal—transfixed beyond space and time. A dog came and sat peacefully nearby, while a mother brought her baby to listen to its sweetness. Even the pigeons seemed to stop and listen. Ravi followed along with his flute, Barbod joined in with his chang, and Aakash kept the rhythm with his drum perfectly.

"Wow, that is powerful," Ravi remarked once they finished the song.

"Brahma is the source of the song. Brahma sang the Vedas into existence," Jaidev declared.

"It is perfect. This music has never been heard in this part of the world. I'm sure Herod will enjoy it," Barbod said.

Mezriani entered the front door of the inn, and the musicians waved for him to come and listen. Mezriani smiled and talked about the winter solstice and Herod's celebration with the Romans. "Herod drinks heavily during Saturnalia with his Roman cohorts. He gives little attention to our Hanukkah."

"My people also celebrate this time when the days grow longer. We call it Yalda Night, the longest night of the year," Khartum said.

Barbod declared he would present Herod with a special bottle of Persian wine, hoping it would help soothe him. Ravi said he would bring some silk.

Mezriani suggested they meet at the temple the following day at two in the afternoon, and from there, they could all walk to Herod's palace.

Before the hour arrived, Jaidev, Ravi, Barbod, Aakash, Ghaffar, Khartum, and Akim made their way to the temple. Suddenly, a group of Roman soldiers emerged from an alley ahead. They turned to encounter Jaidev and the group. Aakash stepped forward and squared his shoulders, ready to defend his friends. A smaller, muscular Roman scowled and made a comment about the group's strange dress and foreign accents.

"Hey, you there! Where are you from?" the soldier commanded.

"We are from the east, a land far from here. We are here to meet with Herod this afternoon," Aakash replied.

The soldier scrunched his nose in disdain. "Well, well," he said with a sneer. "You know Herod serves Rome. If you want to pass this way, you will need to pay homage."

Aakash spotted a bow tied to the back of one of the soldiers. Without hesitation, he challenged them. "I will bet that I can outdo your archer there. We will use his bow and you can choose your target."

The soldier smirked and motioned to Aakash that he accepted the challenge.

The Roman soldiers gathered around them, cackling with laughter. "No one is a better shot than Septius!" one of them exclaimed, mimicking a bow being shot. "He can shoot the eyeballs out of a snake from fifty yards away!" A chorus of jeers followed, and someone asked, "And what do we get if you lose?"

"A drachma for each of you," Ravi replied.

The soldier stood with his hands on his hips and a wide smirk on his lips as he turned to Septius. "Show these easterners what a Roman archer can do," he sneered, accompanying his words with an overly dramatic bow.

Septius held up a waxy, green fig leaf and twirled it between his fingers. "Place this as the bullseye on that tree over there," he instructed them. "Whoever lands closest to its center wins."

"Let us use two arrows each," Aakash proposed.

Septius squinted at the stranger. His face hardened into a

scowl. "One arrow isn't enough for you?" he asked, his voice deep and full of warning. "This will not be a competition."

Aakash had a defiant look in his eyes. "Our first arrow will be with our sight and our second arrow will be blindfolded."

The Romans looked at Aakash with amazement, wondering who would make such a bold challenge. Knowing that he couldn't lose face, the soldier replied, "Agreed."

Septius stood tall, his feet spread apart and firmly planted in the dirt. He held the string of the bow taut, eyes narrowed in concentration as he estimated the distance between him and the target. With a deep breath, he pulled back until the arrow tip almost touched his cheek. Then, he let go, watching with satisfaction as it flew directly to its mark.

"Blindfold me," Septius instructed.

Septius stood still as one of the soldiers tied a cloth blindfold securely around his eyes. With a steady hand, he reached back and carefully grabbed another arrow. His fingers brushing against the bow's smooth surface, he placed the arrow on its string. Slowly, he drew it back, his arm trembling ever so slightly as he adjusted his aim. Then, with a deep breath, he released. All watched breathlessly as the arrow flew off the mark and embedded itself in a tree branch one foot above the target.

Septius raised his eyebrows and grinned. He was pleased with his shot, knowing how unlikely it was that anyone could come as close.

Aakash stepped up to the line and Septius handed over his bow, crafted of dark cherry wood. He examined the two arrows carefully, running his fingers along their shafts and feeling for any slight curves that might affect accuracy. He notched an arrow on the bowstring and aimed at the target. Slowly inhaling, he pulled back further on the string, taking careful aim before releasing it in a smooth motion. The arrow soared through the air and split Septius's arrow at the center of the target.

"Blindfold please," Aakash declared. He closed his eyes as the fabric was tied around his head. He felt the soldier give him a firm tug, trying to move him off his target. Aakash repeated the words of the old saddhu in his mind: *To let the arrow fly, first pull back the bow.* Centering himself, being present with each muscle, and breathing deeply, he pulled the arrow back and released.

Dead center, splitting the second arrow in half.

Septius's mouth dropped open, and his eyes grew as wide as saucers. He shook his head in disbelief, unable to process the amazing skills of the man before him. "Great Mars," he gasped. "I never saw such skill."

Aakash stood relaxed, smiling. He bowed slightly to Septius, handed him the bow, and stepped away.

The lead soldier stepped forward with a stern expression. "You may go. The homage is paid." He motioned to let them pass.

Ravi hugged Aakash by the shoulders. Proud of his friend's accomplishment, he breathed a sigh of relief. They walked past the soldiers without further eye contact.

Herod's palace was a kaleidoscope of festive colors. Green ivy and holly draped the entrance way, its vibrant red berries standing out against the white stone walls. Inside, the white pillars and door frames were wrapped in purple ribbons. An undeniable air of celebration filled every corner of the palace.

"His Majesty, King Herod is awaiting you," a guard announced, gesturing stiffly at the door before them. "Proceed to the great room where you will be welcomed with refreshments."

Mezriani looked around the room with consternation. Romans, Jews, and Greeks all celebrated the festive Saturnalia. Scantily dressed young women walked around carrying silver platters of grapes, cheese cubes, and glasses of golden-hued wine. *Certainly not a Hanukkah celebration*, he thought.

A trumpeter, draped in gold-trimmed scarlet robes, lifted his brass instrument and blew a series of short triumphant notes. He finished with a loud commanding call: "All Arise, King Herod!"

Herod ambled into the great room holding the arm of a young girl dressed in a flimsy gauze toga, her voluptuous body showing through. An air of entitlement surrounding him, he leered at another young servant girl. He whispered something about her to an aide before turning his attention to his guests. "My friends, so glad you have joined our celebration. Come, tell me. What have you found about the birth child?"

Mezriani rose, speaking cautiously, "We have sent word throughout every corner of our kingdom, asking all midwives to watch for the maiden we seek. After weeks of searching, we have yet to identify her."

A scowl briefly flashed across Herod's countenance. "What has been the problem? Don't the stars tell you these things?" he seethed.

"The heavens have revealed to us the coming birth," Jaidev said with reverence, "though exactly who will bring this child into the world remains a mystery that we must endeavor to uncover."

The muscles around the crows-feet of Herod's eyes twitched. "I want answers, not excuses."

Jaidev shifted uncomfortably. "We may have to wait until the day and hour of our prediction to see what babies are born."

Herod caught himself and controlled his rising anger. He forced a strained smile as he spoke. "We are all looking forward to meeting the little one and showing our respect. I want you to come back and report when you have found him. All of Judea will honor his birth."

"Yes, it is a great honor for Judea," Jaidev replied, avoiding agreement with Herod's command to report back.

"Come, let's have some music and gaiety," Herod said.

A drape drew back to Herod's right. As musicians began playing songs that honored Saturnalia, dancers came forward, twirling and dancing to the music. Clapping and cheering erupted from the revelers upon recognizing the music and dance. Jaidev and his group joined in the celebration. After several songs, Jaidev arose and faced Herod. "Highness, my friends and I have prepared to play the music of our homeland."

"Well, let's hear it," Herod replied, sitting on his throne and motioning for them to proceed.

Ravi, Aakash, Jaidev, and Barbod came forward with their flutes, drum, and chang. Barbod unwrapped a bottle and bowed his head. He presented the ornate bottle, etched with intricate designs and inlaid with gold lettering. "Highness, please accept this bottle of the finest Persian wine, aged to perfection."

Herod, now reclining on a large chair draped with velvet, nodded as a rotund servant poured the ruby-red liquid into a goblet and placed it at his fingertips.

Ravi stepped forward, offering a bolt of the purest silk. Herod took it with a transfixed gaze, admiring the exquisite cloth. "You have done well to bring me this, young man. We love silk and this is the finest I have seen," Herod declared.

Jaidev cleared his throat and took a deep breath. "We are going to play some of our favorite melodies from our village," he announced, tapping out a steady beat with his hands. "To end the evening, we will perform a special song that has been passed down through generations. It's said to evoke positive energy and invoke the beauty of nature."

Herod rolled his eyes as Jaidev, Ravi, Aakash, and Barbod began performing the traditional Hindustani classics. He tilted his wine goblet in boredom, holding it with two fingers and barely lifting it to his lips before setting it back down again. His expression was vacant—almost sleepy.

"And this song is a special gift to his Highness." Jaidev began a chant and then picked up his flute, joined by Ravi's flute, Aakash on the drum, and Barbod softly strumming the chang. As the rhythm quickened and faded, Herod's eyes locked on the players. He seemed to be taken to another realm—one of peace, healing, and love. His scowl softened into alertness as he absorbed every sweet note of music. He closed his eyes, rocking gently to the melody. Gradually, his lips curled upward into a smile. When the song concluded, Herod clapped warmly in appreciation, prompting everyone else to join in.

"I have never heard such sweet music," Herod remarked, nodding in appreciation.

Jaidev's eyes were soft and worshipful as he spoke about the music. "Our ancient rishis gifted this music to us," he said, his voice hushed with reverence. "They heard its celestial vibrations emanating from the Song of Creation."

"Thank you for a wonderful performance," Herod expressed, to his own surprise.

As Jaidev and his group prepared to depart, Herod's eyes narrowed. He glanced at an aide standing beside him, who leaned in so Herod could speak quietly in his ear. Suspicion flashed briefly across the King's face as if he feared that the pleasant musical performance had been a ploy to lower his inhibitions.

"Do they think I'm stupid—that some sweet music will make me trust them? Continue to follow them secretly," he commanded the aide. "Let me know if they find that baby. If they do not report back to me, my prison awaits them. Follow them everywhere they go!"

As the group strolled down the cobbled street, Aakash scanned the area for any signs of danger. He caught a glimpse of Herod's men in the shadows behind, and his heart skipped a beat. "We have company," he whispered to Jaidev, nodding towards the two figures trailing them from a distance.

Jaidev's eyes darted behind him, trying to make out any sign of surveillance. "They are probably trailing us to see if we are going to mislead Herod." His brow furrowed in worry as he continued in a low and cautious voice. "Let them follow us—for now. When we find the birth child, we will have to find a way to keep them from reporting back to Herod."

The winter solstice brought not only longer days but also colder weather. "I am looking forward to sitting by the fire at the inn," Barbod remarked, rubbing his hands.

"We must press on," Jaidev insisted. "Three days remain till the maiden gives birth." Worry flickered in his eyes, but determination ran through his every word.

Many of the Jewish faithful from the surrounding area streamed into the temple for Hanukkah. Mezriani, still confident they would be led to the mother and child, said, "Shimon and I must stay here in Jerusalem to continue the search. I don't trust the Sadducees, Pharisees, and Sanhedrin with this quest. They do not understand the language of the stars like those of us who study the Kabbalah. Perhaps the rest of you should head out west to Emmaus for a day or two. Then, if the mother is still not found, head down south to Bethlehem, a village that is a few hours' travel."

Jaidev and Khartum exchanged a knowing glance. "It's settled then," Jaidev replied. "We'll leave in the morning after a sound rest. If our search is successful, we'll send word." With that, they prepared for bed, resting up for what was sure to be a trying few days.

"And tonight, a warm dinner," Barbod added, food always on his mind.

Later that evening, as Barbod lay his head, a meteor fell in the southern sky.

Barbod's eyes snapped open, and he jerked upright. A wavering chorus of voices sang in the darkness, but he couldn't make out any faces. Taking slow steps forward, Barbod swiped his hands in front of him, feeling for obstacles in the thick fog. He tried to speak, but his throat felt full of gravel. Peering into the fog, he could see a faint glow of a fire. When he got closer, the heat from the fire warmed his face and hands. In the center of the flames, a small baby with skin as golden as honey reached out toward him. A calm, steady voice emanated from the flames. "Fear not, Barbod, for you will bear witness to a great event."

An angel appeared before the crackling flames. Its eyes shone with a radiance that seemed to originate beyond the mortal realm. It extended a hand toward Barbod. "Your love of music is the perfect expression of the Song of Creation," it said in a soft but crystal-clear voice. "Your gift of harmony will bring peace and serenity to the newborn."

Ravi walked into the small bedroom and shook Barbod's shoulder gently, calling him by name. When this elicited no response, he grabbed his friend's foot, giving it a gentle but firm tug. Barbod jolted awake, and Ravi smiled down at him. "Come now, my friend. It is time to make our journey to Emmaus in the west."

"I'm coming," Barbod replied, stretching languidly. The visitation in the dream was all too real.

"Jaidev, can I talk with you?" Barbod asked, entering the kitchen.

"What is it? Barbod, you look pretty serene," Jaidev remarked.

"I had another dream about the baby. He was reaching to me from a fire, and an angel was nearby telling me I would play music for the boy," Barbod explained.

"These dreams can foretell our path. What direction were you looking when you saw the baby?" Jaidev asked.

"I could not tell. In front of me was the only direction I could tell," Barbod responded.

"If anything on our journey the next couple of days seems familiar to your dream, let me know," Jaidev instructed.

An hour later, the horses and camels were loaded with supplies and saddled for the journey westward to Emmaus. Jaidev, Ravi, Aakash, Barbod, Ghaffar, Khartum, and Akim departed in the cold morning air under a bright sky.

Barbod rode his camel next to Jaidev. "The angel in my dream said that my love of music was the Song of Creation made manifest.

How is this so?"

"The Song of Creation moves in vibrations as waves of love and bliss. It is these waves of love that become the music and harmony of the Song. For some, these vibrations will never be heard; for others, they will be heard during heightened awareness. For a few, they are ever present in the awareness and heard as the music and harmony that they are. It is because you know the Song of Creation in your heart that it can manifest through your love of music. There is only one Creator of all music, of all art, of all things. You are inseparable from the Song of Creation. Separateness is maya. When we look out into the world and see the sky, clouds, hills, trees, or road, we think it is out there. However, it is actually just the perception of the vibration in here," Jaidev explained, pointing to the space between Barbod's eyes. "That is an in-body experience. You see it through the mind, intellect, and ego when, in reality, there is also no Barbod in there. What you think is you is simply a vibration in your awareness. When you experience a state beyond the ego and mind in meditation, you are not in here. You are everywhere because the Song of Creation is everywhere, and you are the Song. The Song is 'avarnam,' meaning without attributes. All the notes, the attributes, are manifestations of the Song. And the quality of notes does not change the Song. The Song is contained within the notes and the silence the notes emerge from. The Song is all-pervading and never perishes. No unpleasant notes can diminish it, just as the Sun does not burn the sky."

"Yes, I have an idea of what you are describing, but it isn't crystal clear," Barbod replied.

"Just keep meditating and playing music, my friend," Jaidev affirmed.

At last, they entered Emmaus, a small village bustling with activity. Shops and homes intermingled along the street. Goats and chickens wandered about. The air was filled with the smell of dung mixed with the smell of fresh bread baking from a nearby bakery.

"Mezriani told us that Emmaus doesn't have a temple, but it does have a synagogue where the Hebrews worship," Khartum said, adjusting his headscarf to the chill. "Ghaffar and I will go there and ask if any maidens are about to give birth."

"I'll go to the market and ask around," Aakash declared.

"Speak with the elder women," Jaidev added.

Jaidev and the others continued searching for two days without any luck. As darkness fell on December 24th, he called the group together. "Tomorrow we must make our way to Bethlehem. Tonight, I invite each of you to join me in silence and meditation as the Maha Atma enters this world—an event that calls for a reverent acknowledgment from all."

At dusk, Jaidev looked at the sky. Jupiter and Saturn were in the southwest, joined by the Moon in Pisces. Mars was setting in the western sky in Aquarius. After lighting a lamp, he sat on his bed in the meditation posture, closed his eyes, and spent several minutes practicing pranayam, the breathing of a yogi. His mantra started as a clear pronunciation but soon became a faint idea. His heart rate and breathing settled into quietness and observation. He remained in awareness of the Self, in timelessness, for an undetermined amount of time. Jupiter, Saturn, and the Moon grew ever closer to the western sky—to the hour of the Maha Atma's birth.

At 10:50 pm, light filled his mind and awareness. A peace unlike anything he'd experienced before flushed through his body, and a loving presence became all-pervading. Jaidev sat absorbing this transcendent experience—not judging, not interpreting, just being one with it. Upon realizing his thoughts, his observation engaged his mind into activity, and, having been in meditation for a couple of hours, he slowly opened his eyes.

The Maha Atma was born—he was with mankind. Jaidev felt it clearly. The room seemed luminescent. Points of light emitted from every piece of furniture. A glow both within and without the window drew his attention. He stood and walked over to it, his transcendental vision open. In the western sky, Jupiter, Saturn, and the Moon were about to drop below the horizon. In the east, a normally dark sky seemed alive. He noticed this aliveness filled with the Song of Creation. The Song that was within him was everywhere. He did not end and did not begin—he was everywhere. Everywhere was within and without.

Jaidev stood in awe at the window of his room, mesmerized by the sight outside. The courtyard teemed with life—cows mooing, horses whinnying, chickens pecking, cats meowing, and dogs barking. All the animals faced south, their heads turned towards a magnificent golden light radiating from the horizon. A feeling of certainty suddenly washed over Jaidev as he whispered out loud, "South. We must go south tomorrow. Bethlehem is where we will find the Maha Atma. I am certain of it."

As Jaidev peered out, mesmerized, he noticed eyes glittering in the shadows. They peered back at him with an intensity that made his heart skip a beat.

Aakash wrapped his knuckles softly around the door as he called out. "Jaidev? Are you in there? Something is happening. Come look outside. All the animals from the courtyard are lined up and looking southwards. It is like they've gone into a trance. All the birds, owls, nightjars, swifts, and others have been migrating southward together."

Jaidev opened the door. "Yes, Aakash, I have seen them. We leave for Bethlehem at daybreak. We will find the baby there; I am sure of it. Sai Ram."

"Sai Ram," Aakash replied.

"Aakash, I could feel the hairs on my neck stand up as I peered out the window. A chill ran down my spine when I noticed two eyes staring back at me from among the trees, their gaze heavy and unwavering."

"Probably Herod's spies," Aakash muttered under his breath. His heart raced as he realized that as soon as they found the child, these men would run directly to Jerusalem and tell Herod where they found him. He had to think quickly. A plan coalesced in his mind.

Aakash laid out the plan for Jaidev. In the morning, they would begin to head further west to Joppa, not south to Bethlehem. He and Akim would then take care of Herod's spies on the road where no one would see them.

"That will delay us for several hours," Jaidev said.

"Yes, but we will be sure that we misdirect the spies, and they will tell Herod the wrong place to look," Aakash affirmed. "I can use some of Ravi's Nenufar. It causes the world to spin and weave and time is lost. I will intoxicate them with it, and they will take a day or two to recover. By then, we will be long gone and far away. They will think we went to Joppa and Herod will look for us there."

The next morning, Jaidev and the others started down the road to Joppa as planned. A couple of hours into their journey, once Emmaus was far out of sight, Aakash and Akim hid in some bushes, waiting for the spies to come up the road, as the others road ahead.

Soon enough, the spies came around the bend, and Aakash stepped out to confront them. Akim remained hidden in the bushes, his bow and arrow trained on them.

"Looks like you travel to Joppa?" Aakash asked in a disarming tone.

The spies narrowed their eyes at the stranger, recognizing him as one of Jaidev's companions. They shifted their weight uneasily. "Yes," one of them finally replied. "Joppa is several hours away."

"You have been following us for some time. Dismount. You go no further," Aakash commanded, looking them firmly in the eyes.

"There is but one of you and two of us. We think not," one of the spies replied.

"Look again," Aakash declared, placing an arrow in his bow as Akim stepped out from the bush behind them.

Hesitantly, the two dismounted.

"On the ground, hands behind your back," Aakash

commanded.

"Herod will kill you when he finds you," one of the spies threatened.

Aakash quickly tied their hands behind their backs and removed their knives and swords. "Over there, behind those bushes," he ordered them.

Once behind the bushes, Aakash commanded them to sit. He took out the bottle of Nenufar and held it to the nostrils of the bigger spy. "Breathe deeply," he instructed, holding a knife to his throat. After a few deep inhales of the Nenufar, the larger spy fell unconscious. Aakash held the Nenufar to the second spy's nose. Soon, they were both passed out, in deep oblivion to the world around them. Akim led the horses off the road to where Aakash sat with the unconscious spies.

"Akim, ride up and tell Jaidev to turn back towards Bethlehem while Herod's spies are asleep," Aakash said in a low tone so that the spies could not hear him even if they were awake.

Akim kicked his horse into a gallop, the sound of hooves echoing off the rocks and hills. The wind whipped his hair as he approached Jaidev's group, shouting, "Aakash has succeeded! The spies are out cold. We must make haste back to Bethlehem!"

The group turned in unison, hurrying back towards Aakash. Beneath ancient, gnarled olive trees, two limp figures lay motionless near him, the leaves of the low-lying shrubs masking their presence. "Go quickly now to Bethlehem," Aakash commanded. "I will stay here with these two for several hours. If they regain consciousness, I'll give them another dose of the Nenufar."

Aakash watched as the group sped away, leaving him alone with the spies. He kept a vigil beside them, watching for any signs of consciousness. Two hours later, one of the spy's chests rose and fell. Aakash quickly administered a dose of the Nenufar to keep him asleep. He waited with them for several hours until, finally, it was time to leave. He took the spies' sandals, secured their horses to his own, gave one final deep dose of the Nenufar, and spurred his horse towards Emmaus.

Hours later, the spies stirred again. Opening their eyes, their brains foggy and their heads aching, there was no trace of Aakash, their horses, or sandals. Confused and fearful of Herod's wrath, they stumbled barefoot towards Joppa in search of answers.

Aakash hurried to catch up with Jaidev and the others, the sun dipping closer to the horizon by the minute. As they reached the outskirts of Bethlehem, a chill descended on them despite the warmth of the evening.

At the first inn, they asked for rooms but were told it was full. Undaunted, they followed directions to a second inn down several blocks. An air of tired anticipation hung over them as they approached the innkeeper, only to be disappointed once more. "All the rooms are taken," the innkeeper informed.

Barbod looked around, sighing deeply. "We will have to set up camp outside of town tonight," he said. "There aren't any rooms left anywhere." He gestured toward a taverna in the distance. "Let's go back there and see if they can spare us a bite of dinner. Then we can decide what to do next."

The taverna was abuzz, every table filled with people chatting as the door opened. A bell jingled above it to announce the new arrivals, and an elderly woman behind the bar wiped her hands on a cloth. She shot them a tired but welcoming smile. "I'm afraid we've run out of dinner tonight if that is what you came in for. But take a seat and I'll see what else I can rustle up."

"We haven't eaten all day," Barbod said.

"There is cheese and bread, but nothing hot," the old woman replied.

"Cheese and bread will do," Barbod stated. "There are seven of us."

As the old woman hobbled in with a wooden tray of thickly sliced bread and crumbly cheese, Barbod looked around the crowded tavern. "What's going on here? Why is everyone coming into town?" he asked.

The old woman set down the tray and sighed as she wiped her brow. "Caesar Augustus has ordered a census—everyone must come into town to register for it."

Barbod leaned forward in anticipation. "Have you noticed any women who look heavily pregnant or are possibly about to give birth? Have you heard of anyone having a baby recently?" He surveyed the room, waiting for an answer.

"Not in here," the old woman laughed.

The group finished the last crumbs of the loaf of crusty bread and a chunk of sharp cheese and washed it down with warm wine. Then, they set out to the edge of Bethlehem, where they set up camp.

A chill wind whistled through the trees and Ravi pulled his coat tighter around himself. "It's cold tonight," he muttered under his breath, memories of the icy passes in the Hindu Kush mountains flashing through his mind. He shuddered as he recalled that bitter cold.

"Tomorrow, we will have better luck," Aakash declared, pulling a blanket around his shoulders and shutting his weary eyes.

In the morning, everyone gathered. "I have a good feeling about today," Jaidev said, his intuition guiding him. "Let's start in the bazaar and ask if any births have occurred recently."

After several unsuccessful hours, they stopped by an old well to refresh themselves. Two shepherds were filling their clay jugs with water. Barbod walked up to them. "We are searching for a newborn baby," he said. "Have you heard of a birth happening nearby?"

Jaidev could feel the shepherds' eyes sizing him up, assessing if he posed a threat to them. They were two powerful men with faces weathered from years of tending flocks and protecting them from predators. "We come to honor this newborn baby. Fear not," Jaidev reassured them.

The wrinkles around the corners of the older shepherd's eyes deepened as he spoke. "It was two nights ago that we discovered a special birth. The stable on the eastern edge of Bethlehem was humble yet dignified. Golden shafts of moonlight streaming through the open door drew us to look inside. We found a young woman in the hay, cradling a newborn baby boy in her arms as the father stood proudly beside her. The horses and cows huddled around them, providing warmth and protection from the bitter winter air. Even the beasts were aware of something special happening—something miraculous. There was a tangible peace that filled the stable."

Jaidev straightened up, his eyes intent. "Can you give us directions to this stable?"

The old shepherd leaned on his staff and squinted at a distant inn. "It is just behind there, across from a well surrounded by a fence full of bleating sheep. A few thousand steps should take you right to the location." He gestured down the dusty road with the tip of his staff.

"Thank you. We wish you peace, love, and mercy," Jaidev said excitedly.

"You as well," the shepherd replied.

As they neared the stable, Jaidev's mind flashed back to the words of the blind beggar many months ago. When they arrived, they found sheep grazing in the nearby fields and a few mules and cows inside the stable, but no sign of a mother, father, or baby. Jaidev surveyed the scene for a moment before saying, "This is where the babe was born. It appears they have moved on. Let's go ask the owners if they know where the parents went."

Barbod knocked on the weathered door of a small nearby cottage. After a few moments, an elderly woman opened the door and regarded him with suspicion. He cleared his throat and asked if there had been any recent births in the area.

The woman's face softened. "Yes, the most beautiful baby was born here two nights ago. The parents left looking for lodging while the mother recovered and the baby grew stronger."

"So, they are still in Bethlehem?" Jaidev asked.

She nodded; her eyebrows knit together as she chose her words. "They must have found a room somewhere. I hope it's warm and dry enough to keep them safe."

The group set out knocking on cottage doors and inquiring at every well and shop for news of the baby and parents. As it neared late afternoon, the group grew thirsty and tired. They agreed it was time to take a break and find something to eat and drink—before it got too late in the evening and the tavernas ran out of food again.

Jaidev, Ravi, Aakash, Barbod, Khartum, Akim, and Ghaffar rerouted their steps toward the center of town. As they passed a window, Jaidev heard it: the faint sound of a baby's laughter coming from the cottage. He immediately halted and glanced back at the door. His heart skipped a beat as he pointed towards the window and said, "Let's knock on one more door." The group followed him eagerly, hope coursing through their veins.

Jaidev knocked softly but clearly as the others stood back in anticipation. A young woman answered. She had a peaceful, serene demeanor and a glowing complexion. A tall, young man with broad shoulders, soft piercing eyes, and powerful arms and hands stood behind her. The room was aglow with soft light, and Jaidev was overcome with a quiet stillness that seemed to suspend time. Realizing he was at the right home, Jaidev's eyes met hers. They spoke to each other without words, the love in their eyes forming a deep connection. With a tear of joy in his eye, he murmured in awe, "Holy mother, we have seen the birth foretold in the heavens. All of Creation is singing at the birth of your son."

She stood there smiling, framed by the light, her dark hair cascading over her shoulders. The young man stood beside her with his hand resting on the small of her back. "Welcome to our home," she said softly. "I'm Mary, and this is my beloved Joseph. Two nights ago, we welcomed our firstborn son, Jesus, at a nearby stable." She gestured with her arms for them to come closer. "Come and see him.

He sleeps in the manger before us."

"We have come from afar to honor the birth of this Great Soul, delivered to mankind by God's grace. We have traveled for many months over a great distance to honor him," Jaidev declared, motioning to the others to come in.

"God has blessed us. You are welcome," Mary said, nodding her approval to Joseph.

As Jaidev and his group cautiously stepped into the room, a warm ray of sunlight beamed through the window onto the wooden manger, cradling a small baby. His chubby fingers reached up to them, and his laughter filled their hearts with love. The baby clasped his hands together in Sahasrara mudra, his fingertips pressed against each other and thumbs pointing skyward. Jaidev, stunned by the gesture, bowed and reverently knelt on one knee before the tiny being, followed by the rest of the group. In response, the baby humbly draped its hands over its heart in Namaskar mudra.

Overcome with emotion, Jaidev placed his hands near his heart and gazed at the baby. A feeling of ever-expanding love flowed from him to the baby and from the baby to him. He softly recited the Gayatri mantra. "Om Bhur Bhuvah Svah - Tat-savitur Varenyam - Bhargo Devasya Dheemahi - Dhiyo Yonah Prachodayat."

Joseph stepped forward, uncomfortable with the unfamiliar prayer. Jaidev's words were a low whisper in a chantlike rhythm. His eyes were closed, and an invisible energy seemed to emanate from him. Joseph hesitated before asking in an uncertain voice, "What does your prayer mean?"

"It means, 'We meditate on that most adored Supreme Lord, the Creator, whose effulgence illumines all realms. May this divine light illumine our intellect.'"

Joseph absorbed the words thoughtfully. Although foreign to his own prayers, he understood its meaning and nodded in appreciation. Mary watched lovingly, in awe at the mystery her child possessed that men from the furthest corners of the world would travel to his manger.

"We have brought some gifts for the child, if we may?" Jaidev said.

Mary gave a subtle nod of approval, and Jaidev reached into the folds of his cloak to reveal a ceramic jar filled with golden frankincense. He presented it to her with both hands and held her gaze as she slowly lifted the lid and breathed in the sweet, warm, woodsy aroma. She felt a warmth radiating from his eyes and whispered her gratitude.

Ravi slowly rose, pulled out a small cloth parcel from his tunic, and carefully unwrapped it in front of Mary. She gasped at the beautiful carvings along the sides of the box. As he opened the lid, a glimmering light emerged from within—gold coins, rings, and nuggets that shone with an inner fire. Mary's eyes widened with wonder, her mouth still agape as she turned to Joseph for approval. Joseph simply shook his head in awe. He had never owned gold before.

Aakash stepped forward and placed a small clay jar before Mary and Joseph. He carefully opened the lid, revealing a thick green ointment with a pleasant herbal smell. "It is Myrrh. My mother used this for treating babies' rashes. It has many medicinal uses that have been passed on through generations in our country," he said proudly.

With eyes glowing with gratitude, Mary took the small jar. She nodded and bowed to Aakash in appreciation. "You are very generous. Thank you," she said gracefully.

Khartum moved and knelt before the baby, guiding Akim to join him. He reached into his cloak and pulled out a small doll knotted from camel hair. He handed it to Akim to present to Mary. She smiled warmly at Akim and placed her hands over his to accept the gift, whispering, "God's grace upon you."

Ghaffar watched with awe, mesmerized by the peaceful, loving scene.

Barbod stood in the doorway, transfixed. Realizing he had

arrived empty-handed and feeling an overwhelming urge to give something, he stepped quietly outside. Inside the room, the baby cooed and clapped his tiny hands in delight.

A soft, beautiful sound, like a musical bouquet, started wafting through the window behind the baby. He turned his head and smiled widely, kicking his feet gleefully. Mary and Joseph looked out the window and saw Barbod playing the chang, its strings shimmering in the bright sunlight. With eyes prayerfully closed, his fingers danced around the strings with delicate precision. A melodious love song poured forth, filling the air with heavenly harmony, every note creating an invisible bridge between them. Tears streamed down Mary's face as Barbod delivered this heartfelt gift to their newborn son.

Jaidev whispered to Aakash that they needed to warn the family of Herod and his threat to the baby. Aakash nodded, got Joseph's attention, and walked him into a corner of the room. He quietly revealed to him Herod's intentions to find the boy, fearing the baby would pose a challenge to his throne. He told Joseph that they must go beyond Herod's reach as soon as possible, for Herod's spies would not be thrown off course for many days.

"God will protect us," Joseph said resolutely.

Suddenly, loud cracking and popping came from the fireplace. Joseph and Aakash stared hypnotically at the flames dancing wildly in the hearth. Within the flickering light, a vision of a vast desert and long stretches of dunes unfolded before them. They watched in awe as a figure with wings of golden light appeared within the flames, pointing its outstretched arm south and westwards. Without speaking, they both nodded in agreement, feeling a stirring inside that told them this was their destiny.

"Jaidev, Khartum, Akim, Ghaffar, and Ravi, join us. We must make plans," Aakash declared.

Joseph shook his head, his voice heavy with concern. "The baby is only a few days old. We can't possibly take him on a weeks-long journey through the desert."

"We can go east to Qumran. It is only a day's journey. The Essenes can help us," Jaidev assured. "Ghaffar's brother Basil is there. They have no love for the Romans or Herod."

Ghaffar nodded in agreement.

"Herod's spies will only be delayed by a few days. We must leave as soon as possible before he figures out where we are," Aakash urged.

"We should leave at daybreak tomorrow," Jaidev suggested. "We have two extra camels that you can ride."

"I'll leave right away and prepare my brother and the Essenes for your arrival," Ghaffar announced determinedly.

Barbod had an unwavering glint in his eyes as he spoke. "I'll stay with Joseph and Mary tonight to make sure they and the baby are safe." He placed a hand on his chest, determined to defend them from any harm.

Aakash stood with his arms protectively crossed, his voice firm. "I'll watch with you from outside. We will keep the baby safe," he promised.

Chapter 16 - Warnings and Escape

In the foggy night, the warm fire glowed even warmer as Barbod played sweet music for the baby.

Aakash woke everyone an hour before daybreak. "We must get ready for our day's journey. We leave in an hour," he announced. He also suggested that he and Akim ride before them as scouts.

"When we get to Qumran, I want to let Mezriani know where we are and what we have found," Jaidev said.

The group plodded along the sandy desert, each step leading them deeper into a thickening blanket of fog. Mary's heart swelled with gratitude as the impenetrable mist rolled in around them, granting protection from God. She whispered a prayer of thanks for their safe passage, knowing it shielded her son from any suspicious eyes spying on them from the hills or heights above.

As the afternoon sun bore down, the fog lifted, and a watchtower came into sight. "There, that is the watchtower of Qumran. It is a small settlement," Barbod declared.

Aakash and Akim rejoined the group as Barbod waved a blue flag. A small group rode out from the watchtower to meet them, and Jaidev recognized one of the riders as Ghaffar.

"I'm glad you made it safely," said Ghaffar as he greeted Jaidev, Mary, Joseph, and the baby.

"Is this the baby Herod seeks?" Ghaffar's brother Basil asked, stepping forward.

"Yes, and these are the Magi from the east I told you about, brother," Ghaffar replied. "They came seeking a special birth child foretold by the stars. They say the child is a Maha Atma—a Great Soul, a Savior, a Saoshyant."

"Come, let's return to Qumran and talk," Basil offered without hesitation.

Basil and Ghaffar led the group down the winding path into Qumran, the home of the Essenes religious sect. They entered through a stone archway, into a large open courtyard. Ghaffar pointed out the main meeting hall where they would be dining. Inside, white-robed figures huddled around simple wooden tables. Their voices were just above a whisper, sharing stories and muffled laughter over steaming bowls of stew. Ghaffar explained that since the Essenes had renounced all violence and warfare, Herod did not see them as a threat to his kingdom. He allowed them to exist without fear of reprisal.

"You are most gracious," Jaidev remarked. "We have traveled for many months from faraway eastern lands to find the baby the stars foretold. I am Jaidev; this is Aakash, Ravi, Barbod, Khartum, and his son Akim. We bring Joseph, Mary, and their baby Jesus with us. We are thankful to have met your brother Ghaffar and for his invitation to visit you."

Joseph's hand firmly gripped Mary's arm, his eyes scanning the horizon for any sign of danger. "We must find a place to hide," he whispered, his voice as soft as a prayer. "A place where Herod's wandering eyes cannot find us."

The wind rustled the leaves of the scant nearby trees, and dogs barked in the distance. Small rocky peaks rose from the ground like jagged teeth. Basil gestured to the sparse landscape around them—to one area in particular. "We have many caves around the area that one must know well to find. Our sect is not usually welcoming to outsiders, but Ghaffar vouches for you," he said, his voice echoing off the rocky walls. Basil glanced over his shoulder, looking at the others behind him before turning back and offering a smile. "Come, we will show you the way to the caves."

After a short walk along a barren path, Basil pointed grandly to the mouths of several caves, nestled into the rolling hills like small secrets. "You'll find shelter and comfort in these caves," he assured. "I can bring you food and drink shortly." The alcoves weren't visible from a distance; they seemed to appear only in close proximity.

They escorted Joseph and Mary to the first cave. Barbod kept them company. Ravi, Aakash, and Jaidev occupied the second cave, while Khartum and Akim settled into the smaller third cave nearby.

"We will tender your horses and camels while you are here," Ghaffar said. Then, Basil and Ghaffar took the horses and camels for water at a creek that flowed into the sea.

As night settled upon them, the sun faded over the desert they had just crossed. Basil, Ghaffar, and a small group of Essenes brought them food and wine.

"Come sit with me. I have many questions," Basil declared, motioning to Jaidev, Khartum, and the others.

"Ghaffar has told me that your group is called the Children of Light," Jaidev said, curious to hear more from Basil.

"Yes, we look at the Romans and their slavery as a force of darkness, of the evil one. We are known as the Sons of Light, who prepare for the spiritual warfare against this darkness," Basil explained, reluctant to reveal more.

"We also understand the nature of good and evil—of light and darkness. It is a natural understanding of the duality of manifest creation," Jaidev remarked.

"How does your understanding of the stars and the birth of this Maha Atma bring you so far from home?" Basil asked, gesturing to a faraway eastern home.

"Our Holy Book, The Gita, teaches us that whenever dharma is in decay and adharma flourishes, the Lord creates himself in order to re-establish dharma. We see in the stars that this conjunction of Jupiter and Saturn presents all the requirements for the birth of a

Maha Atma, a Great Soul, to restore dharma," Jaidev expounded.

"And our Holy Book, the Avesta, teaches us that a Saoshyant, a savior, will be born—our elders also say under the Jupiter-Saturn conjunction. Jupiter and Saturn are wandering stars that have a significant influence on the affairs of men," Khartum said, pointing at the conjunction in the sky.

"I heard a kabbalist, Rabbi Mezriani, tell also of the stars predicting the birth of a king to the house of David," Ghaffar added.

"Our brothers in Egypt, the Therapeutae, have spoken of a Being of Light, leading a revolution, transforming humanity back to righteousness—a Healer of the world," Basil stated.

"The stars tell us this baby will be a great healer, a hands-on healer. The ruler of the 3rd house, Mars, is in the sign of Aquarius, the 6th house, indicating this." Jaidev pointed to the birth chart he carried in his cloak.

"How do these houses and star placements give you information?" Basil asked.

"The stars that we see are not separate from us but are an extension of our physical bodies. The sign that is rising at birth is the first house and the other houses follow from there. Thus, the twelve zodiac signs define where each house falls. The house gives us information about different areas of life and how karmic life can unfold. In the complete view, our tradition understands there to be three bodies. The physical body is the outermost layer and manifests from the subtle body of the mind, intellect and ego. The subtle body manifests through the causal body made up of the Jiva, or individual soul, the collective soul and the One Universal Soul. So, ultimately, the Creation is a manifestation of the Universal soul, Brahman, the Totality," Jaidev explained.

Basil nodded and stroked his chin as he absorbed Jaidev's words. "We understand and teach that the physical body will be replaced by the celestial body as we ascend. It does this through purification of the physical body."

"Yes, as we evolve and our physical and subtle bodies are purified, the causal body that you refer to as the celestial body emerges," Jaidev explained. "To paraphrase our Katha Upanishad, 'The wise who realize the Self as the eternal, effulgent light within, transcend the cycle of birth and death'."

"I will have to ponder your description of this causal body," Basil replied, blinking his eyes as he considered the different approach to his knowledge.

"We also agree on life after death. You mentioned an ascension," Jaidev continued. "Let me suggest that the ascending body is really the causal body freed from maya, the illusion, of its physical incarnation. Our tradition describes it in many ways, just as creation itself takes on many wondrous forms. So, we use words, which are vibrations, to explain the vibrations of God into the universal creation. I hear it as the Song of Creation. We are the Song of Creation, expressed as a note. We are all the entire Song and the same Song—the silence that the Song emerges from is the silence we share with all."

Basil stared deeply into the campfire, its flickering light dancing on his face. "And you believe this child has come to awaken— to remember the light body, or causal body, as you call it?"

Jaidev watched Basil's eyes slowly move back and forth as he thought deeply. "Yes, we believe he has come to us so we can remember who we really are and what our dharma is."

"The mysteries of the Lord are revealed to each of us in our own fashion," Basil replied, not disputing Jaidev's words. "We have a community in Alexandria, Egypt. We can send the family there while the boy develops. Our Therapeutae will guide his development," Basil proclaimed.

Soft melodies began to emanate from the cave nearby that all could hear. Many of the Essenes gathered and sat quietly outside the cave to listen. Barbod was playing with his eyes closed in a trance like state. His music had a transcendent ethereal quality. Each note was a perfect complement to the one before, bringing the listener to deeper and deeper levels of peace and inner quietness. The flow was effortless. Some of the Essenes had tears welling in their eyes. Others sat with their eyes closed, hands on their hearts in communion with the artist. Mary and Joseph stood over the manger of the baby, who held his hands in a sign of blessing.

Jaidev looked at Basil, who stood enraptured by the sight and sounds before him. Never had he seen and heard such a spontaneous display of synchronicity and coherence. He shook his head in awestruck wonderment.

"What is this?" Basil grasped to explain his appreciation of the surreal scene.

"This is an expression of Bhakti Yoga, the Yoga of Devotion," Jaidev filled the void with his counsel. "Barbod has had an awakening in his heart, and it is showing in his music. We met Barbod when he worked for a caravan that took us across the desert from the east. He plays a rare Persian instrument called a chang. When our caravan leader died, Barbod took over as Kabir."

"God has anointed him to be an instrument for the babe," Basil declared.

"He is a good friend and companion—trustworthy, loyal, knowledgeable, and fun-loving. He enjoys being a provider, and his musical talent is unmatched," Jaidev said, summing up Barbod's personality.

Barbod opened his eyes and looked lovingly at the baby. Mary took the baby from his manger and offered him to Barbod to hold. Astonished, Barbod shirked away, appearing unsure and unworthy. Mary and Joseph smiled and nodded to Barbod that it was okay. With hesitation, he put his chang aside and cradled his arms in acceptance. Jesus cooed and giggled, placing his head on Barbod's shoulder as Barbod brought him closer. The baby closed his eyes and fell into a gentle sleep. Barbod delicately rocked and whispered to the baby. Mary put her hand on Barbod's back, leading him to a seat near the manger. Barbod closed his eyes for a while as the baby slept peacefully. Mary gently took the baby from Barbod's arms and placed him back in the manger.

Aakash and Ghaffar motioned for Barbod and Joseph to join them. "Basil said that the Essenes in Alexandria can protect Mary, Joseph, and Jesus. We must send them there as soon as possible, without them being noticed," Aakash informed.

"Traveling alone would raise eyebrows. If they can travel with a caravan, it will be less noticeable. We go back and forth with traders that move goods between Jerusalem and Alexandria. There is a caravan every couple of weeks. The journey to Cairo takes about 3 weeks and several more days to Alexandria," Ghaffar added.

"I can go with them and help. My life has been traveling with the caravans," Barbod suggested eagerly.

"Yes, Barbod will be the perfect companion. He can take care of all your needs on the journey," Aakash assured Joseph, adding, "It will be dangerous to return to Jerusalem with the baby to join a caravan."

Ghaffar responded, "We can travel to Hebron, about a day's journey south, and meet a caravan there."

Barbod stood with determination and took a deep breath. He glanced to the south—the direction of the caravan—and said, "I will meet with the caravan's Kabir and secure passage for Joseph, Mary, and myself."

Joseph looked over at Mary, who held their newborn infant. Her serene countenance comforted everyone. He said gently, "We can leave as soon as you're both ready."

"When you leave, I will return to Jerusalem and let Mezriani know what has occurred," Ghaffar stated.

Basil's hand raised, commanding attention. "The Romans occupy Hebron on the road to Egypt," he announced with a heavy sigh. "Herod may have sent word out about the baby." He paused before speaking again, his eyes alight with determination. "I know a back road that the Romans won't be watching. If Barbod makes arrangements for Mary, Joseph, and the baby to join the caravan, we can meet up with them on the road after Hebron, before they enter the desert to Cairo. This will keep them safe and out of Herod's sight."

"The stars favor this journey. I see a favorable muhurta to begin travel in a couple of days," Jaidev said with his eyes closed, scanning his inner sky.

A few days later, the group made its way to Hebron. Barbod, Jaidev, Ravi, Khartum, and Akim entered the city, passing an outpost of Roman soldiers who watched the group warily. They continued into the city without being challenged.

Basil led Ghaffar, Joseph, Mary, and the baby along a back road that took them around Hebron. Aakash stayed with them, offering his protection should it be needed.

The narrow streets of old Hebron were alive with negotiating and shouting, as traders from various lands mingled in a vibrant cacophony. Barbod passed tables piled high with spices and herbs, colorful fabrics, exotic jewelry, and handcrafted sculptures. He paused, watching an Egyptian trader haggle with a Greek, the ancient accents of their respective homelands flowing freely through the air. Something about the Egyptian man struck him as familiar.

Barbod squinted his eyes and leaned in close, scrutinizing the face of the haggler. Wrinkles had formed around his eyes and mouth and age had stolen the pigment from his hair, leaving it snowy white. "Tell me," Barbod said, "are you Sadiki, who traveled with Nasir many years ago?"

The haggler looked up and studied Barbod's face, waiting for his mind to recognize the inquisitor. Suddenly, a smile dawned on Sadiki's face. "I remember you. You were in Nasir's caravan. How is that old camel driver?"

Barbod's head hung low, his voice cracking slightly with sorrow. "Sadly, Nasir passed away on our journey from the east. We disbanded the caravan in Damascus. I've been with him for so long, and his absence leaves a large hole in my heart."

Sadiki's eyes lowered, then twinkled with nostalgia as he recalled the time they spent together in the desert. "You were always a great cameleer," he declared. "I remember hearing you play your music at night, filling the air between the dunes."

Barbod clasped his hands, a look of relief on his face. "It is good to see that you are still doing well," he said. He leaned in closer, asking, "Can you tell me who is running a caravan between Hebron, Cairo, and Alexandria?"

"There is a caravan leaving in two days, which I will be traveling with. Omari runs it. You can find him at the north end of the bazaar where they sell papyrus scrolls," Sadiki informed. "You will know him when you see a robed man wearing the amulet of the Eye of Horus. Tell him I sent you over."

The papyrus sellers were a select group of caravan travelers. Papyrus, a delicately woven material imported from Egypt, was sold by vendors known for their intricately painted carriages. They reserved the papyrus for a discerning clientele—a luxury for those in the upper echelons of society.

Barbod strode through the bustling market, weaving between vendors and customers. He soon reached the northern section, where the papyrus sellers set up shop. Many traders in the market were distinctively dressed, with colorful beads and bangles adorning their outfits. Omari stood out amidst his peers, adorned by an Eye of Horus necklace that glinted in the sunlight.

"Omari," Barbod uttered as he approached him. "I'm looking for you—you're the caravan leader, correct?"

Omari ran a shrewd eye over Barbod, his lips upturned in an insolent smile. "You have found me, friend. Can I interest you in some of the finest papyrus on this side of the Nile?" His hands made fluid gestures as he spoke.

"Sadiki sent me over to you. I'm looking for passage for me, my friends, and a family to Cairo and Alexandria," Barbod said.

Omari stroked the necklace as he studied Barbod. "Do you have your own camels, donkeys, and horses, or will we be supplying them?" Omari asked.

Barbod spoke directly and matter-of-factly. "We have five camels and three horses that will be traveling to Cairo. I have worked on caravans my whole life and was the Kabir for a short time on my last one. I know the desert well," he continued. "Sadiki and I met on a caravan from east to west many years ago."

Omari laughed lightly, saying, "I won't hold that against you. We leave in two days at dawn; there are only a few of us in this caravan." He gestured with his hands to illustrate its small size.

"Thank you," Barbod replied, bowing in appreciation. "We will be ready."

Jaidev, Ravi, and Barbod busily bought supplies for their upcoming journey. The night before their departure, Barbod found Sadiki sitting under an open tent. "Old friend, join us for dinner."

Sidiki squinted, recognizing Barbod's voice. "It would be an honor," he accepted.

A few hours later, at dinner, Barbod lifted a clay jug of blood-red wine and poured a cup for Sadiki. His dark eyes shimmered in the fire's light as he asked Sadiki a question, keen for his response. "Tell me, have you seen any Romans or troops of Herod in Hebron?"

"Yes, more than usual," Sadiki replied. "They are looking for someone. The city is thick with rumors and speculation. They say the rebels have found a new king to overthrow Herod."

"So, they are looking for a king?" Barbod probed.

"It is all very mysterious," Sadiki remarked, pausing to sip his wine. "Some rumors say a king, others say a boy king. We don't ask questions. We go about our business and don't draw attention. It's safer to not get involved."

Barbod glanced at his companion and said, "We pass through many lands, you and me, and we see many things. It is better to keep your eyes and ears about you and keep what you see to yourself."

Sadiki nodded his head in approval. "Well spoken. I shall turn in now. The hour is late for an old man. I'll see you tomorrow at sunrise on the south side of Hebron, where the traders gather their camels and carts for the journey."

The morning was gray, a chilling mist filtering through the city. As the caravan formed, Omari checked on everyone. "Four camels in your group are missing," Omari barked at Barbod, frowning.

Barbod explained that they were with the Essenes and would meet the caravan at the crossroads just outside of Hebron.

Omari's scowl lightened. "The Essenes are a gentle people devoted to their beliefs. They always carry themselves with grace and poise, never causing any disturbance."

The caravan snaked its way out of Hebron, the camels shuffling their feet methodically down the road. Roman guards huddled by their campfire to keep warm as they watched the caravan suspiciously. A thick fog was descending, making it difficult to see more than a few feet ahead.

"Tie the animals together," Omari shouted, his voice muffled by the eerie mist.

As they crested a hilltop, the fog lightened. The crossroads appeared below them, where a procession of cloaked figures atop horses and camels waited. Basil, Ghaffar, Aakash, Joseph, and Mary waited patiently to join the caravan, as planned.

Omari gestured for the caravan to stop. "We will rest here briefly while our new guests join the caravan," he shouted.

Barbod beamed as he saw Mary and Joseph, Joseph cradling the baby Jesus in a sling that fit over his shoulders. With eyes full and voice thick with joy, Barbod said, "Mary and Joseph, tether your camels to my Bellows, the strongest and most reliable camel you'll find. She will lead us through this hazy mist." He stroked Bellows's long neck.

Basil and Ghaffar bid their farewells to the group, wishing them a safe journey. "Ghaffar," Jaidev said firmly, "carry this news to

Mezriani in Jerusalem."

"It will be done," Ghaffar assured.

As the caravan resumed its slow trek forward, the fog thickened. Soft wisps of fragrance and angelic wings enshrouded them in a protective haze. Baby Jesus looked wide-eyed and pleased at the rolling vaporous clouds. Barbod softly hummed a melodic prayer to Ahura Mazda for protection and comfort.

"I have not heard that before," Mary told Barbod.

"It's a hymn from ages past that my mother used to sing to me as a child. She called it Ardas and believed that its healing rhythms had the power to soothe even the most troubled of souls. It was her voice that first instilled in me a love for music," Barbod recounted.

Mary seemed to glow, saying, "Your mother was very devoted to you—I can tell."

"Yes," he replied wistfully. "I never had a child of my own, though if I did, I would teach him music. Jaidev has shown me that music is the very Song of Creation." A look of awe and reverence illuminated his face.

Baby Jesus kicked and flustered gleefully at Barbod's words.

"We are fortunate to have your help and comforting music with us on our journey," Joseph expressed.

"When we camp tonight, I have some new music I've been inspired to share with you," Barbod replied.

"We won't make it to Beersheba before nightfall. The fog is slowing us down," Omari announced.

To all within earshot, Aakash declared, "I'm grateful for this fog. It is shielding us from Herod's spies."

Jaidev's eyes blazed, his voice rising as he spoke. "Herod is lost in Rahu's dark illusion of power! Blinded by his pride, he cannot see his own mortality. The fog of illusion that clouds his vision and keeps him from the light is clouding his vision from finding us."

"Our desire is to be guided by the light of God, our Father, the Creator," Joseph proclaimed.

"It was the light of God that guided us to you and the infant," Jaidev affirmed.

As the afternoon sun faded, the fog "lifted enough to reveal the nearby landscape. Omari glanced around, declaring, "This looks like as good a spot as any. We'll make camp here and then tomorrow we can make our way through Beersheba and out into the desert." His voice was firm and vibrant in the still air.

The warmth of the campfires were a welcome respite from the biting night air. Barbod sat cross-legged, his fingers coaxing beautiful melodies from the chang. Despite the cold, he played on, his fingertips numb but his spirit warm. Mary cradled her sleeping baby, swaying gently to the music. When the last notes faded into silence, Barbod rose and made his way over to Jaidev and Aakash, settling in by their fire with a contented sigh.

Hesitantly, Barbod spoke. "We've been through much together. And there's still Beersheba to cross and the desert itself before we reach Cairo."

Jaidev spoke quietly, his voice barely reaching his friends around the campfire. "We have welcomed the Maha Atma into the world as we set out to do. We will tell of this for generations to come. It is time for us to plan our journey home."

A solemn silence fell over them, punctuated only by an occasional sniffle and the crackling fire.

Barbod broke the silence, his eyes firmly set as he gestured slowly. "You may travel by ship, down the Red Sea to India. It would be much faster than going back through the desert, and you would avoid coming back under Herod's searching gaze. The ships are getting larger and faster every day."

Omari, overhearing the word ship, leaned in to join the conversation, drawing attention by clearing his throat loudly. "There is a ship called 'Asteri', captained by a Greek named Gregori, that sails from the port at Myos Hormos on the western shore. I've heard that he takes a direct route down the Red Sea and ends his voyage in

India."

Jaidev nodded in appreciation for the advice. He said that when the time was right, he, Aakash, Ravi, Khartum, and Akim, with their horses, would be on their way to Myos Hormos.

The next morning, a thickening fog once again draped the landscape as the caravan approached Beersheba. Instead of the usual damp chill, this fog had a comforting warmth, surrounding them like a soft blanket. The camels walked slowly and silently across the village, and no one in the caravan spoke. Barbod kept vigilant watch over Mary, Joseph, and the baby. When they reached the south side of Beersheba, the fog gradually lifted. Barbod reflected on how it felt like angels descending from heaven to shroud them from prying eyes.

"Our almighty Father was watching over us and keeping us safe," Joseph declared, "for our baby has a great purpose to fulfill."

Barbod radiated with a newfound joy and his body felt alive from within. A luminescent aura surrounded him that Jaidev could not help but notice. "You have found the path of Bhakti Yoga, my friend," Jaidev expressed warmly. "It is this dharma that will take you closer to God."

Barbod gave Jaidev an inquisitive look. "I don't know about this dharma," he intoned, "but I do feel a strange calm presence— almost as if I am watching my body. What are these Yogas you speak of?"

Jaidev held up four fingers. "There are four primary paths to knowing God as our tradition reveals," he said, slowly enunciating each word. "The path of devotion, the path of the heart, is the path of Bhakti Yoga," he explained, counting on his first finger.

Barbod thought of all the campfire conversations he had listened to over the years—all the arguments and debates about God, and all the Holy books quoted and referenced. None of it spoke to his heart. "I always tried to understand God through my mind, and I couldn't find Him. Now I feel I don't need to find God, for God is impossible to avoid. He dwells in my heart. This child, the Maha Atma, has captured my heart."

Jaidev nodded in agreement and held up his second finger. "Looking for and finding God through knowledge that is processed by the intellect is possible for some. Coming into union with the divine through knowledge is called Jnana Yoga. It is the way my father and forefathers taught our family. That is why we are Brahmin. We study the scriptures and find God within them. It is this study that led us on our quest to find the Maha Atma."

Barbod nodded, absorbing Jaidev's point. "What about the other two ways to know God?"

"Our friends Ravi and Aakash embody the other two ways. Ravi is a Karma Yogi, which is a man of action, so he will know God when he decides to seek God through action. Most men are Karma Yogis, whether they know it or not," Jaidev explained, holding up a third finger and finally a fourth. "Our friend Aakash is on the Royal path, or Raj Yoga. He is bringing the path of meditation and the path of action into one. It is the Yoga that great yogis have followed for generations."

Barbod seemed perplexed, asking, "And what about the child? What is his Yoga?"

Jaidev closed his eyes. An ancient guru emerged within him. Save for the sound of his breath, his body was still. After a moment, he opened his eyes and declared, "A Maha Atma is Yoga. Yoga means Union with the Divine. The Maha Atma is the Divine in Union with the Divine."

Barbod was stunned. The words filled him with an unexpected lightness, his inner knowing nodding in agreement. "I look at him as a helpless baby and wonder what he will bring to mankind," Barbod expressed.

Joseph, listening quietly nearby, turned to Barbod with a pensive expression, his forehead creased in deep thought. "I, too, have wondered the same. I can hardly fathom the glory of the Lord, yet I feel comforted knowing that Jesus brings peace and understanding to those in His presence. I believe He will bring His Word to the entire world, though it is something I cannot yet see or understand."

Mary looked down at the little boy in her arms, peaceful in his sleep. She could feel the love emanating from him and knew it was a sign that all their struggles would soon be gone. Tears of joy and understanding glistened in her eyes as she whispered, "This child will show us how to love. For it is through the love within us all that the clouds will pass from sight."

Jaidev clasped his hands over his heart, bowing slightly. "All glory to the Divine Teacher."

Chapter 17 - Parting

As the group proceeded through the arid expanse of sand towards Cairo, a tranquil hush accompanied them. Beneath the watchful eye of the sun, they strolled in contemplation, while the moon quietly absorbed their conversations on God and the mysteries of creation.

Joseph looked out over the horizon and saw the same desert landscape that their ancestors traversed centuries ago. He remembered stories of a tyrant Pharaoh who enslaved his people until Moses delivered them safely across this desert to the Promised Land. He shook his head in wonder at the irony. Here they were, crossing back into Egypt to escape yet another oppressor. "It's a strange path," he muttered.

Jaidev responded in a low voice, stroking his chin. "The path of karma is unfathomable, our teachings record." He paused and, with a hint of sadness, added, "We will part with your company in a few days and head back to our land."

Joseph restrained his emotion as he addressed the Magi before him. His eyes were bright and full of gratitude. "The gifts you have brought to us we will cherish in our hearts forever," he expressed, his voice growing stronger with each word.

"The gifts are a small token of our honor to be with you, and to be in the presence of your son. Our dearest friend, Barbod, wishes to stay with you. It is with some sorrow that we leave him and you," Jaidev replied, adding, "Perhaps you will see fit to visit our land someday and have your son spend time with us. Barbod knows where our village is and how to find us. The stars favor long trips for your son."

"God willing," Joseph said.

As the caravan drew closer to Cairo, so did the day of separation. Each night, Barbod played sweet songs on the chang, creating new melodies inspired by the baby's presence. Time seemed but a fleeting memory as he strummed each new chord.

A smile spread across Aakash's face as he closed his eyes and swayed to the enchanting sounds. "Your music is like a balm to my soul," he told Barbod, with deep appreciation in his voice.

Barbod stopped playing for a moment. He closed his eyes and let out a calming exhale as he explained, "I can see it all so much clearer in my mind. The music, the baby—they come to me in my dreams, during meditation, and in my daily thoughts. When I'm playing, everything just flows together so effortlessly."

"The Song of Creation manifests effortlessly," Jaidev counseled.

"I can feel that effortlessness when this new music flows through me." Barbod nodded to Jaidev.

"Just as a thought arises effortlessly, the creativity of the Song of Creation arises effortlessly," Jaidev added.

"Yesterday seems like a dream, for today I am awake," Barbod remarked, his eyes squinting with joy.

Joseph came and sat with Barbod and Jaidev, a knowing kinship growing between them. "Your son will have great powers. He will be in command of what our tradition calls Siddhis," Jaidev told Joseph.

"What are Siddhis?" Barbod asked.

"Our tradition shows that those who realize the Song of Creation can tap into it at its most fundamental expression and, with intention, bring the unboundedness of the Song into the manifestation of certain powers. These powers are natural for the realized, although most men view them as supernatural," Jaidev explained.

"Can you give an example?" Joseph asked, his curiosity aroused.

"Yes, some of the natural Siddhis are the ability to view remotely and the ability to walk through something that appears solid, like a wall. There's also the ability to know another's thoughts, to walk on water, to levitate, and to possess a deep, profound intuition. The great saints from our tradition and many others have recorded these abilities," Jaidev said.

"I was hoping the ability to create glorious music was one," Barbod grinned.

Jaidev smiled at Barbod, as if guarding some secret knowledge. "That, my friend, is your special gift. Your Siddhi is the ability to communicate through music. There are dark forces that seek such gifts, or special powers, hoping to use them for their own egoic needs. Most men struggle to access these unique powers, but they are possible for an adept yogi. The Maha Atma is born already possessing these abilities and does not need to search for them. The Maha Atma also can heal illnesses in those afflicted. We can see this power in his astrological chart."

"We have been told that a shepherd was cured of an affliction to his ear after visiting us," Joseph mused.

"When the Song of Creation is heard clearly—when its vibrations are undistorted—it can retune an afflicted note and bring it back into resonance. This is how healing occurs. Just being in the child's presence has a healing effect," Jaidev concluded.

"I don't think I have heard our Rabbis speak of the Song of Creation, as you explain it," Joseph expressed.

Jaidev's eyes shone with profound understanding as he spoke. "The Song of Creation fills the entire universe," he stated, gesturing to the night sky above them. "It exists in every religion and culture. It is an ancient truth that unites us all, for both the Word and the Song express on the silent field of unboundedness. The Song of Creation and the Word of Creation are One."

"I am a carpenter, not a Rabbi and scholar," Joseph said stoically. "I simply hear your words as truth."

With awe in his voice, Jaidev continued. "Just as you can see unlimited things from a tree, such as a bench, chair, child's toy, box, cart, door, and so on, the Song of Creation can express unlimited Songs into manifest Creation. So, it is also with Barbod and his ability to create unlimited songs and music."

Joseph smiled warmly at Jaidev, nodding and absorbing his words.

"Please come to visit me in our land when the child is older. There is much to share with you and him, and much to learn as well," Jaidev implored.

"God willing," Joseph said again.

The last days together passed quickly. The caravan made its last camp about a day's travel outside Cairo. When the horses and camels were settled, dinner prepared and eaten, everyone gathered around the campfire. Barbod played his chang softly near the tent where Mary and Jesus were staying. Jaidev and Aakash meditated quietly nearby. As he came out of meditation, Jaidev chanted in a low voice.

"What is he chanting?" Joseph asked Aakash.

"Mantric prayers—a yagya to bring protection to you and your family," Aakash replied.

"God will protect us," Joseph said.

"Yes, the prayers are to harmonize the protection of God," Aakash affirmed.

On the final night, Omari drew a map on the ground showing the route to Myos Hormos. "Tomorrow, you will part with the caravan and make your way south to the port of Myos Hormos," he advised.

"Yes, it looks like the road is well-marked," Aakash responded.

"You won't have any trouble finding it. The port is becoming a major trade route from the east," Omari assured.

"Our last night together, with Barbod, Mary, Joseph, and the baby is one to be treasured forever," Jaidev said with quiet affection.

Ravi, normally stoic and distant, surprised everyone by squeezing Barbod's shoulders gently. "Barbod, you have become our brother," he declared, his voice warm and sincere.

"And you, mine," Barbod agreed. "My hope is to someday go back to India and be reunited with you."

"You have your path for now," Ravi said with reverence. "Serve the Maha Atma, Mary, and Joseph with all your heart."

"I must. It is my deepest desire," Barbod gushed.

"Come, let's play our music together, one last night," Aakash suggested, breaking the spell of sorrow and taking out his drum.

Barbod strummed the chang, accompanied by Aakash's drum. Ravi and Jaidev joined in the vibrant melodies with their flutes, all playing in perfect harmony. Mary and Joseph watched raptly nearby, Mary cradling their baby. As the music reached its crescendo, the baby waved his arms up towards the night sky. The stars sparkled brightly between the clouds and wondrous shapes formed—angelic dancers spinning around with arms extended as if to take hold of the music and whirl into the air.

Aakash looked awestruck. "It appears the music has awakened the celestial harmony."

"The Maha Atma awakens the celestial harmony. We are just able to witness it," Jaidev said.

"It is a wondrous sight to behold," Khartum remarked, mesmerized by the music and celestial display.

In a motherly tone, Mary softly added, "It is a perfect melody to take to our dreams. Tomorrow will be here soon enough."

The next morning, the sun shone in a cloudless sky as Jaidev packed his horse for the journey. He took his time, cherishing his last moments by the newborn's side. He had grown close to Barbod and was reluctant to leave him behind.

Aakash hefted the last pack onto Ojas. "I'm all packed," he said, nodding toward Ravi, who adjusted the straps of a large woven bag on Tejomaya. Aakash took in a deep breath and exhaled slowly. "When you're ready, we can go over to Mary and Joseph and say our goodbyes."

"Yes, I am ready. Let's go now," Jaidev replied.

Mary tenderly rocked the swaddled baby in her arms, humming a gentle lullaby while Joseph and Barbod bustled about. They loaded the camels securely, tying everything down.

"We come to say farewell," Jaidev announced, Ravi and Aakash standing with him.

Joseph and Barbod stopped packing and joined the group.

Barbod's eyes glistened, the corners of his mouth tugging downward as he looked at each of his friends. "It pains me to say this, for we have been together so long," he began, his voice quivering with emotion. "But I fear our journey together has come to its end."

With a smile full of appreciation for his friend that he could not suppress, Jaidev said, "We could not have made this journey without you. You are truly a blessing from God to us. I pray we will have many more opportunities to share music, laughter, and companionship with you."

"You have become like a brother," Aakash told Barbod, as Ravi put his hand on Barbod's shoulder.

Emotion filled Barbod's eyes as he spoke. "Our meeting has been a great treasure to me, my brothers. I will never forget you and hope that fate brings us together again." He hugged each of them tightly, then stepped away with a smile.

Jaidev held out his hand to Joseph, who shook it warmly and pulled him into an embrace. He moved from Jaidev to Ravi, Aakash, Khartum, and Akim. One by one, he gave each of them a firm handshake, followed by a tight hug in appreciation.

Mary stepped forward with the infant in her arms. Jaidev

bowed his head in reverence as the baby reached his small hands out towards him. Ravi, Aakash, Khartum, and Akim each knelt down and were blessed by Mary with a gentle touch from the baby's tiny fingers. As they rose to their feet, a profound stillness descended over the group.

Barbod joined the group for one last embrace and farewell. With eyes full of love, Barbod gazed at Jaidev and whispered, "I hear it; I hear the Song of Creation emerging from the stillness. It is everywhere and everything."

"Namaste," Jaidev replied simply with a slight bow, acknowledging the Oneness in Barbod.

Barbod's eyes brimmed with joyful tears as the five friends turned, mounted their horses and camels, and ambled down the road. When they reached a bend, Barbod gave one last wave.

"God is with them," Joseph whispered comfortingly as he grasped Barbod's shoulder.

With a nod, Barbod said, "Come, let's finish packing."

Chapter 18 - The Journey Home

The road unfolded before them over hills sparsely dotted with brush, bushes, olive trees, and grassland. No one sought to break the silence pervading the air. As long as they remained silent, the presence of the Maha Atma felt close.

Eventually, Ravi asked Jaidev a question. "What is the purpose of the Maha Atma? I have heard you state our teachings and say it is to reestablish dharma, but how does he do this?"

Jaidev thoughtfully replied, "You have asked a very insightful question. Our shared dharma as men is to know that the deepest part of ourselves is unchanging and eternal. The Maha Atma will bring this knowledge of eternal life to men. This knowledge weaves all mankind together. It is the foundation of all religions and men."

"And how will the Maha Atma bring this knowledge to men?" Ravi asked.

"The Maha Atma will reawaken the deep love that resides in the hearts of all. This love springs from the fullness of the Divine. He will teach men that to follow him is to open their hearts to love. It is the greatest siddhi of all—to have unconditional, unbounded love for all men and women."

Ravi listened to Jaidev's words with reverence and contemplation.

After another long break of riding in silence, Akim spoke next. "I have never been on a boat before."

"I have traveled by boat in my youth—when I traveled with

the caravan. It was unnerving at first—the unsteadiness underfoot, the rocking and pitching with the waves. It takes some time to adjust," Khartum replied.

Ravi joined in excitedly. "We have purchased many goods from the new trading routes the boats traverse. It will be good to see if I can establish a regular trade with different ships and maritime traders." His eyes widened as he thought of the potential for the family business.

"We can sell our camels at the port and buy new camels or horses at our destination," Khartum suggested.

"I couldn't bring myself to part with these horses," Ravi said, fondly stroking Tejomaya's mane. "They've been our faithful companions for quite some time."

After several days, the port of Myos Hormos came into view. The sky was gray and cold, but the warmth of spring peeking through made them realize their journey was nearly over. A group of travelers coming from the port passed by.

"Are you coming from the ships at Myos Hormos?" Aakash asked.

"Yes, we bring spices from the port to Cairo," the traveler replied.

Ravi, always thinking of new trading routes for the family business, asked, "Where are the spices from?"

"India. They are in high demand in Cairo, Jerusalem, Damascus, Rome, and Greece," the traveler said.

"How much further to the port?" Khartum asked.

"A little over a day's travel. You should be there by tomorrow afternoon."

Jaidev squinted as the port of Myos Hormos appeared on the horizon. The faint smell of salt grew stronger with every passing moment, each breath a new mixture of saltiness and cool air. "I have never smelled air like this," Jaidev remarked, eyes wide with wonder.

Ravi inhaled deeply, the salty air overwhelming his senses. "I have heard the travelers at my father's house describe this smell of the sea, though it is much stronger than I expected!" he exclaimed.

"I can taste the air. It is so refreshing," Aakash added.

As they crested the top of a grassy hill, the group halted, awestruck at the endless expanse of sea before them. A ship sailed in the distance, its sails unfurled and billowing in the wind. A port with busy tavernas, shops, and winding streets stretched out along the shoreline, smoke wisping out from the chimneys into the sky.

"We are just a few hours from Myos Hormos," Aakash declared, pointing to the port.

The cry of seagulls proclaiming their arrival at the port echoed off the docks. As they stepped out into the late afternoon sun, a cold misty breeze cut through them like a knife, the damp air causing their skin to prickle with goosebumps.

"Where can we find the 'Asteri'?" Aakash asked a passing sailor.

"She docked this morning. You can find her at the south side of the port," he replied.

"And food and shelter?" Aakash asked.

The sailor laughed and replied, "The Seawitch Inn is where you can find food, drinks, and probably Gregori, the Asteri's captain. If you're looking for a place to stay, most of the houses will put you up. Just turn left at this junction and the Seawitch is right there."

"How will we know Gregori?" Aakash questioned.

"Gregori is the tall one with golden hair."

"Golden hair? This I have to see," Ravi remarked.

As they entered the Seawitch, Gregori was unmistakable— even from across the room. His broad smile and bright blue eyes were almost impossible to miss. His long blonde hair was tied in a knot at the back of his head. Positioned in the corner of the room, he had a drink in hand and his back firmly against the wall.

Aakash and Ravi casually approached him while the others waited behind. "You must be Gregori, the Captain of the Asteri,"

Aakash declared.

"Aye, the finest ship in these parts," Gregori answered.

"We seek passage for five of us and three horses to India," Aakash informed.

"You are a long way from home," Gregori said, sizing up Aakash as Indian.

"Yes, we have been on a long journey, and it is time to return," Aakash replied.

"Three days hence, when we set sail, I shall have a berth reserved for you for a few drachmas in advance. The voyage shall be long and arduous, spanning a month at sea," he announced, his voice full of salt and promise.

"I would like to meet some of your traders," Ravi said, his tone suggesting a request. "I am interested in a new trade route for my family's business."

Gregori took a deep breath, looking at Ravi and his friends. He gestured towards the ship, pursing his lips while nodding and taking a deep swig from his cup. "Aye, come by the ship tomorrow," he said. "At the Indian port, their purveyors wait for us to bring them goods; then we load the ship with Indian goods from their merchants to bring them here. I recommend that you meet my cousin, Patreus, if you want to send goods here. He is the one to deal with. He is honest, but not cheap. Many negotiate a cheap price and then find their goods pilfered."

"I'll come by tomorrow and meet him," Ravi replied.

"Get the fish stew if you are going to eat. I gave the cook my grandmother's Greek recipe. Everyone loves it," Gregori suggested as they walked back to where the others were waiting.

Bright and early the next morning, they headed to the vessel. Gregori stood at the gangplank. "We will restrain the horses in a harness, so they don't slip around on board," he explained. "You will become accustomed to the pitching of the ship soon enough, and after a few days, the boat's motion won't seem strange anymore.

Also, I have an excellent chef. We usually eat stew, bread, cheese, and drink wine," he said with an all-knowing smirk.

In the following days, Ravi established several new channels of trade, bringing Egyptian, Greek, and Roman products over to India by sea. He also struck a deal with Patreus, Gregori's cousin, to ship scents and spices back via the same method.

"Silk will be the most valuable product," Patreus said. "Anyone who provides me with an ongoing supply of silk will be a very rich man."

"When I get back home, I'll see if I can increase our supply and send some to you," Ravi promised.

On the morning of departure, the sun slowly rose, casting a soft orange glow on the small group gathering at the Asteri. The horses stamped their feet as the sailors tightened the rigging, adjusting the slings to keep them from falling. Seagulls swooped through the air, cawing in the cool morning breeze.

Gregori shouted orders and checked the time. "We've got favorable winds this morning!" he hollered. "We leave in an hour!"

Jaidev checked the muhurta and found it favorable for a journey by sea.

As the ship slapped its way through the waves into open water, Jaidev, Ravi, Aakash, Khartum, and Akim watched the shoreline dwindle in the distance, salty air filling their lungs. They could feel the gentle rocking of the waves beneath them as they stood in silence on the bow, their faces turned towards the horizon.

"Ahhhh, this is magnificent!" Aakash exclaimed, breathing in deeply.

Meanwhile, Ravi felt like his insides were turning inside out. His hands flew to his mouth, and he stumbled across the deck, trying to reach the ship's rail before he wretched the contents of his roiling stomach. "All of this rocking has my stomach rocking," he said through gritted teeth, wiping his mouth. Bending over the rail just in time, he vomited overboard again.

Gregori's hearty laugh echoed from the captain's bridge. He leaned against the helm, guiding the ship onward, as he watched Ravi gasp and wretch over the ship's side. "Cheer up, my friend," he said. "Even Caesar has shared his breakfast with Neptune. There's no cure for seasickness other than relaxing and getting used to the motion of the waves. It'll pass before you know it."

On the third morning, Ravi emerged with a healthier color and steadier gait. Watching the bow of the ship slice through the waves of the open sea, Khartum smiled. "I could get used to this," he remarked, placing a fatherly hand on Akim's shoulder.

"I would love to be a sailor," Akim said, imagining new possibilities for the future.

That night, the sky was crystal clear, and the stars twinkled like diamonds reflecting on the open sea. Jaidev, Ravi, Khartum, Akim, and Aakash stood on the deck with their heads tilted back in awe, each envisioning what home would be like.

"We will be home soon, Ravi. What are you looking forward to?" Khartum asked.

Ravi spoke with excitement, his eyes alight as he imagined their return "I can't wait to see my mother, father, and sister," he said. "And I'm excited about the opportunity to expand the family business. Then, I want to revisit the snake dancers and learn about their culture first-hand."

Jaidev knew Ravi's words concealed his attraction to Sonal. Ravi was still smitten by her, and he couldn't disguise his excitement.

"And you, Khartum? What are you looking forward to?" Ravi asked in reply.

Khartum's eyes softened as he spoke her name. "I am looking forward to seeing my wife Parisa, and having Akim back home," he said, his voice heavy with emotion. A knot of worry settled in his chest as he thought of Parisa alone, waiting for their safe return.

"I am looking forward to many more adventures," Akim said eagerly. "Riding with our fabled horse soldiers, discovering the treasures of ancient cultures, and braving the high seas in search of distant lands." His youthful exuberance contagiously made them all smile.

"And what is it you are looking forward to, Aakash?" Khartum asked.

"I carry within my heart the affection of someone I love and hope to marry. I pray to Lord Ganesh, God as the remover of obstacles, that my wish be fulfilled," Aakash expressed solemnly as his hand caressed the cloth in his cloak.

"And Jaidev? All have spoken but you," Khartum acknowledged.

In a voice as old as the stars yet as young as a newborn's laughter, Jaidev said, "I am entrusted with the teachings of our great ancestors and the secrets of the stars, as well as the deep inner knowing that comes from the Song of Creation. I am blessed to have met the Maha Atma, who will bring this ancient knowledge to the western world. It is my family's sacred duty—passed down through the tradition of teachers before me—to awaken future generations to the Song. That is my dharma. The Song of Creation is eternal, beyond space and time, and ever-present."

About The Author

DJ Boyle is a retired firefighter living in Vancouver, WA. He studied eastern astrology under James Braha who brought Vedic astrology to the west.. DJ's journey into eastern wisdom began in 1971 when he learned Transcendental Meditation as taught by Maharishi Mahesh Yogi while studying psychology at Bloomfield College, Bloomfield, New Jersey. The journey is ongoing.

Contact Email: Dennisb364@aol.com